I0819419

the Dread

The Dreadfuls

A. RAE DUNLAP

kensingtonbooks.com

KENSINGTON BOOKS are published by:

Kensington Publishing Corp.
900 Third Avenue
New York, NY 10022

kensingtonbooks.com

All Kensington titles, imprints, and distributed lines are available at special quantity discounts for bulk purchases for sales promotions, premiums, fund-raising, educational, or institutional use.

Special book excerpts or customized printings can also be created to fit specific needs. For details, write or phone the office of the Kensington sales manager: Kensington Publishing Corp., 900 Third Avenue, New York, NY 10022, attn: Sales Department; phone 1-800-221-2647.

The K with book logo Reg US Pat. & TM Off.

First Kensington Hardcover Printing: April 2026

ISBN 978-1-4967-5037-2 (deluxe hardcover)

10 9 8 7 6 5 4 3 2 1

Printed in China

Electronic edition: ISBN 978-1-4967-5039-6 (ebook)

Interior art courtesy of Adobe Stock

The authorized representative in the EU for product safety and compliance is eucomply OU, Parnu mnt 139b-14, Apt 123
Tallinn, Berlin 11317, hello@eucompliancepartner.com

Dedication

For my mother, the teacher

Chapter I
The Anarchist's Daughter

If the world had the decency to display any sense of romanticism, the Whitechapel Hall Reformatory School ought to have been the most dismal place into which I ever stepped foot. The solemn tones of the grand clock perched above the imposing structure would announce my arrival, piercing the misty air. And once I crossed the threshold of the heralded institution, a hailstorm should burst over the city, pelting the windows of the Hall with remarkable intensity. The ferocity of the storm would be punctuated with wild flashes of flame-blue lightning, illuminating every colour with terrible distinctness, turning the hearts of the Hall's inhabitants icy with creeping dread. Claps of thunder reverberating down the dark and gloomy corridors would echo through abandoned vaults and hidden passageways, conjuring the souls of the dead long forgotten, and somewhere deep below (in an ancient dungeon, perhaps?), the rattle of chains would rise up in a ghostly chorus.

But because the world has no such romantic notions, the weather remained belligerently pleasant as my aunt and I were escorted from the grand entryway of the Hall immediately upon our arrival. My heart sank as we were bustled through bright, pristine corridors, the air within them devoid of mildew and decay, instead laced with a heavy undertone of carbolic soap. Beams of brilliant sunlight poured through the polished windows, and it was with an air of utter despair that I discovered the headmaster's office was no better: like the rest of the school, it was scrubbed spotless and flooded with light, giving the room a distinct air of cheerfulness that I detested with every fibre of my soul.

At least our initial sojourn into the Whitechapel district had been appropriately dismal. The streets were filthy, lined with urchins and beggars, and (much to my delight) we'd been forced to step over the corpse of a disembowelled rat lying upon the staircase of the very institution to which I'd been committed. My aunt's already-pale face had visibly blanched, and for a moment, I was filled with hope that my most macabre delights might manifest at last.

Sadly, it was not to be. For apparently within the walls of the Whitechapel Hall Reformatory School, no credence was given to gothic fancy, and instead the place appeared to be governed with the ruthless fist of modern propriety.

It was utterly hateful.

We awaited the headmaster's arrival in stony silence, and I hazarded a glance at my aunt's face, seeking any semblance of comfort there. Seated beside me in serene stoicism, her expression was, as always, unreadable. Even after four years of living as her ward, it was still unfathomable to me that she was my mother's twin. My sunny, boisterous mother, with her shock of auburn hair and honey-hued skin, whose whole persona radiated the glowing warmth of her childhood in far-off Australia, whose voice still carried the singsong accent of her homeland; who'd always seemed so out of place on the dour grey moors of Somerset (where I'd passed my own childhood in her loving care) that she'd seemed a creature from another world entirely.

How was it possible that hers was the same blood as my

aunt, who had so completely conformed to contemporary London standards that her well-coiffed hair, ash-pale skin, and tack-sharp accent would never betray a hint of her wild girlhood abroad? And how could it be that my mother's heart, so bursting with love and affection, had stilled, while my aunt's, which appeared to be fuelled purely out of hardened spite, resolutely soldiered on?

Emotion rose in my chest at the thought. I suppressed it and averted my eyes from my aunt's profile before I could allow myself to continue down a treacherous path of maudlin self-pity at my loss.

Not a moment too soon, the office door swung open and two imposing figures strode into the room, each clad head-to-toe in black. My aunt sprang to her feet and nearly upset her own chair in her haste to turn and offer them a curtsy. I bit back a laugh at her tiresome decorum as I slowly rose to offer my new wardens a considerably more reluctant greeting, scarcely bending at the knee.

"Mrs. Atkins, I assume?" The elder and taller of the two men offered a generous bow and friendly smile in my aunt's direction, the corners of his eyes wrinkling in what I could only assume was manufactured fondness. After all, what reason would this old man have to display graciousness to the family of his prisoner? His genteel demeanour was greatly disappointing, as I'd been expecting a considerably more villainous captor against which to test my wits.

"I'm Headmaster Graves, the director of this fine institution, and this is my esteemed associate, Reverend Barnett." The balding man in vicar's attire with a humourously voluptuous beard extended a bow of his own, but to my relief, he did not smile, and his eyes remained cold. *Perhaps a worthy adversary.*

"A pleasure to meet you, gentlemen."

Graves turned his trite hospitality towards me. "And this must be Miss Adelaide Morton! We've heard so much about you, my dear." He diplomatically neglected to mention that any advance knowledge he had was extracted from a police report, and the old version of me would have been quick to point this out. But careless obstinance had gotten me into this mess, and I was determined to suppress any outbursts that might alert my captors to the danger of my true nature. It was imperative to my plan.

"The pleasure is mine, sir." I ignored the suspicious look on my aunt's face at my uncharacteristic display of civility.

"Please, ladies, do have a seat." With a wave, he ushered us into our chairs, and he and the vicar took their places at the opposite side of the ornate desk dominating the room.

"Now, Miss Morton, it's my understanding that we will be graced with the pleasure of your company for the next nine months." Headmaster Graves gazed down at me with a neutral expression upon his face.

So says the judge, I internally retorted but managed to curtail my response to an unobjectionable nod.

"Do tell me, young lady," he continued with an infuriating air of faux familiarity, as though we were making conversation over afternoon tea. "What brings you here?"

"A court order, sir." As if there were any other reason I would subject myself to this drudgery.

He nodded, a falsified expression of concern overtaking his visage. "For what offence?"

"Stealing."

"Stealing what, dear?"

"Please, Headmaster, she—" my aunt attempted to interject, but she was immediately silenced by a wave of Graves's hand.

"Mrs. Atkins, it is important to us that our pupils take responsibility for their actions; it is the first step towards moral repair. So, tell me, Miss Morton: *What brings you here?*"

I took a deep breath and let the words flow freely. After all, I had nothing of which to be ashamed. "My uncle burned all my books and wouldn't give me money for new ones, so I went out and stole some."

Graves raised an eyebrow. "And why did your uncle burn your books?"

I blinked back at him. *Because he resents the fact that my parents died and left me as his legal ward and takes every opportunity to remind me that my presence is unwelcome.* But I couldn't say such words aloud to be mistaken for a prized pupil eager for reform.

"Because he . . . didn't like them."

"Please, Headmaster, that is hardly the whole of it," my aunt rudely interjected. "In the last four years, my niece has gone from obstinate to uncontrollable. She answers to no one but herself and seeks nothing but indulgence and self-gratification. She scared off no fewer than three governesses with her macabre fascinations, and when we enrolled her at boarding school, she escaped six times in as many months, resulting in her expulsion. She's brought dishonour upon our household more times than I can count, and it's only by the grace of my husband's connections that her latest foray was kept from the papers! We've done everything we can, but nothing helps. We're at our wits' end."

Graves held up a hand, stilling my aunt's airing of grievances at once. "I understand, of course. Her story is not so unlike that of many of our other pupils. Did this all begin with the death of her parents?"

My aunt shook her head vigorously. "Hardly, Headmaster. I regret that the seeds of her moral depravity were planted by none other than her own father and recklessly indulged by my sister. Throughout her childhood, they exposed her to terrible things in the books she read, even as they poisoned her mind. And instead of stopping her, her parents outright encouraged her in these endeavours!"

Graves furrowed his brow. "What sorts of things was she reading?"

My aunt sighed deeply, as if admitting to some cardinal sin. "She began with the penny books they sell on the street—full of filth and delinquency. From there, it was crime broadsides, news of robbery, murder, vice, and perversion, the depths of which I shudder to imagine. When she became our ward, we tried to keep her away from them, but it was like a disease! She cannot help herself, Headmaster, for her constitution has been so affected by prolonged exposure that she can no longer tell right from wrong. It is a moral failing."

"My dear lady, say no more." It was the first time Reverend Barnett had spoken, and his voice was cold, deep, and commanding. "Your niece is not the first to fall victim to the depravity of this literature, and I can assure you, we are all too familiar with her affliction."

My aunt looked flabbergasted. "You are?"

"Of course." The Reverend narrowed his eyes at me, as if he could appraise my condition by the countenance of my face. "An eager perusal of these *penny packets of poison* destroys all sense of virtue. The habit of receiving pleasures without any exertion of thought, by the mere excitement of curiosity and sensibility, may be justly ranked among the worst effects of habitual novel reading. It tends to inflame the passions, pollute the imagination, and corrupt the heart."

My aunt nodded eagerly, apparently enthralled by her kindred spirit. "Precisely, Reverend!"

"Why, just last year two young boys murdered their own parents under the influence of these penny books!"

My aunt clasped her chest and uttered a gasp of despair. (Meanwhile, I made a mental note to attempt to find more details on this crime, as it sounded frankly enthralling. Had they used poison? Or even an *axe*, perhaps? How positively *wicked*!)

The Reverend continued his diatribe, whipping himself into such a frenzy of over-dramatics that it was rather uncomfortable to behold. "Not that I'm implying your life is in danger, my dear woman. But you may rest assured that your niece has come to our institution just in the nick of time! For even if you had weaned her off her dependence, the individual always suffers cravings of former excitement. Within these walls, we can ensure that any such temptation is eradicated before she is returned to your diligent care."

Graves nodded in enthusiastic consent. "Whitechapel Hall is unrivalled in our rate of rehabilitation, and you are fortunate the court has entrusted your niece to us. I can assure you she will be in safe hands."

For a moment, my aunt hesitated. "Forgive me, gentlemen, but you must understand that despite my desperation, Whitechapel does not seem the place in which vices are eradicated. Why, just on our way here we were exposed to the vilest conditions imaginable! How do you endeavour to rehabilitate your wards in such surroundings?"

To my surprise, the Reverend broke into a wide grin. "Mrs. Atkins, your mind is of a most measured temperament, and we understand your concern. But Whitechapel Hall excels at moral rehabilitation *because* of its location, not despite it! Under my tutelage, we have developed a groundbreaking programme for Morality and Temperance Outreach. The pupils are exposed daily to the conditions of the neighbourhood as a warning of what will befall them should they stray from the path of righteousness. It is through this exposure that they learn to reject vice and embrace their position in society as ambassadors of virtue and good will!"

It took every ounce of restraint I possessed not to roll my eyes at the thought of being an 'ambassador of virtue.' I would rather end up dressed in rags begging in a gutter than capitulate to such nonsense. My aunt, however, looked much relieved at the prospect.

Before I could be tempted to object, there were three sharp raps at the office door, and it swung open to reveal a dour-looking woman with brassy-coloured pin-straight hair pulled into such a severe knot that it gave her face a distinctly taut, shrew-like form. Her dark eyes fell on me from beneath hooded lids, and her very gaze caused me to shiver in my seat.

"What perfect timing! Mrs. Atkins, Miss Morton, I'm delighted to introduce you to Miss Kaye, our venerable Religion and Morality teacher and house mother to our girls. She'll be escorting Miss Morton about the school until she gets her bearings."

The woman bobbed briefly in a stilted approximation of a curtsy, still staring at me with such intensity that I knew not how to react.

"A pleasure, Miss Kaye," my aunt chirruped cheerfully from beside me.

"I assure you, madam, the pleasure will be all mine." The tone of her words rattled me. Though innocuous in content, her delivery, spoken in a low, dangerous tone, hinted at much darker intent. She looked fully capable of enacting violent torture upon her wards or perhaps transfiguring into a rat to spy on them . . . *At last*, I thought. *I have found my villain!*

Miss Kaye wasted no time. Within moments, I was whisked from the headmaster's office without the opportunity to bid my aunt adieu. Not that I minded; it was rather thrilling to have a proper adversary upon which to focus my attention, and Miss Kaye rose to the challenge brilliantly. She gruffly paraded me from one end of the school to the other, barking out points of interest in a sharp staccato timbre that made me speculate she was about to drag me by the ear like a spoiled child.

"Kitchen. Bakehouse. Laundry. Dining. Daily chapel that way." I chased the hem of her skirt up a gleaming rounded staircase as she proceeded down the whitewashed hallway.

"These are the classrooms. You'll be at the end there with the rest of the girls your age." She gestured brusquely towards a closed oak door at the far end of the corridor. "Religion, needlework, and daily domesticity will be practised here in the afternoon. Mornings are devoted to work."

I paused, falling behind her unrelenting pace. "And what about academics?"

She turned, her facial expression displaying a distinct air of chagrin. "Academics?"

I floundered. "You know . . . reading? Mathematics? . . . French?"

"Miss Morton, are you under the impression that you are attending an academic institution?"

Her words caught me off guard. "I . . . No, not exactly, but surely we are at least encouraged to *read*—"

"You will read the Bible and appropriate articles on our moral duties as Christian women. That is the policy of this school."

I was gobsmacked. "But . . . Not even poetry?"

Miss Kaye narrowed her eyes, then turned on her heel and stalked haughtily down the hall before taking an abrupt left at yet another staircase, this one far narrower than the first, lecturing all the while.

"Miss Morton, this is a reformatory institution. The educators here are not your childhood governess. In the Hall, you will learn exemplary morals, the value of hard work, and the domestic skills with which you may obtain respectable employment following your sojourn here. That is all. Nothing more."

It dawned on me for the first time that this was indeed my aunt's plan all along: She and my uncle had no intention of supporting me into adulthood. I was to be abandoned to this institution and then left to fend for myself as a domestic servant, of all things!

But then I paused, a savage retort dying on my tongue. *After all, wasn't this the way of it?* It was the sad fortune of every heroine in my beloved penny bloods to be up against such odds. Just as they did, it would be up to me and my wits to escape this terrible fate, make my way in the world through sheer will and courage, and of course, eventually claim my rightful inheritance, which surely had been hidden by my scheming relatives.

In that case, I reasoned, this setback was simply all part of the plot. I must simply remain calm, composed, and compliant.

Until such a time that I was not.

We reached the top of the staircase and passed through a large, open chamber lined with two long rows of wrought-iron beds, each neatly made in simple white linens.

"This is the Girls Dormitory, but sadly, we are at capacity. As such, the headmaster has instructed that you shall temporarily reside in the annex. This way." I tore my gaze from the bleak lodgings to see Miss Kaye disappear around a bend at the far end of the hall. Hastening my gait, my heart leapt into my throat as I watched her ascend a twisted iron staircase so steep it was nearly a ladder.

Could it be that at last my romantic notions had come to fruition? Was I truly fortunate enough to be locked away in a dismal tower, isolated from my peers, left alone to scheme upon my escape in precious solitude? I was breathless and flushed with excitement (and frankly, the exertion of the climb) as I ascended into what appeared to be an ancient belfry, and to my deepest satisfaction, the space was gloriously gloomy.

The belfry had none of the fashionable modernity of the lower floors. In lieu of the polished tiles and gleaming marble below, the floor here consisted of dangerously rotting wood. The windows were small and opaque, the glass smoky with a layer of grime that cast a woeful vignette upon the drab view. The vaulted beams supported walls of crumbling brick that held up a decrepit roof thirty feet overhead, and I could distinctly make out a few patches of sunlight creeping through where the structure had given way to the elements. In the mild weather of the day the space was merely devoid of charm, but I imagined as soon as we were blessed with rain the tableau would be wonderfully bleak and draughty indeed.

It was perfect.

No sooner had the thought crossed my mind than a voice from over my shoulder startled me nearly out of my wits.

"Miss Kaye?"

Miss Kaye turned, and I followed her eyes to a figure emerging from the deep shadows at the far end of the tower. For an instant, the juxtaposition of light and dark was too strong for me to find shape to the form, but everything changed the moment it stepped into a strong beam of sunshine projecting from a crack in the rafters far above, and in that instant, I was struck breathless.

It had never occurred to me until that moment that the distressed damsels exalted in the pages of my penny books might be reflections of true persons, for they were simply too beautiful, too innocent, too pure to exist in a world as mundane as ours. Yet here before me stood a girl so dazzling in her perfection that my vision swam in the angelic glow emanating from her radiant visage.

She resembled a fragile flower, her white-blonde hair a halo crowning a face that would have formed a study for the rarest sculptor that ever Providence gave genius to. Long, silken lashes cast pallid shadows upon her impeccable cheeks as eyes of celestial blue laced with inquisitiveness peered at me, an intruder in her sanctuary. She would make an exquisite victim for the dastardly vampire that stalked the pages of my serials.

"Ah, Miss Fitzroy, there you are. I present to you Miss Morton, our newest boarder. Miss Adelaide Morton, this is Miss Philippa Fitzroy. You two will be sharing the annex until such a time that beds become available in the dormitory. Miss Morton, the staff will be assembling a bed and delivering your belongings after supper. Miss Fitzroy, I shall entrust you with Miss Morton's timeliness until she becomes familiar with our schedule."

"Yes, Miss Kaye." She curtsied with the grace of an angel,

and I recoiled at her meek disposition. Was she not incensed to have her private sanctum invaded by a total stranger? I would have been irate at such an imposition were I in her place.

"Very well. Miss Morton, Miss Fitzroy is an exemplary pupil. With her guidance, I have no doubt that you will thrive here at Whitechapel Hall." And with that, she turned and receded down the stair.

A ringing silence ensued. Miss Fitzroy blinked at me, apparently taking stock of her new charge.

I glared back. It would seem I was not fated to be the solitary heroine locked in the tower, as this tower was already occupied by an infinitely more sympathetic character, one whose beauty and manner eclipsed the whole of my own in every conceivable way. I couldn't believe my misfortune; how dare this lump of saccharine piety usurp my narrative?

Miss Fitzroy offered me a smile that was perhaps intended to be welcoming, but her placid willingness to accept my presence unchallenged irritated me deeply. "You can call me Pippa for short," she offered in her sweet singsong voice.

I narrowed my eyes. "Dell."

"Oh, lovely! But your full name, Adelaide—is that like the place in Australia? I read a book about it once. It was fascinating: gold mines and cowboys and kangaroos!"

"Yes."

Her prim hand rose to her lips with excitement. "Really? Is that where you're from?"

"No. My mother was born there. But her family came to London when she was a young woman." It struck me then for the first time that I was now the same age my mother had been when she came to England. In my childhood, her adventure had always seemed that of a mature woman, whereas I currently felt adulthood to be a world away from my trappings.

"Oh." To my satisfaction, Pippa looked visibly disappointed, but sadly this affliction was short-lived. "Well, at least you must know some wonderful stories about it!" Her assumption that I would be willing to share these stories only irked me further. Was she truly so delusional as to think we'd become bosom friends?

"Not really."

"Oh."

At least that shut her up. Another silence stretched out between us, and I revelled in it. After all, the more I could make her dislike me, the more urgently she would aspire to vacate the annex and leave me alone to do my plotting.

An idea came to me at once. "Have you heard of Blue Cap?"

A delicate crease appeared between Pippa's eyebrows. "Why, no! Who is he?"

I bit back a smile, recalling a recent edition of *Blue Cap the Bushranger.* "Oh, just one of my favourite Australian heroes. He ran the most fearsome gang in all of New South Wales, robbing hotels and taverns and the like, and having shootouts with police."

"He sounds fearsome."

I shrugged. "As highwaymen go, he was the worst of them. Rumour has it I'm related to him." Her eyes widened ever so slightly at this improvised flight of fancy. "Sadly, he was chased down by the law and died stranded in the outback, mummified by the blazing sun, eyes plucked out by vultures and guts devoured by dingoes."

Pippa recoiled. "That's disgusting."

"It's my greatest aspiration to one day return and find his body, give my dear old granduncle a proper burial . . ." I gazed wistfully into the distance, as if transfixed by the thought. Pippa opened and closed her mouth a few times, but to my supreme satisfaction, I had struck her speechless.

Just then, a shrill clang emanated from the floor below, and we both jumped.

"Well." Pippa averted her gaze and smoothed the nonexistent

wrinkles from the front of her frock. "That'll be the bell for supper. Follow me." She marched to the stair and descended into the hall below. It would seem my story had repelled her enough to scorn any notions of a burgeoning friendship between us, much to my relief.

Pippa was an unfortunate obstacle to be overcome, for without her, my placement in the annex would be an incredible stroke of luck. If I could evict her from the space, I would have hours of unsupervised freedom with which to plan my getaway. For my mission at Whitechapel Hall was hardly simple: I would not, as I had at boarding school, give in to flights of fancy and make hasty, ill-advised attempts at escape.

This time would be different: I was a child no longer, and nothing in my new circumstances would allow for the hare-brained half-measures I'd employed before, leaping out of unlocked windows or recklessly bolting towards every open door. This time, I would follow in the footsteps of my penny blood heroines: I would of course apply courage and cunning, but above all, I would apply patience. I would earn the absolute trust of those around me, until I'd had time to perfect my scheme. My willing compliance was to be my great disguise.

I would escape Whitechapel Hall by a method and means yet to be determined. Once outside, I would stow away aboard a train bound for Portsmouth. There, I would use my wits and wiles to gain passage to Australia, where I would join the police force as their first-ever lady detective, using all I had learned in my so-called *penny packets of poison* to solve the most heinous crimes in the territory. Acclaim, fame, and fortune all awaited me, and I could hardly wait to get started!

But wait I must. I would be clever. Cautious. And above all, *patient.*

With an air of grim determination, I dutifully followed Pippa down the stairs.

Chapter II
Vice and Its Victim

We arrived to find the dining hall already near capacity, with six long tables arranged in the shape of a horseshoe around a lectern. The hall was oddly silent, devoid of the chatter I'd expect from the clusters of girls diligently taking their place in accordance with some invisible seating chart to which I was not privy. It was with a twinge of resentment that I found myself anchored at Pippa's heels, chasing her ice-pale plait through the throngs of identical black frocks and lace collars until we came to two vacant chairs at the far end of the table closest to the lectern. Pippa came to stand stiffly behind one, and with a curt nod of her head, I took my place beside her.

The hush of the room swelled to a crescendo, and a moment later the oppressive silence was broken by the crisp *clack* of heels against the floor. From the door by the kitchens, Miss Kaye emerged and made her way to the lectern before raising her hands as if to silence an inaudible cacophony. I cast a glance around at my fellow pupils, but their eyes were all locked upon Miss Kaye.

"You may be seated." Her voice was drowned out by the sound of six dozen chairs scraping across the floorboards as her wards all moved in perfect synchronicity. I was subjected to a moment's mortification as I attempted to take my seat from the right, only to collide with a scandalised Pippa.

"From the *left*," she hissed through clenched teeth, and I blushed as I scrambled to rectify my oversight. Though I had no aim to impress her or our surly house mother, I at least aspired to make it through the meal without attracting unwanted attention; there would be no gain in causing a scene over something as mundane as manners. I would pick my battles wisely.

As the clatter faded, the kitchen doors swung open once more and a parade of girls clad in the school attire emerged carrying steaming bowls of porridge and platters of bread, which were distributed upon each table. The girls then vanished back into the kitchen as suddenly as they'd emerged, and I wondered for a moment if they were allowed to eat back there, or if this was some sort of punishment they were enduring. I'd just opened my lips to inquire of Pippa when Miss Kaye's voice reverberated through the hall once more.

"We continue our reading this evening with Proverbs." She cleared her throat, and her spindly fingers gripped either side of the lectern as she lowered her head to read.

> *Pride goeth before destruction, and an haughty spirit before a fall. Better it is to be of an humble spirit with the lowly, than to divide the spoil with the proud. He that handleth a matter wisely shall find good: and whoso trusteth in the Lord, happy is he . . .*

To my surprise, the girls around me wordlessly picked up the serving bowls and began to pass them back and forth, then tucked in in stony silence. It would seem there was to be no gossip at mealtimes, no idle blathering about the cadence of our days or silly gossip about the goings-on within our prison, as had been the case during my ill-fated stint at boarding school. At Whitechapel Hall, apparently, mealtimes were devoted to penance.

No matter, I concluded quickly. After all, trivial conversation was a waste of my precious time. I could instead devote these otherwise squandered hours to devising and perfecting my schemes, for did I not now have a nemesis to thwart? I forced myself to shut out Miss Kaye's sombre droning and focus on planning my next assault upon Pippa's delicate sensibilities.

My thoughts returned immediately to the priceless volumes that my uncle had so heartlessly set aflame. While there were a few scattered works that had escaped the inferno by virtue of being squirrelled away in my wardrobe (hidden beneath my undergarments), much of my bounty had lain in the carefully curated library hidden beneath the floorboards which my uncle, upon its discovery, had destroyed in its totality. Tragically for him, my memory was not so easily erased, and there was no shortage of stomach-churning violence in those absent tomes that I could recall nearly word-for-word.

But which to adapt for my purposes of frightening Pippa away once and for all? I risked a sidelong glance at her, and all it took was a glimpse of her upturned nose and perfect posture to reignite my irritation. Her innocence irked me beyond measure. I almost felt sorry for her, but my plot to alienate her from the annex was for her own good. She'd be much happier in the dormitory below in the company of the other girls than locked in the tower with me as I planned my escape. As my nemesis, she was bound to be a tattletale, and left unchecked, she would thwart my plans before they were fully formed. My resentment grew as I envisioned her inevitable betrayal.

Turning back to the task at hand, I recalled the contents of some of my most prized volumes for inspiration. There was the one in which the heroine learned ventriloquism to convince her captors that she was plagued by demonic hauntings and killed them all of fright (an intriguing prospect, but I ultimately deemed learning ventriloquism too time-consuming to be of use in the short term), the one in which the heroine trained the house dog to poison her wicked stepfather's wine (too far-fetched even for a simpleton such as Pippa to believe), the one in which the heroine dressed as a paperboy to murder her scheming relatives with a pistol wrapped in newspaper (rather lacking in originality; I could do better), or perhaps the one in which the heroine slit her jailor's throat with a hat pin (sensational, but was it believable?) . . .

Alas, none of these stories would suffice to repurpose as my own. For Whitechapel Hall did not house murderers, merely *ladies suffering from incurable delinquency*, and there was no way Pippa, dullard as she was, would believe that I had committed such a heinous act and was merely sentenced to nine months of simple reform.

At last, it came to me in a rush of delighted memory: a tale wicked enough to frighten Pippa clear out of her wits but clever enough that she would suspect I could execute such a crime without detection. If I could convince Pippa that I had gotten away with cold-blooded murder, she would undoubtedly take extraordinary measures to escape the annex but would be so riddled with fear that she wouldn't risk divulging my 'secret' to Miss Kaye.

I must have uttered a breath of satisfaction aloud, for the next thing I knew, Pippa was throwing a bony elbow into my ribs and shooting me a furious glance from over her half-eaten porridge. I managed to feign a halfhearted cough in response, but I could feel Miss Kaye's eyes dart in my direction, daring me to disrupt the proceedings. I stiffened my spine and took a bite of my lukewarm meal, a placid expression of innocence upon my face.

A few mindless mouthfuls later, Miss Kaye, apparently ruled by some invisible timetable, slapped her Bible shut with an air of finality. All around me rang the clatter of spoons dropping back to the table in unison as every girl pushed back her chair and rose to stand.

"You are dismissed. Miss Morton and Miss Fitzroy, a word, please." I could feel Pippa's trepidation as the other pupils shuffled towards the exit, but with downcast eyes she nudged me towards the lectern. I steadied myself and approached.

"Yes, Miss Kaye." Pippa fell once more into a stiff curtsy, and I offered a stilted bob myself as a gesture of fleeting goodwill.

"Miss Fitzroy. Now that Miss Morton has joined us, you have been assigned as partners in the Reverend's Temperance Outreach programme. You will report to the kitchen for market duty with Cook at six sharp. Understood?"

"Yes, Miss Kaye." This time, I joined Pippa in the chorus, and a flicker of what could almost be described as satisfaction moved across Miss Kaye's face.

"Very well, girls. To bed."

With another curt bob, Pippa and I exited the hall and wound our way up the stairs towards the dormitory. We had barely cleared the first landing when Pippa clutched my arm with an excited squeal and proceeded to shake me with such vigour that I nearly missed a step and fell to my untimely death.

"Oh, can you believe it? *Market duty*, as our first assignment! What luck!" Her eyes sparkled so brilliantly that I had to avert my gaze, lest I be infected by her grating enthusiasm.

"Market duty is good?" Anything with the word *duty* in it sounded frankly unappealing.

"Oh, yes! I imagine you haven't heard much about the Temperance Outreach programme—"

"Reverend Barnett may have mentioned it," I interjected before she could start blathering on *ad nauseam.*

She remained infuriatingly undeterred. "Oh! Well, it's an excellent opportunity to engage with the public and be upstanding examples for those less fortunate around us."

I raised an eyebrow incredulously. "You think we're going to be *examples* for the people out there?" I gestured towards the nearest window overlooking the sordid streets below. "I'm pretty sure seeing us prancing about in our uniforms isn't going to inspire the morale of the hard sleepers and loose women I saw lying about."

Pippa pursed her lips prudishly and clasped me by the elbow as we continued our ascent, as though I were simply pitifully misguided about the state of the streets upon which our prison was perched. "Now, now, Reverend Barnett says that merely demonstrating moral purity affects those around us in ways invisible to the eye, seen only by the soul."

"I'll bet," I muttered under my breath.

"Look." She lowered her voice conspiratorially, as if telling me a saucy secret. "Every pupil must have a partner to participate in Temperance Outreach. I didn't have one before, so I was assigned to clean the floors. By myself. It's been wretched! My knees are in such a state, and just look at my hands!" She thrust her fingers in front of me and to my surprise, they were not so unblemished as I'd previously assumed; her nail beds were raw and tattered, and her knuckles bruised. "Anything will be better than cleaning the floors, trust me."

For the first time, I was rather inclined to. Just as I was about to reply, we pushed through the heavy door of the dormitory, and to my surprise, Pippa suddenly pitched forward and landed in an all-out sprawl, skidding two full feet before coming to rest at the foot of the nearest bed. I nearly went down with her but managed to right myself at the last moment, the heat rising in my cheeks at the sound of raucous laughter erupting from around me.

"Oops." I whirled around to see a plain-faced girl with ebony hair and an impish grin flick up a broomstick from where she'd clearly just thrust it into Pippa's path. "Sorry, Batty. Didn't hear you coming. Figured you'd just fly on back to your belfry tonight." Another chorus of laughter resounded as Pippa struggled to her feet, her face a flaming shade of scarlet, and she whirled to face her assailant.

"Shut up, Beatrice!"

"Oh, don't take it personally, Batty. Accidents happen. But if it makes you feel better, you can write a letter to your daddy and cry about it. Though I don't think he'll answer, do you?"

"I said, shut up!" To my shock, Pippa charged forward and gave Beatrice a mighty shove upon the shoulders. Beatrice let out an infernal shriek as she stumbled backwards and nearly pitched over upon her own bed, but at the last moment she steadied herself and swung her broomstick at Pippa, who dodged it by mere inches but collided with me in the process.

Up until that point, I'd been watching the scene unfold with an air of horrified disbelief as every previous assumption I'd had about Miss Philippa Fitzroy summarily turned on its head. Was it possible that she wasn't the prim, poised, popular perfectionist I'd pegged her for? One look at the crazed expression upon her face confirmed that there was clearly more to Pippa than met the eye.

"Oi!" By some miracle I managed to catch her arm just as she raised it to strike. "Pippa, stop!" Though I had no insight into the cause of their feud, I couldn't imagine that allowing Pippa and Beatrice to beat each other senseless until Miss Kaye intervened would end well for any of us.

A series of gasps rang out from the other girls at my intervention, and it was only in that moment that I realised they'd circled around us to watch the scene play out. A heavy silence ensued, and I loosened my grip on Pippa's wrist. It occurred to me for the first time that she just might be more insane than myself.

Pippa's head whipped in my direction, a mutinous, feral look in her eye. Her hair, previously so well styled it appeared to have manifested from an oil painting, had somehow sprung loose from its braid, framing her angelic features in a tangle of wild waves. Her nostrils flared in her upturned nose, her lips pulled back into a sneer, and for one mad moment, I thought she might strike me, too.

But then she blinked, and as quickly as it had appeared, her madness was gone. Her hand fell limply to rest in mine, and she issued a soft gasp, as if resurfacing after being trapped beneath the water.

"Yes. Right, of course, Dell. We'll just be going."

With her head down and my hand clasped resolutely in hers, she marched forward, parting the throng of onlookers and guiding me the length of the dormitory and up the spiral stair to our annex, leaving nothing but the echoes of nervous tittering in our wake.

The moment we were back in our sanctum, Pippa released my hand and retreated to the small vanity tucked in the corner of the belfry. Seating herself, she picked up a comb and proceeded to fuss with her hair.

I had no idea what to say. Our encounter with Beatrice in the dormitory below had upended my understanding of the school's pecking order, and for the first time I pitied Pippa for something besides her perceived naivete.

"I'm sorry you had to witness that." Her voice had returned to its normal mellifluousness, her mercurial nature so unexpected I could scarcely believe what I had witnessed with my own eyes.

"It's fine." I cleared my throat and looked away, feeling very much as if I had somehow invaded her privacy. My eyes fell upon my trunk, which had appeared during supper and was situated at the foot of a newly assembled bed identical to the ones in the dormitory downstairs. I pounced on it instantly, glad to have a distraction. Popping open the trunk lid, I ran my hand along the upper lining until my fingernails caught on an errant thread.

With a satisfied huff, I gave it a tug and watched smugly as three dozen crime broadsides poured out of my secret hiding spot, littering the floor.

My heart felt lighter at once, knowing my contraband had

made it safely into the school. I ran my fingers lovingly over each one as I picked it up, reuniting with old friends after an unjust separation.

"What are those?"

I turned to see Pippa gazing curiously at me from her seat at the vanity, daintily fastening pins into her now-perfect hair.

"They're crime broadsides. I like to use them for decor," I added flippantly as I propped a few up on the window ledge nearest my bed.

Pippa rose to her feet and made her way over to my bedside, stooping to pick one up. "*Execution of M. Atkinson at Durham*?" she read incredulously.

"Oh, that's an excellent one," I said, plucking it from her fingers and positioning it on the sill. "He murdered his wife, but they botched his first execution and had to hang him again. It's not very often they get to do it twice, you see."

"That's absolutely ghastly." Much to my surprise, Pippa did not immediately retreat. Instead, she bent and picked up another. "*Confession of the Barbarous Murder, Committed by John Holloway on the body of his Wife, and Cutting Off Her Head, Arms, and Legs.*"

"Oh, that one's really rare!" I exclaimed. "It comes with a doggerel verse."

"A what?"

"It's a little poem about the murder and who committed it, his punishment, and a warning to all laymen to avoid the same fate. It's funny, see?" I pointed to the rakish prose positioned beneath a graphic image of the executed murderer.

To my surprise, Pippa giggled. That was not at all the reaction I'd intended to produce, but I was finding it harder to disgust her than anticipated.

"Where on earth did you get these? There haven't been public executions since before we were born!" She appeared genuinely intrigued.

"I collect them from antiques shops," I replied simply. "And my father used to find them for me at village markets when he travelled." I swallowed the lump in my throat at the fond recollection.

"How perfectly horrid." She handed John Holloway's card back to me with a sly smile. "Does your father still send them to you?"

"No, he's dead. And my dastardly uncle set the rest of them on fire."

"That's a pity," Pippa mused as she stooped to help me gather a few more off the floor.

My moment had arrived; this was the golden opportunity to divulge my *darkest secret* to Pippa. But to my surprise, I felt a slight tug of remorse within my chest at the thought of expelling her from the annex. If our encounter in the dormitory were any indication, she was hardly welcome there, though for what reason I couldn't discern.

Stop it, I scolded myself. I had only been in captivity mere hours, and it was already making me soft! I needed to remain devoted to my cause and make no excuses if I was to escape Whitechapel Hall successfully. I hadn't the time to mess about with waifish maidens in distress.

"Well, I made sure he paid for it," I whispered conspiratorially.

Pippa raised her eyebrows and leaned in closer. "How so?"

"The night after he burned my broadsides and my books, I poured laudanum into his evening whiskey. Then once he was asleep, I snuck into his room and pushed a coffin spike straight up his nose and into his brain. The coroner never found it. And that's how *I* got away with *murder*."

Pippa stared at me, her azure eyes wide as saucers, petal-pink lips parted in awe, wholly aghast. I held my gaze steady.

Then Pippa threw back her head and cackled.

She laughed with a reckless abandon I could never have expected from her, a gleeful, irreverent sound, light and bright and honest, pearly teeth exposed and a mischievous glimmer in her eye.

It was contagious. Through my astonishment, I started laughing, too.

"You are utterly full of shit," she managed between giggles, and her crass language only shocked me into laughing harder, to the point we were both clutching one another and struggling for breath. "My God, where did you even hear such a tale?"

My cover was ruined; there was no way I could carry on the farce if Pippa insisted upon finding my tall tales amusing rather than terrifying. "It's a detective tale from an old penny dreadful," I mustered. "Called *How to Get Away with Murder.* It was a real masterpiece, but my bastard of an uncle burned it, along with the rest of my collection. He even burned my favourite detective fiction, *Revelations of a Lady Detective*, which my mother had passed on to me from her own girlhood. I got caught trying to steal a new copy of that one. That's . . . that's the real reason I'm here."

Pippa wiped away tears of mirth with her sleeve, shaking her head. "You're an absolute lunatic, you know that? And to think they call *me* Batty."

Composing myself further, I allowed myself to ask the question that had been pestering me since our encounter with Beatrice. "Why *do* they call you Batty?"

Pippa shrugged. "Because I live in the belfry. 'Bats in the belfry,' and all that. Get it? So clever."

Her response was elusive. Of course, I understood the 'joke,' but she'd stopped short of admitting why she, in her posh, pristine perfection, was the brunt of it. But before I could query further, she thrust the handful of broadsides she'd collected from the floor at me.

"Any more good ones in here?"

I flipped through them. "A few. But look, if you like these, I've got something even better." I tossed the cards onto my bed and returned to my trunk, pulling out the few possessions I'd been allowed to pack and dumping them on the floor. Once I'd emptied it out, I gripped a loose tab of fabric in the bottom corner, pulled the upholstery back, and revealed the precious stash of my few remaining penny dreadfuls with a flourish.

"Sadly, I lost most of my collection when my uncle destroyed it, but these escaped unscathed. Have a look." I plucked out *The Link Boys of Old London*. "This one's a rollicker. It's got a barber who murders his patrons and then bakes them into meat pies."

"Sounds delicious," Pippa retorted, but she accepted the offering without hesitation.

"And this one! *The Adventures of a Notorious Burglar*. It's about a man named Charles Pearce, who is devoted to an extraordinary life of crime."

Pippa snatched it up eagerly, her eyes alight as they flicked across the text. "It looks marvellous."

"It is! Oh, and these, too," I added, thrusting a few random editions of *The Illustrated Police News* at her. "The murders are gloriously gruesome, and better yet, they're all real."

"Ew." She wrinkled her nose as her eyes scanned the scandalous illustrations, but she appeared otherwise undeterred. "These are excellent."

"They really are," I concurred with a satisfied smile.

Suddenly, Pippa's brow knit with consternation. "We must hide these well. They search the annex for illicit materials too, you know, not just the dormitory. We can't risk being caught with these."

I glanced wildly around the room. "Perhaps under our mattresses? Or maybe under the floorboards?"

Pippa rolled her eyes. "Despite your taste in books, you're clearly an amateur in the realm of the criminal; those are the first places they look. Come on, grab your broadsides, you can't leave those in the window here. I know just where to put them."

With a devilish look in her eye, she rose and helped me to my feet, and we quickly gathered up all my precious contraband. "Follow me."

She led me to the furthest back corner of the belfry, partitioned by an elegant dressing screen. Her own bed was tucked discreetly behind it, positioned beneath a singular large arched window illuminated by the fading light outside. Much to my surprise, she strode confidently up to her bed, stepped squarely upon her own mattress, hoisted herself up onto the window ledge, and then swung daintily onto the nearest crossbeam without missing a stride. I scrambled to catch up, only to observe in astonishment as she proceeded to walk the beam like a tightrope across the expanse of the belfry until she arrived at a small circular window on the opposite side. She reached up and pushed it open, then pulled herself up and through, petticoats disappearing into the twilight.

Heart in my throat, I mimicked her circus act as best I could, though my fear of heights made traversing the beam a far more tedious undertaking for me. By the time I reached the circular window, my brow was damp with sweat, and I could barely muster the strength to clamber through it.

But when I did, I gasped in awe.

For to my surprise, we were perched upon a stone ledge no more than three feet in width which extended the length of the building in both directions. Though narrow, the ledge appeared sound, and all thoughts of safety quickly evaporated when I took in what lay before me.

The view brought the whole of Whitechapel to our feet; I could see for miles in every direction, the maze of streets buzzing with life below us. My eyes darted from scene to scene, from the lamplighter making his rounds, to a trio of women with linked arms singing off-key as they stumbled down an alley, from the cop on the corner shouting at a vagrant to the jovial laughter of a troop of sailors huddled outside a pub. To the east, the rail yard teemed with activity as labourers rushed to load an idling train, steam billowing forth from the engine as a lonesome whistle announced its imminent departure. The plush glimmer of sunset still sat low on the horizon. I could see everything, the whole world spread bare before me, and the feeling was intoxicating.

Pippa's hand upon my shoulder startled me back to reality, and I jumped.

She laughed. "Easy, now. This isn't the place to lose your balance. Come on." She guided me further along the ledge to a place where a large outcropping protruded beneath the face of the clock. Crouching low, her fingers traced the mortar between bricks in search of something.

"Here." She shimmied out a loose brick, revealing a perfectly hidden cubbyhole behind it, then turned back towards me, her expression one of wild delight. "Your things will be safe here."

"Pippa, this place is amazing!" There was no other way to describe it.

"I know, right? And they wonder why I'm not put out being stuck up in the belfry alone." She tucked her armful of penny dreadfuls into the cubby before reaching in and pulling out a weathered pipe box. "Fancy a smoke?"

I nearly swooned. Was it possible that Pippa not only spoke with the foulest language I'd ever heard from a lady's mouth but smoked like a hell-born babe as well? The only woman I'd ever seen smoke was none other than the incomparable Mrs. Paschal—the Lady Detective herself, pictured upon the cover of my favourite penny blood of all time, cigarette in hand as she coyly flashed her petticoat at the beguiled reader. The book had once belonged to my mother in her youth before she'd gifted it to me on my tenth birthday, and it had long been the crown jewel of my collection. Watching it go up in flames at my uncle's hand had been a loss to me nearly as momentous as losing my mother herself.

"Dell?" Pippa was staring at me, her expression one of mixed confusion and amusement, and I realised I had been staring at her in a most uncouth manner.

"Oh! Um, yes, yes please," I consented, and then pretended to busy myself hiding my broadsides within the cubby, while in truth I was observing transfixed as Pippa expertly packed the pipe with a generous pinch of tobacco—an act which I'd never seen performed by a woman. Pippa, however, appeared to have no deficit in such knowledge.

Tossing the box aside, she strode up to the very edge of the ledge, and my heart leapt at seeing her in such proximity to danger. She looked every bit the part: a princess cruelly locked in her tower, sequestered above her realm, her beauty only magnified by her isolation as the wind stirred tendrils of fawn-soft curls across her distant expression. Yet the moment was fleeting; she flopped down upon the outcropping, feet dangling over the edge, and produced a matchbook from the pocket of her frock. "Coming?"

"Right," I muttered, breaking free of my trance and steeling my courage. I felt hot and cold all at once as I took a few tentative steps towards the edge, my heart racing and breath short. Yet one beckoning gesture from Pippa, and before I knew it, I was lowering myself beside her, refusing to look down at the plunge that would surely be my death, and instead focusing upon her encouraging grin as she offered me the packed pipe. I took it and lit it, inhaling the way I'd seen my father do a thousand times before, and promptly fell into a fit of coughing.

Pippa laughed merrily as she took the pipe back, and I was relieved to see there was no trace of mockery in her eyes. "It's an acquired taste."

Regaining my composure and wiping my watering eyes, I shook my head. "It'll grow on me, I'm sure." I could picture myself looking as devastatingly daring as Mrs. Paschal someday; it would merely take practice.

Pippa took a long, smooth drag and released the smoke into

the chilling air, the juxtaposition of such a masculine act balanced against her feminine form an irresistible sight to behold. "It reminds me of my father."

I cleared my throat. "Mine, too." I paused, remembering Beatrice's cruel words earlier that evening. "Yours isn't dead, is he?"

Pippa gave a derisive snort. "Good as. To me, at least." She took another pull of the pipe and then offered it back to me, and I accepted it warily and took a light puff.

A long silence stretched out between us. With a rumble and a groan, the train in the railyard shuddered into motion, chugging off towards the distant skyline, and for a moment I allowed myself to envision escaping upon it, bound for Portsmouth, for freedom . . .

"He's the reason I'm here," Pippa suddenly continued, apropos of nothing.

"Oh," I replied, my reckless thoughts returning to the present.

"My mother disappeared. Left him in a bout of madness, some would say, but personally I think she was the sane one." The story was not unfamiliar to me, a classic tale in the gothic style. Pippa was lucky to be of such poetic origins, I concluded.

"Less than two months later, he had her declared dead and married my governess."

I choked on my pipe smoke. "He *what*?"

"Married my governess, who, I might add, is a mere three years older than me. I'd thought of her as a sister. And then . . . no more."

"That's awful." I paused to mull this over further.

"What's more, she then insisted he send me here."

I turned to her aghast. "Here? But why? You weren't sentenced here by the court?"

"Nope. She somehow convinced my father that I was out to get her, and the only solution was to send me to a reformatory institution."

"But what about finishing school?" I still couldn't comprehend what sort of father would send his own child to a penal school willingly.

"I was too incorrigible, according to her."

A relevant question dawned on me. "Well, *were* you out to get her?" The memory of Pippa's expression as she'd attacked Beatrice was still fresh in my mind, despite her current state of civility.

Pippa rolled her eyes. "You mean, was I putting laudanum in her coffee and pushing coffin spikes up her nose? No, I was not." We shared a mutual chuckle at this. "But I may have swapped the sugar for salt in her coffee once or twice or dropped a bit of aniline in with her wash."

"Those hardly seem sins fit for a reformatory."

Pippa sighed and leaned back on her hands, tipping her face up towards the sky as if searching for something among the stars. "And on that point, we agree."

I considered this. "Is that . . . um, is that why Beatrice . . . said those things to you?"

Pippa didn't look down. "Her and all the rest of them. Being a voluntary boarder here is a stamp of shame in their eyes. They're all here because they have to be. I'm here because my family doesn't want me."

"I'm sorry." And I truly was. For as much as I'd been determined to despise Pippa with every fibre of my being, I could feel a connection between our souls, born of the same alienation from our families. While the cause of our separation differed, the pain felt no doubt the same. "For what it's worth, I don't think any less of you for what your dastardly father has done."

"It's fine." She sat up and dusted the gravel off her hands. "Besides, now you're here! And what's more, you're stuck with me." She turned and gave me a winning smile. "Tomorrow morning, we get to go out in the city together. And to market, no less! Can you imagine the grand adventures we'll have, you and me?" Her face was alight with promise, brighter than the stars above.

I smiled back at her. "You and me."

Drat, I thought. *So much for deposing my nemesis.*

Though perhaps I could use an accomplice.

Chapter III
Mysteries of London

I slept poorly my first night at Whitechapel Hall. Whether it was from the excitement of the day or the scratchiness of the woollen blanket or the burning sensation in my chest induced by ingestion of pipe smoke, I could not be sure. The only certainty was that when I heard the clanging of the bell from downstairs, I could have sworn it must only be moments after midnight.

Pippa was clearly of a different view. She emerged from behind her dressing screen fully clothed and coiffed what felt like mere seconds after the initial chime and waltzed over to my bedside to poke me most ferociously.

"Oi!" I snapped and yanked my threadbare bedding over my head. I was unaccustomed to rising before dawn, but judging by the warm pink glow filling the belfry, the sun had yet to make an appearance over the horizon.

"Come on, Dell! Now's not the time to lie about, we're going to market!" I suddenly found my blankets stripped clear off the bed. With a howl of protest, I shot bolt upright, glaring at an infuriatingly delighted-looking Pippa, cradling my bedding in her arms.

"What's so bloody great about market?" I moaned, my toes curling against the frigid floorboards as I begrudgingly rose to my feet, whether to dress myself or murder Pippa still a toss-up in my sleep-addled mind.

"Merely that we get to go out in the city—completely unsupervised, I might add—and mingle about the neighbourhood!" I flinched as Pippa managed to strike me square in the face with a pair of wool stockings she'd plucked from my trunk. "What makes you so sure all this mingling is going to be fun?" I muttered as I hopped about on one foot, attempting to yank on the stockings. "I'm not sure you've noticed, but this neighbourhood doesn't seem the type of place girls like us make dear friends."

Pippa just rolled her eyes and thrust my blouse and stays into my hands before turning her back to retrieve something from the rickety wardrobe propped in the corner, giving me a moment of merciful privacy to pull them over my chemise. "It's not all bad around here, you know. Of course, there are streets to avoid, but most of the households nearby are perfectly respectable."

I opened my mouth to argue with her but realised if she had been observing the whole of Whitechapel from her perch beneath the clock tower for months now, then she probably knew her surroundings much better than I.

"Besides," she continued, turning back around after having procured a plain black wool frock from the wardrobe and thrusting it at me, "I've heard the girls downstairs talk about their adventures on outreach. They've seen outrageous things out there! Trollops and gamblers and gangsters; stuff straight out of your penny books, I imagine."

I giggled at the thought, pulling the dress over my head. "And the Reverend allows this?"

"Oh, they never tell the Reverend," Pippa replied with a wink. "As far as he knows, they spend all their time interacting with penniless widows outside the Salvation Army."

Despite the early hour, Pippa was doing a decent job of

arousing my excitement. What's more, I would undoubtedly gain essential knowledge of the streets, bringing me one step closer to perfecting my eventual escape plan—though that angle I knew I must protect from Pippa at all costs. Eager to be on our way, I grabbed my two spare hairpins and attempted to wrestle my unruly mane into some semblance of a plait.

"For heaven's sake, Dell, have you never learnt to fashion your own hair? Come here." Pippa plopped me down at her vanity and picked up her comb, running it through my tangled locks. I winced, but she remained undeterred and briskly fashioned the frazzled strands into an elegant coil.

My breath caught at the sensation. My aunt had never had time to do much with my hair besides a simple youthful braid. But back when she was alive, my mother had always taken the time to fix my hair properly, even when I was a child. My fondest memories were of sitting with her just like this, her gentle fingers brushing against my scalp, so soothing and familiar as we laughed at some triviality shared just between us. It was an intimacy I missed with every fibre of my being, and something inside me trembled with longing for it.

"There!" Pippa pronounced proudly, jolting me back from my memories. "What do you think?"

I admired my reflection in the mirror. While my clothing was undeniably dour, Pippa's elegant handiwork gave me a surprising air of sophistication. "It's lovely. You'll have to teach me."

"Gladly. It suits you," she said warmly, tucking an errant strand behind my ear. "Now come on, we'll be late!" And with that, Pippa grabbed my hand and yanked me down the stairs.

Cook was exactly as she should be, if written up in one of my stories. Stout, sour-faced, and with a northern accent so stiff I could scarcely make out her instructions as she spat them at Pippa and me, all whilst wielding a large cleaver to chop a stack of mealy-looking potatoes so vigorously I feared for the safety of all appendages involved.

"You'll be on butcher duty," she pronounced, flinging a fistful of the potatoes into a boiling pot. "I always do it myself, but now the Reverend says I've got to trust it to the two of you, God help us." She shook her head but ploughed on, not even pausing for a breath. "You'll expect two pounds of beef liver, three of kidney, and three of sausage. Then whatever he'll offer of stew lamb and chicken bits as well, provided it's in the budget. Butcher Levy knows what we pay him for the month, so don't let him tempt you with more or we'll be broke within a fortnight." She wiped the sweat from her brow with a doughy forearm, sighing mightily. "And always ask if they've got stripped knuckles, but only if they're free. And don't forget the receipt," she snapped haughtily, reaching into her apron pocket and thrusting a scrap of paper with the scribbled order into my hands. "And don't you dare muss it up, the dinner depends on it. God knows why they've decided to put the two of you in charge, but the Reverend must know best."

I exchanged a glance with Pippa. Cook certainly seemed resentful of having such a sacred task withdrawn from her authority.

Pippa, ever charming, dropped into a graceful curtsey. "Yes, Cook. Very well, Cook."

Cook's expression softened ever so slightly, and I was once more struck by the power Pippa could wield merely through her demure beauty. I could envisage all the marvellous ways we could use this to our advantage in the future; while I may not possess any of her charms myself, I was more than happy to ride her petticoats in that respect.

"Alright then, off with you both. Miss Kaye will meet you at the door to see you off."

"Yes, Cook." This time, Pippa and I curtsied in perfect unison before scurrying out of the kitchen towards the entrance hall.

As promised, Miss Kaye was stationed by the door,

shepherding a few other girls out into the world. She turned, and her eyes fell upon us, narrowing disapprovingly. "Ladies, you are late."

Apparently, this villain was not as susceptible to Pippa's charisma as Cook. "Apologies, Miss Kaye. Cook was providing us with our instructions, and they were quite complex." Pippa's voice had taken on the sweet, melodic tone I'd come to recognise as the one she used when placating our superiors.

On cue, I held up the receipt to corroborate her tale, my expression one of innocent befuddlement.

Miss Kaye pursed her lips. "Very well. It is your first day. Just don't be tardy again tomorrow, or it'll be detention for you both."

"Yes, Miss Kaye," we chirruped.

"First, your map." This she handed to Pippa, but I managed a glance. It was a simple, hand-drawn affair, highlighting the route that would presumably take us to the butcher's shop. "Do not lose this, it is your lifeline through these streets," she dictated, impressing upon us the gravity of our task as if it were not a simple stroll to market such as could be undertaken by a child servant of seven in most monied households.

"Next, you will need these." From a row of hooks running the length of the hallway behind her she procured two forest green hooded travelling cloaks and handed one to each of us. As I swung it about my shoulders to clasp it, I noted the initials *WH* embroidered boldly upon the left breast in rich gold thread.

"Now girls, these cloaks are not simply for propriety," Miss Kaye droned. "For when you go out into society wearing the emblem of Whitechapel Hall, you become an *Ambassador of Virtue*. Our Temperance Outreach programme is only as respected as the young ladies who represent it, and starting today, *you* are two such ladies."

Pippa and I exchanged a glance. To our credit, we did not smirk. "Yes, Miss Kaye."

"Listen carefully. The rules are such: You shall travel directly to your destination and back via the route that has been provided to you. You shall not take detours. You shall not engage in commerce with anyone besides the merchant to whom you have been assigned. You shall not provide monies nor trinkets to the beggars that approach you; instead, you shall offer them solace in prayer. You are to stay together. And most importantly, you are not to deviate from your route for any reason whatsoever. Understood?"

"Yes, Miss Kaye."

"And above all: If one of you runs off, the other must report her and will be rewarded handsomely. If you both run off, it's six weeks' detention and a notice to the court; bear in mind that judges do not take well to runaways. It displays a most abhorrent deficit in character; detention will be the least of your worries if the judge decides jail is a more suitable sentence."

Pippa and I nodded solemnly. "Yes, Miss Kaye."

"Very well. Off you go, and do hurry back; I'm afraid you are hopelessly behind schedule." With that, she fetched two matching white bonnets, two woven baskets, and two sets of gloves from a shelf beside the doorway and placed them into our outstretched hands. And then just like that, the door swung open, and we were at last free upon the streets of Whitechapel.

The first thing I noticed as we descended the stairs was that the rat carcass was gone. I wondered if it had been picked up by a stray cat, or if this street was, as Pippa had suggested, so reputable as to employ a street-sweeper.

Pippa, meanwhile, had her nose buried in the map. She took three steps to the right, then switched left, then right again whilst rotating the map ninety degrees.

"What are you doing?" I hissed as we nearly collided with one another, changing direction once more. I could feel the eyes of passersby upon us, whether drawn by our uniforms or by our obvious obliviousness I wasn't sure. "I thought you'd know these streets back to front after watching them from your perch."

Pippa shot me a nasty glare. "Well, they look quite different from up above, you know."

"Give me that." I snatched the map from her, and though she uttered a squeak of annoyance, she didn't fight me for it. "Look here, it's simple. The school is behind us, so this must be Buck's Row. We take a left towards the station." Steadying myself, I linked my arm with hers and steered her in the right direction.

For a moment, I thought she was cross with me, but a quick glance at her face revealed the hint of a smile upon her lips. "It's lovely, isn't it?" she mused.

I yanked her to an abrupt halt to avoid a cluster of cattle manoeuvring through a cross-street. "It's . . . quite something, I suppose?"

Pippa sighed. "I forget that you only arrived yesterday. I've been locked inside for six whole months."

"Six *months*?" I was aghast. It honestly hadn't occurred to me until that moment how long she'd been sequestered prior to my arrival. "All because you didn't have a partner to accompany you on outreach?"

Pippa shrugged. "Apparently I'm quite the flight risk, as I have an allowance."

"You have an allowance?" I was agog once more; Pippa was certainly full of surprises.

"It's the only benefit of being a voluntary boarder. But they'll only let me have a penny or two at a time, no matter how much Father sends me. That was the only way they'd trust me."

"Does your father know that?"

"I doubt he cares."

Interesting. If Pippa had an allowance, perhaps she would be less tempted than most by the so-called reward offered by Miss Kaye in exchange for reporting a runaway.

The cattle cleared, and we proceeded down the road. The

street was wide and well paved, the south side consisting of shabby but neat two-story cottages overshadowed by tall warehouses towering to the north. As Pippa had predicted, the people out and about did not seem to be of a lowly station; the desperation and decrepitude I'd witnessed on my carriage ride the previous day was concentrated closer to the river.

We passed the station, and I took the opportunity to discreetly assess its defences. It was surrounded by tall iron gates that remained locked, presumably a deterrent against unscrupulous thieves and careless children. It would be considerably more difficult to stow away upon a freight train than a passenger one, I reluctantly concluded, unless I could perhaps disguise myself as a boy with gainful employment there, much like the heroine Johanna Oakley in *A String of Pearls*—

"Dell? What are you doing?"

I realised my pace had slowed nearly to a stop, and I quickly shook myself from my scheming. "Nothing! Sorry, just . . . distracted. I'm just so fascinated by trains, you know?"

Pippa shot me a quizzical look that implied she did not at all believe me, but I took the opportunity to bury my nose in the map once more. "Here, a left on Church Street." Pippa followed me lockstep along a cobbled residential street, pleasantly serene compared to the commotion of Buck's Row, the windows lined with flower boxes and the stoops well swept and even. "Just here, I think, another right." And sure enough, we emerged victorious into the rumpus of Whitechapel High Street.

The energy was contagious, and Pippa and I both grinned from ear to ear as we wove our way through the crowd. We made our way along the row of bustling businesses: shoemakers, lightermen, greengrocers, chemists, china sellers, wheelwrights, dairymen, blacksmiths, and masons all advertised their services with ramshackle signs, and a pleasant bustle filled the air as patrons hurried to and fro. I was mesmerised by delicious scents emanating from sugar shops and bakeries, and the din of chatter was a welcome respite after the oppressive silence that permeated Whitechapel Hall. Pippa was right; it was indeed a lovely privilege to be out among it all.

Just then, a paperboy darted into our path. "*Link Boys! Link Boys of London*, newest edition! Penny each! Penny papers, get your penny papers here!"

My heart galloped in my chest, and my fingers itched at the sight of the familiar font emblazoned across the wood-pulp paper. I yearned to hold it—or at least, to glance upon the headline . . .

But wait! My head whipped in Pippa's direction. "Pippa! Have you got your allowance?"

Pippa gave me a sour look. "I have but one penny on me, Dell, and I'm not spending it on that." Turning up her nose, she continued her steadfast march down the street.

"But . . . but . . ." I ran to catch up with her. "Come on, it will be fun, you'll love reading it! You liked those others, didn't you?"

Pippa didn't slow her pace, and to my disappointment the paperboy disappeared into the crowd, my opportunity lost. "Of course I did, but I'm also nearly out of tobacco, and I can't keep stealing it from Cook's cupboard when she's out for Sunday Mass."

I giggled at the thought, and Pippa took my arm in hers once more, our animosity forgotten. "Fine, then, I guess. But someday, you owe me."

"Of course, Dell. Someday."

We carried on, Pippa maintaining a brisk near-trot, whether out of concern for our timeliness or her desire to prevent me from becoming tempted by further distractions, I couldn't be sure. We crossed Minories Street and instantly saw what I could be certain was the plot on our map labelled BUTCHER'S ROW: a series of stout brick storefronts, each with a brightly coloured canopy extending over the walkway from which dangled the carcasses of various fowl and viands.

"Which one's ours?" Pippa posited, leaning over to consult the map in my hand.

"Number 44, it seems," I replied, gesturing towards the burgundy awning near the end of the row, festooned with garlands of goose necks. We approached the window and peered inside, our elation somewhat muted by the presence of so much slaughter: The display was stacked high with racks of lamb, fresh-plucked chickens, and sides of beef glistening obscenely beneath an oscillating cloud of houseflies. I swallowed hard and looked away, seeking a distraction.

"What do you think *cah-sher* means?" I gestured towards a sign affixed to the front door.

She tilted her head inquisitively. "I think it means 'Jews'?"

I furrowed my brow, but a quick glance up and down the storefronts of the row indicated the same bold KOSHER etched across every one of them. "You don't suppose we have to be Jews to enter, do you?"

Pippa bit her lip. "I shouldn't think so. The Reverend wouldn't have sent us if we did."

I pondered this for a moment. I knew very little of Jews, only a few unkind words I'd overheard my uncle say regarding his business dealings. It had never occurred to me that I might one day come face-to-face with one.

Another thought popped up in my mind, and I lowered my voice to a whisper. "Do they speak English, do you suppose?"

"Of course they speak English, Dell, don't be obtuse." Pippa's tone, however, appeared far less certain than her words, and I was sure she'd had no more experience with real-life Jews than I. She took a moment to adjust her hat and set her shoulders before lifting her chin haughtily in what I now easily recognised as a posture of feigned confidence. "Right, then. Shall we?"

"After you." I pulled open the door and ushered a reluctant-looking Pippa inside.

The interior of the shop was cramped, and we had to shuffle nearly sideways to navigate between shelves stocked with tinned spices and bottled wine. Before we could reach thc counter, however, we were halted in our tracks by a duo of raised voices emanating from behind it. They were arguing, that much was clear, but in a lilting, guttural tongue foreign to my ear. Pippa paused behind a tall rack stacked with bricks of lard, hesitating. "What are you waiting for?" I hissed. Though barging in on an argument between the proprietors would undoubtedly be awkward, it would be infinitely more so if we were caught eavesdropping in the aisle.

"We shouldn't interrupt them!" she whispered, panic painting her features. "It's not proper."

From behind her, one of the voices rose to a shout. It was clear that the disagreement was between an older man and a more youthful one, presumably the butcher himself and a young apprentice. We both flinched as the younger man attempted to interject, only to be silenced by his master's continued outburst.

"What else can we do? We can't return to Cook empty-handed, and Miss Kaye will have our skins if we're tardy."

Pippa glanced around wildly for a solution. "We could try one of the other shops?"

"With what money?" I retorted. "I doubt your penny will cover the debt."

"Fine, then *you* interrupt them, if you're so sure!" She clasped me firmly by the shoulders and swung me around to give me a push in the direction of the counter. At the last moment, my will faltered and I stumbled to a halt, inches from revealing myself. Flummoxed, I sank to a crouch and peered around the corner as discreetly as I could, determined to ascertain the perfect moment for us to divulge our presence.

I could not have chosen a worse moment to do so. As soon as the tip of my bonnet cleared my line of sight, I observed with horror as a tall, broad-shouldered man clad in a fat-streaked apron (Butcher Levy, I presumed) raised his fist and delivered a savage backhand across the face of his young apprentice. My heart clenched in fear at the sudden violence, and I froze, rooted in mortification and fear, watching the scene before me play out.

The apprentice staggered slightly but remained upon his feet. He murmured something quietly in the same strange tongue in which they'd been arguing, eyes downcast and cheekbone reddening from the strike. Apparently satisfied, the butcher stormed off in a huff, disappearing through a curtain blocking a door behind the counter.

The silence that followed was suffocating. I didn't dare move, let alone turn to divulge to Pippa what I had just witnessed. How were we to extricate ourselves without subjecting the poor apprentice to even more distress? I watched as he stood stock-still in silent contemplation, raising his fingers to trace the edge of his inflamed cheekbone, his gaze distant, and for just a moment, everything was still.

Then he simply sighed, shook his head, straightened his apron, and called out in pristine, unaccented English, "May I help you?"

I prayed that he was speaking to someone else. But the silence that followed affirmed my worst fear: not only was the apprentice aware that we were in the shop, but he was also aware that we were currently hiding amidst the jarred fats like a pair of unrepentant snoops.

Swearing under my breath, I rose from my crouch and emerged, carrying myself with as much dignity as I could muster. To my relief, I could hear Pippa's footfalls in step behind me as I approached the counter.

"Good day, sir. We're here on orders from Whitechapel Hall."

The young man gave me an appraising nod, but his gaze quickly pivoted to Pippa, who positioned herself beside me with an air of disinterest. And who could blame him? I could now easily discern that he was our age (or perhaps a year older, if that), his features fine and angular, his tousle of dark hair a debonair accent offset by hazel eyes. His rumpled muslin shirt made him appear stylishly dishevelled, like a swashbuckling hero from a maritime adventure. He was objectively pleasant to behold, if one were interested in gentlemen of his sort. Much to my chagrin, Pippa appeared to be very much interested, judging by the blush forming high on her pale cheeks as she met his eye with a decorous curtsy and discreet smile. Were they characters in one of my penny bloods, the two of them would be eloping within a fortnight. I resisted the urge to roll my eyes.

Any pity I'd felt for him after witnessing the abuse by his master instantly dissipated as I found myself rendered invisible in the throes of their silent flirtation. I cleared my throat loudly, producing Cook's order from the pocket of my cloak and thrusting it at him with perhaps a bit more force than necessary, but I was in no mood to watch some stranger moon over my companion like a star-crossed lover.

"Our order, if you please, sir."

My curtness clearly caught him by surprise, and with a brisk bow he plucked the list from my fingers. "Of course, miss. Right away." He turned and busied himself wrapping stacks of meat in rough brown paper, his attention deliberately focused upon his task.

Pippa leaned over to whisper in my ear as he worked. "Why are you being so rude? He seems perfectly genteel, and we're here to demonstrate our virtuous conduct in the presence of our Whitechapel neighbours."

I longed to be indignant on my own behalf, but my defence caught in my throat. *I didn't like the way he looked at you* sounded unforgivably childish, and I realised if I were to maintain my status as Pippa's bosom friend, I could not allow petty jealousy to dictate my behaviour. She would have countless admirers, and I could not attempt to fend each of them off with a dismal attitude, lest Pippa begin to resent me.

"I was just . . . eager to get back to school," I fumbled, and Pippa shot me a withering look.

I turned my attention back to the apprentice, determined to rectify the situation. "I'm Dell, by the way," I offered. "And this is my friend Pippa." A first-name introduction ought to improve our familiarity, I concluded.

The apprentice tossed an incredulous glance over his shoulder, clearly confused by my unsteady temperament. "Pleased to meet you both. I'm Noah. Noah Levy."

"Levy?" I was startled. "Is this your family's establishment?"

"Indeed," he responded wryly, keeping his focus fixed upon the links of sausage he was measuring out. "That was my father you saw earlier. He's the proprietor."

"Oh." I was at a complete loss for words. It felt unforgivably familiar to say *I'm sorry*, but short of that, what was left to be said? Desperately, I glanced around for a distraction, and to my delight my eyes landed upon a familiar folio resting behind the counter.

"Is that this week's edition of *Link Boys*?"

This got Noah's attention at once. He turned back to face us, an incredulous expression on his face as he wiped his hands upon his apron. "Indeed. Are you a subscriber as well?"

"Why yes, for years! But I've missed the last three weeks on account of—" I stopped myself short, realising that the tale of my uncle's retaliation and my subsequent arrest and sentencing to a penal institution was not appropriate fodder for polite conversation. "On account of unfortunate circumstances. I'm terribly behind on the story now, and I fear I'll never catch up."

Noah's face brightened. "I just so happen to still have the lot! I use them to feed the fire once I'm finished, but the warm weather has spared their fate all summer. You're welcome to have them, if you'd like."

I could scarcely believe my luck. "Are you serious? Yes,

please, a thousand times!" I realised too late that my level of enthusiasm was borderline unladylike, but Noah just smiled.

"But how will you get them into school?" Pippa piped up from beside me. "They'll search our packages for contraband upon return."

I paused to mull this over, but before I could conjure a solution, Noah interjected. "I can place a second layer of wrapping around your meats, with the folios hidden in between. You'll just discard the first layer before you deliver the goods to the kitchen."

I stared at him in amazement. "Did you learn that from *The Demon Detective*?"

Noah laughed and clapped his hands with delight. "The very same! I didn't much care for the series, to be honest, but some of the tricks they pulled are quite handy."

I stared back at my kindred spirit with unbridled glee. "No doubt, but have you read *Revelations of a Lady Detective*? Why, I could rob a bank myself after reading all the clever ploys described in that one."

He shook his head earnestly. "I've only heard of it. Isn't that the one where the Lady Detective, Mrs. G, solves the case of a sleepwalking nurse who murdered a baby?"

I rolled my eyes. "No, Mrs. G is from the series *The Female Detective*. Common misconception."

Noah quirked an eyebrow. "And *Revelations of a Lady Detective* is so different?"

"Completely!" I exclaimed. "As a detective, Mrs. G is a dismal failure. Did you know that in the whole series, she never catches a single criminal? One is let off, two get away before the crime is discovered, one is let go because they simply can't think of a way to track him down, one kills himself, one murder was an accident, and in the last case there is no criminal, but the noncriminal escapes anyway. It's utter rubbish."

Noah laughed. "And your Lady Detective—"

"Mrs. Paschal," I interjected.

"Mrs. Paschal—she has more success?"

"She's brilliant! You really ought to read the series if you like detective stories at all."

Noah appeared quite taken by my description. "Could I borrow your set?"

I felt the elation dissipate immediately as I recalled my edition's sorry fate. "I'd loan it to you, but alas, it . . . caught fire."

Noah gave me a quizzical look but didn't pry. "The only series I hold onto is *Dick Turpin*—it was the first serial I ever bought. A good highwayman's tale will always capture my heart."

"Are you just saying that because Dick was the son of a *Whitechapel butcher*?"

"Ha! You truly know your penny bloods, Miss Dell," he replied, beaming. "No doubt you've also read *The Blue Dwarf*, but have you considered—"

"Ahem."

Our heads swivelled towards Pippa, who was staring at the two of us with exasperation. "Apologies for the interruption, but Dell, must I remind you that we're on a rather strict schedule?"

"Of course, of course, Miss Pippa. A thousand apologies. It will just be a moment, let me grab my folios, and I'll have you on your way in no time flat." With that, Noah dashed off up the stairs, leaving Pippa and me alone once more.

I glowered at Pippa. "*Now* who's being rude? I was just trying to be polite and connect with our *Whitechapel neighbour*."

Pippa pursed her lips. "I simply want to avoid a reprimand. This is our first day on outreach, we shouldn't be irresponsible."

I wanted to believe her, but a part of me suspected that her displeasure was less to do with our timeliness and more to do with the way Noah's attention had been so easily diverted from her. Perhaps I was not the only one to experience jealousy at the threat of exclusion.

I clasped her elbow and gave her a reassuring smile. "Of course, you're right. We mustn't compromise our freedom so recklessly."

Noah bounded back in, waving a stack of pages in his hand. "As requested, Miss Dell, the last three editions of *Link Boys*, coming right up." With a flourish, he commenced wrapping them neatly into the bundles of meat.

At once, Pippa piped up from beside me. "Noah?"

"Yes, Miss Pippa?"

"You wouldn't mind hiding a penny's worth of tobacco in that wrapping, would you?" She pulled a coin from the pocket of her frock and placed it squarely upon the counter.

Noah's eyes widened, his expression one of surprise mingled with amusement. "Of course." He paused to pluck a satchel off the shelf behind him, then carefully folded it into the paper beneath the sausages. "Here you are, ladies." He pushed the stack of parcels over the counter, and Pippa and I tucked them into our baskets.

"Much obliged, Noah," Pippa offered with another curtsy, and I followed suit.

"So, I shall see you both again tomorrow?" He sounded cautiously hopeful.

"Indeed, provided our little secret is not discovered," I replied.

Noah grinned. "I look forward to it." For a moment he hesitated, then resolved to continue. "I must say, you are not at all what I expected when the Reverend informed me of your assignment. You are both quite full of surprises."

Pippa shot him a grin just this side of wicked. "You don't know the least of it." And with a coy wink, she linked her arm with mine and guided me back down the aisle.

We somehow managed to keep our composure until we were

well out the door before collapsing into giggles at Pippa's unabashed flirtation.

"Ooh, I think he *likes* us," Pippa crowed. "See? I told you outreach would be fun. You just must learn to trust me."

"I promise, Pippa, from here on out, I shall."

"Then our future in Whitechapel seems quite bright indeed." Yet as we made our way arm-in-arm through the bustling crowds, still revelling in our newfound freedom (and each carrying a basketful of glorious contraband), I could not help but feel a tight twist of guilt in my stomach. For how could I break the news to Pippa that I had no intention of staying at Whitechapel Hall a moment longer than I must? That the instant I was able, I would turn to run and never look back, leaving her alone in the belfry with nothing but her perch and pipe smoke for company?

But planning an escape for myself was dangerous enough; plotting for two was out of the question. And as much as Pippa had endeared herself to me, could I truly risk trusting her completely after knowing her for only one day?

Of course not. Sentiment could play no role in the equation. I must simply carry on as if I were the friend Pippa believed me to be, until such a time that it was revealed I was not. Otherwise, I was doomed to perpetual imprisonment, if not in Whitechapel, then at the hands of my dastardly relatives or, worse, eventual servitude. And no girlish delights could justify that.

So, I simply squeezed Pippa's arm and smiled, hoping she would not see the regret in my eyes.

Chapter IV
The Misfortunes of Virtue

For the next fortnight, I settled dutifully into the rhythm of life at Whitechapel Hall, which turned out to be maddening. Far from the gothic house of horror I'd yearn to escape, the place was instead morally unobjectionable and relentlessly dull. Pathologically devoted to silence, cleanliness, and godliness, the daylight hours were a blur of suffocating tedium, with nothing to differentiate one day from the next. I'd long believed that a penal institution would be the perfect setting in which to manifest my heroine's destiny, but to my continued dismay, there was no torturous labour to endure, no dungeon from which to abscond, and no simmering underground mutiny brewing amongst my fellow inmates yearning to overthrow our cruel overlords. Instead, there was simply silence, complacency, and boredom.

Each morning following our return from market came breakfast, a sombre affair consisting of either gruel or stone-ground bread and lard, accompanied by the monotonous drone of Miss Kaye's Bible recitations. Afterwards, Pippa and I were employed in the kitchen for three hours straight, assisting Cook with the preparations for supper. An occasional moment of levity could be captured between us if Cook had the decency to leave us unattended for a moment or two, but otherwise, we were condemned to work in silence, eyes downcast and palms worked raw as we chopped, ground, boiled, and scoured our way through our tasks.

Then it was off to chapel, a predictably joyless affair during which Reverend Barnett regaled us with countless cautionary tales of fallen women and their woeful fates (most of which, I was disappointed to note, were considerably less gruesome than those of the virtuous victims in my penny bloods). Afternoons consisted of "lessons" in needlework, laundering, and home-making, an excuse to subject us all to more labour under the stern supervision of our supposed instructor, Mrs. Dolmer, whom I strongly suspected was in fact merely the housekeeper on the take, charged with keeping the inmates occupied with menial tasks lest we summon the will to revolt.

But worst of all was Miss Kaye's Morality class, an hour-long slog through even more Bible passages, made infinitely worse than what we were subjected to at mealtimes as we were expected to debate these venerable moral teachings and debunk any doubts over the absolute dichotomy of right and wrong. It had been barely two weeks of such torture, and I'd already lost track of the times I'd had to bite my tongue to keep from piping up in dissent over some supposedly infallible interpretation of the text that my fellow inmates seemed either too stupid or lazy to contradict. Bed check was at an unreasonably early eight o'clock sharp and served as yet another opportunity for Beatrice to tattle upon anyone not in compliance.

I found myself wistfully recalling my life before imprisonment; as insufferable as my aunt and uncle had been, the banality of life with them was no match for the doldrums to which I had been exiled. With each passing day, my desperation for escape increased. I remained staunchly committed to my plan to exercise restraint, but mornings at market and evenings in the annex (bright spots that they were) barely provided sufficient distraction from the tedium of our captivity.

I had remained vigilant, knowing from years of diligent study in detective fiction that even in a place as dull as Whitechapel Hall there must be formidable foes in our midst, but thus far none of my suspicions had come to fruition. I had become momentarily elated when I noticed that a wanted bank robber whose likeness was plastered upon every window on High Street bore a distinct resemblance to Headmaster Graves, only to be disappointed when the outlaw was apprehended two days later and the headmaster remained in employment (Pippa mocked me relentlessly for my gullibility, but I remained secretly convinced that Graves had a criminal twin). I was overjoyed when I spotted Mrs. Dolmer in possession of Miss Kaye's prized watch, certain she had schemed to pick her cohort's pocket, but it was soon after revealed that she had borrowed the watch with Miss Kaye's full knowledge after her own had ceased to function and she needed to maintain our laundry schedule. For forty-eight breathless hours I suspected that the Reverend had murdered his own daughter based on a clandestine conversation I overheard outside his office, only to discover that she was simply abroad on her honeymoon. And in one final blow to my withered psyche, only moments after I discovered Miss Kaye was caught deep in a web of gambling debt and owed a great sum to her bookie, it was revealed that her 'bookie' was simply the son of the grocer whom she paid weekly for a delivery of the hateful carbolic soap whose sterile scent permeated everything within the Hall. All in all, I had made no progress on my detective career, and even less on my escape plan. Two weeks into my nine-month sentence, my morale was already in tatters.

"I'll eat my bonnet if that actually works."

I looked up to find Pippa casting a sceptical glance at my handiwork: I'd expertly separated the cover of my Bible from the pages within and was currently attempting to affix the latest issue of *Link Boys* we'd received from Noah that morning to the now-tattered binding.

We were sprawled across Pippa's bed surrounded by our contraband bounty, and the clock had just chimed eleven—well past our bedtime, but thanks to our isolation in the annex, we'd quickly discovered we need only keep our lamp stowed behind the dressing screen next to Pippa's bed to avoid detection following Miss Kaye's bed check. We'd therefore developed a delightful evening routine: Following our dour supper in the dining hall, we'd retire to our secret spot upon the roof for a well-earned smoke, soaking in the last throes of summer sun as we observed the goings-on upon the streets below.

There was never a dull moment in Whitechapel, it seemed; from our perch we'd watched a truly brilliant array of vignettes unfold. One night a band of bawdy women rounded up by the local constables managed to break out of the jail cart and rough their captors about, outnumbering them five to one and sending the police into fierce rage before abandoning their prospects of arrest altogether. On another, we watched transfixed as a gang of pint-sized pickpockets made their rounds, dazzled by their dexterity as they lifted no fewer than twelve hats directly off the heads of unsuspecting women in the span of less than half an hour. We'd even witnessed a brazen robbery followed by a thrilling manhunt, and it filled us with giddy elation to observe as the culprit stowed away upon a passing train, leaving the lawmen flummoxed in his wake. Intoxicated by the excitement of it all, we were untouchable, omniscient, our tower transformed from a prison to a portal as we bore witness to thrilling events rivalled only in the pages of our penny bloods.

And the penny bloods were not to be done without! Noah was as good as his word, not just securing the latest edition of *Link Boys* for me but sneaking in older serials as well, apparently keen to replenish my diminished collection. Much to my delight, Pippa consumed them with voracious enthusiasm, and we often stayed up long past midnight poring over the pages together, squealing with horror at the most lurid tales of violence and collapsing into scandalised giggles at the romantic ones.

On this particular night, however, the streets had been dull and quiet, brought to stagnation by an oppressive heat that had settled upon the city for the past three days. The evening brought no respite, no merciful breeze to cool us nor whimsical hijinks to distract our minds. We'd stayed out on our perch as long as the light allowed, reluctant to return to the stale stuffiness of the annex, but had been forced inside by the prospect of navigating the ledge in total darkness.

We'd stripped down to our chemises and assumed our positions on Pippa's narrow cot. I'd told Pippa to read on her own and leave me in peace as I devised a new plan to make our days more bearable, though now it would seem she could not keep her thoughts to herself.

I huffed in exasperation, blinking furiously in the low light. "It's not ideal, I know, but I think if I just weather the pages a bit, there's a chance it's passable."

"But honestly, Dell, is it truly worth it? We have our evenings together to read as much as we please, why can't you just muddle through the day with your head down like the rest of us? If Miss Kaye catches you, we'll both be under scrutiny; she'll surely want to know how we got our hands on these." She waved her faded copy of *The Illustrated Police News* (bearing a truly horrific illustration of a decomposed head on the cover) in my direction.

"It will be worth it," I declared with a sense of finality. "You'll see." Pippa looked unconvinced, but she dutifully cast her eyes back to her own pages, allowing me to return to my endeavour in peace.

A pang of worry clenched in my chest. After all, Pippa was right: Were I to be caught reading such filth in lieu of my Bible, I might find myself squarely in the crosshairs of the deplorable

Miss Kaye, making any plans of escape more dangerous by tenfold. And yet I could not bring myself to carry on as I had been, for while my mornings at market and evenings with Pippa were undeniably a source of joy, there was no way I could envision enduring weeks of this on end. I needed to find a way to keep my mind occupied until I had given a convincing impression of trustworthiness.

With a sigh, Pippa tossed her manuscript aside and rolled languidly onto her back to stare up at the ceiling. "I'm starving."

"Should I be worried that reading about the discovery of a rotten head in the Thames makes you peckish?"

She gave my arm a playful push. "Don't be morbid. I just miss real food sometimes, you know?" Indeed, I did. The culinary offerings at Whitechapel Hall were as bland and monotonous as everything else about the place. Of all the things I missed about my old life, I would willingly place the food at the top of my list.

"What's more," Pippa continued bitterly, "Beatrice has been on market duty as well, and today I saw her handing out apples that she somehow purloined from her stock."

"*Apples?*" My eyes flew open wide at the prospect. Nothing we'd seen in the kitchen resembled anything that could be consumed without first being mercilessly boiled, baked, fried, or stewed beyond recognition. The idea of fresh food was unthinkable. "How on earth did she get her hands on apples?"

Pippa continued to stare mournfully up at the ceiling. "They're for the staff, or anyone with money. They used to let me to purchase them from Cook with my allowance, until the Reverend deemed it unbecoming for me to have such indulgences while the other girls had none." She sounded bitter at the recollection.

I pursed my lips in contemplation. "But where do they store the fruit?"

Pippa shot me a sidelong glance. "You've never found it odd

that Cook doesn't allow us into the pantry? No doubt she keeps the staff stock locked away in there."

I was upright in an instant. "I'm getting us some."

Pippa remained disappointingly supine. "And how, precisely, are you going to do that?"

I shrugged, the sluggish haze brought on by the heat suddenly dissipating with the prospect of a mission to test my spy skills. "I'll take the lamp and sneak downstairs. It's well past bed check; I doubt Miss Kaye stays up for the sole purpose of prowling the halls at night to catch disobedient pupils."

Pippa propped herself up onto her elbows but still looked unconvinced. "I'm all for making a bit of trouble, Dell, but as I said, the last thing we need is you bringing Miss Kaye's scrutiny upon us, now that we have all this." She gestured towards our stacks of serials.

"It's a matter of principle," I replied defiantly. "Beatrice and her gib-faced cronies don't deserve all the spoils. Besides, I'm hungry, too." Intention set, I snatched up the lamp, covered it with my shawl, and scuttled down the staircase before Pippa could utter another word of protest.

Reaching the bottom of the stairs, I paused to gather myself. While I had no concrete plan, I'd read enough of Mrs. Paschal to know a thing or two about clandestine quests. Though I had no cleverly crafted dark-lantern with which to guide my way, I concluded that I might achieve a similar effect by parting my shawl just enough for a sliver of light to split the darkness. I could barely make out the slumbering forms of the other girls in the periphery, and the illumination was just enough to guide me between the narrow rows of cots towards the heavy door at the far end of the hall. Holding my breath, I slid my stockinged feet upon the ground in slow, smooth shuffles, to avoid the incrimination of a footfall. Heart throbbing in my chest, the nobility of my mission spurned me on.

To my utmost relief, not a single soul stirred as I spirited past them, and I arrived at the far end of the dormitory in mere seconds. Barely daring to exhale, I wrapped my fingers around the heavy iron knob of the door and gave it a resolute twist—

Only to find it locked. I let out a crude curse (though only in my mind), half incensed by the circumstance and half furious with myself for not anticipating it. Of course, our captors would not be so careless as to leave their wards to roam free; what sort of dull-witted villains would leave a tower full of maidens unattended? And while I was not new to picking locks (I'd picked a fair few cupboards at my aunt's when she'd first begun locking up my books), I'd never found myself up against a proper mortice lock before; it would require a level of agility greater than my previous conquests.

Fully wrapping my lantern to shroud myself in the darkness, I paused. *What would Mrs. Paschal do?* Certainly not abandon her prospects at the first obstacle she came upon! A true detective must use the tools at hand to orchestrate her success.

So, what had I at hand? No tools at all except my lantern, which suddenly offered a tempting solution. Swiftly, I knelt to the ground to huddle beneath my shawl and pressed the latch to release the lantern door with a soft *ping.* Upon closer inspection, the pin holding the hinge was just the right size to leverage the lock. But how to remove it? I issued a desperate glance at my surroundings; I had nothing but the shawl and the clothes upon my back. A hairpin would be perfect for the task, but alas, I'd let my coils down hours ago and hadn't the foresight to bring one with me.

I paused. Though I hadn't a hairpin on my person, I was in a dormitory full of young ladies. Surely any one of them would have hairpins aplenty! Cautiously, I lifted the corner of my shawl to assess my surroundings. The nearest bed was that of Beatrice, and the idea of lifting the item in question from her private stores was more than a little satisfying. With the vigilance of a rogue, I swiftly crouched and made my way to her bedside, careful to direct the beam from my lantern towards her nightstand. I cast my light across its surface, but to my dismay, I found it vacant aside from her extinguished lamp.

Just then, the unmistakable sound of rustling bedsheets erupted behind me. There was no time to hesitate; I immediately dropped to the floor and rolled beneath Beatrice's bed, dragging my lantern with me as I frantically re-draped my shawl around it to smother its glow, my breath coming in ragged gasps that required all my concentration to control. For a seeming eternity, I froze.

And then: nothing. No more movement from the figure above me, nor any sign of restlessness from those surrounding me. Ever so slowly, I allowed my limbs to relax, and my heart gradually receded from where it had lodged itself in my throat. With some effort, I managed to roll over onto my stomach and commenced shimmying my way out from my hiding place as furtively as I could, careful not to upset my lantern in the process. Just as I was about to raise myself to stand, my hand pressed down upon something hard and sharp. An exclamation of pain died on my tongue when it dawned on me what the offending object was: none other than a hairpin, carelessly discarded beneath the bed, seemingly poised for this precise moment in time! I couldn't have written it better myself were I in the pages of Paschal's book!

With silent glee, I pocketed the hairpin and resumed my post by the door. The tool served its purpose superbly; I was able to eject the pin from the lantern latch in one swift stroke and then, with the handle of my lantern clutched uncouthly in my teeth, I was able to pair it with the hairpin to make quick work of the mortice lock. With a satisfying *click*, the bolt shifted, and the door at last swung open.

The halls were silent and abandoned, the marble of the floors blissfully cool beneath my stockinged feet. Unlike the draconian dark of the dormitory, the moonlight streaming through the tall windows of the hallway provided plenty of light as I slipped silently down the main staircase. Past the eerily still entrance hall, through the desolate dining room, I moved silently as a spirit until at last I came to the kitchen.

Letting out a breath I scarce realised I'd been holding, I withdrew my shawl from the lantern and allowed myself a proper look about the place. The room was hot and stagnant, the last remaining coals still flickering in the great stone fireplace, and the stale cabbage-watery smell which always infests such domestic offices hovered heavily in the air.

I made my way past the larder and to the pantry door, tucked into the furthest corner of the room. To my surprise, there was no lock in place (though upon reflection, it stood to reason that Cook never left us unsupervised long enough for us to enter this forbidden sanctum). Pulling it open, I couldn't contain a gasp.

The shelves were lined with food—real food! There were of course the dreary sacks of flour, potatoes, salt, turnips, and cabbage, but there were also jellies, jams, saveloys, bacon, sugar, and fruit! Apples and oranges both, glistening brightly in a basket affixed to the far wall, so tempting my mouth watered at the mere sight of them. Unable to contain myself, I rushed forward and plucked up a pair with my hands. It took every ounce of willpower I possessed not to sink my teeth into the juicy flesh right then and there, but no, I had promised Pippa a treat, and I intended to deliver and enjoy my success in her doting company.

I tied the hem of my chemise into a loose knot to create a pocket for my prize, then hastily shoved two apples and two oranges inside; it was, by my estimation, the most I could take without their absence being rendered noticeable to the undiscerning eye. Elation thrumming through my veins, I'd turned to grab my lantern from the shelf upon which I'd abandoned it when my eyes fell upon a most unexpected sight.

There, in the furthest corner of the pantry, was a door.

It was small, less than half the size of a standard entryway, with an ornately carved surface and thick brass handle. Curious, I pulled it open and found myself face-to-face with a small wooden platform and a pulley rope. A *dumbwaiter.*

An unforgettable scene from *A String of Pearls* leapt instantly into my mind: Mark Ingestrie, the heroine's true love, had been kept prisoner in Sweeney Todd's basement, baking pies from human flesh to sell to unsuspecting patrons. But in a dazzling display of wit and daring, he escaped via the lift used to transport the pies upstairs, undoing Todd's dastardly operation once and for all.

I gave the device a more discerning look. It was indeed large enough to fit a small person—a tight fit, no doubt, but considering it was apparently used to transport heavy sacks of goods, I reasoned I could fold myself inside without much ordeal. I could lower myself using the rope, just as Mark had done in the pages of my folio, and I would be transported directly to freedom via the alley below.

I blinked rapidly. I could hardly believe that such an obvious path to escape had presented itself to me unbidden, and I stood simultaneously thrilled and terrified by the option now laid before me.

I could leave now. The prudent part of me wanted to push the thought from my mind, yet the temptation persisted. I had vowed to be more cautious in planning my impending escape than I had in times past, but how could I pass up such an opportunity? I was here, alone and undetected, well after midnight, and the whole school was asleep. If I made a run for it now, I could put plenty of ground between myself and Whitechapel by daybreak, when my absence would be detected. The only one who would miss me before then was Pippa.

And what of Pippa? Guilt struck me to my core imagining her upstairs, whiling away the hours awaiting my return, wondering if I'd been caught and our sanctuary was moments away from a raid conducted by an irate Miss Kaye.

Would Pippa believe me capable of escape? Surely the thought had crossed her mind, though we had never discussed it outright. But she would not dare report me tonight, whether out of loyalty or self-preservation it mattered not. While the thought of leaving her behind pained me greatly, there was no way I could guarantee such a fortuitous confluence of events could be replicated later with her at my side—and that was if she even agreed to go with me. My moment was now or never.

Decision made, I assessed my prospects: I could make it out of the building, but then where to? I had only my chemise and shawl and the stockings on my feet; there was no way I'd make it far in such unusual attire, even in Whitechapel. I needed a covering were I not to be mistaken for a complete derelict and arrested for indecency.

I pulled the purloined fruit from my apron and returned it to the basket. Freed of that burden, I sprinted out of the pantry, through the kitchen, past the dining room, and out into the entrance hall. Hanging in a row by the door like a parade of impatient ghosts were twenty-four identical cloaks and matching bonnets. I plucked up a set and quickly yanked them on, then grabbed a pair of gloves off the shelf and stuffed them into my pocket. While it was hardly a perfect solution, my outfit would at least not attract attention—provided the bystanders ignored my feet, which were still woefully bootless.

The boots were a problem. Not only would my stockinged feet give away any feigned air of respectability, but there was also no way I could manage any type of escapade (say, hopping aboard a moving train) without them. I stewed upon this thought as I made my way back to the pantry and, alas, came to but one conclusion: I couldn't make it out of Whitechapel tonight. I had no shoes, no money, and no proper plan. But I could at least escape the school, which would be a vast improvement from my current situation. I simply needed somewhere to run *to*, a place to bide my time until I could find my footing . . .

Noah. His name came to me as a sudden epiphany. He would understand the nobility of my escape! Any chivalrous soul who'd read a single penny blood would feel pity for an imprisoned heroine in distress, and Noah's heart seemed tender enough; he could be my protector, hero of his own tale. I would not ask him for much: simply shelter, for a time, until I could procure the funds to leave the city (how I would go about that remained inconclusive, though I had to admit watching the pickpockets snatch hats directly off ladies' heads had given me a taste to try my hand at the art. After all, was it truly stealing if it were for a cause as worthy as my freedom?).

My plan wasn't perfect, but it was just brazen enough to work. Before I could hesitate, I gripped the edge of the dumbwaiter and hoisted myself up and in. It was a tight fit, but the interior was taller than it looked, and I was able to assume a seated position with relative ease. Taking one last look to ensure the hem of my cloak was safely tucked beneath me, I yanked the door shut, gripped the rope between my fingers, and pulled.

The process was slow but steady. My breath came in excited gasps as the comforting light of my abandoned lantern faded from the edges of the door frame, encasing me in total darkness. For a moment, I nearly panicked: what if I were to become stuck, and no one knew where I was trapped? How often did Cook take deliveries from the alley below? Would I be saved at daybreak, or found weeks later, mottled and decomposing? Shaking such morbid thoughts from my mind, I concentrated on placing one hand below the other, lowering myself into the unknown depths. After what seemed an eternity (but was realistically no more than a minute), I jarred to a halt. Fumbling in the darkness, my fingers closed around the blessed shape of a doorknob. With a twist and a shove, the door flew open, and I tumbled out into an unfamiliar landscape.

I was, as I anticipated, in an alley, or at least something akin to one. It was narrow and dark, the ground beneath my feet dirt instead of the familiar cobblestone of Buck's Row. The well-worn carriage tracks indicated that it was a thoroughfare of some sort, but it was lined with bulging sacks of refuse heaped carelessly in the looming shadows on either side.

How absolutely vile. I had spent little time in alleys; I knew them only as clever getaways utilised by the protagonists in my books when outwitting their nefarious nemesis, and none of my tomes had taken the liberty of mentioning the godforsaken smell. Choking back a gag, I hastily made my way towards the opening at the far end of the lane, leading to what I assumed would be Buck's Row.

Just then, the hem of my cloak caught upon something protruding from one of the discarded sacks, and I swore under my breath as I turned to untangle myself. To my surprise, I looked down to find my hem in the grasp of five filthy fingers.

"Eh there, pretty creature, fancy a flight?"

In an instant, the realisation dawned on me that the 'sack' gripping me was no sack at all but a man, his face obscured by darkness but rapidly taking shape as my mind caught up to what my eyes were perceiving. Two bloodshot eyes leered up at me, framed by a mop of greasy hair and a menacing grin full of teeth so jagged they appeared more wolf than human.

I stumbled backwards and tripped over another 'sack,' which promptly sat up and shouted a string of expletives in my direction. To my compounding horror, all the other sacks in the alley began to shift and shuffle, a menacing rumble swelling under the cover of darkness. Why, these were no sacks of refuse at all, but people!

A scream caught in my throat. I whirled around and pelted towards Buck's Row with all the speed my legs could afford me. The phantom clutch of the wolf-man's fingers tore at my cloak as I raced through the gauntlet of filthy degenerates huddled in the shadows, sure that each moment was my last. Pumping my arms, I willed myself to move faster than their malevolent intentions could catch me.

I burst out onto the Row with a cry of relief, the light of the streetlamp welcoming me in its familiar glow. Though this section of road was now deserted, I knew from my watch with Pippa that there were policemen aplenty patrolling these parts. I had initially intended to avoid them at all costs for the duration of my escape, but the presence of a constable suddenly seemed a much more favourable prospect than before; Whitechapel after dark was a more treacherous landscape than my morning sojourns to market had led me to believe.

Gathering my wits, I made my way towards High Street with haste, my stockinged steps affording me a degree of secrecy as I skirted the pools of lamplight as closely as I dared. I had no desire to be observed, but my encounter in the alley had rattled me considerably, and I was forced to confront the precariousness (I refused to entertain the prospect of *foolhardiness*) of my mission. The city itself could be just as formidable a foe as my prior captors had been, and caution was now as essential as cunning.

I turned onto Court Street with a degree of relief; though shadowed, its residential nature offered a semblance of safety, and I could see the lights of High Street beckoning ahead. High Street was never vacant and would offer me both anonymity and protection. I gathered my cloak and skirt in hand and broke into a brisk trot. Just then, a voice echoed down the street from behind me.

"You there! Halt!" I whirled around to discover a policeman was standing at the corner of Buck's Row, holding his lantern aloft in my direction.

I froze. What reason had he to interrogate me? The answer seemed suddenly obvious: I was scampering down a residential street, shrouded in darkness and silent as a spectre, at a time of night when only the unseemliest figures in Whitechapel were out and about. He no doubt mistook me for a burglar, up to petty tricks under the cover of night.

I could not heed his command. All it would take was one look at my cloak to know that I was a ward of Whitechapel Hall, and I had no ready excuse for my state of undress or the absence of my boots or my presence out on the street at such an hour. He would return me immediately to my wardens and leave me to face whatever excruciating punishment they could conjure. Such a fate I could not tolerate.

In for a penny, in for a pound, I muttered under my breath, then turned and sprinted in the opposite direction of my pursuer. I bore down towards High Street like a woman possessed, brimming with conviction that if I could only make it that far, I could disappear easily into a tavern or boarding house long enough for him to give up the chase. Ignoring the shouts behind me, I dodged a discarded barrow, hopped over a sagging stoop, ducked beneath a dangling flowerpot, and flung myself around the corner—

And somehow directly into the arms of none other than *Miss Kaye*. For a moment, she blinked, too stunned to speak, but then realisation spread across her face, only to be replaced by outright fury.

I was caught!

Chapter V
The Silent Witness

Our return to the confines of Whitechapel Hall was not what I had expected. I expected Miss Kaye to be apoplectic with fury, to berate and threaten me, or to drag me bodily through the streets like a petulant child. But instead, she simply reached forward, grabbed my arm in a vise-tight grip, spun me around, and marched me straight back to the premises in seething, ominous silence. She offered a curt nod to the policeman who'd pursued me as we passed by him in the dim light of Court Street; apparently satisfied that I was no thief and instead simply a reckless urchin under the stern supervision of my mother, he allowed us to pass with only a nod in acknowledgement.

Miss Kaye's clutch did not lessen as we turned back onto Buck's Row. To my surprise, she did not lead me up the stair to the main entrance, but instead steered me to a stout wooden door situated adjacent to the stable yard that bordered the school. Across the door sat a heavy metal bar fitted snugly into a latch affixed to the door frame. With her free hand, Miss Kaye lifted the bolt, then procured a rough-hewn iron key from the folds of her cloak. With this, she unlocked the door and pulled it outwards, thrust me inside, and then followed me in, pulling the door firmly shut behind her. Outside, I could hear the metal bar clank back into place; it was clear this door was meticulously secured against students angling for a getaway. Locking it behind her and pocketing the key, she guided me up a rickety set of wooden stairs and through a doorway which deposited the two of us directly into the back of the chapel. I had seen this door before in passing but always assumed it simply led to a closet; the idea that it led to the outside world was a rather embarrassing oversight.

"This way." Those were the first words she'd uttered since our chance encounter, and her voice was low and dangerous. She guided me down the moonlit passage to the entrance hall, stopping before the row of cloaks, the peg at the end conspicuously empty. "Return your things at once."

Sheepishly, I shed my cloak and bonnet, then produced the gloves and plopped them back into place. Miss Kaye's eyes narrowed at my woeful state of undress. Still, she said nothing. She simply took my arm back into her ruthless grasp and guided me up the staircase. The silence was so heavy it rang in my ears as I contemplated my sorry fate.

What was my punishment to be? Would I be whipped? Locked in some undiscovered vault or maimed by a torture device like the ones I had read about in a particularly juicy penny blood detailing the barbarism of the Middle Ages? Would I be expelled and sent to jail to serve the remainder of my sentence? Each prospect was worse than the last, and I could see no future that was not full of suffering and solitude.

And solitude! My mind returned instantly to Pippa, who by this point had surely given up all hope of my return. Would she comfort me if I were whipped, visit me if I were imprisoned, rescue me if I were tortured, or mourn me if I were banished? Or would she be so incensed by the betrayal of my escape that my name would become as a curse to her, the mark of a traitor as fickle as her own father, who had abandoned her to fulfil his own selfish designs? The thought was so hateful I could not bear it, and for the first time since my capture, my eyes welled with tears.

We'd no sooner rounded the corner at the top of the stair than I received my second great fright of the night as we nearly collided with none other than the headmaster himself.

"Miss Kaye!" Graves exclaimed, clutching his heaving bosom in surprise. "Why, what in Heaven's name are you doing up? I'd thought you returned hours ago! And as I live, is this Miss Morton? What is the meaning of all this?"

"Apologies, Headmaster. I was just assisting Miss Morton with an urgent matter in the kitchen." I was too stunned to react to this blatant lie and instead simply stared dumbly up at my captor.

Graves's brow furrowed, and he squinted incredulously at the two of us, me in my chemise and stockings, and Miss Kaye still in her cloak. "The kitchen? At this hour?"

"Yes, Headmaster. Cook informed me this afternoon of a pressing matter involving the bread dough which required attention tonight. It slipped my mind until just now, and I took it upon myself to rouse Miss Morton to address it at once. Otherwise, we were to be subjected to unleavened loaves for four days straight, a fate by which, I'm sure you'll agree, Cook would not kindly abide."

A flicker of a smile appeared on Graves's face; Cook's diligence regarding her bread was well known by all who crossed her path. "Of course, Miss Kaye. I do trust your discretion. But please ensure Miss Morton returns to bed promptly; the hour is unduly late. Now excuse me, I must be off. Urgent business with the Reverend." And with a tip of his hat, he pressed past us and proceeded down the stairs.

Miss Kaye continued our silent march to an undesignated destination, guiding me through yet another doorway and up an unfamiliar staircase to a part of the school I had never accessed. The hall into which we emerged was dim and narrow, a shoddy lamp burning feebly where it hung on the wall, and I was conducted into a small room before the flimsy door snapped shut at my heels, plunging us both into darkness. Summoning all the courage I could, I aspired to convey the bravery of my Lady Detective despite my precarious lot. I must have *nerve and strength, cunning and confidence*. Now was not the time for remorse—at least, not until I could perceive my opponent's aims with clarity, for at present they were as unknowable as my fate.

Miss Kaye turned and lit a lamp, and for the first time, I was able to perceive my surroundings. We appeared to be in her personal office, a small, cramped room outfitted with a handsome desk, two chairs, and a row of bookshelves sparsely stocked with ecclesiastical volumes. In the far corner was a narrow door, which I assumed led to her private chamber. A brass coat rack was positioned in the corner, and upon it she deposited her own cloak and hat, then situated herself rigidly in the chair positioned behind her desk.

"Miss Morton. Be seated." I did so immediately in the chair opposite hers.

She carried on without pause in her soft monotone. "Miss Morton, I am going to ask you a series of questions. If you answer me promptly and truthfully, I have no doubt that our exchange will be a productive one." She paused, allowing the silence to ring loudly between us.

"Yes, Miss Kaye."

"But if you attempt to deceive me or perjure yourself, you will find yourself in quite a precarious position, as this institution does not tolerate deviance. And what I witnessed from you tonight was no doubt an act of wilful deviance, was it not?"

"Yes, Miss Kaye," I whispered.

She paused. "Again, Miss Morton. I can't hear you. *Were you not engaged in an act of wilful deviance?*"

I paused; perhaps my approach was all wrong. Looking up, I met her glance and returned it unflinchingly. "Yes, Miss Kaye." This seemed to satisfy her. "Indeed. So, first and foremost: How did you escape?"

My mind reeled with possibility. I could, of course, simply tell her the truth. But my plan had worked flawlessly until a twist of dumb luck had foiled it; would it not be to my advantage to keep my method secret to make a second attempt later? To have time to procure some money, plot a destination, and for God's sake, *put on boots* (the soles of my feet throbbed at the thought, the roughness of the cobblestones having done them considerable harm).

"I . . . I picked the lock." It wasn't a total lie, and I fashioned my expression into one of earnest penance. Like Mrs. Paschal, I knew I must carry myself as an accomplished actress through the adversity of my interrogation.

Miss Kaye's brow knitted ever so subtly in the flickering lamplight. "Now, Miss Morton, that's simply not true. The lock to the entrance hall has been tested by the best locksmith in London, and the only one who holds the key to get in or out is Headmaster Graves himself. No one leaves the premises without his knowledge. Furthermore, the door to the staff entrance is barred from outside, an unfortunately necessary precaution, as I'm sure you'll agree. You did not pick any lock." The severity of her gaze provided no opportunity for misinterpretation: she was not a gullible subject.

I changed my tune in an instant, buying time. "No, no, not the front door, ma'am. The door to the dormitory. I picked the lock of the dormitory."

Her expression softened slightly. "I see. Go on."

"And then . . ." I grasped at straws. "I . . . Well, you see, earlier this evening I stole the headmaster's key from his key ring. And . . . I used that."

Miss Kaye wearily removed her spectacles and produced a

lace kerchief from her pocket. Sitting back in her chair, she proceeded to polish them in silence. The lull dragged on forever, and she showed no indication of continuing her questioning. Instead, she simply sat, leaving me to squirm. Eventually, I could take it no longer.

"Miss Kaye?"

"Yes?"

"Did you . . . have any further questions for me?"

"Not at the moment, Miss Morton. I was simply waiting."

"Waiting?"

"Waiting for Headmaster Graves to arrive."

"Why would Headmaster Graves arrive?"

"Because you and I have just encountered him on his way out to the Reverend's. And once he arrives in the entrance hall and discovers his key is missing, he shall be in dire need of assistance in locating it. I imagine he will arrive imminently and deliver this news. Will he not?" With that, she replaced her spectacles upon her face and blinked back at me expectantly, her expression one of manufactured innocence.

Drat.

"I . . . Well, yes, but I— "

"Miss Morton, if you intend to convince me that you somehow performed a magnificent sleight of hand during our encounter in the entrance hall and returned the key to its rightful place without myself or the headmaster being any the wiser, you are either much more dim-witted than you seem or believe me much more dim-witted than I am assured I appear, and I am not certain which of those two scenarios you feel would help your present case."

I bit my lip, resisting the flush I could feel rising in my cheeks. Miss Kaye leaned forward, folding her hands primly upon her desk. "Allow me to make myself perfectly clear. If you continue to lie to me, I shall have no choice but to report your transgression to the headmaster. I cannot stand by, knowing that there is an unsecured method of egress from this school; it is a liability which I have no desire to shoulder alone. And I must tell you from experience, the headmaster will imminently send a statement to the judge overseeing your case, and your sentence will be rightfully amended, and you shall serve time in jail for violating his orders. Is that what you want?"

Jail. The idea shook me considerably. Until that point, my petty acts of rebellion felt harmless—if not to my aunt and uncle (and the bookseller I had swindled), at least to me. But for the first time, I realised acting in contempt of my legal sentence was perhaps a bridge too far.

"No, Miss Kaye." For the first time, I spoke the truth.

"Good. Now tell me, how did you come to be out on the streets of Whitechapel tonight?"

At last, I resigned myself to my fate. "The dumbwaiter in the pantry." Miss Kaye's eyebrows rose a fraction of an inch, barely discernible in the flickering lamplight, but I could tell she was intrigued. "Cook never allows us in the pantry, but . . . I'd snuck in for some . . . refreshment. I wasn't planning to run off, upon that I swear." It wasn't a lie, technically, and I was eager to plead my case. "But then I saw the door, and I was all alone, and there was . . . opportunity."

Miss Kaye pursed her lips. "So, am I to understand this was not a premeditated effort?"

"No, not at all," I rushed to assure her. "Why, if you go to the kitchen now, my lantern will still be upon the counter where I left it, pointing straight to my hideout. It was not my intention to run off, but I must confess, it's . . . well, it's habit."

Was it possible that the edges of her lips turned up ever so slightly at this admission? Surely the light was playing tricks on me. She sat in silence for a moment more, carefully turning my story over inside her head.

"Very well. And what was your plan, once you were outside?"

"I hadn't a very good one, ma'am."

"In the absence of your clothing and boots, I'd imagine not," she retorted. "Was anyone else aware of your designs?"

My mind flitted to Pippa, no doubt lying awake upstairs, but she was innocent in all of this. "No, ma'am."

"Very well." She sat up straight once more and looked me squarely in the eye. "Absent any grand design or ill intent, I see no reason to inform the headmaster of your momentary lapse in judgement tonight." I exhaled for the first time since my interrogation had begun. "*However*," she continued sternly, "this deed will not go unpunished. Detention, here in my office, nightly for the next three weeks following your dismissal from supper." I wanted to squawk with indignation, for that was my time to spend with Pippa upon our perch, my favourite moment of the day! Luckily, I was able to regain my composure before any incriminating sound of protest could escape. "And Miss Morton, I will have Cook seal up the dumbwaiter first thing tomorrow morning, so let the thought of a second attempt at such folly be scrubbed vigorously from your mind."

"Yes, ma'am."

"And last, but most importantly: I implore that you do not tell your fellow pupils of the offence you committed tonight. Word spreads quickly here, and were the headmaster to discover our little agreement, he will be disinclined to give you any further benefit of the doubt."

"Yes, ma'am."

"Thank you, Miss Morton. Now off to bed, the hour is late." With a flick of her hand, I was dismissed and soon found myself treading the now-familiar moonlit halls leading back to the dormitory, my thoughts a jumble of confusion. What had just happened? Why had Miss Kaye lied to the headmaster for me? What motive had she to protect my reputation?

And what's more, what had Miss Kaye been doing out upon the streets so late herself? It would seem the headmaster was aware of her departure from the school, but it had been well past dark by the time I encountered her; what could a woman of her esteem be up to upon the streets at such an hour? And Headmaster Graves himself! He had been fully dressed despite the time, apparently intent upon an urgent audience with the Reverend, and made no excuse for his odd manner. It was a curious encounter indeed! Had I not already pardoned them both of my prior suspicions, I should think each was up to something quite scandalous.

Before I knew it, I was slipping through the dormitory and fumbling my way in the darkness towards the stairs to the annex, using every ounce of grace I possessed to avoid crashing into a bed and awakening the girls. At long last, my fingers grasped the familiar railing of the spiral staircase, and with one last breathless press, I ascended to my sanctuary.

"Dell!" I had barely cleared the top stair before I was practically bowled over by Pippa, her near-violent embrace as stifling as it was surprising. "God in Heaven, Dell, I'd thought you were lost!"

I managed to loosen myself from her grip just enough to perceive her face. To my shock, her eyes were glistening with tears, and her lower lip trembled with emotion. It was clear that my prolonged absence had had a great effect upon her, and guilt once again washed over me at the prospect of her abandonment.

"Oh, Pippa, it's alright, I'm here." I pulled her close and stroked her hair, willing myself not to notice how she shook with suppressed sobs of relief in my arms.

"You were gone for ages!" she mustered through muffled tears.

"I'm so sorry, I'm so sorry . . ." I held her to me, comforting her as best I could.

At long last, her tears subsided, and she pulled away once more to study my face. "Oh, Dell, what happened? I was certain you were caught. You frightened me half to death!"

I let out a long exhale. "That's the thing . . . I was. Caught, that is."

Pippa's eyes flew open with horror. "Caught?! By whom?"

"Miss Kaye. But Pippa, you must listen, the strangest thing just happened . . ."

And I told her, in as general terms as I could, about my odd encounter with Miss Kaye. I left out the bit about my attempted escape and instead conveyed a tale in which I was simply caught in the act of stealing fruit. After all, it was hardly my crime that was the curious part; I was entirely more focused upon Miss Kaye's bizarrely altruistic reaction to my misdeed.

When I was finished, she let out a deep sigh and lowered herself to sit upon my cot. "That was lucky, Dell. Extremely lucky. She could have told the headmaster! You might have been expelled!"

I settled beside her, tucking my feet beneath me so that she might not notice the shredded soles of my stockings. "I know. But isn't it odd about Miss Kaye? She's always so strict, but tonight—"

"Dell?" Pippa's eyes had turned stern, and she firmly clasped my hands in hers. "This time? Let it go."

"But don't you think it's strange—"

"Yes, Dell, of course it's strange! But just this once, I don't want to wonder if it's because Miss Kaye is a foreign spy or a murderer on the lam or an escaped convict from Newgate. I want her to just be our teacher, who did a kind thing and did not take my only friend in this world away from me."

Any words of protest died in my throat. Her plea was so sincere, I was powerless to argue with her. "Alright, Pippa. I'll let it go. This time."

"Good." And with that, she dropped her head to my shoulder, and I rested mine upon hers. There were no more words to say.

We nearly slept through the bell the following morning, having drifted off side by side on my cot well past the stroke of one. It was a struggle to rouse ourselves for market, even with the promise of more contraband from Noah.

"I'll be dead on my feet all day," Pippa moaned as we shuffled blearily down the stairs to Buck's Row, still tugging our bonnets on as we attempted to make up for our slow start. My mood was similarly dismal. The swollen soles of my feet throbbed from the events of the previous night, and my eyelids felt lined with lead. Even the promise of a fresh pinch of tobacco and the latest *Link Boys* was hardly enough to cheer me.

"Oi! Coming through." I elbowed my way through a tight crowd spilling over from the entrance to the stable yard, a jam presumably caused by yet another herd of damn cattle wallowing about. The streets had lost their lustre for me today, and one glance at Pippa's pinched expression and sallow eyes confirmed she felt the same.

We arrived at Noah's with our sour dispositions intact, and I was unamused when we had to ring the bell no fewer than four times before we heard the telltale sound of his footsteps upon the back stair.

"What is taking so long? I'm bound to fall asleep standing up at this rate." Pippa leaned forward and buried her head in her arms upon the counter, a most unladylike posture, but her flair for drama did make me giggle.

Noah burst into the room with his usual exuberance, but for once, his expression was not one of fond anticipation. Instead, he appeared unnaturally pale and short of breath. "Pippa! Dell! What are you doing here?"

Pippa did not raise her head off the counter, so I took it upon myself to respond to his odd line of questioning. "It's seven o'clock, of course. Why wouldn't we be here?"

Noah shook his head vigorously. "Haven't you heard? There's been a *murder*, right here in Whitechapel!"

Chapter VI
Whispers of Blood

We positioned ourselves strategically upon the staircase outside the door that led to Noah's family's dwellings upstairs. Prior to our arrival, he'd been eavesdropping on a conversation between his mother and two local men who'd brought the grim tidings straight from the site, but Pippa and I had sadly interrupted Noah's snooping with our arrival. It took little persuasion for us to join him in his attempt to hear all the gory details. It was a moment I'd dreamed of all my life. A murder, in my very neighbourhood! And here I was, lucky enough to hear the details from men who had seen it firsthand! Noah and I settled silently upon the stair and pressed our ears against the door. Pippa, meanwhile, drooped against the bannister and rested her head upon my knees, apparently content to receive the news secondhand.

I furrowed my brow, attempting to untangle the muffled words I was hearing from the other side of the door. After a few seconds, I pulled away in exasperation. "I can't hear anything," I hissed to Noah. "At least, nothing I can understand."

Noah shot me a quizzical look. "They're speaking Yiddish, Dell."

Well, that made sense. "Oh."

Noah just chuckled and shook his head, then pressed his ear back against the door. At last, he began to translate.

"The victim was a woman. Nickelson? Nichols. They found her with all her insides torn out, right there in the street, like a . . . butchered cow—or beast. Animal. She was found by the . . . over by Brown's Stable Yard. Gracious, that's close to you lot, isn't it?" I nodded breathlessly, and even Pippa sat up and looked alert at this revelation. Noah leaned in closer, grimacing with the effort to make out the words. "New Scotland Yard is on the scene. They . . . They have a suspect? No, that can't be right." He muttered something to himself (presumably in Yiddish) under his breath. "They're . . . asking questions. The police are asking questions." With that, he promptly pulled back from the door and gestured wildly at the two of us to retreat. Clambering to our feet, Pippa and I raced down the stairs and back out into the shop, situating ourselves in front of the counter and looking as innocent and unflustered as we could. Noah quickly followed us and busied himself wrapping up our order, whistling innocently.

Sure enough, no sooner had we assumed our positions than two men, each with a sullen grimace upon his visage, descended the stairs and exited the shop, without so much as a tip of their hats in our direction. We all exhaled in unison as the door closed behind them.

"Here." Noah slid our wrapped packages across the counter with a pointed stare. "Sorry, no serials today, Dell—I can't risk plucking about upstairs."

"That's quite alright," I replied as Pippa and I collected the day's meat supply into our baskets.

"Wait—here!" With that, Noah turned and grabbed a pouch of tobacco from the shelf behind the counter and tucked it in amongst my stock. "Just in case."

I cocked my head, confused. "In case of what?"

A look of sadness flickered across Noah's face. "In case I don't see you for a while."

Pippa looked as confused as I felt. "Why would we not see you for a while? We'll be back tomorrow, as always."

Noah looked unconvinced. "You think they'll still let you out and about with a murderer loose on the streets?"

I shrugged. "Hard to say. Perhaps we'll run into him and can teach him the *virtues of temperance*."

Both Pippa and Noah burst out laughing, and I was relieved to see a spark of joy light up Noah's face. But after we said our farewells, his words of concern weighed heavily upon me as we made our way back home. How were Pippa and I to survive if they locked us up in the school, prisoners with no recourse, unable to experience the outside world (or obtain the sweet contraband it provided)? And more importantly, how was I to learn all the grisly details of this murder if we were forbidden from the streets? Time was of the essence; this outing might be our last, and I was determined not to let it go to waste.

"Come on, Pippa," I chided, pulling her along by the elbow. "If we hurry, we might be able to make it back to Buck's Row before the body's removed!"

"And what good will that do us?" Pippa whinged, though she quickened her step to keep up.

"We'll get to see a real murder scene, of course! Not just an illustrated one like in the news."

Pippa pulled a face. "No offence, Dell, but your serials are gory enough to give me nightmares already. Why would you want to see something like that up close?"

I contemplated this as we briskly made our way up Court Street. "Because I have to know what it's really like, not just how the papers tell it. If someday I am to be a detective, I shall come face to face with such atrocities all the time! It's best I strengthen my stomach now in preparation." Pippa looked unconvinced. "Besides, aren't you the least bit curious what someone's insides look like? I saw you mulling over that folio on the execution of Sawney Bean," I said, referring to the famous Scottish cannibal who'd been drawn and quartered.

Pippa's expression betrayed a smirk despite her best effort to hide it. "Fine, maybe a little. But it's on your head if I faint."

As it turned out, her concern was woefully unwarranted, as by the time we arrived back at Buck's Row the body was gone and the crowd was already dispersing, save for a cluster of familiar green cloaks huddled near the front of the New Cottage next to the stable yard. Quickening our step, we ran to see what the fuss was all about.

"Oh, Reverend, whatever shall we do? Shall I fetch the police?" Agatha Miller, a short, squat girl with a sour face and a disposition to match was wringing her hands in distress as a dozen other pupils looked on eagerly. Agatha was rarely seen outside of Beatrice's shadow, and I cast my gaze about for a full few seconds before I identified where, precisely, Beatrice had disappeared to. She was lying supine upon the cobblestones, her head cradled in the Reverend's hand as he knelt to assess her prognosis.

"What happened?" Pippa murmured breathlessly to our closest fellow onlooker, a quiet girl called Cora whom I was fairly certain I'd never before heard speak.

Cora looked shaken indeed. "Beatrice and Agatha were bound for the market, but they saw the crowd and went to look. And they saw . . . they saw . . ." Her eyes brimmed with tears. I leaned in, hanging on every word. "They saw . . . *the body.*"

"The body of the murdered woman?" I replied breathlessly.

"Yes!" Cora replied, her face pale. "It must have been so awful. Beatrice swooned and fainted on sight! Agatha fetched the Reverend, but what can he do? One can't unsee something so horrid." Blinking back tears, she turned away to watch the proceedings.

"Are you kidding me?" I muttered furiously under my breath.

"What?" Pippa queried, craning her neck to try and catch a glimpse of Beatrice's limp form.

"Not only did Beatrice get to see the body for herself, but now she's just putting on airs about it. I guarantee you she's not actually faint; she just wants to get out of laundry duty this afternoon."

Just then, Beatrice sat up with a dainty cry, and the crowd of onlookers burst into relieved murmurs.

"There, there, my dear girl. Up you get! You've had quite a fright, I'm sure." The Reverend patted her back dotingly.

"Oh, Reverend, it was horrid!" Beatrice wailed, her face a perfect picture of feminine frailty. I rolled my eyes.

"Of course, of course. Come along, we must get you to bed right away. Miss Kaye will call the doctor." And with that, he hoisted Beatrice to her feet and parted the crowd to guide her through as she clung helplessly to his arm. Such a fine performance it was, I almost didn't notice her smirk as she passed.

Beatrice did indeed get out of laundry duty, as well as needlework, chapel, and Morality class. I could scarcely stand the injustice of it all, but Pippa kept glaring daggers at me every time I complained about Beatrice's good fortune in witnessing the gruesome scene, so by supper I'd taken to holding my tongue. The only bright spot in the day was the revelation during chapel that we were not, in fact, to be sequestered in Whitechapel Hall until the murderer was brought to justice. It seemed the unfortunate victim was a woman of poor moral standing, and as such, the Reverend concluded that her fate was no threat to any of us but was simply a helpful anecdote to reinforce his opinion that so long as we did not stray from the path of morality, we were not in danger. But for any girl who dared question the virtues of his teachings . . . Well, we now only had to look out our own front door for an ending to that sorry tale.

I was in a low mood by the time I reported to Miss Kaye's office for my detention, though Pippa had promised to wait up for me so that we might still have our nightly smoke together and discuss the details of the crime—a small consolation after a day fraught with frustration. I found Miss Kaye seated placidly behind her desk, spectacles slipping down her nose, which was buried in (what else?) her Bible. I rapped gently on the door frame, and she raised her head, her expression betraying no hint of the altruism she had extended to me the night before.

"Miss Morton, right on time. Please, be seated." She gestured towards the chair opposite her own, and I obeyed. "You have brought your Bible with you, I presume?"

"Um . . ." I had it with me, of course (we were never allowed anywhere in the Hall without our holy book in tow, should the need arise for immediate moral guidance), but my thoughts quickly turned to the ragged leather binding now containing last week's edition of *Link Boys* and considerably fewer proverbs. "Yes?"

"Excellent. Please open to Mark 7:20." Swallowing hard, I flipped open my Bible, mentally saying my first *sincere* prayer of the day that by some miracle, Mark had been spared during my bout of butchery.

No such luck. Blinking down at my heretical contraband, I forced a smile back at Miss Kaye, hoping that perhaps she'd simply tell me to commence reading silently.

Miss Kaye cleared her throat.

> *That which cometh out of the man, that defileth the man. For from within, out of the heart of men, proceed evil thoughts, adulteries, fornications, murders. Thefts, covetousness, wickedness, deceit, lasciviousness, an evil eye, blasphemy, pride, foolishness. All these evil things come from within, and defile the man.*

She looked up at me expectantly. "Your turn, Miss Morton." She wanted us to read aloud *together*? Oh, I was well and truly doomed. Stalling for time, I cast my mind to the first retort I could conjure. "I have a question."

She startled, clearly not anticipating my willingness to engage with her upon the subject. "Yes, Miss Morton?"

"Today in chapel, the Reverend said that the murdered woman, Miss Nichols . . . He said that she sinned and was guilty of immorality, and that is why she died. As God's punishment."

Miss Kaye appeared unmoved. "Indeed."

"But what about Ellen Atkinson, whose husband beat her to death and dismembered her simply because she let the hearth fire go out? Her husband was wicked, but she seems innocent enough. Why was she punished?"

Miss Kaye blinked back at me stoically. "There are innocent lambs of God upon whom great suffering falls through no fault of their own. But it is the sinfulness of her husband, Mr. Atkinson, upon which we should focus. Now please, Miss Morton, if you'll read—"

"And what of Dick Turpin, the highwayman?" I interjected desperately.

Miss Kaye looked even less amused this time. "What of him?"

"Well, he stole things, of course, but he also helped people in distress, and he only robbed rich people when he really needed the money."

"Miss Morton, if there is one takeaway from Mark 7:20, it's that it should not be up to man's fallible discretion to whom wealth is bestowed; that is God's choice."

The indignation stewing within me after weeks of her morality lectures was too potent, and I could no longer hold it back. "But there are many modern ways of making money that are infinitely worse than taking it by force in a highway robbery. What about the cheating done by lawyers and brokers whose clients trust them to their own sorry disadvantage or the corrupt men in positions of power who levy blackmail to gain influence—"

Miss Kaye cut me off sternly. "Miss Morton, you are woefully misguided if you believe in the morals of your dastardly *penny dreadfuls* over the word of God." I must have looked surprised, for she continued without pause. "Yes, the headmaster informed me of the reason for your internment here, and I find myself unsurprised that your character has been corrupted so. After all, penny dreadfuls are filled with nothing more than anguish, degradation, and brutality, then balanced by a lavish helping of sentimentality, which is more than enough to confuse young and impressionable minds such as yours."

"But they're *not* immoral!" I retorted vehemently. "Yes, some may be bloody and a bit gruesome, but in the end, good always prevails against evil. And what about the anguish, degradation, and brutality of the Bible?"

"What of the two boys that murdered their own mother under the influence of penny dreadfuls?" Miss Kaye shot back. "I've yet to hear a tale of children murdering their parents due to influence from the Bible."

"That's because in the Bible, the parents do all the murdering," I muttered, and for just a moment, I could swear I saw a flicker of something resembling amusement cross Miss Kaye's visage.

"Very well, Miss Morton. If you are so certain of your convictions, you may defend them to me in a written essay."

"A written essay?"

"Yes. As I recall, when you first arrived here at Whitechapel Hall, you were dismayed at the lack of academic tutelage in our curriculum. I'm now giving you a chance to rectify that by writing me an essay, of no fewer than five thousand words, explaining to me just how the slaughter and sin in your penny books are beneficial to your moral edification. You may leave it on my desk a week from today in lieu of detention, and once I review it, we shall debate its merits. I'm looking forward to it greatly."

"Is this a trick?" I could not see what possible reason she would have for letting me air my grievances so blatantly.

"I should think not. You and I are still strangers, Miss Morton, but I believe once you get to know me, you shall find me quite reasonable. I am not here as your warden or your mistress or your keeper. I am here to advise you on your spiritual recovery from the deviance that landed you here in the first place. If I am not willing to defend my own beliefs, then how should I expect you to embrace them?"

This seemed to me a highly well-reasoned argument, and I could find no fault in it. "Very well," I capitulated.

"Very well indeed," she affirmed. "In that case, you are dismissed."

"Yes, Miss Kaye."

"Good night, Miss Morton."

"Good night, Miss Kaye." I rose and, with an awkward curtsy, retreated from her office.

I joined Pippa on our perch just as the final streaks of daylight were painting the sky over Whitechapel an enchanting shade of pink. She appeared lost in thought as I approached, as pristine a vision as ever with her golden curls tangling in the wind, her porcelain skin glowing in the rosy light. I took my place beside her. Wordlessly, she handed me the freshly packed pipe and a box of matches, breaking her angelic facade with a conspiratorial grin.

"How was your detention?" She casually swung her feet to and fro where they hung off the side of the ledge, the heels of her boots clicking against the stone. After two weeks, the height was still enough to make me wary, but Pippa's cavalier confidence always put me at ease.

"Strange," I replied, taking a long drag of the pipe. "Though when it comes to Miss Kaye, I'm discovering that 'strange' might just be normal."

"So, you will not attempt to convince me that she's at the top of your list of murder suspects?"

I barked out a laugh at this, and Pippa smiled cheekily at me.

"No, don't be ridiculous. Besides, she has an iron-clad alibi: She was with me, berating me for stealing fruit."

"Fair point." Pippa plucked the pipe from my hand and took a puff for herself. "She didn't threaten to report you to the headmaster?"

The cause of Pippa's concern was clear: My attendance at Whitechapel Hall was still contingent upon Miss Kaye's silence. "Not at all," I rushed to reassure her. "But speaking of the headmaster, isn't it odd that I saw him leaving the Hall last night at such a late hour, and then this morning, there's a body practically on our stoop?"

Pippa rolled her eyes. "Come on, Dell. I know you're eager for a case, but what cause would Headmaster Graves have to disembowel a lady of the night?"

"Haven't you read *any* of the penny bloods I've lent you? There are a million reasons: Perhaps he had an affair with her and needed to cover it up! Perhaps she stole money from him, and he wanted revenge! Perhaps he's a secret madman, and this is his twisted idea of fun! Perhaps— "

"That's all fine and good, but as a detective, don't you need some sort of proof?"

I sighed dejectedly and reclaimed the pipe, taking a pensive draw. "You're quite right. We must formulate a plan and work the case properly. First, we must produce a list of suspects." I nodded at Pippa expectantly, encouraging her contribution; if she was to be my accomplice in crime solving, she'd have to learn the protocol.

"So . . . Headmaster Graves?"

"Yes, he's a good place to start on account of his odd behaviour the night of the murder. Who else?"

"Um . . ." Pippa cast her eyes down towards the streets below us, still bustling now that the heat had broken. "The . . . lamplighter? He's out late at night."

It was a far-fetched idea, but I entertained it for the sake of her encouragement. "Good thinking! We'll have to keep an eye on him from up here and see if he does anything suspicious. Who else? Think about the culprits you read about in our broadsides."

"Her husband?"

"Precisely!" She was a quick learner.

"But the Reverend said Miss Nichols had left him and was living in sin!"

"Exactly! Don't you think that's a possible motive?"

"Perhaps, but how will we find him? They lived apart, and we've no familiarity with the neighbourhood. We don't know anyone who knew her, let alone anyone who knows him."

"*We* don't." I mulled this over, an idea taking shape in my mind. "But we know someone who might: Noah. He knows the neighbourhood as well as anyone; surely, he can offer us a clue."

Our walk to Noah's shop the following morning was markedly different than it had been in the past. The streets were crawling with policemen, and I yearned to stop and interrogate each one of them about what they knew of the case, but Pippa refused to let us be deterred, steering me doggedly towards High Street with grim determination. We arrived at Noah's well before seven, only to find the shop doors locked and the counter vacant. We wasted at least five minutes knocking with escalating degrees of urgency, until I was forced to take matters into my own hands.

"Do be careful," Pippa implored as I collected a fistful of pebbles from the gutter and took aim at the window situated above the shop's awning. "I shudder to think how Noah's father would react if you disturbed him." The risk was not lost on me, but I had no desire to return to Whitechapel Hall empty-handed, and I wasn't just referring to the meat.

Taking steady aim, I let loose a pebble, and it struck the window frame with a disappointingly soft rap. I swiftly fired a second, this time connecting with the glass with a satisfying *ping.* Seconds later, the window flew open, and Noah's head emerged.

"What are you doing?" he hissed down at us.

"We're here for our wares, obviously," I shouted up. "Beef knuckles and the like? Or anything else you have on offer today?"

"We open at seven," he retorted saltily, and slammed the window shut.

Pippa and I exchanged a confused glance; his disposition was utterly unlike the usual affable Noah with whom we traded news and jests each morning, but we could do nothing more besides retreat under the awning to wait.

We were not delayed long. Moments later, the door swung open, and an elderly man in a splendid wide-brimmed fedora and frock coat shuffled out, supported by a handsome walking cane. He was accompanied by a tired-looking woman in a worn woollen dress, her hair fastened firmly beneath a paisley scarf. The two exchanged a few words in Yiddish, and the woman curtsied, low and solemn, her eyes downcast. With a tip of his hat, the elderly man turned and disappeared into the crowd. The woman, meanwhile, cast a withering glance at Pippa and me before turning and disappearing back into the shop.

No sooner had the door shut behind her than Noah appeared to open it once more and usher us wordlessly inside. We arrived at the counter just in time to see the woman disappear through the door in the back of the shop, followed by the echo of her footsteps upon the stairs.

"Your mother?" I asked quietly. Noah nodded but remained silent until the sound of the upstairs door closing broke the sombre mood.

"Apologies," he murmured, his expression one of sincere regret as he met my eyes for the first time since we had entered the shop. "It's been a difficult morning." His shoulders drooped in a most defeated posture, and I was compelled to uncover the source of his distress.

"What's going on? Is it to do with the murder?"

"Indeed," Noah responded sullenly. "The police believe they have a suspect."

"Really?" My heart beat double-time, and Pippa and I exchanged an excited glance. "Why, that's good news, is it not?"

"For the police, maybe," Noah replied, pulling out the paper to start packaging our order. "But for us, not so much."

"What do you mean?" Pippa pressed earnestly.

With a sigh, Noah proceeded, all whilst keeping his gaze cast firmly upon his work, as if ashamed of his report. "The police believe they have sufficient reason to suspect a man who goes by the name Leather Apron. He's been a menace to the women of the streets for months now, and they believe his behaviour is disturbed enough that it may have escalated to the point of murder. And perhaps not just this one! There have been two more brutal killings in Whitechapel since April last, though it was thought they were the work of street gangs. Now, though, the police believe all three may be tied to the same man."

I was flummoxed. "But why does this news weigh so heavily upon you? Surely you have nothing to do with this dastardly villain."

"I certainly don't, but the trouble is, Leather Apron is a greener—that is to say, a Polish Jew from our neighbourhood. And the public rarely makes the distinction between a single Jew and our people as a whole. If one Jew has done this, we'll all pay."

"Is that why your mother looked so worried?" Pippa inquired, her eyes wide with sympathy.

Noah hesitated but steadied himself to reply. "Yes. That was the rabbi you saw leaving just now: He's making house calls, urging us all to be vigilant. As if we need a reminder of what happens each time our people are the source of suspicion." His tone was bitter and guarded, and for the first time I recognised that despite our effortless companionship with him, the worlds in which we lived were separated by more than a few city streets.

"Surely this will all pass as soon as Leather Apron is apprehended," Pippa offered encouragingly, and Noah shot her a wan smile over his shoulder in return.

"Yes, I'm sure it will." There was no conviction in his voice.

Pippa turned towards me. "Well, that certainly eliminates our theory."

"You had a theory?" Noah turned and deposited our day's supply upon the counter, which we commenced loading into our baskets.

"The husband," I replied with a shrug. "It's always the husband."

Noah laughed at that, and I was relieved to see this first sign of amusement since we'd arrived. "And if not the husband, then certainly the lover."

"Precisely! But if this cad has indeed butchered three women in the span of a few months, it's certainly unlikely that he was tied to each of them, unless he is a foremost rake and libertine."

"Now, that I doubt," Noah confirmed. "Those who have seen him claim he is excessively repellant."

"Does this mean we can eliminate Headmaster Graves from our suspect list as well?" Pippa continued.

Noah's expression turned dark once more at this admission. "You suspect your own headmaster of such a thing? Is your treatment at Whitechapel Hall truly so dismal?" His concern for us was evident upon his face, and I hastened to dissuade him from such fears.

"Hardly," I countered. "It was simply a case of ill timing, in which I witnessed him engaging in a peculiar quest at an inopportune time."

Noah still seemed unconvinced, but his manner improved as he procured something from beneath the counter. "Just for you ladies, a parting gift: this morning's copy of *The Star*."

I snatched the paper greedily from his hands, the headline WHITECHAPEL MURDER! splashed tantalisingly across the top of the page. I trembled with anticipation at the chance to read it and discover all the grisly details of the scene which had played out upon Buck's Row. "Oh, Noah, you shouldn't have!" My voice quaked with excitement, and beside me, Pippa laughed.

"For Heaven's sake, Dell, at least wait until we're home."

With a conspiratorial grin, Noah wrapped up the paper with a few spare stripped knuckles and pressed it into my eager hands.

Chapter VII
Buried Secrets

A week later, we were disappointingly no closer to a breakthrough on the case. Though I'd devoured each and every scrap of news that Noah was able to provide us, Leather Apron continued to elude the police, and I had grown frustrated with my continued relegation to the role of spectator despite my tantalising proximity to the crime. Each night from our perch Pippa and I spied upon the streets of Whitechapel from above, but Leather Apron appeared to have retreated into the shadows for the foreseeable future. I yearned to work the beat as Mrs. Paschal would have done, interviewing the police, interrogating the boarders at Miss Nichols' former residence, or perhaps going undercover in the hopes of luring the culprit from his hiding place, but alas, my duties at Whitechapel Hall made any such progress impossible. Even worse, the local laymen had formed a vigilance committee dedicated to capturing Leather Apron in the act, but there was no way I could sneak out of my prison to attend their meetings and was instead forced to hear all about it secondhand from Noah, who relayed all the details to me as I seethed over every wrong-footed approach.

"I can't believe someone suggested placing *spring-loaded*

dummies filled with blades in the alleyways to serve as bait," I moaned to Pippa one evening as we sat sequestered in the annex. I was working on my essay for Miss Kaye, which of course I'd put off until the night before, and Pippa was indulging herself with that morning's copy of *The Illustrated Police News*, which boasted a dazzling new array of illustrations portraying Miss Nichols' sordid activities the night leading up to her murder. "As if they'll catch a murderer with a childish booby trap! It's ludicrous." Pippa, clearly already tired of my endless bellyaching, offered only a faint hum of affirmation.

"They ought to be more sensible about these things," I grumbled, recalling Mrs. Paschal's sage advice. "They ought to *deliberate carefully, so that by reflection they should hit upon the right path which will eventually lead them to success, if such a consummation could be achieved by mortal means*," I quoted.

"What are you on about?" Pippa sighed in exasperation.

"Nothing," I muttered to myself, bending to add a few words to my essay about the prudence of patience.

The tones of the clock struck midnight, and Pippa tossed her paper aside, a resolute expression upon her face. "Come on, let's go have a smoke."

I groaned. "I can't. I have this wretched essay due tomorrow, and—"

"And you've deprived me of your company all night, and I'm absolutely gasping for a whack at the pipe. Come on, we're both exhausted. You can finish your essay tomorrow, after chapel." That was a lie; we both knew that there was no respite between our obligations under the strict supervision of our taskmasters, but I hadn't the inclination to argue with her. I cast my pen aside with a sigh of relief and followed her up to our hideout.

This wasn't the first time we'd reposed upon our perch after dark, but we didn't make a habit of it, as the journey along the ledge was far more precarious without the benefit of daylight.

Even so, the peril was worth it on nights such as this one, and we worked easily in tandem to share our lantern's light between us as we took our post.

I cast my eyes down upon the maze of streets below us, searching the glow of the streetlamps for any sign of the insidious butcher and his trademark apron. What I would do if I spotted him was uncertain, but I was determined to be vigilant in my watch. Beside me, Pippa packed the pipe and took a long, slow drag before handing it over to me and resting her head upon my shoulder with a weary sigh.

"I do wish they'd catch him," Pippa murmured quietly. "It weighs on Noah so."

I opened my mouth to reply but found myself momentarily confounded. I had not taken Noah's emotions into account as I devoured every morsel of information he could offer about the case. What Pippa said was astutely observed: upon reflection, Noah had been considerably less jovial these past few days, his tone more guarded in our presence. Pippa was a good friend to have noticed.

I patted her hand encouragingly. "They will. And I'm sure Noah's fears for his people are unfounded; as soon as the culprit is caught, it will be as if this never happened."

"I hope so, for his sake." She sounded deeply melancholy, and for a moment something hot and sharp flared in my chest at the thought of her harbouring such tender sentiments for our companion and confidant. I cared for Noah, too, after all, but his concerns felt to me all too remote.

I was about to reply when a flash of light from the alley beside the school caught my eye. I was not the only one to see it, for Pippa suddenly sat bolt upright and craned her neck to search for the source. To my dismay, the flame of a lantern appeared from the receded door frame which I knew to be the entrance to the dumbwaiter. Moments later, a cloaked figure emerged from the alley onto Buck's Row, scurrying along the edges of the shadows in the direction of Hanbury Street. Though her face remained covered, there could be no mistaking her clothing or stature; it was none other than *Miss Kaye*.

Pippa issued a soft gasp, and I sprang at once to my feet, intent upon tracking Miss Kaye's path on her clandestine adventure. At six stories high, Whitechapel Hall was by far the tallest structure in the neighbourhood, but Miss Kaye disappeared all too quickly behind a row of dilapidated warehouses.

My fear of heights was immediately eclipsed by the thrill of the chase, and I turned abruptly to face the clock tower, testing the fealty of the rough bricks in my hands. I needed to get *higher*. Casting caution aside, I raised myself up and began to scale the side of the tower.

"Dell, for God's sake, what are you doing?" Pippa's voice was frantic, but I didn't dare turn around.

"We have to see where she's going!" I called back as loudly as I dared.

"Are you out of your damned mind? You're liable to fall!"

Now was not the moment for caution or cowardice. There was malice afoot, and I was determined to get to the root of it. The bricks were easier to climb than I'd dared to hope, and it took me no more than a minute to reach the recessed ledge beneath the face of the clock. Heartbeat thrumming in my ears, I pulled myself to safety and turned to mark my quarry.

Sure enough, from this angle Miss Kaye's figure was still clearly visible as she made her way further down Hanbury Street. I tracked her every move as she manoeuvred past a rowdy band of sailors gathered outside the row of gin palaces, then crossed the street to avoid two filthy urchins whom I knew from my daily observations were among the most reckless pickpockets in the neighbourhood. Wherever Miss Kaye was going, it was somewhere she had been before; she navigated the streets with the intelligence of a woman familiar with them.

"Can you see her?" Pippa hissed from down below.

"I can," I confirmed. "She's— " And at that very moment, I made the terrible mistake of looking down. Though Pippa was not more than fifteen feet below me, behind her the ledge dropped off into a precipitous fall all the way down to the steps of the school. I swooned, and my knees went weak. The next thing I knew, I was pressed against the clock face in a defensive crouch, shaking from head to toe.

"Dell? Dell, are you alright?" Pippa's tone had grown more frantic.

I swallowed hard. "I'm fine. I'm fine, I just . . ." I took a few steadying breaths. "I just . . . looked down is all."

At that, Pippa laughed, and her laughter calmed me considerably. A few moments later, I was once again steady enough to resume my watch, and I rose resolutely to my feet and cast my gaze back to the street.

Only to discover to my dismay that Miss Kaye had vanished. "Damn it all!" I cried out.

"What?"

"She's gone! I looked away for just a moment, and she disappeared into thin air! Somewhere near Brick Lane is all I can tell," I conveyed forlornly.

"Perhaps that's for the best, as I have no intention of watching you risk life and limb in the pursuit of something we don't even understand! Now, will you please come to your senses and get back down here this bloody instant?"

For once I agreed with Pippa's assessment, but it turned out her commands were easier said than followed. For while I had scaled the tower with a burst of bravery brought on by the thrill of the chase, I was now forced to contend with my descent in a much more fragile state. Thankfully, Pippa was eventually able to coax me down as one would a kitten from a tree, though the entire process did little to secure my reputation as a fearless female detective. My only consolation was that Pippa did not poke fun at my folly, and I trusted she would tell no one of my foible.

Safely ensconced back in the annex, my mind was ablaze with theories. I wished for nothing more than a few hours to mull them over in stoic silence, but Pippa clearly had other ideas.

"Where do you think she was going, Dell? A gambling den? A music hall? A tavern?"

"I fear it may be far worse than any of that," I posited as we took our places side by side on Pippa's cot. "What if Miss Kaye herself is the murderer?"

Pippa shot me an exasperated look. "Dell, I know you're eager to solve the case yourself, but there's no way Miss Kaye had anything to do with the Nichols murder. She was with you that night, remember? Giving you detention for stealing fruit."

I bit my lip, unsure of how much I could divulge without confessing what I'd truly been caught doing that night. "There's . . . there's something I've not yet told you. About the night I was caught in the pantry."

Pippa's eyes grew bright with curiosity. "What is it?"

"When Miss Kaye found me amongst the food stores, she was not simply angry that I was stealing. She suspected that I was trying to escape."

"Escape? How?"

As vaguely as I could, I conveyed the existence of the dumbwaiter to Pippa, taking care to downplay its role in my crime and punishment.

"Miss Kaye told me that the dumbwaiter would be sealed from that moment on, but it's clear that she was lying; she used it just now! What if that night, she took the idea for herself and stole out after midnight to commit the murder? And for all we know, she's off now to do it again!"

Pippa pursed her lips sceptically. "As much as I'd like such a simple solution, what is her motive? What is her method? Why would a woman tasked with teaching morality at a reformatory school kill a lowly woman on our doorstep?"

It was a fair question, and I scrunched my nose as I attempted to conjure a plausible reason. "To teach us all a lesson, of course! You heard the Reverend's sermon the day the body was discovered; he made an example of Miss Nichols to us all!"

"Be that as it may, there's a difference between making an example and taking a life, and we've no reason to suspect Miss Kaye is so desperate in her quest to lecture us into compliance that she'd kill someone for it."

I paused to consider this. "Maybe. But the coincidence seems uncanny. Why else would she be using the dumbwaiter?"

"There are a thousand reasons for a woman to want to escape the confines of this Hall! Perhaps she fancied a stiff drink or a flit about the dance floor with a handsome suitor or a toss of the dice!"

I mulled this over in my mind. Any of these exploits seemed at odds with Miss Kaye's austere disposition, but I was reminded of our exchange the evening of my detention; she had presented herself as highly capable of reason and flexible in her interpretation of biblical law. Was it possible that she was not, in fact, as devoted to temperance as she publicly claimed?

We had little else to say that night and eventually prepared for bed in an amicable silence. But as I drifted off into an uneasy sleep, I couldn't shake the feeling that there was something more sinister in the mystery before us than the evidence conveyed.

Chapter VIII
A Very Bad Woman

Pippa and I arose early the next morning, eager as ever to connect with Noah. Though I hadn't dismissed my suspicions of Miss Kaye, more news of Leather Apron could sway my opinion on the matter; I would be a poor detective indeed if I narrowed my suspect pool so early in the case. We made our way downstairs before most of the girls in the dormitory had even dressed, only to find the front door barricaded by a cluster of activity.

Three police constables stood in the entryway, speaking in hushed tones with Headmaster Graves, Miss Kaye, and the Reverend, all of whom wore expressions of stricken shock upon their faces. For a moment I considered attempting to pull Pippa down behind the wide stone bannister to eavesdrop upon the conversation, but I was not fast enough; Headmaster Graves looked up and spotted us, summoning us down with a wave of his hand.

"Ladies, ladies, please, don't be frightened." Pippa and I shared a wary look but quickly obeyed, descending into the foyer and dropping into curtsies before the legion of outsiders.

"Miss Morton, Miss Fitzroy, these constables have kindly

stopped by to ensure the safety of our pupils. Now if you please, proceed immediately to the chapel; the Reverend will address the student body as soon as we are all assembled."

"But our market duty," I protested before I could stop myself. "Cook will be expecting her delivery—"

"You are all excused from your outreach today," the headmaster continued stoically. "Now, ladies, please; I must have a few words with the constables in private. Miss Kaye, if you'd be so kind as to escort the girls to chapel?"

"Of course, Headmaster." With a brisk nod of her head, Miss Kaye ushered us swiftly down the corridor.

"Miss Kaye, what's going on?" I queried, strangely less intimidated by her despite my suspicions than I had been before discovering her penchant for secret excursions.

"Nothing of concern to you, Miss Morton," she replied, absent the trace of familiarity she'd revealed during my detention. "Take a seat. The Reverend will address us shortly."

Slowly, the other girls filed in, each looking as confused as the last, and soon the pews were buzzing with anxious whispers that dropped off into rigid silence the moment the Reverend walked down the aisle and took his place behind the pulpit.

"Ladies, I stand before you this morning with news of a most sobering nature. Last night, there was another murder here in Whitechapel." A ripple of murmurs broke out among us, and beside me, Pippa gripped my hand, her face paling as we shared a knowing look.

"Now, now, silence, please, *silence*," the Reverend commanded. "As shocking as this is for all of us, I must emphasise that none of you need fear for your safety. The victim was, once again, a degenerate: a lady of the night, stricken with vice, caught in the inescapable fate of those who turn their backs upon the word of the Lord. The police have assured us that they are on the heels of the criminal responsible and will be making an arrest imminently." I hazarded a glance at Miss Kaye, who was stationed in the front pew, nodding solemnly along with the Reverend's oration, her expression betraying nothing of her villainous deed. My blood ran cold at the thought; the police were clearly on the wrong trail, and the true culprit was here in our very presence!

"Even so," the Reverend continued. "Out of an abundance of caution, we will suspend our outreach for today, though I am confident we may resume our mission tomorrow. The Devil never rests, and nor shall we! For today, however, the police have assured us we can be of most help to our brothers and sisters in Christ by raising our voices in prayer for the salvation of the innocents. *Our Father, who art in Heaven . . .*"

The day proceeded in a most frustrating manner. Pippa and I were not afforded a single moment alone to discuss this latest turn of events: Cook was beside herself in the absence of her daily produce delivery from our outreach at the market and lorded it over Pippa and me as we scrounged up a makeshift dinner of boiled cabbage, week-old potatoes, and stale bread, never allowing the two of us to share so much as a private glance. Chapel was an even more dismal affair, the Reverend's condemnation now buoyed with the sordid details of the life of the deceased, one Miss Annie Chapman, whose drinking and philandering provided a convenient target for his fire and brimstone orations. I had high hopes that we'd have laundry duty that afternoon, as the ruckus in the washrooms often provided an excellent cover for gossip, but we had no such luck: Mrs. Dolmer made us darn stockings for three hours straight in solemn silence as she observed us, arms folded, from the back of the classroom, as if daring any one of us to raise our voice in protest.

The singular highlight was Morality class. I entered the classroom eager for the chance to observe a real-life *murderer* up close and took my seat with rapt anticipation. Disappointingly, rather than engage us in a lecture and debate, Miss Kaye simply set an essay on the dangers of Purgatory and appeared content to busy herself behind the barricade of her desk, nose buried in her Bible, avoiding any interaction with us. Despite this, I did my best to observe her with a detective's eye, but she was by all accounts flawless in her performance of innocence. I could not help but admire the carefree demeanour with which she held the book that wholly condemned those who sinned as she did, her lips upturned as she leafed through the pages, as though finding solace in the passages that threatened her murderous soul with hellfire. Something within me quivered at the concept of so callous a human, but after all, she was the first killer I had encountered in person! She had the cold detachment of a prowling predator, lurking in our midst. I simply kept my mouth shut and observed, for I could not predict when I would have another golden opportunity to study such criminal behaviour firsthand.

After a long day of merciless oppression, it came as no surprise that the moment we retreated to our dormitory following an interminably sombre supper, an explosion of excited squeals erupted at an unprecedented volume as soon as the door shut behind us.

"A madman, loose on the streets!" cried Agatha.

"They say he's a *cannibal—*" countered Cora.

"Not just a cannibal, a *vampire*; the victims were bled dry!" piped up another girl, whose name eluded me and whom I'd previously thought was a mute on account of her perpetual silence.

"Don't be ridiculous," Beatrice interjected, instantly commanding the attention of her army of minions. "It's clearly the return of Spring-Heeled Jack!"

I rolled my eyes at their childish obsession with the supernatural. Their heads were filled with fantastical drivel, the stuff of nursery stories, at the expense of logic, a disposition I found most unflattering from a detective's perspective.

"He can jump six stories high," Cora murmured, her eyes wide with fear.

"Precisely," Beatrice affirmed. "None of us is safe! He's liable to leap straight through the window!"

"And what of Leather Apron?" Pippa piped up from beside me, much to my surprise.

Beatrice rounded on her in an instant. "Who's to say they're not one and the same? Leather Apron is a Jew, isn't he?"

"And what of it?" Pippa countered venomously.

"Spring-Heeled Jack has horns and claws, just like a Jew," Beatrice retorted.

"Jews don't have horns or claws, don't be stupid."

"How would *you* know?"

"Because our butcher is a Jew, and he's perfectly lovely."

"*Perfectly lovely?*" Beatrice raised her eyebrows as a chorus of *oohs* rose up around us. "Sounds like he's charmed you with his Jew-magic. Have you ever checked under his little hat for horns? You ought to, before you run off and *marry* him—"

"Go to Hell, Beatrice," Pippa spat, then grabbed my arm and stormed off in the direction of the annex, dragging me gape-jawed behind her. Crossing the threshold of our sanctuary, Pippa released my arm and gave her trunk a solid kick, uttering a frustrated cry and then shaking her fist at the sky.

"Curse that pompous bitch and the broomstick she rode in on!"

I was growing familiar with Pippa's drastic change in personality following her interactions with Beatrice. I knew better than to counter her and remained silent, waiting until she'd regained her head.

"Can you believe her audacity? It's dim-witted ratbags like her that are causing Noah and his family so much strife."

"Well, she'll just be double-shamed when we prove Miss Kaye is the true culprit," I offered in hopeful consolation.

Pippa paused amidst her tantrum and gave me an odd look. "You don't honestly believe Miss Kaye did all this, do you?"

I stared back at her, gobsmacked. "Why of course I do! You saw her sneak out last night, and sure enough, this morning there's another body!"

"But Dell, you haven't a shred of evidence to support your theory, besides the fact that Miss Kaye happened to leave the school the same night that a murder occurred. Isn't it more likely that she simply likes to sneak out to a tavern and has done so every night since your encounter in the pantry without our notice? We were only out late last night by coincidence."

I bristled at the insinuation that my intuition had led me astray. "Then we must commence sleeping in shifts and have one of us always on the lookout."

Pippa issued a withering sigh. "Look, I know how much you want this to be about *us*. About our school, our headmaster, our teacher, something, *anything*, to make our internment here at Whitechapel Hall more bearable. Why, I seek refuge from the drudgery with my own imagination all the time! But you've read the papers, same as I have: the culprit is a mad butcher from the dodgy part of town who's been known to police as a menace for months. That's *it*, Dell. Case closed."

"It's anything but! The police say Leather Apron's their man, but then where is he? Some mythical demon Jew with a blood-spattered apron and a butcher's knife? He's just as much a spectre as Spring-Heeled Jack! The truth is, the police haven't got a clue, and they're looking for a scapegoat. But what *we* have is *evidence*." I crossed my arms and glared mutinously at my opponent.

Pippa cocked an eyebrow. "We have *evidence* that our teacher was one of hundreds of people out on the streets of Whitechapel last night. Where's the murder weapon? The bloodstained garb?"

She had me caught. Internally, I cursed myself for letting her read too many of my penny bloods for her own good. Just then, a nascent realisation entered my mind. "That's it! Brilliant thinking, Pippa."

"What's 'it'?"

"Miss Kaye must have the knife and her bloody clothes hidden somewhere in the school. Nowhere accessible by the students, of course. I'll bet in her private chamber."

Pippa paled. "Oh, no. Dell, don't tell me—"

"I'm breaking in."

"And how do you plan to do that? Wait until she sneaks out again?"

"Obviously not. If she sneaks out, she'll have the knife with her to commit another murder, which misses the point entirely!"

"So, then what?"

I raced over to my desk and picked up my now-delinquent detention essay. "I'll approach her under the guise of handing this in and say I forgot earlier." This was partially true, though my tardiness had more to do with the fact the essay was, technically, unfinished, but that hardly seemed to matter.

"And then?"

"And then I'll tell her . . ." My mind raced, conjuring the various scenarios in which my beloved detectives had thwarted their targets. "I'll tell her I heard Beatrice planning to escape through the dumbwaiter and question whether it's now truly as impenetrable as she informed me it is."

"And what will that do?"

"She'll have to go check it, of course! She knows it's not secured if she's been using it herself, and the threat of a student escaping via her own method of egress would threaten to expose her."

"And you think she'll leave you unattended with access to her private chamber?"

"No, but I happen to be quite proficient at picking locks," I proclaimed, plucking two hairpins off the table and pocketing them, thinking as I went. "I'll simply hide in the hallway until she makes haste downstairs, then I'll crack the lock to her office, slip into her chamber, and have a look about."

Pippa shook her head ruefully. "That's a terrible plan. You'll be caught in an instant!"

"If I hear her coming, I'll vacate her chamber and return to her office right away. Then I'll simply say I forgot this." I snatched up my pen and thrust it into my pocket as well, congratulating myself on this stroke of brilliance. "She'll be so flustered she'll assume she simply left her office unlocked behind her."

"And what happens if, as you predict, you find a great bloody knife and a pile of gory frocks?"

Drat. I hadn't thought of that. "I suppose I'll engage her in fisticuffs. If I must."

Pippa refused to dignify that with a response.

"Look, if you're right, nothing will come of this, Pippa! Her chamber will be as spartan as a nun's, you'll have proven me wrong, and if we're lucky, we might just get Beatrice in trouble." Pippa's lips twitched upwards at this. "If I find nothing there tonight, I won't question Miss Kaye's innocence again, I promise."

To my delight, cracks were showing in Pippa's defiant disposition, evidenced by the coy tone of her response. "Really? You mean, if she's not the murderer, you have no desire to solve the mystery of where she steals away to at night? Because I must confess, Dell, even *I* thirst to know what she's up to."

I shot back a conspiratorial grin. "Fair point. We'll solve the mystery of Miss Kaye one way or another, but for now"—I held my essay aloft—"I've a caper to commit."

It was easy to slip past the gaggle of girls gathered around Beatrice's bed, still in the throes of wild speculation about the identity of the killer, as Miss Kaye had not yet done her nighttime rounds to demand lights-out and lock the dormitory door. I made my way directly to Miss Kaye's office with my essay clutched to my chest like a shield, prepared to whet my silver tongue on whomever challenged my presence, but my passage was unimpeded.

Miss Kaye's office door was closed when I arrived, and I issued three sharp raps upon it before I could give myself a chance to back down. Seconds passed. I knocked again. Still nothing. I cursed under my breath; this was not part of my well-laid plan. Even so, I refused to be discouraged. On a wild impulse, I reached up and tried the doorknob.

To my shock, the door swung open without protest, revealing a vacant office behind it. Taking a few cautious steps inside, I cast my gaze about for any sign of Miss Kaye. Her lamp was still lit, but her desk was clear aside from her ever-present Bible, and her hat was missing from its rack in the corner, suggesting she was still out and about within the Hall.

I had but a split second to make my choice: I could turn back to the dormitory and attempt to execute my plan the following night, but I would run the risk of Miss Kaye demanding my essay in advance of that, destroying my alibi completely. Or I could simply proceed. After all, opportunity must be seized. It would be frankly irresponsible of me as a detective to squander such favourable circumstances smiling upon my investigation.

Intention set, I crept to the other side of Miss Kaye's desk and rifled through the drawers as quickly as I could. While I did not expect to find the murder weapon stashed within them, it seemed quite possible that she might keep a secret diary of some sort, in which she would unravel the evil web of thoughts that compelled her to kill her fellow woman; in my readings, it was inevitable that the criminal must confess their deeds in such a fashion. Alas, I found nothing but spare paper, pens, a few bottles of ink, last year's calendar, and somehow, *another* Bible. I slammed the drawers shut with a disappointed sigh and gave the shelves a hasty glance, but there was nothing overtly suspicious upon them that warranted a closer look. I was unsurprised, for it would take a lazy criminal indeed to leave evidence displayed in such a public space, and Miss Kaye seemed far too clever for that.

That left only my final destination to consider: her private chamber. I approached the doorway on tiptoe to give myself the opportunity for retreat were I to hear footsteps echoing down the hallway, but no such warning sounded. Taking a deep breath to steady my heart, I reached up and turned the knob.

Once again, the door was unlocked and swung open without fanfare. I entered a room so stark it more closely resembled a prison cell than a bedroom. In the centre was a cot made up with the same coarse linens as those that graced the beds of the inmates, along with a bedside table topped with a basin, pitcher, cup, and lamp. At the foot of the cot was a travelling trunk, and wedged into the corner was a plain wooden wardrobe devoid of any flourish of decoration. Hanging from the wall was a cheap unframed mirror, a clock, and a crucifix. It was, in sum, the blandest, most dismal living quarters I could have imagined, but at least it would make my investigation easy.

The trunk was obviously the first place to check. I snapped open the clasps and peered within, but the contents were disappointingly mundane: a tartan shawl, a spare pair of worn boots, opera glasses, a swansdown muff, and a black lace mourning veil were tucked neatly inside, with no sign of a knife or bloodstained cloak.

Disappointed, I returned the lid to its original state and pivoted my attention to the wardrobe. When I pried open the doors, the contents appeared to be predictable enough: three identical black frocks hung in a row, each paired with a high-collared white blouse beside it. Folded smartly on the high shelf were a few plain chemises and pairs of drawers, the sight of which made me blush despite my pragmatic intentions, and a spare petticoat lay uncharacteristically crumpled upon the floor, appearing to have simply slipped off a hook affixed to the interior of the wardrobe door.

Even though there was nothing incriminating strewn about in plain sight, I knew from my years of research that criminals were rarely so careless; as a detective, it was my duty to perform due diligence despite the lack of obvious evidence. As thoroughly as I could, I rifled through the stacks of undergarments in case the murder weapon was cleverly encased within their creases, but I came up empty-handed. Undeterred, I moved on to the dresses, upon which I scrutinised each hem and sleeve for the presence of blood but could detect none. The petticoat was last: I plucked it off the ground and inspected every inch of the trim, hunting for the telltale splash of red that would confirm I had my culprit, but I found nothing besides pristine (if cheap) lace.

Deflated with defeat, I moved to fling the petticoat back to its place, but before I could release it something peculiar caught my eye. Pushed back into the corner encased in shadow was an ornately carved wooden box inlaid with ivory, larger than a standard jewellery box but about as deep. As the only item I'd yet come across that displayed any sort of decorative flourish, it stood out in stark contrast to its own surroundings. And was it possible that the petticoat had not innocently slipped off its hook, but was strategically placed in such a way as to prevent the box's discovery? I dropped to my knees and pulled the box out of the wardrobe to hold it closer to the light. Heart racing, I pried open the lid.

At first, my eyes did not comprehend what I was seeing; I merely registered that the contents were not, in fact, a bloodied dagger. Instead, the box contained a bottle made of dark brown pharmacy glass, an ivory comb, a small sponge, and a single pair of spectacles. My curiosity was piqued as I plucked up the bottle and held it before the lamp, but it was sadly unlabelled. Unscrewing the lid, I took a whiff of the contents: the scent was sweetly floral with a hint of spice. Concluding that if it were poison it would probably not be the type to burn the flesh from my bones, I tipped the bottle and poured a drop into my palm. The liquid was a brilliant golden-yellow and viscous to the touch.

How incredibly strange! My gaze wandered from the fluid on my hand over to the teeth of the comb, and then to the sponge, which I observed were both tinted with the same signature yellow hue. All at once, my eyes flew open wide with realisation: The liquid was *hair dye*. I'd never encountered the substance, but in Mrs. Paschal's adventure *Incognita*, she finds herself up against a villain who used just such a method to alter her own appearance. I shivered with excitement at the thought that Miss Kaye may be engaged in just such a deception herself.

I pivoted my investigation to the spectacles. At first glance, they appeared innocent enough; nearly identical to the model that Miss Kaye currently wore, although a bit dated in style. As I pulled them from the box, something shifted beneath them, and to my surprise, it was revealed that they were sitting atop a pair of spare lenses. Confused, I pulled one loose lens from the box and held it up to the light, comparing it with the lenses within spectacles.

It was only then that I could see the true deceit. The loose lens in my hand was curved to correct near-sightedness, but the lenses placed within the frames were perfectly flat; they did nothing to alter the vision whatsoever. I gasped with the weight of this revelation: the spectacles were *fakes*! They were not intended to improve the eyesight of the wearer, only to alter her looks.

The puzzle pieces fell into place all at once. While I may not have discovered proof that Miss Kaye was the murderer, in my hands was undeniable evidence that she was employing a disguise to change her appearance, a fact which apparently she so wished to keep guarded that she hid the implements of her deception in a secret box buried at the bottom of her wardrobe. *But to what end?* Why was Miss Kaye wearing a disguise at school? Who was she hiding from? And why did she go to such lengths to keep anyone from finding out?

The sound of footsteps in the hallway shook me from my

ruminations. Face flushed and pulse racing, I thrust the box's contents back into their resting place, tossed the petticoat upon them, then snapped the wardrobe shut and scuttled out of the room, pulling the door closed behind me in the very same instant that Miss Kaye strode into her office, her signature glower transforming into an expression of shock as she registered my presence there.

I stood rooted to the floor, mute and terrified. Had she heard her chamber door close behind me? Did she suspect my inquisition into her innermost secrets? Just how dangerous was she? The revelation that she was clearly residing at Whitechapel Hall under a false identity offered no consolation to my palpitating heart, and I surrendered my fate to circumstance as I was confronted face-to-face with my suspect.

Miss Kaye looked me up and down, eyes narrowing as she searched my person for signs of mischief or malevolence. I painted an expression of earnest innocence upon my face and prayed that it would be convincing, though my knees trembled at the precariousness of my predicament.

"Miss Morton, what are you doing in my office at this hour?" Miss Kaye's voice was soft and even. She did not seem angry, but she also did not seem prone to mercy.

"I came to . . . turn in my essay. Just here." I gestured towards her desk where I'd deposited the document in question.

She rounded her desk, the lamplight dancing upon her pin-straight tresses as she took a seat. For the first time, I registered that the odd brassy blonde hue was undoubtedly manufactured, for it was a colour I'd never once witnessed in nature. She adjusted her spectacles as she peered down at my work, and I noted that the reflections within them were not warped with contour; the glass was flat, the accessory fake. I licked my lips, my mouth oddly dry, and I could feel a cold sweat forming upon my brow. The woman before me was a master of disguise, and I was currently at the mercy of her temperament.

"Miss Morton, while I appreciate your adherence to deadline, surely you're aware that the extenuating circumstances of today have warranted an extension."

I cleared my throat and shifted nervously from foot to foot, attempting to conceal the trembling of my knees. "Yes, I suppose so, but I'd worked so hard on it, you see, it seemed unnecessary to neglect it any longer."

Miss Kaye raised her gaze from the paper to meet my own. "I see. In the future, however, please be advised that my office is strictly off-limits if I am not present to grant you entry."

"Yes, Miss Kaye." I bobbed an unsteady curtsy.

"I look forward to discussing your essay's merits with you once I've had a chance to review it."

"Yes, Miss Kaye."

"Very well. Straight to bed, Miss Morton. Bed check is in ten minutes, and I'll be forced to add to your demerits if you are tardy."

"Yes, Miss Kaye. Thank you, Miss Kaye."

In that very instant, I could have sworn her gaze darted past me to fall upon the door to her chamber. I didn't dare breathe, I didn't dare move, I didn't dare question what she perceived, but a thousand ill-fated scenarios danced through my mind. What if I'd failed to latch it properly? What if I'd carelessly left some telltale sign of my presence of which only she would be aware? What if she could hear the frantic rhythm of my heart over the unearthly stillness that had fallen between us?

The silence felt eternal. At long last, she blinked, and the spell was broken. "You are dismissed, Miss Morton. Good night."

"Good night, Miss Kaye," I murmured, then darted out the door as swiftly as I dared.

Chapter IX
A False Scent

"But I don't understand what any of it means," Pippa shouted over the melee in the street the following morning on our way to Noah's shop. As promised, we'd been permitted to resume our outreach that morning on account of hardly being the type of targets upon which Leather Apron set his sights, and we'd been so eager to reconvene with Noah that we'd arrived in the entry of the Hall so early we were forced to wait for the headmaster to show up and unlock the front doors.

The neighbourhood was in chaos in the wake of the latest murder. The thoroughfares were crawling with police, and around every turn, paperboys thrust volumes emblazoned with grisly illustrations beneath our noses, tempting us for a penny apiece. The morning shoppers weren't bustling about on their daily errands as usual; instead, they congregated upon the corners, speaking in hushed tones, casting suspicious looks at all those who passed by. I could practically feel the fear reverberating through the air, and it titillated my senses and made my head spin with apprehension. I had been so eager to work a case, and now it appeared I had two at once, for I was no longer convinced that Miss Kaye's deception was connected to the murders after all.

"I've no idea," I confessed reluctantly as we were parted by a parade of shrieking schoolchildren waving an *Illustrated Police News* above the ringleader's head (I yearned to snatch it from his grasp and have it for myself but drew the line at roughing up a child in my pursuit of information). "It's clear that Miss Kaye is employed at the school under an assumed identity, but I didn't discover any evidence of what, precisely—or *who*—she's evading."

"So, what now?" Pippa grasped my elbow as we were at last reunited, turning the corner onto High Street.

"I haven't quite deduced that yet," I admitted.

Before Pippa could interrogate me further, we both stopped in our tracks in front of Noah's shop, horrified by the spectacle before us.

The large display window was boarded over, and bits of glass and brick littered the sidewalk beneath the awning, which had been stripped of its festive goose-neck garlands. The shops to the left and right had fared no better: the windows were in a similar state, and Number 46 had the words DOWN WITH THE JEWES scrawled across the door in black paint. The storefront was in such a state of disarray, I was unsure whether we would be able to enter.

"Dear God," Pippa murmured, her face pale and eyes wide. "Dell, what happened here? Do you think Noah's alright?"

I was overwhelmed with remorse for not taking Noah's worries more seriously. All he feared had come to pass: his people were under attack, and his business had been destroyed. A sick feeling swelled in the pit of my stomach and terror gripped my heart, but I knew I must be strong for Pippa—and for Noah, if by any luck he were still alive and had escaped unscathed.

"Come on." I took Pippa's hand firmly in mine and guided her towards the entrance, picking our way through the glass with caution. An arc of sidewalk devoid of debris beneath the door indicated that we were not the first to have entered the shop since the incident.

Just then, the door burst open on its hinges and a flood of people spilled into the street, catching us by surprise. Far from being vacant, the tiny shop had apparently been crowded with people, all of whom were talking over one another in a combination of Yiddish and English, creating a din so cacophonous that for a moment I froze, finding myself nearly trampled in the process. Luckily, Pippa regained her wits more quickly than I did and pulled me aside to let the assembly pass.

The first to exit were three constables arguing loudly over something one of them had written in his notebook, upon which the others apparently vehemently disagreed. Next came the rabbi I'd seen on our previous visit, surrounded by several other men I recognized as Jews only by their hats, deeply engaged in some sort of quarrel based on their tone. Bringing up the rear was Noah's mother, looking worn and weary but very much alive and apparently unharmed. A wave of relief washed over me, and as soon as they had cleared the entryway, Pippa and I rushed through it, eager to check on our friend.

We found Noah at his post behind the counter, but his pleasant demeanour had been replaced with one of stunned shock. He was seated upon a stool, hands folded before him, staring down at his fingers with glazed, unseeing eyes. He looked unfathomably sad.

"Noah!" Pippa was the first to speak, pulling away from my grasp and racing towards him as I followed at her heels.

He looked up, and upon seeing us, his melancholy expression transformed into one of disbelief. "Pippa! Dell! You're here!" In an instant, he jumped over the counter and ran forward to clasp our hands in his, a joyful exchange which we gladly embraced. To my surprise, tears sprang to my eyes at this gesture of fondness; I had not realised until that very moment how dearly I valued Noah's friendship, far above the value of the silly contraband he so generously provided to us. His kindness, his humour, and his insight were a source of purest joy to me, and his encyclopaedic knowledge of all things grim and dreadful reminded me daily that I was not *such* a strange bird, when for most of my years I'd felt utterly alone in my passions. Pippa and Noah had become, in the span of a few short weeks, my closest companions in all the world.

He pulled away from us at last, still shaking his head incredulously. "I can't believe you're here. I thought I'd never see you again! How did you escape the school?"

I shrugged. "They simply let us continue with our outreach as planned. Leather Apron apparently has little appetite for young ladies of *upright moral standing*."

Noah's smile faded. "But haven't you heard? It's not him."

Pippa and I exchanged a nervous look. "What do you mean?"

Noah sighed heavily, the sadness returning to his eyes, and his shoulders sagged as if burdened with an invisible weight. "Leather Apron. He's not the murderer."

"But how do they know?" I couldn't believe the case had taken such an unexpected turn overnight.

"I can tell you everything, but first, we've got to find you some meat. Everything in our display was destroyed, and I haven't had a chance to replenish our stores."

Pippa glared at him. "How can you be thinking about our goods at a time like this?"

"Look, your being allowed out of the school at all is a turnup so lucky I can scarcely believe it. Do you think they'll let you return if I send you back empty-handed, and you're forced to explain to them that this shop was the site of a riot? Come on. There's a gentile butcher two streets down. I'll explain on the way."

We emerged back into the bustle with Noah beside us, guiding us through the throngs at a purposeful gait. Pippa and I flanked him, eager to uncover the details of whatever had transpired since we'd last spoken.

"Yesterday morning, the police finally caught up with Leather Apron. He'd been holed up at his brother's house on Mulberry Street for the past two days, ever since word caught up with him that he was the prime suspect; he feared mob retribution if he were spotted in public."

"But if he's been on Mulberry Street for two days—" I began.

"There's no way he could be responsible for the murder of Annie Chapman," Pippa concluded.

"What's more," Noah continued, "he has an iron-clad alibi for the night of the Nichols murder. He was at Crossman's lodging house, and multiple patrons corroborated his story. The police had to release him, with no charges pressed. And that's when the trouble began."

"What sort of trouble? Is it to do with what happened to your shop?" Pippa implored.

Noah continued to stare straight ahead, as if ashamed to meet our eyes, and he relayed his tale in a steady monotone. "A crowd had formed outside the police station as soon as word of Leather Apron's arrest spread—as it turns out, he wasn't wrong to be concerned with mob justice. By the time the police let him go, there were a lot of very angry men gathered there, and they were all looking for answers. When the police could provide none, they jumped to their own conclusions: That Leather Apron may be innocent, but *No Englishman could have done it*, as the papers are so fond of saying. Therefore, the culprit must be some *other* Jew. *Any* Jew. The mob marched from Hanbury to High Street, torches in hand, throwing bricks at any establishment harbouring *foreigners*. Our shop was hardly the worst of it; we were lucky, this time."

"Noah, I'm so sorry." I reached out and clasped his hand, and Pippa linked her elbow with his in solidarity.

"Surely the police will provide your people with more protection from now on," Pippa offered in consolation, but Noah just scoffed.

"To be honest, I think they were relieved to have a scapegoat. If the mob hadn't attacked our shops, they would have set their fury on the police themselves. The streets of Whitechapel are stained with blood, and the mob won't rest until there's been retribution. I can only pray that justice arrives soon, as my family . . . we are more vulnerable to this danger than most."

I was confused. "But why would the mob target your family in particular? You said they were bent on attacking *any* shop owned by Jews."

A dark expression formed on Noah's face. "That's just the thing, Dell, it's not the mob I'm afraid of, it's our own people."

"Your fellow Jews? But why?" Pippa seemed as lost as I was.

Noah hesitated before speaking again. "There's something about my family I haven't told you—"

Just then, Noah was practically tackled from our arms by a tall, sandy-haired young man who had just emerged from a shop on the corner. For a split second, I was concerned he was being attacked, but a shout of raucous glee from Noah indicated otherwise.

"Noah! Thank God you're alright! I wanted to come right away, but our herd was at the stockyard—"

Noah waved off the explanation, grinning wider and looking lighter than I'd seen him all morning. "It's fine, it's fine. I'm alright."

"And your mother?"

"She's as well as she can be, considering."

"And . . . your father?"

Noah's joyful expression flickered just a fraction, and with a shake of his head, he dismissed the inquiry. "Never mind that, I'm being unforgivably rude! Henry, these are my friends, Dell and Pippa. They go to the school on Buck's Row. Dell, Pippa, this is Henry Winthrup. He and his family own this fine establishment"—he gestured towards a cheerful-looking shop with striped awnings and a whole roast pig displayed in the window—"and I'm hoping he'll be able to spare some goods to fill your order today."

"Say no more, my friend!" Henry replied, clapping Noah fondly on the back. "Anything you ladies need, it's yours." With a flourish, he escorted us through the doors of his shop, which was at least five times larger than Noah's and stocked with a dazzling array of meats and exotic shellfish—including, I noted, the pork that Noah and his family didn't sell.

"I think for today just some sausage will do, about ten pounds," Noah mused as we made our way to the counter. "That ought to be enough to hold you over until tomorrow, won't it? By then I'll be back on my feet."

"Anything you need, as long as you need it," Henry offered as he commenced packaging our order. "Are you sure you'll be up and ready by tomorrow? What can I do to help?"

"We'll be alright, I think," Noah replied. "The men from the synagogue will be over this afternoon to help with the repairs, and the lad from the stockyard says he can replenish our supply by tomorrow morning."

"Glad to hear it," Henry beamed as he handed me the wrapped meat with an amiable bow. "Miss Dell, your order."

"Thank you so much," I replied as I tucked the meat into my basket, before a terrible realisation overtook me. "Wait, Noah, I haven't got any money—"

"Put it on my credit, won't you?" Noah replied.

"I absolutely will not," Henry countered. "On the house. Please. It's the least I can do."

Noah's relief was evident upon his face. "Cheers, Henry. Say . . . you wouldn't mind throwing in yesterday's copy of *The Star*, would you?" He gestured towards a discarded newspaper tucked behind the till.

"Anything for you," Henry replied with a wink, and handed it over. It took every ounce of willpower I possessed not to snatch it from Noah's hands, but I managed to restrain myself. We exchanged a fond farewell with Henry and made our way back out onto High Street. I noticed Noah's spirits had lifted considerably, but our pleasant encounter had not made me forget the fact that he had been on the cusp of divulging some terrible secret before we'd been interrupted.

"Henry seems lovely," Pippa offered, and I was reminded that on occasion, tact was a far more persuasive approach than outright interrogation.

Noah grinned in response. "Our families have owned shops here for three generations apiece; I'm lucky to have a companion like him in these uncertain times."

"Speaking of uncertain times," I countered, attempting to steer the conversation as casually as I could.

Noah sighed, and his gait slowed. "The thing is . . ." he began, then shook his head in apparent defeat.

"Noah, whatever it is, you can tell us," I assured him.

He chuckled at this, but the sound was devoid of joy. After a pause, he finally commenced with his tale.

"The thing is, my father is unwell. He has been for quite some time. Two years ago, he took a turn for the worst. He was committed to an asylum in Essex." At this, my stomach dropped, and Pippa audibly gasped, but we did not dare interject. Noah carried on stoically. "He'd become violent and unruly, towards not only my mother and me but strangers alike. He complained of hearing odd noises, he cried out for no reason, he felt compelled to act in such a way that his conscience could not stand. He had formerly been a shrewd businessman, but he could not sleep at nights, and he wandered the streets aimlessly, searching for purpose. He was sent away, and I took over the shop in his absence. It was . . . difficult. I was only fourteen."

I took a moment to calm my nerves before replying. "Was he cured of his ailments while he was away?"

Noah's expression was distant as he contemplated this. "When he returned a year later, he was different, that much is certain, but nothing remains of the man he was before his affliction. I remember him from my childhood: he was a kind soul, gentle and patient, and he loved me and my mother dearly." My mind could not reconcile this pleasant memory with my own (albeit brief) encounter with the man, whom Pippa and I had witnessed slapping his son across the face as we cowered behind the market shelves on our very first day of outreach.

"When he returned from the asylum, he was indeed somewhat changed for the better. He no longer wanders the streets or talks to voices no one can hear, but the mean streak in him wrought by his madness remains—at least, where my mother and I are concerned."

"But certainly you do not suspect your father of the crimes that have been occurring upon the streets of Whitechapel," I countered, and at this, Noah laughed.

"Of course not. For all his faults, I do not suspect my father of murder. He is far from perfect, but a killer he is not."

I paused to consider this. "Then why do you fear that your family is in any more danger than that of any other Jews in the neighbourhood?"

"My mother and I have learned to endure his lingering cruelty, but it appears our neighbours are not so forgiving. Nor have they forgotten the transgressions he committed before he was interned in Essex. To them, he is a prime target for the police to investigate now that Leather Apron is off the hook. His madness is a liability to himself, and that makes him a liability to *all* our people. The neighbours have asked the rabbi to bring him before the *beth din*."

"What's—" Pippa and I began in unison.

"The beth din is a Jewish court of law, separate from the

official court of England. Normally it's used to prosecute religious infractions, acts not in keeping with our faith. But other times, it's a preemptive measure, an effort to prevent outsiders from intervening in matters which the council believes are best handled by our own people."

"Your neighbours truly believe your father to be culpable?" Despite the harshness I'd witnessed that first day in the shop, it was a far leap from a backhanded slap to cold-blooded murder.

Noah sighed heavily. "I cannot say for certain. A part of me wants to believe that they believe it! For if they honestly felt my father was such a danger, it would be well within their right to seek justice."

"But you don't think they really believe he's the killer," I ascertained.

"And there's the rub: No, I don't. I think they're more than willing to let an innocent scapegoat be convicted by the beth din and handed over to the gentile lawmen as a sacrifice in the hopes that we'd then be left alone."

"Is there any chance of changing the rabbi's mind?" Pippa queried meekly. "About bringing your father before the beth din?"

"My mother and I have argued staunchly against it, but the rabbi continues to press the matter. The riots last night are simply another straw on the camel's back. I'm afraid my whole family is living on borrowed time." In unison, Pippa and I reached out to clasp Noah's shoulders as comfortingly as we could, though he could barely muster a sad smile in return.

"Is there anything at all we can do to help?" Pippa offered, her brow furrowed, and her beatific visage painted with concern.

Noah issued a hollow laugh. "Catch the real killer for me, won't you?"

We had to sprint back to Whitechapel Hall, having only minutes to spare before we were tardy for kitchen duty. My progress was considerably impeded by the rolled-up day-old edition of *The Star* stuffed in my stocking, a parting gift from Noah that excited me so greatly I'd thrown my arms around him in a fit of giddiness quite unbecoming of a lady but had fortunately only amused him.

Throughout the tedium of the day, my mind kept turning back to Noah and his predicament. First and foremost, I was struck most keenly by this first instance of true madness to which I'd ever been exposed. In my penny bloods, madness was a most romantic affliction, suffered by hapless maidens locked away in secret attics. The madness suffered by Noah's father, however, was far different. It was tragic, visceral, and dangerous, and I could not comprehend how he could so stoically convey its reality to us without shedding a tear. I thought back to my own departed father: his kindness, his gentleness, his patience . . . What would it be like to witness all that slip away beneath some invisible veil, to have it drained from him like blood by an incorporeal vampire, to have it stolen by a shapeless fiend?

This invariably led my thoughts to Pippa, who had lost her own mother to some affliction of madness as well, leaving behind only the hollow aching to which I now bore daily witness. Her subsequent abandonment by her father was callous enough, but what toll must her mother's indifference have taken? How must she feel to have a mother who was lost but not *lost*, gone but not *gone*?

My own grief was not inconsequential, of course, and I missed my parents each waking hour. But they had been stolen from me swiftly in a matter of days, a turning of tides so abrupt that I could scarcely comprehend when I was suddenly underwater. For Noah and Pippa, however, their losses were enduring, jagged, and incomplete. I could see now that our mirrored grief was two sides of a coin, two halves of a broken heart. We were fated to understand one another, and I was struck by simultaneous sorrow and gratitude.

The conversation with Pippa on our perch that evening was predictably solemn. Try as we might, we could offer no resolution to Noah's predicament besides the capture of the real killer who, despite our nightly vigilance, we were no closer to apprehending than we had been to start with. Now that Leather Apron was no longer implicated, a gaping chasm of plausible suspects presented an insurmountable obstacle. I could not pin it upon a husband, a lover, or a fantastical spectre who jumped six stories high and had nails like razors; for once, my penny bloods provided no plausible explanation. There was no simple solution, and instead of feeling omniscient as we gazed down upon the fated streets below us, we felt more powerless than ever.

It was with an air of resignation that we retired to the annex that night. I had hatched a half-witted scheme that involved escaping the school via the dumbwaiter and infiltrating Vigilance Committee meetings in the hope of gleaning a better lead, but Pippa had promptly discouraged me by noting that the meetings occurred in the middle of Morality class, making our absence from the school rather conspicuous, and I'd been forced to begrudgingly resign the point.

Pippa drifted off into a peaceful slumber soon after we retired, but I found myself restless. For lack of a better option, I relit my lamp and pulled out the edition of *The Star* that Noah had so generously bequeathed me that morning. Pippa and I had of course reviewed the leading article about the Chapman murder already, but I reasoned I ought to comb through the corroborating articles, in case there was some thread of evidence left dangling that could be woven into the larger tapestry by a more discerning eye than that of the average reader.

The ghoul-like creature who stalks through the streets of London is simply drunk with blood, and he will have more . . .

Pursing my lips, I plucked my pen off my bedside table and circled this passage, my mind replaying Pippa's argument with Beatrice the previous night. *Ghoul-like*. Conjuring images of Spring-Heeled Jack, of course, but also invoking an undeniable parallel between the revolting appearance of *this* monster and the cruel rumours of the Jews' invisible claws and horns. "*No Englishman could have done it*," Noah had recited bitterly. But how could anyone be sure, when no one had caught so much as a glimpse of the perpetrator?

With a sigh, I moved on, skimming each breathless article for relevant facts.

> *She was lying on her back with her legs outstretched. Her throat was cut from ear to ear. Her clothes were pushed up above her waist and her legs bare. The abdomen was exposed, the woman having been ripped up from groin to breast-bone as before. Not only this, but the viscera had been pulled out and scattered in all directions, the heart and liver being placed beside her head, and the remainder along her side.*

I circled this as well, ignoring the churning in my stomach as I envisioned the scene. It was a fair bit grislier than anything Mrs. Paschal had been up against but hardly more grotesque than the crime scene descriptions in the average *Illustrated Police News*. I forced myself to be objective. What could we deduce from the scene? That the culprit not only used a knife, but that he seemed extraordinarily fond of it; in most of the stabbing reports I'd reviewed, the purpose of the blade was to extinguish a life. But in this case, it seemed to me much more than that: a unique delight in the aftermath of the act, far beyond simple retribution. He did not disembowel his victims for the purpose of disposing of the body, like John Holloway tearing his wife up limb for limb to stash her in a trunk. No, this was something far more sinister than it was practical. I dutifully took note.

It was evident at a glance that the murder had been done where the body lay. The enormous quantity of blood and the splash on the fence, coupled with the total absence of stains elsewhere, made this clear.

He must be swift with his actions: the nightly patrols of Whitechapel were now so persistent, Pippa and I had timed the constables' rounds to seven minutes apiece. To kill a woman within view of the route and still make a clean escape required a swift hand, indeed.

Our representative went to the Ten Bells, in Bricklane, where as the gossip goes, the unfortunate creature spent her last night. The barmaid said she opened the place at five o'clock, and served Dark Annie throughout the night, along with an unnamed companion.

I circled the name of the tavern and made a note to query Noah about it. Though he didn't frequent taverns himself, perhaps he would know more of the clientele, which might at least lead to a worthwhile interview or two.

She had three rings on when she left the house: One a wedding ring, and the other two chased. These had disappeared, having evidently been mistaken for gold and stolen by the assassin.

I furrowed my brow at this. It seemed highly unlikely that anyone would mistake the jewellery upon the hand of a lady of a night for real gold. What, then, would be the motivation for taking her rings? I drew a question mark in the margin, determined to reflect more upon the riddle later.

> *For several hours past, the occupants of the adjoining house have been charging an admission fee of one penny to people anxious to view the spot where the body was found. Several hundreds of people have availed themselves of this opportunity, though all that can be seen are a couple of packing cases from beneath which is the stain of a blood track.*

I suppressed a cry of excitement at this revelation: It was possible to *see* the scene of the crime? Immediately I began conjuring excuses to give Pippa as to why she and I simply must go there and view it for ourselves, even at the expense of her precious allowance. There was a slim chance I could convince her that we might be able to salvage a few clues if we were just given the opportunity to review the evidence with our own eyes, but unfortunately Pippa was becoming more attuned to my fanciful larks with each passing day, and it was doubtful that she'd believe I had any motive other than to gawk at the sight of fresh blood.

With a sigh of resignation, I folded the paper closed and reached to extinguish my lamp, but just before my fingers turned down the wick, the title of an article buried upon the bottom of the back page caught my eye.

Mysteries of Albion: The Missing Murderess
September 1888; Strange Murder Case Recalled

> *A MURDER MYSTERY which aroused intense interest in its day is the subject of new scrutiny in the wake of the culprit's release from prison and subsequent disappearance.*

In 1860, Samuel Saville Kent, with his second wife and his large family, lived at the village of Road, in Devon. His first wife, the mother of Constance and of a number of other children, had been insane for some years before her death. The second wife had been the governess of Constance.

On June 30, 1860, it was found that Francis Saville Kent, a son of the second marriage, aged nearly four years, had been taken from his bed and brutally murdered. The child had been stabbed multiple times in the chest, and his throat slashed so deeply as to suggest decapitation. After suspicion had turned in various directions, Constance, then aged 16 years, was arrested three weeks later, chiefly because she was unable to account for some of her clothing which had been missing. She was tried by a bench of magistrates, but was released on bond days later.

The boy's nurse was charged, and evidence was heard, but she was not committed for trial. There were other inquiries, some unofficial and absurd. For years public suspicion was divided between the nurse and the child's father. The father was followed by crowds which yelled and hooted, and called "Who murdered the boy?"

On being released, Constance had stayed at first at a convent in France, then at an Anglican religious retreat in England; until five years after the murder she confessed that she had committed it. Even now doubt is expressed by some students of the case whether the confession was not caused by a morbid state of mind, or whether Constance was not insane. A lady superior and a clergyman associated with the retreat gave much evidence about what the girl had said, and they talked at the same time about "the seal of confession." It was stated that she had affirmed jealousy of her stepmother as the cause, but in court she denied jealousy, while apparently admitting anger.

Constance had received £1000 on coming of age, and the clergyman, when the question was raised, stated that she wished to apply it towards the charities of the retreat, but he had refused it. He later added that a sum of £800 was found in one of the alms boxes of his church, and he ascertained that it was placed there by Miss Kent.

The Star, upon reviewing the evidence, has concluded that both the lady superior and the clergymen, while careful to avoid laying any injunction on Miss Kent, were all the while forcing her into a police court; and much value cannot be attached to public confessions obtained by such means. Other leading journals have similarly deplored that there had not been a trial in which the case was thoroughly investigated.

On her own confession, Constance was found guilty of murder, but the sentence of death was commuted to imprisonment for life. She was released in 1885 after 20 years of incarceration during which she displayed exemplary behaviour, and nothing definite is known of her contemporary life. Romantic stories are told of a marriage and happiness, or that she entered an Anglican sisterhood, where she remains hidden today. But could it be that the mysterious murderess now walks free among us, her identity disguised to her oblivious acquaintances? Such remains the mystery of the Road Hill House Murder.

And there beneath the article was a sketched portrait of a young woman with pin-straight hair fastened into a severe chignon at the base of her neck, dark, hooded eyes that glared broodily into the distance, and a dour expression I would recognize anywhere.

It was none other than *Miss Kaye*.

Chapter X
Crime and Punishment

"I can't believe it." Pippa's eyes, which had just moments earlier still been bleary with the vestiges of the slumber I'd urgently interrupted, were now blown wide and brimming with terror as she stared down at the newspaper clutched in her hands.

I bit back the triumphant *I told you so* threatening to escape my mouth, and instead settled for a far more neutral, "We were right to have suspected her."

"But of *this*?" Pippa looked up from the article. "Dell, this is so much worse than simply teaching here under an assumed identity or sneaking out for a bit of fun after-hours. This is dangerous. This is *deadly*."

"I know!" I could scarcely contain my glee. I'd solved not one but *both* mysteries in a single swoop, a feat so impressive that surely even Mrs. Paschal would be impressed.

"But whatever shall we do? She could commit another murder this very night! We ought to alert the headmaster immediately."

This gave me pause. I knew of course that Pippa was right—the obvious course of action would be to turn Miss Kaye in right away—but part of me was hoping for a rather more climactic conclusion to the story; perhaps catching her in the sordid act of killing or, short of that, cornering her with the evidence of her deceit in such a public manner that she was forced to confess her sins before the whole school.

"I suppose . . ."

Pippa was already out of bed and pulling on her frock, leaving me grasping at straws for reasons to delay. "You said you can pick the dormitory lock, right? We'll simply bring the paper down to Headmaster Graves, and he can send for the police tonight."

"But how will we account for having the paper?" I protested. "We'll be in trouble if we have contraband."

Pippa shot me an exasperated look as she pulled her boots out from under her bed and proceeded to fasten them. "I think he'll be quite willing to overlook the source of the evidence once we inform him that there's a madwoman teaching under his roof and wreaking havoc upon the streets outside."

"Ugh, *fine*." I capitulated and rose to pull a dress from my wardrobe.

"Have you got a better idea? For Heaven's sake, it's clear that Miss Kaye—Miss Kent—whoever she is—will stop at nothing in her quest for blood. Why, she could have a go at any one of us if she's not stopped."

"I know that, I just thought . . ." I trailed off, unsure of how to tell Pippa my true feelings.

"That we'd capture her ourselves?"

"Well, yes. That."

"We did, Dell! Well, you did. You uncovered Miss Kaye's secret identity, you solved the mystery of the Whitechapel murders, and you'll have saved Noah's father from an undeserved fate! What more do you want?"

I paused to consider this. "Maybe a spirited chase through an underground labyrinth or a bloody confrontation at the scene of a crime?" I offered, recalling some of the better third acts in my fictions.

"For God's sake, you're hopeless. Come on."

Our escape from the dormitory was uneventful, and we made our way swiftly through the moonlit corridors as upstairs, the clock chimed ten.

"What if he's asleep?" I wondered aloud as we traversed the entrance hall. It had never occurred to me before whether Headmaster Graves's chambers were adjacent to his office as Miss Kaye's were, or if he resided somewhere else in the school entirely.

"Unlikely. I've known girls brought before him for detention at all hours of the night; he seems perpetually vigilant during the nocturnal hours, perhaps even more so than during the day."

"Right." I tightened my clutch on the rolled-up edition of *The Star* in my hand and noted that my palm was considerably sweatier than the draughty chill of the hallway would merit.

We arrived at his office moments later, and just as Pippa had predicted, a merry light was glowing from behind the heavy door. Pippa turned to me and gave me an encouraging nod, which I returned with a tight-lipped smile before raising my hand and delivering three sharp knocks.

There was a pause, followed by the sound of footsteps upon the floorboards, and then the door swung open to reveal none other than—

"Miss Kaye!" Startled, both Pippa and I stumbled backwards in unison, matching expressions of shock manifesting upon our faces as the impossible nightmare before us materialised.

"Miss Fitzroy! Miss Morton! What are you both doing out of bed? And how did you get out of your dormitory?"

My mouth had gone dry, and my cheeks flushed hot, my head spinning with the terrible improbability of this latest encounter with my nemesis.

"Where is Headmaster Graves?" I turned to see that much

to my relief, Pippa appeared far more composed than I felt and had taken on the haughty, prissy demeanour that seemed to so charm our superiors.

"He is out of town on urgent business."

My stomach dropped, and an icy panic began to work its way up from my toes. "For how long?"

"Indefinitely. Now will one of you ladies please explain to me precisely what you are doing out of your dormitory at this hour, demanding an unscheduled audience with the headmaster?"

"We were . . . We simply wanted to . . ." I hazarded a panicked glance over at Pippa who, despite remaining mercifully poised, was staring back at me with her mouth sealed firmly shut. My mind reeled, desperately searching for a plausible excuse for our presence.

"What's that in your hand?" To my compounding horror, Miss Kaye's eyes firmly fixed upon the rolled journal clutched in my fist.

"It's nothing." Desperately I tried to hide it behind my back, but it was too late. Miss Kaye snatched it from my grasp and unrolled it, her eyes flicking across the salacious headlines.

I scarcely dared breathe. The article detailing her crimes was buried upon the back page, but all it would take was a thorough reading and Pippa and I would be doomed at the hands of an unhinged murderess. My imagination took flight at the thought: How would our demise play out? Would Pippa and I fight and grapple for our lives, or was Miss Kaye already armed—perhaps with a switchblade, hidden in the folds of her petticoat—ready to slit our throats before we could so much as scream in protest? Should I attempt to thwart her before she discovered that we knew her secret? We could run, but how far could we get, knowing that the front doors were sealed and that the dumbwaiter, while still operational, could only fit one of us and was far too slow for a successful escape? Should I attempt to gain the upper hand by attacking first? Perhaps if we could simply get the jump—

No sooner had the wild thought crossed my mind than Miss Kaye sighed, closed her eyes briefly, then strode across the room to toss the newspaper directly into the fireplace, the flames consuming the incriminating tome in a matter of seconds.

A cry of indignation escaped me, and Miss Kaye turned to glare at me over her shoulder, her black eyes cold with fury. "And *this*, ladies, is precisely the type of derelict *filth* that we do not tolerate in this institution. Why, just last night I had three girls pounding down my door moments before bed check, claiming to have seen a fire-breathing demon outside the window of the dormitory! And the night before that, it was a knife-wielding succubus supposedly lurking outside the Reverend's church, stalking the girls charged with maintaining the garden there. You are at Whitechapel Hall by the grace of God, to reform your morals and walk the path of holy salvation, yet you allow your minds to be sullied by all manners of indecency pedalled upon these streets!"

Pippa and I were still so startled by this sudden turn of events that neither of us could formulate a rebuttal.

"You are meant to be *Ambassadors of Virtue*, proselytising the Word of God to the degenerates you walk among, and instead I find time and time again that not a single pupil here has the constitution to forsake the temptations of sin, and instead you take every opportunity you are afforded to soak up the indecency and depravity like a sponge! Why, I fear I have no choice but to suspend our efforts at Temperance Outreach immediately—"

"No!" Pippa and I both cried out in unison, and the vigour of our response appeared to catch Miss Kaye off guard enough that she momentarily suspended her tirade.

With a sigh, she turned from the fire and took a seat behind the headmaster's desk, the low light casting a malevolent shadow across the pall of her face. "Of course, the Temperance Outreach programme is so dear to the headmaster's heart, I do hate to interfere so forcibly in his absence. But the proof is too palpable to ignore: The world outside of Whitechapel Hall has not done you one whit of good. It has been nothing but open floodgates to temptation."

Pippa cleared her throat and batted her eyes, a daring display of innocence so captivating that I nearly believed her myself. "Our apologies, Miss Kaye. It was simply that . . . we found the newspaper in the dormitory, in Beatrice's trunk. We shouldn't have been snooping, obviously, and it was wrong of us to have taken it, of course, but we were indeed tempted by the headlines, for they terrified us so. But as soon as we read it, the horrors were so upsetting, we could think of no other recourse than to bring it here and report the transgression to the headmaster. We had no ill intent in reading it, that much we swear! It was simply curiosity, which is of course a vice unto itself, but Dell and I are intending to walk the path of salvation, Miss Kaye, you must believe us, we've been good, it was a momentary lapse in judgement— "

"Enough." At that, Miss Kaye held up her hand, and for one terrifying moment I thought she might regale us with the story of my attempted escape in rebuttal to Pippa's assertion. But much to my relief, she simply gave us both one more solemn survey, as if buying time before formulating her reply.

"To bed with you. There will be no punishment for your transgression, as you made the correct decision in bringing this dire matter to my attention."

"Yes, Miss Kaye, thank you, Miss Kaye," we parroted in unison, the relief in our tone nearly palpable.

"That said, starting tomorrow, the Temperance Outreach programme will be suspended indefinitely."

"But Miss Kaye, please— "

"Don't fret, ladies, I'll not implicate either of you or your discovery of this dangerous contraband in my decision. But it's my belief that until order has been restored to the streets of Whitechapel, the potential for corruption is too high to allow you to carry on in good faith."

"But Miss Kaye, we simply—"

"There is nothing more to say on the matter. Good night, ladies."

Pippa and I stood there for a moment longer, the words of protest we yearned to utter suppressed only by terror as the reality of our plight began to settle in: We were captive inside the school with a murderess, with no avenue for rescue. If we objected too fervently to her ruling, there was no one to stop us from being the next slit-throated victims to be arranged in an unholy display upon the steps of Whitechapel Hall.

With stiff curtsies, we turned and exited the room, carefully closing the door behind us. Without exchanging a word, we took off in a full-tilted sprint towards the safety of the annex.

For the first few minutes following our return, we could only sit in stunned silence, the enormity of our predicament washing over us in oscillating, nauseating waves. Headmaster Graves was gone, our outreach had been suspended, and we were trapped inside the Hall with a cold-blooded killer. Not only that, but my fears were compounded by the one secret I could not tell: that Miss Kaye would undoubtedly be eying me with more suspicion than most, as I alone knew of the secret dumbwaiter and had previously not hesitated to use it. It was imperative that I regain her trust completely, or I would no doubt suffer the same fate as her own little brother, whom she had apparently unceremoniously beheaded for no reason other than simple jealousy. I shivered at the thought.

Pippa wrapped her arms around me in a gesture of warm comfort, and my regret for ever even considering leaving Whitechapel Hall without her welled up within me, choking me on the weight of all the words I dared not say. She had been nothing but loyal and true since the first day I had met her, and in a moment of pure selfishness, I had risked it all for my own gains; and now I could not even confess to her the true source of my distress. *I'm sorry*, I thought. *I'm so sorry*.

"We have to get out of here." My words pierced the ringing silence and seemed to echo through the rafters of the clock tower.

"And go where? We've no funds, no connections, nowhere to run *to*." Pippa's tone was so laced with bitterness that it scarcely sounded like her at all.

A million scenarios swirled through my head, each as unlikely as the last. Despite my initial obsession with escaping my internment, I had admittedly been too distracted by the excitement of the previous week to have spent much time contemplating a future attempt.

Resigned, I opted for the least bombastic scheme. "We just need to make it outside the walls of the Hall and find a constable. We'll tell him about Miss Kaye—Miss Kent—and the police will no doubt come to our rescue."

At this, Pippa let out a rancorous cackle. "Oh, please, are you really so blind to our position here? We are *inmates*, Dell, prisoners sentenced by the court to serve our time at this so-called *reformatory institution* that's known to all for what truly it is: a children's prison. Of course, the headmaster loves to send us out onto the streets to masquerade about as upstanding citizens, but do you know why he does it? Because it gives him fodder to ask the courts for more money! Every week that passes without an escape, the school is granted an additional ten pounds, did you know that? He lets us out just to parade us around and prove that he can make us come back."

I blinked at her uncomprehendingly. Was that true? Was it possible that the headmaster did not believe wholeheartedly in our moral reform but was instead using us to milk the court for money?

"How do you know all of this?"

Melancholy overtook her, and for once it was my turn to clasp her hands in mine for comfort. After a long spell, she finally spoke, her voice soft and broken with sadness.

"When I first arrived here at Whitechapel Hall, I met a girl called Sally. She was a year or two younger than me and had been here for nearly as long as she could remember. She was an outcast, too, but I liked her. I did not know her well, but we would always share a laugh or two on laundry day."

I nodded, unsure of what to say.

"One day, Sally went missing. It was a big to-do, as you can imagine, as the Reverend and Headmaster pride themselves so on their immaculate record. Much to their relief, she was returned that night by the police. She'd run off but had been captured and returned. After that day, she didn't speak any more. Try as I might, she would never tell me where she'd gone to, or why."

Pippa took a deep breath and closed her eyes, and I squeezed her palms in mine, her pain visceral to me. "Four days later, she was found hanging in the laundry room courtyard. She'd killed herself and left a note upon her pillow."

"Dear God," I murmured.

"The note explained everything. Before Miss Kaye was employed here, we were overseen by a schoolmaster by the name of Mr. Samuels. As it turns out, he had been taking liberties with Sally for months. She'd told the Reverend and the headmaster, but they ignored her. Unable to endure it any longer, she escaped and made her way to the police. And what did they do? Turned around and *sent her back*." Pippa spat out the final words like they were poison on her tongue. "And you know what they found when they took her body for examination? *She was with child*. Here, locked in Whitechapel Hall, with only the faculty to blame. Of course, they covered it up and sent Mr. Samuels away, all very hush-hush, and no one ever spoke of it again."

"Pippa, I can't even . . . that's terrible."

Pippa sighed. "I know that. What happened to her was unforgivable. But don't you see? When we walk these streets, with our silly cloaks and bonnets, people don't see us as *Ambassadors of Virtue*. To them, we are liars, cheats, and whores. Why, even if you *could* find another copy of *The Star* and you found a magistrate and shoved it under his nose, he'd laugh in your face and march you right back here to face the music. We can't trust the police on this, Dell. We're on our own."

I paused to contemplate this. "We have to get to Noah."

Pippa gave me a withering look. "He can't take us in, Pippa. His family is in dire straits as-is."

"No, not to lodge us, to help us catch Miss Kaye. We must let him know what we've discovered about her! If we're trapped in here, perhaps at least he can work the case from the outside."

"But how are we going to get all the way to High Street to alert him? If Miss Kaye knows you know about the dumbwaiter, there's no way she'll be so careless as to let the likes of you at it."

"Then we'll wait here. If we disappear, he'll come to our rescue; he believes in true chivalry." Defeated, we spoke no more as the walls of Whitechapel Hall closed in ever tighter around us.

Chapter XI
Unravelling a Tangled Skein

The ensuing three days were torturous as we endured our daily routine with superficial calm, lest we draw any more attention from the murderer hiding in our midst. Pippa and I performed our kitchen duty with Cook in solemn silence, sharing a knowing glance over the packages of meats that Cook now had the lone pleasure of procuring, our mutual yearning for Noah's company palpable only to the two of us.

Another blow came via news from the Reverend: he had been appointed to a leadership position on the Vigilance Committee and taken a sabbatical as our spiritual leader. Miss Kaye delivered this news from the pulpit where she'd prepared a sermon of her own, and I knew I was not imagining the smirk of satisfaction on her face; her coup of the leadership was complete.

Lastly, when we showed up for afternoon housekeeping, we were abruptly informed that Mrs. Dolmer had temporarily resigned her position, fearing to walk the streets of Whitechapel alone until the killer was caught, and therefore Miss Kaye would be our sole supervisor for the foreseeable future. Laundry, needlework, and cleaning took on an ominous undertone as Pippa and I toiled shoulder-to-shoulder with our classmates who remained oblivious to the danger posed within the supposed sanctity of the Hall. Our isolation was complete, the fear of Miss Kaye's retribution suffocating any cry for help.

While rumours and gossip about the Whitechapel killer still dominated the nightly conversations in the dormitory, our quarantine deprived us of any new information, and the speculation only grew wilder the longer we remained ignorant. I yearned to know anything of the world outside: Was Noah safe? Was his father still free? And above all: *Had Miss Kaye killed again?* Within the confines of our prison, we were trapped in an infernal darkness, invisible to all except each other.

The morning of our fourth day of internment, we reported to the kitchen with an air of grim resignation, faced with the prospect of more time slipping through our fingers as Miss Kaye smugly dallied, her control over Whitechapel Hall uncontested, her reign of terror on the streets unimpeded.

What neither of us expected when we shuffled into the kitchen was to find ourselves face-to-face with Noah himself, arms wrapped around a basket of freshly prepared sausages, chatting up Cook with a winning smile upon his face.

"Oh, ladies, there you are! Thank goodness you're early. Butcher Levy here has kindly offered to deliver our daily meat supply until this dreadful business has passed and your outreach resumes. Mr. Levy, please, the girls will show you where to put it all. Now I must be off: not all our vendors have been as generous as you, kind sir, so I must make it to the market myself if we're to have so much as a turnip to go with supper." And with that, Cook hastened off, leaving the three of us alone in stunned silence.

"*Noah!*" Pippa was the first to break, running forward and throwing herself into his arms as he dropped his basket of wares to catch her. I followed on her heels, wrapping them both in an embrace equal parts relief and joy.

"Oh, Noah, we knew you'd come! We've such news, but we've been locked away— "

Noah pulled away and grinned down at the two of us. "Yes, yes, Mrs. Dillinger told me all about it. Luckily, she was only too eager to take on my offer to make the deliveries myself."

Pippa and I exchanged an inquisitive look. "Who is Mrs. Dillinger?"

Noah appeared lost. "Your . . . your cook? Why, I thought you two worked for her in the kitchen every day?"

"Oh!" I exclaimed with a laugh. "You know, it never occurred to me that her name was anything besides *Cook*."

Pippa and Noah joined me in my chuckle, but our mirth was short-lived; we had far graver matters to attend to.

"Though my heart is glad to see you both safe, I'm afraid you'll be sorely disappointed with my lack of news. There have been no more killings, but the rabbi has still not given up on the prospect of bringing my father to trial— "

"Never mind that!" I interjected (perhaps a bit rudely, considering the expression on Noah's face, and I was momentarily abashed for my callousness but reasoned our pressing news could not wait). "*We've found the killer!*"

Noah quirked an eyebrow. "You what?"

"We figured out who the killer is!"

"I . . . *what? How?*"

"It's our teacher here at the school, Miss Kaye—or, as she's really known, Constance Kent." Pippa revealed this information with a look of eager excitement, such that Noah's confounded disbelief seemed to dissipate slightly.

"What makes you think your teacher is stalking the streets at night murdering degenerate women?" Noah was still guarded but clearly intrigued.

"She's done it before," I divulged, lowering my voice to a whisper despite the fact we were very much alone. "Twenty years ago, she went to prison for stabbing her own infant brother to death, slicing his throat so deeply she nearly decapitated him."

Noah looked aghast. "So, what is she doing teaching at Whitechapel Hall?"

"She's in disguise, you see . . ." As briefly as I could, I revealed what I'd discovered during my investigation in her chambers. "I initially suspected her of the murders because we saw her sneaking out of the school the night of the second killing, but then I found an article in the old copy of *The Star* you gave us about how Constance Kent was released from prison and disappeared three years ago. The pieces all fell into place: Miss Kaye *is* Miss Kent, she was unreformed during her stay in prison, and now she's back to her old ways. She's insane, and what's worse, she's taken over Whitechapel Hall! The headmaster is gone, quite possibly murdered himself— " (this theory had admittedly just occurred to me, but in the moment I could picture him dismembered and stuffed into his own travelling trunk with such clarity that the conviction in my voice offered no doubt) "the Reverend is exiled, and she's put us all in total captivity!"

Noah let out a long, low whistle and leaned heavily back against the counter. "What do you propose we do? You can't expect me to go to the police: They'll never believe a Jew whose own father is a suspect."

"Of course not," I assured him. "But now that we know who's responsible, we can track her movements and catch her in the act!"

"How are you going to catch her if you're locked up in the Hall?"

"Erm, well . . . that's just the thing: We'll need you to be our man on the street. You could patrol the area outside Whitechapel Hall, so the next time Miss Kaye sneaks out, you could follow her and catch her in the act. It shouldn't be difficult: With the headmaster gone, she'll simply use the key to exit the main doors. Easy!"

To my surprise, Noah did not leap at the opportunity to be the hero detective. Instead, he looked even more dubious than before. "Perhaps for a few nights I can sneak away without my parents realising something is amiss, but I have responsibilities of my own, Dell. The shop, my mother, everything with my father— "

"But we're trying to save your father, don't you see— "

"I *do* see, Dell, but what you *don't* see from within the walls of your cloisters is that everything in my life is hanging by a thread! It is a race against time to see which happens first: to have my father brought before the beth din, my family disgraced, and our business brought to ruins, or another murder, in which case I won't have to worry about any of the rest of it, because our shop will be burned down by a damned mob and we'll be stoned to death in the streets anyway!" To my surprise, anger flashed in his eyes, and for the first time I noticed the dark hollows beneath them. Once more, my romantic notions of crime solving were dashed by the sour reality of injustice.

"Surely it won't be for long, Noah." Pippa's sweet tone cut through Noah's bitterness. "The killings have been only eight days apart. By that logic, we are due for one within the week! And just think, if you catch Miss Kaye red-handed, all will be right as soon as she is apprehended! We will be free, your father will be proclaimed innocent, and everything will be as it was!"

I pretended not to notice the melancholy intermingled with Noah's smile as he gave Pippa an affirmative nod. "Fair enough. I'll commence my watch tonight. The sooner we catch her, the sooner it will all be as it was. But make no mistake: I cannot make a habit of being away at night. It's not safe."

Fortunately, we did not have to wait long to test Noah's commitment to our plan. The following night, at precisely four minutes past midnight, from atop our perch Pippa and I witnessed the sight which we'd most desired and feared in all the world: Miss Kaye emerging from the front door of Whitechapel

Hall, cloak pulled tight about her shoulders and her bonnet draped with her black lace mourning veil as she stole off into the night.

For a moment we held our collective breath, eyes peering into the darkness. And then, from deep within the shadows, the figure of a young man emerged and followed Miss Kaye down the street.

"Do you think this will work?" Pippa whispered.

"There's only one way to find out: We wait."

And wait we did, for three eternal hours, each strike of the clock an icy dagger of dread in our hearts. A thousand anxieties gnawed at me in the oppressive silence that laid upon the two of us: Shouldn't we have heard a police alarm by now? What if Noah had failed to track Miss Kaye, and she was out there slaughtering another innocent victim as we sat in helpless impotence? Or worst of all, what if *she* had found *Noah*, and our dearest companion now lay slain in some dark alley, his life simply one more trophy in Miss Kaye's maniacal quest?

It was nearly four o'clock, the streets finally vacant and the city asleep, when our deepest fears were confirmed: Out from the stillness emerged a familiar cloaked figure. She made her way up the steps of the Hall, procured the key, and let herself inside, then shut the door with a sickening slam, the sobering sound of our imprisonment reinforced. Then there was only silence.

"Oh, God . . ." whispered Pippa. "Where is Noah? Oh, Dell, do you think he's alright?"

"I'm sure he is." I spoke with a confidence I in no way possessed.

"But we've heard nothing," Pippa countered, the pitch of her voice rising in panic. "If he'd caught up with her, we would have heard the police summons!"

"Of course," I capitulated. "But he may not have caught up with her at all! For all we know, she lost him in a clever dodge, and he's still out there scouring the streets for a sign of her."

"But what if he caught her in the act and she's killed him, too?" I could not pretend that the thought had not crossed my own mind, but I forced the fear back down. "Noah isn't like her other victims. He's not a child or a drunkard or a lady of the night. He's strong, smart, and capable. He can look out for himself, Pippa, or he'd never have agreed to our plan in the first place." *Unless he was desperate to save his own father*, my inner voice contested, but I willed it away.

"I suppose." Pippa looked unconvinced.

"Come on," I said, rising to my feet and offering her my hand. "We're both exhausted. We must try and get a little sleep before daybreak. What has been, will be. We can't save anyone tonight."

Reluctantly, Pippa joined me, and I led her back down to the annex. We curled side by side in my cot and drifted off into an uneasy slumber.

The morning bell was as jarring as it was unwelcome, but the two of us wasted no time in reporting to the kitchen. We raced out of the dormitory at a record pace, footsteps accelerating as we darted down the stairs, hearts in our throats as we contemplated what awaited us. Would it be Noah confirming that he had been unable to locate his target on the streets below? Would there be news of another murder as a result? Or worst of all, would there be news of Noah's own murder?

We were hardly able to suppress our mutual cries of relief when we arrived downstairs to find Noah already positioned in the kitchen, chatting amiably with Cook as he unloaded a pile of parcels from his basket.

"Hello, Noah!" Pippa's cheeks were flushed at the very sight of him, and he turned to greet us with a fond salutation.

"Miss Fitzroy, that is *Butcher Levy* to you. The help does not employ *given names* upon addressing one another!"

"Ahem. Apologies, Butcher Levy." Pippa dipped into a low curtsy, the depth of which would have been considered cheeky by anyone a degree more observant than Cook.

"Good morning, *Butcher Levy*," I parroted, curtsying myself.

"Miss Fitzroy. Miss Morton. A true pleasure." With his exaggerated bow, the three of us exchanged knowing smirks.

"Much improved, ladies. Well, I'm off to market! A pleasure, as always, Mr. Levy." With that, Cook tottered off, leaving nothing but a pregnant silence in her wake.

I was the first to speak, unable to contain my breathless excitement a moment further. "Noah, what news? Miss Kaye returned last night unscathed; did she lose you out upon the streets?"

"Hardly," Noah replied. "I was able to track her straight down Wilkes Street, just past the row of warehouses."

I nodded eagerly, recalling that was the same street upon which I'd lost sight of her the night we'd spied upon her from above.

"And then?" Pippa continued breathlessly.

"I followed her into a pub."

"A *pub*?" I could feel myself deflating at the prospect. "She simply went out for a drink?"

"Not exactly. It was clear right away that she wasn't there for the drink; she kept her visage hidden beneath a lace veil. It would seem she had reason to remain unrecognised."

"I know that veil," I affirmed. "I found it in her trunk when I searched her chambers. It did seem rather odd to me that she kept it so readily at hand."

Noah nodded in affirmation, then continued. "She ordered a gin but barely touched it and spent the entire time chatting up the strangest eccentrics in the place. And here's the rub: She was asking them about Annie Chapman."

"The latest victim?" Pippa seemed entirely flummoxed. "What reason would she have to seek details about someone she's already killed? And why would she be doing so in a lowly tavern?"

An astute recollection came to me in that instant. "Do you remember the name of the pub?"

"Of course I do. Ten Bells, on Brick Lane."

"That's it!" I exclaimed. "That's the pub Annie Chapman was drinking in the night she was killed. I read about it in *The Star*."

"Apparently, so did Miss Kaye," Noah surmised.

"But that doesn't resolve why she was asking questions about her previous victim. Why should Miss Kaye care what Annie Chapman was up to the night that she killed her?" Pippa rightfully inquired.

It was an odd turn in the case, and no immediate hypothesis materialised in my mind as we all lapsed into a contemplative silence.

"I'll go back to the pub tonight," Noah interjected at last. "I'll interview the patrons about Miss Kaye and see if she's been there before. Perhaps there is some rhyme or reason to her fascination with the place."

"Oh, I wish we could go with you!" I moaned. A proper round of interviews at the last known port of call of the most sensationalised murder victim in London's history was so tantalising, I could hardly bear the thought of missing it.

"Is there any chance you could sneak out and join me?"

"Dell, *no*." Pippa cut me off before I could even contemplate it. "It's dangerous enough that we're locked in this school with Miss Kaye, and what's more, I have a feeling she suspects we're up to something ever since she caught us with the newspaper. We can't risk our own capture again, it's too reckless."

With a sigh, I was forced to concur. "Fine. But Noah, you must return at dawn tomorrow and tell us everything."

Chapter XII
The Devil's Receipt

"No one at the Bells knew her name, but that certainly wasn't the first time she's been there," Noah conveyed breathlessly the following morning as Pippa and I hung on his every word. We were standing shoulder-to-shoulder in the kitchen, busying ourselves unwrapping the day's wares, Noah still throwing nervous glances over his shoulder at the door Cook had disappeared through moments earlier.

"I spoke with no fewer than six patrons who recalled seeing a veiled woman making the rounds since the start of the month, chatting up the regulars and mining them for information. But here's the best part: This didn't start with Annie Chapman! The first week in September, the same woman in black was asking for any information pertaining to—"

"Mary Ann Nichols!" I interjected. "Sorry," I added, seeing the look of exasperation on Noah's face at my having stolen his glory again.

"What sort of information was she looking for?" Pippa queried. "It hardly makes sense for her to want to get to know her victims *after* she's killed them."

"It's odd," Noah continued. "She wanted to know where

they lived, their occupations, the names of their next-of-kin. Most patrons assumed she was another reporter; apparently, they've been swarming the place since the press picked up that both victims drank there."

I took a moment to mull this over as I stacked the day's cuts of liver on the counter. "She's not picking her victims at random, then. I mean, if she were just prowling the streets looking for derelict women, what are the odds that both would have spent the night at the same pub before she murdered them?"

Pippa paused and looked up, a pensive look upon her face. "Maybe she's picking them *because* they're at the Ten Bells?"

Noah and I exchanged a confused look. "What do you mean?"

"We don't know why Miss Kaye is going there after she kills her victims, but what if she's also been going there before, and she selects her target from among the patrons of the pub? Then she follows her out onto the street until she turns into a dark alley, and—" She gestured dramatically towards the set of knives hanging above the counter.

Noah nodded slowly. "That makes sense."

"It would also explain the veil," I added. "She doesn't wear it when she goes there to hunt her prey to avoid attention, then she disguises herself when she returns so that no one there will recognise her. Good thinking, Pippa." At this, Pippa blushed and shot me a pleased smile. She was becoming a rather valuable accomplice.

"Why the Ten Bells, though?" Noah mused. "What's her connection to the place, and what's she got against the women who frequent it?"

"Perhaps she's simply a religious fanatic," I posited. "The Reverend's sermons about the victims were merciless in his condemnation of their 'degenerate lifestyle.' Why, you'd almost believe they *asked* to be murdered, simply for having the audacity to live apart from their husbands! It's not so far a leap that

Miss Kaye not only believes the women deserve to be murdered but that she is the one who should deliver God's punishment."

Pippa nodded in affirmation to a quizzical-looking Noah. "It's true about the Reverend's sermons. Though he never condoned committing violence, he certainly believes that suffering is warranted by those who live in sin."

"So, you think your teacher decided to take matters into her own hands? Some sort of vigilante vendetta against vice?"

I shrugged. "Maybe. Or maybe she's simply a born killer, and ever since her release from prison, she's been searching for an excuse to continue her spree. She could simply twist the Reverend's words into an endorsement of her actions."

"It's an idea," Noah concurred. "These latest crimes feel like a far cry from murdering her own little brother, but who are we to comprehend the mind of a lunatic?"

"But that's just it, Noah! As any good detective knows, understanding the mind of the culprit is imperative to capturing them!"

"Capturing whom?" A voice from behind us rang out of nowhere. The three of us whirled around to face the kitchen door, only to find ourselves in the presence of the very woman we feared the most.

Pippa screamed and dropped the string of sausages she'd been trimming, sending them rolling across the kitchen floor in what would have been a highly comedic fashion had we not just found ourselves cornered by the madwoman we were attempting to outwit.

"Good gracious, girl, what is your affliction?" Miss Kaye glared at Pippa, who promptly scampered to collect the rogue sausages.

"Apologies, Miss Kaye, I was . . . startled. With the murderer on the loose, my nerves have been most affected." Pippa's voice was high and tight, a far cry from her usual aloof complacence in the presence of the faculty.

Miss Kaye cocked an eyebrow. "And what, you suspect he infiltrated the Hall—the most secure building in Whitechapel besides the bank—and decided to make your end here in the kitchen?"

Noah and I mustered a round of nervous laughter, still too shocked by Miss Kaye's sudden appearance to play off our uneasy demeanour with anything resembling witty banter.

"Of course, you're right, I'm being foolish. Sincerest apologies, Miss Kaye." Pippa wrangled the last of the sausages into her arms and righted herself at last, attempting to regain her composure despite the telltale flush of her face.

"Miss Morton!" Miss Kaye's eyes set upon me, and I froze in mortification. Next to me, I could feel Noah's shoulders tense.

"Yes, Miss Kaye?"

"I came here to notify you that I've at last had a chance to review your essay."

". . . Oh?" I had no idea how to respond to this inane declaration.

"You may serve the remainder of your detention tonight. In my office, directly after dinner. Don't be late."

With a squeak, Pippa lost control of one of her sausages, which somehow ejected itself from her arms with alarming velocity and projected itself a full three feet before hitting the ground and rolling away beneath the stove. Pippa scampered to retrieve it, dropping three more sausages in the process, and I could distinctly hear her swear under her breath as she fell to her knees to collect them.

Tearing my eyes from the unfolding folly, I met Miss Kaye's gaze once more. "Yes, Miss Kaye. Understood."

"Excellent." Her eyes narrowed as they fell upon Noah, who did his best to look nonchalant despite having been caught in the act of socialising with her wards. "Butcher Levy, allow me to escort you out. I see your services have been duly rendered for the day."

"Yes, ma'am, of course, ma'am," Noah replied, collecting his basket and bustling out of the kitchen without so much as a backwards glance, and Miss Kaye turned to follow before offering a word of parting to Pippa, who was still scrambling about on her knees, attempting to wrangle the sausages.

"Take care to wash those before you use them."

"Yes, Miss Kaye."

"And Miss Fitzroy? Do collect yourself. A woman of weak nerves is unattractive indeed."

"Yes, Miss Kaye." And with that, she was gone.

The moment the kitchen door shut, Pippa sprang back to her feet, abandoning her mission and allowing the sausages to scatter haphazardly upon the floor as she turned to me, the wild terror evident in her eyes.

"Dell, what are you going to do?"

My heart was still galloping within my breast from the sudden nature of our brief encounter, and I had not yet begun to wrap my mind around the dire nature of my predicament. I took a deep breath and collected my thoughts. Reason must prevail above all else in an investigation, or else it was liable to go astray.

"I shall report for detention as directed, of course."

Pippa looked at me with horror. "But . . . but she'll certainly kill you! She'll cut your throat and pull out your insides and toss your body out onto the street, and I'll be trapped in the annex and forced to watch the whole scene play out from six stories up!" At this, she burst into tears, and I wrapped her in my arms with as much tenderness as I could muster despite her asinine concerns.

"Pippa, come now, you mustn't be foolish about this. Why would Miss Kaye kill me tonight? She hasn't killed any other pupils, though she's had every opportunity since the headmaster left and Mrs. Dolmer resigned. What reason would she have to take my life?" As I spoke the words aloud, the more certainly I believed them myself, and my heart slowed its frantic clamouring as I allowed reason to prevail.

Pippa sniffled wetly against the collar of my frock. "Sh-sh-she certainly suspects us of something. Did you see the way she glared at Noah before she escorted him away?"

"Miss Kaye glared at Noah because we were being overly familiar with him," I concluded. "After all, he is a handsome young man, and we were fraternising in his presence without supervision."

Pippa pulled back from my shoulder, wiping her red-rimmed eyes with her sleeve. "You think Noah is handsome?"

That hardly seemed relevant to the conversation at hand, but I was eager to console her so we could get back to the far more pressing business of planning my strategy for the evening. "Of course, he is objectively pleasant to gaze upon. Why, do you not find him so?"

Pippa's expression visibly soured. "He is pleasant enough, I suppose. I just thought . . . I just thought perhaps you didn't notice."

I was utterly befuddled by her line of questioning. "Of course I noticed. Why, didn't you?"

"Yes, but it's not like I want to *marry* him or anything!"

"Is this about what Beatrice said the other night?" I suddenly recalled Beatrice's chiding about Pippa's affections for Noah and wondered if it had perhaps struck a nerve far more sensitive than Pippa had let on.

"No, of course not." Pippa crossed her arms defensively. "Do *you* want to marry him?"

A bark of laughter escaped me before I could hold it back. "Marry him? Are you mad? Of course not! I adore Noah as our friend and occasional partner-in-crime, and while I objectively perceive that he is probably deemed attractive to the impartial observer, no, Pippa, I have no aims to marry Noah. Or anyone else for that matter; I must confess, outside of my readings I do not much understand love or passion between the sexes, and I loathe the idea of marriage. As soon as I am released from Whitechapel Hall, I fully intend to embrace the challenges and opportunities of glorified spinsterhood."

"Oh. Well, that's . . . that's good to know." With that, Pippa promptly knelt and began gathering the scattered sausages once more.

I dropped to my knees beside her, and we exchanged a coy smile. I could feel the last of the tension between us dissipate into fond familiarity, laced with nervous excitement. "So. For the interrogation tonight . . ."

At precisely quarter past six that evening, I readied myself outside Miss Kaye's office clutching Pippa's Bible, which she had generously lent me on account of mine still consisting of more *Link Boys* than scripture. Summoning all my courage (and inevitably, a healthy dose of Mrs. Paschal's), I raised my hand and knocked.

"Come in."

It was unfathomably strange: nothing in her office had changed since the last fateful night I had been inside, but now with the affirmed knowledge that it was the lair of a savage killer, every element took on a more sinister undertone. The coat rack in the corner seemed suddenly oddly sharp, its prongs resembling nefarious blades poised to strike. The rows of books lining the shelves, with their innocuous titles such as *Hymns Ancient and Modern*, *The Christian Year*, and *The Kingdom of Christ* seemed now a taunt instead of a symbol of piety. The crucifix upon the wall cast an imposing shadow that loomed over the entire ominous scene, and a shiver ran down my spine as I took my seat at the chair opposing hers as she gazed up at me from behind her phoney spectacles.

"Miss Morton. Thank you for joining me this evening."

I cleared my throat, gripping Pippa's Bible to steady my nerves. "With pleasure."

"I have read your essay and was most intrigued by your argument regarding the moral benefits of consuming penny dreadfuls, particularly those detailing hideous crimes and acts of human degradation."

I hesitated; surely this was some sort of trap. "Um . . . thank you?"

Miss Kaye removed her spectacles and polished them with her kerchief before propping them back upon her narrow nose. I averted my eyes, lest they betray my knowledge of her trickery. "Though I've read none of these penny dreadfuls myself, I take it upon good authority that some of the finest fruits of the finest minds are found in this field of literature, encumbered though it is by heaps of vilest trash."

"Trash?! It isn't trash at all! It extolls the superiority of virtue, condemns crime and vice, and exalts redemption and transformation! While it may not be serious literature, it's hardly trash." Had she not read a word I had written?

She sighed wearily, as if my well-reasoned argument was merely an inconvenience. "Tell me, Miss Morton: Before coming here to Whitechapel Hall, how often did you read your Bible or other scholarly works of modern theology?"

I paused to consider this. "Well, not often, to be honest, but that's hardly unusual."

"Alas, in this day and age, it's sadly not. People of all walks of life, young and old alike, are so enthralled with sensational tales of crime and murder that their minds cannot see the value in text that isn't riddled with violence and gore."

"But that's hardly a product of modern times, is it?" I retorted boldly. "One hundred years ago, before it was banned, a hanging would draw a crowd of thousands. Two hundred years ago, public torture was considered entertainment! Why, in the twelfth century, one tournament of knights before the royal court resulted in no fewer than sixty casualties! Violence and gore aren't new. And in many ways, penny dreadfuls replace the need for all that real violence with something of redeeming quality."

"To that end, Miss Morton, what redemption do you find in them?"

"Well . . . They warn of the dangers of vice, such as gambling, drinking, and seduction. And they promote the consequences of crime, highlighting the inevitable downfall of those engaged in immoral actions. The criminals are always punished, through legal means or violent retribution."

"So, not so dissimilar to the judgement of God in the Bible, then?"

I considered this. "No, I suppose not."

"And what of the highwaymen, the pirates, the thieves and rascals that so often take top billing?"

"They're all good at heart," I replied. "While they may not always follow the law, they only break it when their actions are justified."

Miss Kaye cocked her head at this. "So, you believe that there are times when breaking the law, or behaving in opposition to authority, is justified?"

The breath was knocked out of me as if I'd been punched in the stomach. For a moment I'd nearly forgotten the stakes of our debate; I'd allowed myself to be roused by Miss Kaye's inflammatory line of questioning, and now I'd been tricked into admitting my penchant for delinquency. Miss Kaye was much better at this than I'd given her credit for.

I allowed myself a moment before I continued. "The stories merely assert that corruption can occur at any level, and it is up to those of clear moral conscience to question that authority and root it out, like the wicked kings and pharaohs of the Bible." I spoke as plainly as I could, devoid of passion, eager for her to pass this point by entirely.

"I see. And do you see yourself in this moral worldview, as presented by this 'literature' you so vehemently defend?"

I paused. "What do you mean?"

"You were sentenced to Whitechapel Hall for stealing, Miss Morton. Do you believe your actions were justified? That the corruption of your chaperones required your rebellion for the sake of moral retribution?"

"I . . . I mean, no, not exactly, it was a foolish action, childish and brash. But I . . . but I want to. See myself as virtuous, that is. I'm . . . I'm working to. I want to be better. I want to be a conduit for good." There was an air of truth in this that I had not previously realised, considering my professional aspirations.

"That is indeed reassuring to hear."

There was a heady pause, and for a moment, I faltered in my conviction. I considered leaving the conversation at that, simply hoping for an early dismissal, so that I might scurry back to the safety of the annex and away from the villain that stalked within our midst. But that would be cowardly indeed, and I could not allow it.

"Do you?"

Miss Kaye narrowed her eyes. "Do I what?"

"Do you believe that there is good and evil, and that good people deserve good things, and evil people deserve any horror that befalls them?"

To my surprise, Miss Kaye leaned back in her chair, the inklings of a smile playing at the corner of her lips. "I believe in good and evil, yes, as any good Christian will attest. But I'm afraid the Bible takes a far more complex view of this dichotomy than your trivial penny bloods. And that, Miss Morton, is why I am encouraging you to broaden your mind by reading this"—she rested her palm upon her Bible with an air of inexplicable fondness—"instead of your far more salacious fare."

I hesitated. "So . . . you don't believe that, say, Mary Ann Nichols and Annie Chapman deserved what happened to them?"

I half expected her to break, to lunge at me and wrap her hands around my neck and demand exactly what I knew of the matter, for in any of my penny bloods, this would no doubt be the moment in which the villain, unable to maintain her charade of innocence any longer, would break. Yet my anticipation led me astray, for Miss Kaye simply shook her head, an air of melancholy settling about her that was most at odds with her undeniably criminal nature.

"As much as the Reverend may implore us to, no. *Deserving* is an odd concept, is it not? We humans cast judgement upon each other, attempting to extrapolate the will of God based upon the circumstances of our fellow man's fortune or misfortune, and all the while we ignore the subtleties of His mysteries. We prefer the black-and-white narrative of your penny bloods, instead of the far more complex realities that surround us."

For a long moment I considered this, puzzle pieces of my past sliding into place with a clarity I'd not before considered. "Perhaps that's why I prefer the penny bloods. They offer a clear distinction: criminal and victim, villain and hero. Death is a deserved sentence, not a random act of fate, whereas in the real world, when someone dies, the only culprit is an unfeeling God who hasn't the decency to show remorse or let Himself be dragged to the gallows."

Miss Kaye appeared unfazed by my blasphemy. "Ah, yes. The perceived caprice of an ambivalent God is difficult to comprehend for anyone, Miss Morton, not just yourself. Open your bible to Romans 7:15, and read it aloud, if you please."

I followed her instructions and took a deep breath.

> *For that which I do I allow not: for what I would, that do I not; but what I hate, that do I. If then I do that which I would not, I consent unto the law that it is good. Now then it is no more I that do it, but sin that dwelleth in me. For I know that in me (that is, in my flesh,) dwelleth no good thing: for to will is present with me; but how to perform that which is good I find not.*

Miss Kaye held up her hand to stop me and gave me a small smile. "Does this sound familiar?"

I nodded, my thoughts racing as I dissected the verse. Is this how Miss Kaye felt about herself? Did she hate that she was a murderer but could not stop herself from committing more? Did she feel helpless in her sins, unable to rise above them and live out her better intentions? Did she truly believe she was incapable of ceasing the evil she felt compelled to do?

"Human nature is a complex thing, Miss Morton, and it is *that* which concerns me most about your choice in literary fare. Even outside of the Bible, centuries of philosophers and theologians have grappled with moral ambiguity, and how it relates to our relationship with God. Nothing is cut-and-dry; no one is as good or evil as they seem. To see the world as it's described in your penny bloods is to disregard its nuances in favour of simplicity." She stood and turned towards her shelf of books, plucking one out and depositing it on the desk in front of me.

"*Eternal Hope*?" The title was unfamiliar to me.

"I'd like you to read this, the next time you have a hankering for one of your penny books. I'd be interested to hear your thoughts."

I picked up the volume and flipped through it sceptically. "Do I have to?"

Miss Kaye laughed, and I found myself taken by surprise at her increasingly friendly demeanour. "No, Miss Morton, you do not; after tonight, I will consider the terms of your detention fulfilled. But I do enjoy conversing with you, and I hope you'll consider indulging me upon this point."

"I . . . I will. Thank you, Miss Kaye."

"Very well. Now, it's getting late. Off to bed with you."

"Yes, Miss Kaye. Good night."

Chapter XIII
A Feast of Blood

My audience with Miss Kaye, while a success in that I had not ended up disembowelled upon the street, was hardly the breakthrough we desperately needed in the case. I'd come no closer to detecting a pattern to her kills, for if she were content to simply repeat herself, there should have been another murder the very next night, yet she failed to make an appearance outside the school. She did sneak out of the Hall twice the following week, leading to a great deal of excitement for Pippa and myself as we watched from our perch as Noah tracked her through Whitechapel like a hound on the scent, but both times she merely repeated her veiled charade at the Ten Bells, forsaking any attempt at claiming another victim.

What's more, within the walls of our prison, she took to treating me with a strange, earnest *kindness* that caught me off guard. She nodded to me when we passed in the hallway, complimented my arguments during Morality class, made an example of my needlework during our domestic chores, and one evening went so far as to inquire before bed check as to whether I'd had a moment to peruse *Eternal Hope*. She appeared sincerely disappointed when I said I had not.

"She must be spying on me, I know it," I impressed upon Pippa later that same night as we sat upon our perch passing the pipe. "Why else would she be observing me so diligently?"

"Maybe Miss Kaye likes you," Pippa mused cheekily, blowing a smoke ring up into the darkness like a wicked halo above her head. "Maybe she sees you as her creepy kindred spirit, and she's training you up to be a little baby murderess, just like her!"

"Oh, sod off," I replied, shoving my shoulder against hers.

On the street below, we watched Noah pace his beat from one streetlamp to the next. I prayed that Miss Kaye would make another attempt at a murder soon, for Noah's ability to stay on as our lookout grew more tenuous with each passing day. ("The rabbi has agreed to hold off the beth din now that things have quieted a bit, *Baruch Hashem*," he'd confided to us that morning. "But my mother is no fool; she says I've been acting odd, and Heaven knows she's right. I'm dead on my feet during the day, exhausted from the watch. I can't keep this up much longer."

"You won't have to," I'd assured him, with a confidence I barely possessed myself. "Miss Kaye is six days past due for a kill; surely tonight will be the night." Noah had nodded but looked unconvinced, and I knew it was only a matter of time before our cherished lookout would be forced to resign his position permanently.)

"Whatever the motive for her kindness, I wish she'd just reveal herself already. Noah needs his sleep. We're in dire straits, indeed."

Pippa sighed and passed me the pipe, then leaned back on her hands to tip her face up towards the stars. "Maybe it's over."

"Maybe what's over?" I asked around a mouthful of smoke.

"The murders. Maybe Miss Kaye had some weird vendetta, she got her revenge, and now everything will go back to normal."

I shot her a sceptical look. "If there's one thing I know for certain about murderers, Pippa, it's that they don't just stop killing. It's a compulsion for them. I mean, look at Miss Kaye! She killed for the first time when she was our age, she was locked away for twenty years, and then upon her release barely lasted three years before she started up again!" I paused, a new, more horrifying idea materialising in my mind. "And who's to say this is the first time she's killed since being out of prison? We have no idea where she was stationed prior to Whitechapel Hall. She could have been killing since the moment she stepped back onto free soil."

"Maybe," Pippa shrugged. "Or maybe she just had a grudge, and it's over now."

"No offence, but I think we'd best leave the detecting up to me." I glowered as, above us, the clock chimed two. Down below, Noah looked up at our perch and gave us a defeated wave before disappearing back into the night, headed home to his shop. We reluctantly resigned ourselves once more to defeat and headed inside to bed.

Sleep eluded me that night. It was clear as day that my current plan wasn't working, and what's more, it was putting Noah more at risk each time he snuck out to take his watch. Miss Kaye remained an uncrackable nut: My interactions with her had yielded nothing but my own increased paranoia and muddled conscience. An escape from Whitechapel Hall remained as elusive as it was impractical, yet I could no sooner abdicate my responsibilities as a detective on the tail of a murderer than I could turn my back on Pippa. Something had to give, I resolved, and I vowed that in the morning I would approach Noah and Pippa with humility and ask their advice, as so far, my detective's instincts were failing us all.

As it turned out, my resolve to reform was entirely unnecessary, for fate intervened before I could so much as utter a word of my *mea culpa* to my co-conspirators. Pippa and I arrived for our kitchen duty to find Noah already stationed at the counter unloading his wares, but the moment he turned around, we both gasped in horror.

His cheekbones were a mottled mess of bruises, and a dark gash spanned the bridge of his nose. His throat bore telltale signs of abuse as well, well-defined fingerprints in a haunting aubergine hue wrapped menacingly around his windpipe, and both eyes were blackened and puffy. He looked as if he had one foot in the grave.

"My God, Noah, what happened?" I wanted nothing more than to rush forward and pull him into a comforting embrace, but as Miss Kaye was now well aware of our companionship and apparently keen to stomp out any further familiarity, I was forced to show restraint. "Was there another mob?"

"My father caught me sneaking back home last night." His voice was gravelly, whether from crying or the crushing of his throat, I could not be sure.

"I'm so sorry." Pippa was the first to regain her resolve and resolutely took her place by Noah's side. I quickly followed suit, flanking him as we turned to busy ourselves with the preparation of the day's stock, a welcome excuse to remain in one another's proximity.

"How did he find out?" I murmured as I unrolled a tightly wrapped parcel of beef knuckles.

"I'd been using the window above the alley to escape. Hardly a brilliant scheme, but it worked until now. For some reason, last night my father awoke after midnight and noticed me missing. He sat in the darkness until I returned and caught me clambering in through the back window at half past two. He was displeased. He demanded I tell him where I'd been."

"What did you say?"

Noah sighed heavily and gave a resigned shrug. "I told him I'd been to see a *shiksa*." He whispered the word as if it were dirty, only to be met by bewildered expressions from Pippa and me. "A . . . a gentile girl, that is."

Pippa looked appalled. "And that's why he beat you so badly?"

"He beat me because that's what he does. That's what he's always done, since he lost his mind. It doesn't occur to him to do anything else." He paused, swallowing around his emotions. "You know, when he was locked away, I used to hope he wouldn't come back."

Pippa and I shared an uneasy glance behind his back as he hunched over the counter in apparent defeat.

"It's blasphemy to admit, but I prayed that he would die in Essex. Then my mother and I could do what we've always wanted to do: leave this godforsaken city and never look back."

"Leave?" Pippa implored. "But where would you go?"

"My mother wanted to go to Paris. Her sister lives there. I imagine she'd be very happy."

"And you?" I pressed.

At this, he shot me a sly grin. "Me? I'd go to Australia with Henry."

"He's going to Australia?" I exclaimed. "But what about his family? His own shop?"

"He has six siblings, he's better off getting out of the family business than fighting to stay in it."

"But whatever is he going to do in Australia?" Pippa pressed.

"Seek his own fortune, become his own man. Do things I could only dream of." Noah's tone shifted perceptibly as he returned his attention to unwrapping the package of kidney before him.

"There's nothing stopping you from pursuing the same dream, Noah," I offered, resting my hand upon his shoulder as delicately as I dared. "You should. Leave with Henry, I mean."

"The Talmud commands us to honour thy father and thy mother. And what do you think would become of my mother if I left her to my father's whims? She'll end up beaten to death or sleeping hard on the streets once he runs the shop into the ground. You know, he used to threaten to burn the place down with all of us inside it. Sometimes I wish he had." Tears gathered in the corners of his eyes, and my heart twisted in my chest in sympathetic pain.

"You stop that right now, Noah Levy," Pippa interjected, her voice sharper than I'd ever heard before. "You deserve so much more than your father gives you credit for. For what it's worth, these two *shiksas* are rather fond of you." She wrapped an arm around him, and we all shared a mutual smile.

"Come, now. You're just tired. You've been running yourself ragged attempting to catch a damned murderer on top of running your own shop and keeping your family afloat." Pippa's voice grew gentler as she offered words of comfort. "You need some time off. Dell and I can handle the watch for the next few nights. Until you've had time to recover."

I nodded in affirmation, despite the fact I currently had no idea how we would catch Miss Kaye without him. "It's true. While the information you've gathered at the Bells has been invaluable, there's nothing more we can do until Miss Kaye makes a new gambit. We've nothing to do now but wait."

I could not ignore the expression of relief that settled upon his face with the abdication of this responsibility, and once again I felt a pang of guilt at asking so much of Noah and offering nothing in return.

Assuming our watch from the perch that night was a notably more dismal affair than usual. Noah was not the only one upon whom the late hours were taking their toll; Pippa and I lolled groggily against one another as we lazily passed the pipe back and forth, the minutes ticking by like years as we fought the temptation of sleep.

We'd been sitting in solemn silence for nearly an hour when Pippa finally spoke. "Maybe we should take shifts."

"Hmm?" I rubbed my eyes blearily, reluctant to admit that they'd perhaps fluttered shut (an unforgivably stupid oversight, considering my feet were dangling off a ledge six stories above ground).

"I take watch one night, and you take watch the next. Or maybe you do the first hour, and then you wake me . . ."

I scowled at the thought. "I mean, we could, but . . ." The protest died on my tongue. The truth was, even when nothing of significance was happening on the streets below, whiling away the hours with Pippa beneath an enchanting shroud of moonlight had become a source of great joy for me. To undertake the endeavour alone seemed very lonely indeed. "But two sets of eyes are better than one," I concluded.

"Two sets of eyes for what, exactly?" Pippa shot back. "There hasn't been a murder in over a fortnight!"

"Of course not, because Miss Kaye isn't stupid. She's biding her time until the police back off."

"Well, it's making our surveillance a rather dull endeavour."

"And what, you expected it to be nonstop thrills?" I snapped, my patience wearing thin. "This is what detective work is like, Pippa. Hours of nothing and waiting and hoping and then, finally, if you're lucky, it all pays off in the end."

"But what if we're not?"

"Not what?"

"*Lucky*, Dell. At the end of the day, we're just two girls trapped in a reformatory school with a madwoman, yet we've grown delusional enough that we're convinced that we have any semblance of control over what happens next! We don't have control over this, Dell—over any of this! What Miss Kaye does upon the streets under the cover of night is a crime of the highest order, but our lowly station in life means we're powerless to stop it. Our families have abandoned us, the law mocks us, and the men tasked with our spiritual reform care for nothing but money and reputation. And you know what? Maybe I don't care anymore. Maybe I don't care if Miss Kaye kills again."

I sat there mutely, gobsmacked by her outburst, and unable to get a word in edgewise even if I'd wanted to, as it appeared her tirade had just begun.

"Maybe it doesn't matter that she's a murderess. Because the only people she kills are lowly whores, maybe none of this even matters—" To my shock, tears brimmed over in Pippa's eyes, weeks of fatigue and frustration all manifesting in one epic outburst.

Just as I opened my mouth to calm her, a noise from below startled us both back to attention. A sliver of lamplight sliced through the darkness as the front door to the Hall swung open, and a moment later, Miss Kaye appeared. She diligently secured the door behind her, then scurried off down Buck's Row, but much to my surprise, she didn't turn right towards Hanbury Street, as was her customary route to the Bells. Instead, she took a left in the direction of High Street and quickly disappeared into the shadows.

"Did you see that?" Pippa's eyes were wide with disbelief.

"She's not headed to the Bells," I whispered.

"Oh, God—Dell, we have to stop her!" In an instant, Pippa was on her feet, tossing our smokebox into the cubby hole and making haste back through the window to the annex.

"But—damn it, wait up!" I protested as I chased after her, dropping down onto the beam of the annex with as much grace as I could muster. "Pippa, what are you doing?"

"I'm putting up a chase! Are you coming or not?"

"You want to escape the school and chase Miss Kaye ourselves? Two minutes ago, you told me none of this mattered because they were just 'lowly whores'—"

"I didn't mean it, alright?" Pippa rounded on me, eyes flashing with a combination of panic and frenzied excitement. "This is our chance, Dell! Our one chance to catch Miss Kaye, save a life, and spare Noah's family once and for all! Now come on, to the dumbwaiter! We must be quick!"

Our pursuit was straight from the pages of my most exhilarating fictions. Pippa and I moved quickly but silently to disarm the dormitory lock and sprint through the hallways of the school, caution tossed aside now that we knew our adversary was absent. With the spirited bravery and dogged conviction of two heroines in pursuit of justice, we bolted downstairs to the dumbwaiter.

Walking the streets of Whitechapel felt like a dream after being sequestered in the Hall for so long. Pippa and I emerged from the alley more closely resembling a pair of skittish fox kits than two lady detectives in pursuit of their mark, and I did my best to shake the feeling of anxiety that was rapidly settling over me. Outside the walls of our cloisters, the nature of our mission was suddenly becoming very real, and I resisted the urge to falter. Gripping Pippa firmly by the elbow, I steered her in the direction of High Street. The night air was cool and damp, a light mist adding an eerie glow around the streetlights, and for a moment I regretted not grabbing our cloaks.

"So, what's the plan?" Pippa sounded breathless with excitement and was clearly of the mindset that I had somehow predicted just this situation and devised a brilliant scheme to navigate it. I was in no way inclined to inform her otherwise and attempted to recall everything I'd read in my penny bloods about the pursuit of a suspect.

"We last saw her heading towards High Street, so we'll start there. There's still plenty of people about, so she'll no doubt be trying to blend in, lose herself in the crowd. Lying in wait in the darkness would only draw attention; it's my guess that she tracks her target through main thoroughfares, then attacks as soon as they deviate from the beaten path."

"Right, of course," Pippa concurred with an air of confidence that I in no way possessed.

"And keep your eyes peeled for a glimpse of her at any taverns we pass. While the Ten Bells may be her preferred hunting grounds, she could have chosen a different locale tonight for any number of reasons."

Pippa gave a resolute nod of affirmation.

"And most important of all: make note of every policeman and patrol we see. So far, she's managed to elude both the police and the members of the Vigilance Committee; she clearly clocks them when she plots her crimes to avoid detection. Any time we don't have a copper or a patrolman in sight—that's when she'll endeavour to do the deed."

"Right. And Dell?"

"Yes?"

"What do we do if we see her murdering someone in an alley?"

It was a valid question. In our rush to pursue our subject, neither of us had thought to grab so much as a kitchen knife on our way out of the Hall.

Even so, I replied with all the conviction I could muster. "We shall act as a team, of course. One of us will make haste to alert the nearest policeman or member of the Vigilance Committee. The other will stand at the entrance to the alley and scream to deter Miss Kaye from further violence before the victim can be incapacitated."

"Excellent." Pippa appeared placated by this haphazard plan, which should probably have been a source of concern for me, yet I could think of no other option than to continue improvising as best I could.

I had no sooner resolved myself to this fact than a familiar figure emerged from the doorway of a tavern no more than twenty paces ahead of us. With a yelp, my hand tightened around Pippa's elbow, and she cried out in surprise.

"Pippa, look!" And sure enough, there on the steps of the Queen's Head pub stood an unmistakable silhouette. Though her face was obscured by a black lace mourning veil, her posture betrayed her instantly.

"Come on!" I yanked Pippa off the walkway into a pool of shadow that had formed between two storefronts. From the darkness, we watched in fascination as Miss Kaye surveyed the street from the stoop of the tavern, her head swivelling to and fro, as though searching for a familiar face among the crowd. I did my best to disguise the shiver of excitement that ran up my spine; though we were undoubtedly in more danger than ever, the fact that we had managed to locate her at all was a sign that our interference was destined. After a long moment, she stepped out into the street, took a right, and began making her way towards Commercial Street.

"Come on," I whispered to Pippa, and we fell in step behind her at a distance of half a block.

"Can you see who she's following?" Pippa asked, bobbing her head around a small band of patrolmen in front of us, all carrying a rather menacing assortment of pitchforks, pipes, and torches.

"No, but it doesn't matter currently. There are far too many lookouts here for her to have a go. She'll wait until we reach a quieter spot; we must be patient."

We followed her as she turned onto Commercial Street. The area was noticeably less crowded considering the late hour; the shops and warehouses were closed, and the taverns were fewer and farther between. Pippa and I fell back a few paces as the members of the Vigilance Committee in front of us peeled off to continue their patrol along Alie Street, a darker and less inhabited thoroughfare that undoubtedly to them seemed the more likely scene for an attack; I chuckled at the irony that the subject of their search was no more than fifty feet in front of them, her unassuming appearance the perfect disguise.

Miss Kaye's pace slowed slightly as she made her way down the street. More than once, I caught her peering into the cross streets to her left and right, as though she, too, were searching for someone. Was it possible that she had not already selected her victim and was hoping to catch a poor woman alone in an alley simply by chance? It seemed an odd *modus operandi*, but perhaps if it had worked thus far . . .

Seemingly apropos of nothing, Miss Kaye took a sudden detour onto a narrow side street shrouded in shadow, the only light emanating from the open doors of what appeared to be some sort of social establishment halfway down the block. From within, we could hear the raucous sounds of a multitude of voices, and a few patrons milled about outside. Pippa and I paused at the corner and watched with fascination as Miss Kaye wove her way past them, pausing ever so briefly to peer inside the building, but promptly carried on quickly enough that none of the gentlemen congregated on the street gave her a second glance.

"She's looking for someone specific," I murmured as much to myself as to Pippa. "She's not gravitating towards the most isolated place she can find, as we'd expect if her kills were a crime of opportunity."

"You think she's looking for someone who frequents . . . what is this place, anyway?"

I squinted up at the faded street sign. "Berner Street? I've never heard of it. Let's go find out." Miss Kaye's figure grew distant but still visible on the narrow street, and I gauged that we were far enough behind her as to not arouse suspicion. We made our way towards the source of the light, until the sign hanging above the open doors was legible.

"*International Working Men's Educational Club*?" Pippa read incredulously. "What business could Miss Kaye have with anyone here?"

I took in the scene before me, more confused than ever. It was obvious that the club was for gentlemen only, and what's more, I noted that the snippets of conversation I could overhear were all in Yiddish. It was most peculiar and provided no valuable clues as to the identity of Miss Kaye's target.

"It's strange, indeed," I mused. "But come on, we mustn't lose sight of her." We continued past the milling men outside the club doors, drawing nary a second glance from any of them. Just as we cleared the pool of light cast upon the street, I looked ahead and saw a sight that made my blood run cold: Miss Kaye had turned around and was walking straight towards us.

I resisted the urge to scream, but Pippa's clench of my elbow indicated that she was aware of our immediate peril. Though we were still at least a hundred feet away, the darkness would not cover us forever. We would have to make an escape without attracting attention. In desperation, I cast a glance to my right, and to my amazement my eyes landed upon a gated passageway which was miraculously still propped open despite the late hour.

"This way," I hissed, and pulled Pippa in behind me. We pressed ourselves against the wall, the cold damp of the stone frigid even through the wool of my dress, and I shivered violently. Beside me, Pippa was stiff and still as a statue, and we scarcely dared breathe as we waited for Miss Kaye to pass.

The minutes ticked by like years as we awaited the telltale sound of Miss Kaye's boots on the cobblestones, and yet . . . nothing.

"She should have passed us by now," Pippa whispered.

"Maybe she turned back around?" I posited uncertainly.

"Well, I'm certainly not sticking my head out there to find out," Pippa countered obstinately.

"Let's just wait another minute or two. We don't want to lose her . . ." My instincts were warring within me, part of me too scared of being caught to emerge from our hiding place, but the other desperate to not lose track of our mark. My palm grew sweaty where it was clasped in Pippa's hand, and I could hear every irregularity in her breath as we waited for a certainty that would never come.

We had yet to move a muscle when, out of nowhere, a shriek erupted from behind us. Startled, we whirled about to confront its source. The short, narrow passageway in which we were hidden appeared to open at the opposite end into a small yard from which the cry had emanated.

"What was that?" Pippa's voice was trembling with anxiety.

"*Shh!* Hold still," I hissed.

We stood hand-in-hand, hidden by the shadows and petrified in fear as from the yard, a woman's figure emerged and stumbled into the passageway. Her face was pale and her expression shocked, and her hands clasped around her throat. She stared at us for a moment, blinking uncomprehendingly as her eyes adjusted to the darkness. Then she took another step forward and opened her mouth to form words, but no sound emerged.

"Miss?" I took a tentative step towards her, letting go of Pippa's comforting grasp. "Miss, are you alright?"

In that moment, the woman released her hands from her throat, and a fountain of blood cascaded from a ragged gash, spilling down the front of her dress and spattering onto the dirt at her feet. Her eyes were wide with terror, her mouth agape in an unspoken scream. Before I could react, a cloaked figure appeared behind her and yanked her backwards into the blackness of the yard, her hands outstretched towards Pippa and me in a silent plea.

Though every bone in my body cried out to *scream, run, escape*, the desperation upon the woman's face compelled my resolve. Casting a frantic glance around, my eyes fell upon the only makeshift weapon I could locate: a stack of discarded crates piled and the end of the passageway.

I turned to Pippa. "Run. Get help."

Pippa stared back at me, pale as a sheet and shaking from head to toe. "Not without you!"

"Pippa, *go*." And with that, I shoved her towards the street and ran towards the yard, snatching up a crate as I went.

My target was not hard to find. The bleeding woman was still on her feet but stumbling unsteadily, Miss Kaye making a valiant attempt to reel her in by her shawl as she struggled to escape. Summoning every ounce of courage I had, I charged forward, lifted the crate as high as I could, and brought it crashing down upon Miss Kaye with an unholy *crack*.

Everything seemed to happen all at once. The wounded woman crumpled in a heap, and Miss Kaye let out an unholy wail of pain as she staggered backwards, flailing frantically, knocking me to the ground before I could retreat. With a curse, Miss Kaye reeled, the blade of her knife flashing menacingly as she rounded on me, intent upon enacting revenge on her attacker.

It was only then that I fully comprehended the scene. For the knife-wielding maniac looming above me was not, in fact, Miss Kaye, but a complete stranger. He was a thin, pale man with black, empty eyes, hollow cheekbones, and a long dark cloak that nearly touched the ground. His expression was wild, his teeth bared in a feral snarl as he raised the knife above his head, poised to strike a fatal blow.

If interrogated upon the subject beforehand, I would have believed that my final thoughts before succumbing to death would be profound, reflective, or perhaps full of transcendent clarity. Instead, my frantic mind could only conjure one thought: *How unfair*. How perfectly unfair, that despite my prodigious detective skills, I had somehow gotten it all so utterly wrong. And now I was to be the next victim of my very own subject of fascination—and what's more, I would never be able to solve the case! It was all so dreadfully unjust, I could not comprehend it. Instead, I simply brought my arms above my head in a vain attempt to ward off the blow and braced for the inevitable.

A furious roar startled me from my defensive position, and I looked up just in time to see none other than Pippa attack the man from behind, wrapping her legs about his waist and capturing his neck in the crook of her arm, causing him to rear back, lurching unsteadily under her unexpected weight. To my horror, he quickly regained his composure, lifted his knife, and slashed it across Pippa's forearm, raining a spray of blood down on me from above, her subsequent scream echoing off the walls of the yard.

"*No!*" Without thinking, I scrambled forward onto my hands and knees and threw myself bodily at his legs, endeavouring to hinder his retreat, but it was no use. He issued a fierce kick to my cheek, sending me sprawling backwards into the dirt, and I righted myself just in time to see him hurl Pippa's unresisting body to the ground, adjust the grip on his knife, and throw himself upon her.

"Pippa!" I was woozy from the blow but willed myself to move. My heart was hammering against my ribs and my limbs felt foreign and clumsy, but the sight of such malice poised above my dearest friend was enough to rouse me to action.

Summoning the strength I had left, I launched myself at our attacker, but I was easily rebuffed with a swift swing of his blade, forcing me into a hasty retreat, but at least his attention was now upon me instead of Pippa, still lying disconcertingly motionless beneath him.

"Come on, then!" I shouted, the fear and the fury combining into something that felt quite like courage as I staggered to my feet, gripping a shattered shard from the crate in my hand. "Come at me!"

At this provocation, the man's lips turned up into a sneer, and to my shock, he laughed. It was a low, wicked sound, and the next thing I knew, he bounded to his feet and lunged at me, blade aloft. I braced for his impact, only to be startled by yet another wild cry. The next thing I knew, the man was bowled over sideways by a fearsome blow to the head from behind, sending him careening off-course and slamming into the stone wall bordering the yard. For a moment he froze, stunned and unmoving, staring at the tableau before him with a look of disbelief. Then he righted himself and sprinted off down the passageway into the lingering dark.

I blinked into the shadows, still gripping the shard of crate in my hand, attempting to discern who had delivered the deciding blow. "Who's there? Show yourself!"

To my shock, a black-clad figure shrouded in a lace veil stepped out from the gloom, a length of pipe in her hand which she quickly deposited on the ground. She raised her hands and lifted the veil, revealing herself at last.

"Miss Kaye? What are you doing here?" Nothing made any sense, and the world around me tilted dangerously, reality swimming in and out of focus. I had thought she was trying to kill us, and yet she had been the one to save us.

"I could ask the same of you, Miss Morton, but now is not the time." She strode forward and crouched down beside the collapsed woman, rolling her onto her back and peering down at her intently. "Come here."

I complied instantly, too stunned to question her command. She leaned down and ripped off a strip of the woman's soiled apron. "Take this. Press it upon her neck. Don't let her move."

"Right." With trembling hands, I received the rag and looked down at the figure before me. Her skin was a strange, dusty grey colour, but her eyes were still bright and wild with fear, and she was making an odd gurgling sound as she struggled for breath. As gently as I could, I reached down and pressed the fabric against the gash at her throat, from which a sickening swell of blood pulsed rhythmically onto the dirt beneath her. The copper-bright tang of its scent filled my nostrils, and I retched but held the compress firm.

I looked up to see Miss Kaye tending to Pippa, wrapping her bloody forearm in the length of black lace she'd removed from her bonnet. Much to my relief, Pippa was sitting, and while undoubtedly shaken, her life did not look to be in immediate peril.

Beneath my hands, the woman twitched and jerked, and my eyes were riveted to meet hers. Her expression held nothing but fear, and without thinking, I reached down to clasp her hand in my own. "You're alright," I whispered, the lie slipping smoothly off my tongue as I attempted to comfort her. "You'll be alright. The police will be here soon, and the doctor. There's nothing to be afraid of. This will all be over soon."

She made an odd sort of whimpering sound as another shiver wracked her body, and I could feel the hot slickness of her blood upon my hands as the rag soaked fully through.

"Shh." I squeezed her hand and smiled as reassuringly as I could, willing the terror out of my own eyes. "Just hold still. Just . . . just hold still."

Her gaze held mine, and a single tear trickled from the corner of her eye. In the next moment, her hand went slack, and the light left her once and for all. I knelt, trembling, my hands covered in blood, unable to comprehend what was happening, too shocked to so much as remove my hand from her throat.

"Miss Morton." The sound of Miss Kaye's voice snapped me from my trance, and I looked up to see her helping an unsteady Pippa to her feet. "We have to go. Now. He might come back at any moment."

"Right. Right." I shook my head to clear it but still found myself unable to let go of the woman's lifeless form beneath my hands.

"Dell. *Now*. We have to leave her; there's nothing more we can do."

"Right. Of course. I'll just . . ." I clambered to my feet and swayed briefly before finally tearing my eyes away from the bloodied figure at my feet. Pippa was at last fully upright, one arm slung around Miss Kaye's shoulders and the other in a makeshift sling constructed of the lace veil. Relief so acute I could have choked on it welled up inside me, and I rushed forward to take my place at Pippa's side, wrapping my arm around her waist to support her as best I could.

"Drop that." Miss Kaye issued a furtive glance down at the blood-soaked rag in my hand, which I obediently tossed aside. "Quickly. Back to the Hall. We mustn't be spotted." Miss Kaye's tone left no room for protest, and Pippa and I nodded in assent. We quickly made our way back down the passageway, stopping only briefly to retreat into the shadows as a pony and barrow clamoured past, and I could hear Miss Kaye swear beneath her breath. "Hurry. The body will be spotted soon; we must be well clear of this place before the police arrive."

It did not occur to me to protest. It did not occur to me to do anything besides put one foot in front of the other as we darted from shadow to shadow until we were safely back in the embrace of Whitechapel Hall.

Chapter XIV
Expedition to Hell

Nothing felt real. Though everything was just as it had been when we left—the gleam of the freshly polished floors, the gay flicker of the oil lamp beside the door, the smell of carbolic soap, the ringing stillness that permeated the entryway in the absence of the bustle of pupils and staff—I felt as though I were trapped in some uncanny parallel world that had replaced the one in which I had whiled away so many hours in what I could now perceive were the throes of girlish innocence. As Miss Kaye spirited us towards the kitchen, I spared a glance down at my own body, a blood-spattered aberration grossly contrasted against a backdrop of order and calm. To my right, Pippa was no better off; while the veil had slowed the bleeding of her arm, her face was ghastly white and her clothing a gruesome patchwork of mud and blood. Opposite me, Miss Kaye's expression was unreadable.

This was not how it was supposed to be. In my penny bloods, the heroine arrived in the nick of time, thwarted the villain, saved the damsel, escaped unscathed. It wasn't supposed to come down to this: to gore and grit and a grim alliance born of unspeakable fear. It was never supposed to be like this.

"Miss Fitzroy, come here and be seated." Miss Kaye pulled

out Cook's stool and propped Pippa upon it. "Let me look at your arm. Miss Morton, fetch a flannel and wet it with water." Miss Kaye's voice was a welcome source of normalcy, and I tethered myself to it like a lifeboat in a storm. I followed her commands automatically, my eyes unseeing and hands unfeeling as I procured the requested item.

"Thank you, Miss Morton. Miss Fitzroy? Deep breath." Pippa complied automatically, and in tandem with her breathing, Miss Kaye removed the last of the improvised bandage.

Pippa hissed through her teeth, and Miss Kaye's brow furrowed in consternation. It was easy to see why: the gash upon Pippa's forearm was long and deep, and while it was no longer bleeding profusely, the well of deep crimson blood threatened to overflow the moment the lace was pulled away.

"Ah, I see, I see." Miss Kaye peered down at the wound intently, and for the first time, I noted she was not wearing her fake spectacles. "Miss Fitzroy, we will clean this here and then return to my chambers to administer some stitches. Miss Morton, the flannel, please."

I handed it to Miss Kaye. She swiped it over Pippa's arm in swift, gentle motions, but despite her best efforts at mercy, Pippa whimpered softly.

"It's alright," I murmured, and took my place by Pippa's side, clasping her free hand in my own. "It's going to be alright now. Just a little more, and you'll be fine."

Pippa let out what may have been an aborted sob and buried her face in my shoulder, but it allowed Miss Kaye ample opportunity to finish cleaning her wound as I squeezed her hand and stroked her hair as soothingly as I could, ignoring the way my blood-encrusted fingers left incriminating streaks of scarlet in her pristine platinum locks.

"There now. All finished with the washing." Miss Kaye wrapped Pippa's forearm in the damp flannel, pressing it gently to staunch the bleeding, and issued a pat upon her shoulder which would almost have seemed maternal had it not been delivered by a convicted murderess.

"Ladies, we must retreat to my chambers immediately. I have the materials for the stitches there. Miss Fitzroy, are you able to walk?"

Pippa at last withdrew her face from where it had been buried against the crook of my neck and nodded muzzily before rising to her feet, a bit unsteady but otherwise unimpeded.

With an approving nod, Miss Kaye turned away from the two of us, then promptly approached the coal bin beside the fireplace and shovelled two heaping scoops onto the smouldering embers. In an instant, the fire roared back to life.

"Before we go, we must dispose of your dresses."

"What?" In my state of disorientation, I could not comprehend her logic.

"Your dresses, Miss Morton. We must remove them and dispose of them at once."

I cast another furtive glance down at my vestments and could immediately see Miss Kaye's motive: both Pippa and I were soaked with an unholy quantity of blood, and if there was to be any hope of denying our involvement in the night's events, our dresses could not be seen in such a state.

I lifted the hem of my dress and pulled it off over my head, leaving me clad in nothing but my chemise and stockings. As if in a trance, I approached the fireplace and threw the offending garment into the flames, and I watched devoid of any emotion as it was consumed and reduced to ashes right before my eyes. Then I turned to Pippa, rendered lame by her injury, and aided her in yanking her frock up over head and subjecting it to the same fate.

We turned to face Miss Kaye, who was briskly emptying the basin of its damning contents down the sink. "Very well. Quickly, now, to my chambers."

She ushered us through the hallways with the same brisk

efficiency that she did all her pupils on any unremarkable afternoon, and I took solace in her steady gait and dispassionate demeanour. A part of my brain knew I ought to question her motives, for was she not the one and only Constance Kent, the murderous monster whose tale of treachery I had so serendipitously unearthed?

And yet there was no question that she had saved our lives and risked her own in the process. Whatever the sins of her past, it was clear to me now that she was not the spectre stalking the streets of Whitechapel. Her methods and motives remained elusive as ever, but I could not object to her gentle shepherding as she led us through her office into her bedroom and guided Pippa to sit upon the cot. Pippa nearly collapsed upon it, swaying slightly with the effort of staying upright. I knelt at Pippa's feet and pulled her good hand into my own, smiling up at her with what I could only hope was a convincing imitation of reassurance. Pippa's eyes met mine, but her expression remained alarmingly distant.

"Miss Morton, please prop a pillow against the headboard and assist Miss Fitzroy in reclining and removing her boots." I obeyed immediately and from the corner of my eye watched in stunned silence as Miss Kaye cast aside her own bonnet and cloak, hiked up her petticoat, and removed an imposing-looking knife from a sheath fastened about her calf. For one wild moment, I thought she was going to end Pippa and me right then and there, but instead she promptly knelt and lifted the bottom corner of the mattress to stash the knife beneath it, then withdrew a small glass pharmacy bottle and a lean metal flask from the same clandestine location.

Hidden beneath the mattress. The most obvious place of all. How could I have been so stupid as to miss it during my search? I nearly laughed aloud recalling how Pippa had berated me for considering stashing my own contraband there; it was an ironic turn, indeed.

Miss Kaye righted herself and deposited the bottle and flask upon the bedside table, then retreated to her office. She returned a moment later carrying a sewing kit and positioned it on the bed beside Pippa as I worked to unlace her boots. Pippa looked a bit less pale now that she was reclined, though she still winced in obvious pain as Miss Kaye removed the flannel from her wound and picked up the lantern to examine it more closely.

"Miss Fitzroy, I'm afraid we have no choice but to stitch this up. It will hurt, but it is the only way it will heal."

Pippa nodded, still betraying no true signs of emotion. "Very well. Miss Morton, bring the basin over here and position it beneath Miss Fitzroy's arm." I quickly procured the requested item and watched in fascination as Miss Kaye unscrewed the top of the flask.

"A deep breath, please, Miss Fitzroy." Pippa complied, her eyes fluttering shut, her delicate lashes casting a web of shadows across the peculiar pallor of her face. Miss Kaye tipped the flask over her forearm, and a dark, bitter liquid poured forth, filling the gash from top to bottom. Pippa let out a cry, the first true expression of emotion I'd heard from her since we'd returned to the Hall, and I reached out to clasp her free hand in my own—an action I almost instantly regretted as she proceeded to squeeze it so hard I heard my knuckles crack.

"Shh, it's alright, Miss Fitzroy, but you must remain calm. Have a sip of this, it will dull the pain."

To my dismay, Miss Kaye offered Pippa the flask, which Pippa was only too eager to exchange for my hand. She tipped her head back and took a long, fortifying swig, downing it without a sputter before handing the flask back to Miss Kaye and allowing her head to loll back against the pillow I'd positioned behind her.

"Go ahead. I'm ready." Her voice was hoarse, but I could see a glimmer of her dogged determination in her expression, which reassured me greatly.

Miss Kaye pocketed the flask and produced a needle and thread from her sewing kit. "Miss Morton, I'll need you to hold the lamp steady. And Miss Fitzroy, should you find yourself tempted to scream—"

"I won't." Pippa's tone left no room for argument, and my heart swelled with affection at her bravery. Miss Kaye appeared surprised but did not argue.

I held the lantern aloft above her arm. Miss Kaye, still forsaking her spectacles, leaned forward and plunged the needle into Pippa's perfect porcelain skin.

Blood welled around each puncture as Miss Kaye wove the needle in and out over the gaping gash, but Pippa did not flinch, and I did not demur. A part of me yearned to look away, but my eyes remained riveted to the place where Miss Kaye was mending Pippa's wound as dispassionately as if it were a torn petticoat. The three of us settled into a silence fortified by our strange new alliance, the nature of which I could not comprehend but the certainty of which I could feel settle in my very bones.

At last, the deed was done. Miss Kaye tied off the thread and severed it with a pair of sewing shears, then rose to pull a clean chemise out of her wardrobe, from which she tore a strip and wrapped Pippa's arm with the length of it. Once secured, she gave an approving nod.

"Well done, ladies. Miss Fitzroy, you must get some sleep. Here." She plucked up the glass bottle from the table and, from it, produced two small white pills and held them out for Pippa to take. Pippa hesitated and shot me a furtive look. I intuitively understood the question in her eyes: *Do we trust her?*

I gave a reassuring nod, my best answer to the unasked question. "Go on, Pippa. Here, have some water." I filled the cup on the bedside table from the pitcher and offered it to her, and I could not mistake the gratitude in her eyes as she placed the pills upon her tongue and chased them with a fortifying drink of water. I helped her lower the pillow so that she could recline fully, and Miss Kaye covered her with the wool blanket folded at the foot of the bed. Pippa retired willingly, and I could see her expression grow hazy as I helped settle her injured arm beside her. Her eyes were closed before I could even bid her good night.

Miss Kaye remained all business, bustling about to collect the pitcher, basin, flask, and bottle. "Come, Miss Morton. Your friend is in dire need of rest. Let us retire to my office." Reluctantly, I rose to follow Miss Kaye out of the room, leaving my slumbering companion behind.

Miss Kaye busied herself placing another scoop of coal upon the fire in her office as I hovered uncertainly in the centre of the room. The scene had once again taken on a surreal, dreamlike quality, and I was rendered mute and dim-witted by the enormity of it all. It seemed impossible that a mere two hours ago I had been biding my time on the smoking perch, the horrors unfolding upon the streets below no more real to me than the pages of Mrs. Paschal's latest adventure. But staring down at my own hands, where the blood had congealed from scarlet to a dull, coppery brown, I could now feel the horror viscerally. It was stuck beneath my fingernails. It seeped into my pores, burned itself into my eyes, inflamed my nostrils, and caused my ears to ring. I blinked, but nothing changed. I could not wake up.

"Miss Morton, why don't you wash up? I'll pour us a drink."

I tore my eyes away from my hands and met Miss Kaye's gaze. Her voice remained steady, and I could feel my body move in response to her instructions, despite my mind's lack of comprehension.

I poured water from the pitcher to fill the basin and lowered my hands into it. The water was cold and devoid of comfort, and I watched in fascination as ruby-pink plumes billowed out from where it contacted my skin. For a moment I just stared. Then I began to scrub.

I scrubbed and scrubbed, working my way from my fingertips up past my wrists and to my forearms, observing in detached contentment as my skin emerged from its sanguinary baptism. I do not know how long I carried on for, except that I was startled to feel a hand upon my shoulder. I spun around to find myself face-to-face with Miss Kaye, who was holding out a fresh flannel with which to dry myself. I blinked again and accepted it.

"Have a seat, Miss Morton." Miss Kaye gestured towards the chair in front of her desk, and I was startled to note that two glasses of the same strong-smelling dark liquid she had provided to Pippa had materialised upon its surface seemingly from nowhere. I absently wondered how long I had been washing my hands for.

"Please." Miss Kaye's tone was stern, and my body obeyed her command without question. I appreciated the fact that she was still giving orders. It made things simpler. Easier. Better.

Miss Kaye took a seat in her own chair opposite me and picked up one of the glasses. I followed suit and watched as she raised hers towards me before swallowing half of its contents in a single go. I lifted my own and took a swill, immediately dissolving into a fit of undignified coughing. The spirit was obscenely bitter, and while I'd only ever tasted wine, this drink did not appear to have anything in common with that.

"Easy there, Miss Morton. Your first brandy?" I managed to nod through teary eyes, and was surprised to find Miss Kaye gazing at me with an expression I could only describe as *sentimental.* "It's an acquired taste, I'm afraid. I suggest you perhaps resort to sipping it from here on out."

"Right," I croaked, and Miss Kaye pressed her lips together as if suppressing a laugh before her experience turned serious once more.

"Miss Morton, I need to know why you and Miss Fitzroy left the school tonight."

"I'm sorry." The words bubbled up out of me from nowhere, but the moment I uttered them, I realised I'd never spoken a truer phrase in my life. I *was* sorry: sorry I had left the Hall, sorry I had doubted her, sorry I had dragged Pippa into the whole sordid mess, and above all else, sorry that I had been too late to save the woman whose life had been extinguished right before my eyes.

"Were the two of you running away?"

Miserably, I shook my head.

"No. We were following you." Her eyes narrowed. "Why were you following me?"

I swallowed. "Because . . . because we thought . . . we thought you were the Whitechapel killer."

"Why in God's name would you think that?"

I paused. The silence stretched between us, heavy and dark. Behind me, the coals crackled in the fireplace, and for one mad moment, I imagined throwing myself upon them and evaporating up the chimney in a cloud of smoke just as my dress had done.

"Because I know who you are."

Miss Kaye's head tilted, the familiarity of her demeanour shifting into something far more calculating. "Who might that be?"

"You're Constance Kent."

For a long time, she did not speak. When she finally endeavoured to move, it was to reach forward, pick up her cup, and drain the remainder of her drink in a single swallow. "Well, then. This does complicate things a bit, doesn't it?"

She did not look angry, but she certainly didn't look pleased. Even so, I was suddenly reminded of the fact that while she had spared my life when it had been threatened by the Whitechapel killer, that didn't necessarily mean that she wouldn't proceed to kill me for her own selfish reasons. There could be more than one murderer in Whitechapel, after all.

"It doesn't have to!" I rushed to assure her. "I mean, just

because . . . well, just because of the thing with your brother, that was so long ago, I realise now you probably don't even do murders anymore, since prison and all, and you're here reforming the rest of us, and now I know you're not the Whitechapel killer, so I can just forget all about it and never mention it to anyone again!"

Miss Kaye raised her eyebrows, and I blushed furiously, realising how absurdly foolish I must sound. "Miss Morton, while I deeply appreciate your discretion, I must assure you of one thing: I have never murdered anyone in my life."

I paused, confused. "You're not Constance Kent?"

Miss Kaye sighed heavily and leaned back in her chair, looking hopelessly sad. "Truth be told, Dell, yes, I am Constance Kent. I've not used that name in quite some time, for reasons I imagine are all too clear to a prodigious mind such as yours. But I was framed for a crime I did not commit and have spent twenty long years awaiting my chance to enact justice."

"Is that what you were doing out on the streets?" I inquired breathlessly, leaning forward despite myself, the thought of Miss Kaye—Constance—as some sort of vigilante crusader suddenly painting my mind with a thousand wild fantasies.

Miss Kaye just issued a wan smile. "I'll explain everything tomorrow, once we've both had some rest. But for tonight, all you need to know is that I am not a danger to you or any pupil in this school. I would willingly lay down my life for any one of you girls, and it has been my greatest priority to keep you all safe despite the chaos on the streets and the headmaster's absence."

I paused and took a sip of brandy, contemplating my next inquiry. "Where exactly is the headmaster?" If Miss Kaye hadn't killed him and stuffed him in a trunk, I was at a loss for where he may have disappeared to.

"He is out soliciting donations for the school."

"But why? I thought the school was funded by the courts."

"It is. Or rather, it was. But due to an incident last year involving some unseemly behaviour on the part of a faculty member that has since been dismissed, the continuation of the school's operation has been called into question."

I furrowed my brow. "Is this about Sally?"

Miss Kaye did not hide her surprise well. "How do you know about Sally?"

I shrugged. "This is a reformatory school for delinquent girls. Gossip isn't exactly hard to come by around here."

"It would seem not." Miss Kaye rubbed her eyes but did not deflect. "To answer your question, yes, it's to do with Sally and the reputation of the entire school. But the headmaster firmly believes in our mission, and he's taken it upon himself to secure private funding until the issue with the courts has been resolved."

I took a moment to contemplate this and realised that for once Miss Kaye was treating me not as a pupil but as an equal. It was a gesture that I did not take for granted and, as such, declined to press the issue further. "I see. But then why did you leave the school tonight to— "

Miss Kaye held up her hand. "As I told you, I'll explain everything in the morning. But for now, it is late, and you need rest. Tomorrow will be here soon enough. You and Miss Fitzroy may remain in my chambers until then."

I paused. "You might want to bring Noah Levy up in the morning, too."

"The butcher boy?"

I nodded. "He's been helping me and Pippa with the case, you see, and he'll be dreadfully worried if there's news of another murder and then Pippa and I don't report to the kitchen. He knows who you are, too," I added bashfully.

Miss Kaye closed her eyes and pinched the bridge of her nose, and for a moment I feared she was going to berate me. Luckily, she composed herself once more. "Very well. I shall bring the butcher up, too. But for now, Miss Morton: bed." She plucked the glass bottle up off her desk and shook two pills into her hand and offered them to me.

I was tempted to decline. My thoughts were still racing, the events of the night so surreal in their enormity that the detective in me wanted to simply sit and stew in them until some of it began to make any sort of sense.

But I would have no further answers until the morning. And every time I blinked, the haunting, shocked expression of the dying woman peered at me from the backs of my eyelids, and I could not contemplate facing her as I sought a much-needed rest.

I plucked up the pills and downed them with the rest of my brandy. Miss Kaye led me by the elbow to her chamber, where I climbed into the cot and curled up next to Pippa, careful not to jostle her injured arm. Miss Kaye tucked the blanket over me, and her face was the last thing I saw before the dark pulled me under for good.

Chapter XV
The Accidental Murderess

I awoke groggy and disoriented, light streaming through an unfamiliar window to illuminate an equally unfamiliar room. It was far past dawn, too late for the morning bell—why had no one come to awaken me? I pulled myself upright and took solace in the one familiar sight I could find: that of Pippa, still sleeping beside me. She looked angelic as always, the sunlight dancing merrily along the strands of her golden locks, casting elegant shadows along the lines of her perfect cheekbones. She should by all accounts have seemed divine, untouchable and remote, but instead I delighted in the familiarity of the warm intimacy of her form. My friend was at peace, and therefore, so was I.

Voices rumbled from behind the closed door. Still struggling to make sense of my surroundings, I reached up to rub my eyes and let out an involuntary yelp as a violent shock of pain reverberated from my cheekbone, ricocheting through my skull like a marble in a game of ring taw. My exclamation startled Pippa, who sat bolt upright as well, took one look at me, and let out a shriek. The suddenness of her movement took me by surprise, and I let out a shriek in response. It was only then that the chamber door burst open, revealing a frantic-looking Miss Kaye, who stared down at the two of us as though we'd lost our minds.

"Ladies! What in God's name are you screaming about in here?" Miss Kaye seemed considerably less concerned once she'd discerned that neither of us were in immediate peril.

"Apologies, Miss Kaye," Pippa replied hastily. "But . . . but look at her *face*!"

"What's wrong with my face?" I retorted, horrified, and jumped out of bed to check the mirror on the wall. Upon encountering my own reflection, I let out another shriek: my right cheek was a swollen mess of bruising, a deep purple aberration that stretched from my temple to my lips. I raised my fingers to touch it and hissed at the sensation.

With a withering look, Miss Kaye approached me to peer at my cheek. She cupped my face lightly in her hand, turning it to and fro, then leaned forward as if inspecting the pupil of my eye. "Well, Miss Morton, you may look a mess, but your cheekbone isn't broken. I will check to see if the headmaster has any arnica in his stores. In the meantime, you and Miss Fitzroy must get dressed at once." She turned and pulled two of her identical black frocks out of her wardrobe, tossing them casually to each of us. "We mustn't keep Mr. Levy waiting."

"Right," I replied breathlessly, the events of the night before sliding into place in my mind, the fear and shock and revulsion and confusion all intermingling into a lead weight of dread that positioned itself squarely inside my stomach. Miss Kaye left us in privacy and pulled the door shut behind her, and I turned to find Pippa unsteadily rising to her feet, the delicacy of her movements clearly conveying her pain from last night's altercation.

"What is Noah doing here?" she whispered as she struggled to yank the opening of the skirt over her head using just her good arm.

"I told Miss Kaye to bring him up when he arrived with the morning delivery. She knows we all know she's Constance Kent."

"What?!" Pippa yelped, flailing awkwardly, stuck half-in and half-out of her dress, one arm flapping over her head where it was protruding from the neck hole.

"Come here and calm down," I chided, and stilled her with a firm grip before assisting her in righting herself within the garment. I lowered my voice and raced to catch her up. "It's true Miss Kaye is Constance Kent, but here's the thing: She claims she's innocent and that she never murdered her brother."

Pippa's head popped through the collar, a sceptical expression upon her face. "And you believe her?"

"Pippa, she saved our lives last night and fought off the Whitechapel killer herself!"

"Fair point, but what has she been doing sneaking around outside the school these past few weeks?"

"That's exactly what she's promised to tell us," I reassured her as I turned to don my own dress. "Hopefully now we'll get the answers we need."

"Like who the man is that tried to kill us last night?"

An image of his face flashed before my eyes, the darkness in his gaze sending a chill down my spine, even hours later in the sobering light of day. "I hope so. If she knows who he is, then he can be stopped."

"He couldn't last night." Pippa's eyes met mine, and I knew that she, too, was reliving the terror of watching that innocent woman perish as we looked on helplessly from the shadows.

I reached out and clasped the hand of her good arm in my own and gave it a squeeze. "But he can be. He *will* be. We'll find a way to stop him, I promise."

She gave me nothing but a wary smile in return. "Let's hear what Miss Kaye has to say."

We emerged from the bedroom to find Miss Kaye already

positioned behind her desk, a pot of tea and four cups having replaced the flask of brandy from the night before. There were now three chairs positioned in a row opposite her, but Noah had forsaken them in favour of pacing back and forth, his cap twisted in his hands. The bruising on his own face had receded slightly. Upon seeing the two of us, his expression turned to one of profound relief.

"Dell! Pippa! Thank God." He lurched awkwardly in our direction as if to meet us in an embrace but stopped himself before he could, his brow furrowing at the sight of my bruised face and Pippa's bandaged arm. "What happened last night? You both look a breath from death!"

"We're quite alright," I assured him as steadily as I could. "But it was a near miss. We found him, Noah. The real Whitechapel killer—we caught him in the act, but he attacked us, and we couldn't stop him."

"You tried to *stop him*?" Noah's eyes were wide with horror. "After the stunt he pulled last night, the fact you're both still alive is nothing short of a miracle!" With that, he produced from his back pocket the day's edition of *The Star.* Splashed across the front page was the headline:

Whitechapel: The Murder Maniac Sacrifices More Women to His Thirst for Blood

Pippa and I both gasped and rushed forward for a closer look. Snatching the paper from Noah's hands, I read the article aloud:

The series of blood-chilling tragedies which have shocked the public mind and sent a thrill of horror throughout the land, have been crowned by murder more foul than any of the former crimes. Two more poor unfortunate and degraded women have fallen victims

> *to the knife of the hellish fiend who stalks abroad in Whitechapel leaving a track of blood behind him. At one o'clock on Sunday morning the body of a woman is found with her throat cut in a yard in Berner-street, Commercial-road. At a quarter to two a second victim is found hacked, mutilated, and disembowelled in Mitre-square, Aldgate. Everything points to the fact that both murders were the work of the same hand—that fiendishly cunning hand, which not many weeks since massacred Mary Ann Nicholls in Buck's-row, and butchered Annie Chapman in Hanbury-street.*

I whirled around to face Miss Kaye. "Miss Kaye! Did you see this? He killed again last night, after you disposed of him at the first murder scene!"

"After you *what?* Noah rounded on Miss Kaye, who remained as austere as ever as she lowered herself into her chair and commenced pouring the tea. "Will someone please enlighten me as to what on God's earth is going on here?"

Miss Kaye glanced up at us over her fake spectacles, which I noted she'd taken the liberty of donning once more. "Gladly, if the three of you are done gossiping like schoolchildren over that drivel in the press."

Abashed, I folded the paper and deposited it on the desk, the recollection of why we were all truly gathered here rushing to the forefront of my mind in a tidal wave of regret. "Right. Of course. Apologies."

Miss Kaye managed a small smile at my return to civility. "No apologies required, Miss Morton. Miss Fitzroy, Mr. Levy, have a seat."

The three of us complied without protest, taking up the cups and saucers that Miss Kaye pushed in our direction and settling into an apprehensive silence.

"Sugar?" Miss Kaye gestured towards a small sugar pot and

spoon, the first of its kind I'd seen since entering Whitechapel Hall—no such niceties were afforded us at our normal meals. The indulgence felt so strange at such a solemn moment that I automatically shook my head without thinking, and Pippa and Noah followed my lead.

"Very well." Miss Kaye took a spoonful for herself, stirred it vigorously into her tea, and took a sip. "I know you all have questions, but first, I have a few of my own. If you are honest with me, I will return the favour. After what you witnessed last night, there must be no secrets between us anymore. Can we agree on that much?"

"Yes, Miss Kaye . . . I mean, Miss Kent?" I replied, perhaps too much in earnest.

"Miss Kaye is fine for now. First, I must know how you uncovered my real name. I have taken great care to distance myself from my past, so I must admit I was quite startled that you put the pieces together so decisively."

I took a deep breath and let all the secrets that had settled upon my chest over the previous weeks spill forth. "Well, even before the murders started, Noah had been providing us with contraband," I began, and turned to see a scarlet blush spread across Noah's cheeks. "Nothing sordid!" I quickly clarified. "But he enjoys penny bloods too, and he'd sneak us the latest edition of *Link Boys*, or the *Illustrated Police News*, that kind of thing. But then a few weeks ago, buried at the bottom of an edition of *The Star* was an article about . . . well, about *you*. It didn't give the details of your current whereabouts, of course, but the sketch would be familiar to anyone who's come across you, even with your hair and your spectacles."

Miss Kaye looked impressed but did not interject. "By then Pippa and I had already witnessed you sneaking out of the Hall multiple times, and twice your absence coincided with a murder. We simply drew the most obvious conclusion given the evidence at hand."

Miss Kaye gave a thoughtful nod and took another sip of her tea. “A logical assumption, considering the circumstances. Go on.”

I steadied myself and continued. “We devised a plan to have Noah tail you every time you left the school.”

At this, Miss Kaye let out a wry chuckle. “Ah, yes, I thought I’d spotted you skulking about at all hours upon the streets, Mr. Levy, and I do commend your commitment to the task. You’re a tough man to shake.” At this, Noah gave a lopsided grin, and I could feel his posture relax in tune with Miss Kaye’s increasingly familiar demeanour.

I carried on. “But last night, Noah was unable to take his usual watch. When we saw you leave the school, we endeavoured to follow you, out of fear you were . . . well, about to commit a murder.” Miss Kaye reacted with nothing but a dispassionate sip of her tea at this allegation, and once again the strangeness of the situation made the room swim in and out of focus. Mere hours ago, we’d been convinced that Miss Kaye was a diabolical madwoman, and now we were all sitting down for tea and a proper confessional with her. I took a drink of my own tea to steady my thoughts.

“When at last we caught the true criminal in his element, we realised our mistake, but it was too late.” I turned to Noah, determined to confess the whole of what had transpired. “Pippa and I attempted to thwart the killer, but he overpowered both of us. Were it not for Miss Kaye’s intervention, we would have been his next victims.”

Noah gasped at this revelation. He turned his attention to Miss Kaye, his eyes wide and earnest. “And for that, ma’am, I am eternally indebted to you. Had I not absconded from my duties as watchman, Dell and Pippa would never have been in danger, and none of this would have happened. For that, I am sorry.”

“And for doubting your motives and believing you a killer . . . For that, we are even sorrier,” Pippa chimed in, looking sincerely abashed for once.

Miss Kaye dismissed them with a wave of her hand. "Please, there is no need to apologise. For now, it is clear to me why, through your eyes, you believed me to be the killer and went to such lengths to prevent further bloodshed. You are a commendable trio of detectives, all of you, but I'm afraid now I must be the fly in your ointment, the unexpected plot twist at the end of the second act. For as I told Miss Morton last night, nothing about my story is as it seems." With that, she removed her spectacles and placed them upon the desk and tucked an errant string of brassy-blonde hair behind her ear. She reached for her teacup once more, clasped it firmly between her palms, leaned back in her chair, closed her eyes, and began to speak.

"It's true that I am Constance Kent. I served twenty years in prison for the murder of my half-brother, Saville. But I was framed by the very man who now wreaks havoc upon the streets of Whitechapel: my own brother, William Kent."

The three of us shared a wide-eyed look at this revelation, but we dared not interrupt. Miss Kaye, as unflappable as ever, continued.

"By all accounts, Wills—*William* and I shared a happy childhood. We were healthy, safe, and loved. But our lives were turned upside down when our mother died. It seemed to me that everything changed in an instant, and our grief was compounded by the fact our father barely mourned. Instead, he remarried quickly and shipped us 'spare' children off to boarding school." Upon hearing these details, I spared a quick glance at Pippa; her story and Miss Kaye's aligned so closely it was uncanny.

"He wasted no time in replacing us, producing three children in quick succession with his new wife: two girls and one boy, Saville. Of course, being the youngest and the only son, Saville was doted upon by everyone in the household . . . except for William. He grew increasingly convinced that the only reason he and I had been sent away to school was so that he could be more easily usurped in the family line by Saville, whom he viewed as a rival for our father's affection.

"Even at the time I found William's jealousies unfounded, but he was my brother and my dearest friend. There was no love lost between myself and my stepmother, so it was easy to side with William as he ranted against the unfairness of it all, and I confess my head was turned against the rest of the family by his spite. Soon it felt like it was just him and me against the rest of the world.

"The summer of my sixteenth year, William and I were home for the summer holidays, and our welcome had been predictably bleak. Making matters worse was little Saville, only three at the time, who had become quite the escape artist. One morning he slipped from his nursery under the nose of his nursemaid, tottered down the hall, and made his way into William's bedroom, where he proceeded to tear the pages from several valuable books on the desk. Our stepmother blamed William for leaving the books out, and our father declined to intervene.

"William was livid at the injustice. He suggested we stir things up a bit by playing a little prank: That night, we'd take Saville from his room and let him outside to wander the grounds. There was no true danger in the jest, for William insisted he'd supervise Saville while I created a believable scene back at the house to make it appear Saville had escaped on his own. We would simply scare our stepmother a bit, have a laugh at her expense, and put it all behind us, he insisted, and I agreed.

"At the start, everything proceeded just as we'd planned. William snatched Saville from his crib and spirited him outside to the gardens while I unlatched and opened the front door. Then I waited for William's signal to awaken my stepmother: a match struck beside the garden gate, indicating that he and Saville were clear of the house.

"But the signal never came. I waited in earnest for half an

hour, perhaps more, my anxiety growing with each passing moment, but I didn't dare deviate from our plan for fear of disappointing William. So, I stayed put. I waited. And eventually, Wills came home.

"When he walked through the front door, I knew in an instant that something was terribly wrong. Saville was nowhere to be seen. William was wearing my nightdress, holding a razor, and soaked head to toe in blood. But the strange thing was, he was not at all panicked. He simply ordered me not to scream, then escorted me swiftly to my bedroom. Once safely inside, he divested himself of the nightgown, wiped off the razor blade, sat me down on my bed, and explained to me that Saville was dead, and he and I would never have to worry about him bothering us again. And then he smiled, awaiting my gratitude.

"That was the moment when everything changed. It was as if for years I'd been living beneath a veil, and in that moment, it was torn away, and the world came into focus for the very first time.

"A thousand moments from our childhood resurfaced, changing shape and tone in light of my sudden revelation: The tea set that seemingly shattered itself when I refused to let Wills share it. The dollhouse that mysteriously caught fire the day after Christmas, when I'd refused to leave it behind to have a snowball fight instead. The missing pet mice and birds and cats that always seemed to show up dead on the rocks in the garden when I doted upon them too fiercely.

"And it only grew worse as more pieces fell into place. There was the time when I was only nine and had made my first friend outside the family: a girl called Emma who'd moved into a neighbouring cottage. We became fast friends and had been inseparable for weeks when she nearly drowned while the two of us were playing in the river with William. She insisted *something* held her underwater, but Wills claimed he'd been the one to pull her back to the surface, saving her life. But Emma never came back to our house after that day, and William never mentioned her again.

"When we became teenagers, he persuaded me to run away from home with him after overhearing my father discussing plans for my future after boarding school, insisting that we were better off stowing away at sea than being separated by my eventual marriage. I had been young enough to believe him then, but the moment I saw him standing in my bedroom, covered in Saville's blood, I realised that my whole life, I had been the pawn of a monster. And what's more: he believed me to be a monster, too."

The silence in the room was resounding as Miss Kaye's eyes fluttered open and she gazed back at us, dazed, as if awakening from a dream. I turned to see the expressions of my companions: Pippa's was a mask of shock, but to my surprise, Noah appeared unmoved.

"So why didn't you tell anyone?"

I was taken aback by his brazenness, but Miss Kaye did not appear offended by his inquiry. "Believe me, I wanted to, but by then William had capably cast the two of us as the black sheep of the family; I no longer had my father's trust, and my stepmother was my sworn nemesis. What's more, William wore my nightdress while committing the deed, and it was covered with incriminating evidence. That night in my room he insisted that it was because it was the easiest garment with which to cover his own clothes during the crime, and no one would ever suspect me, so it was simply a matter of pragmatism. But I knew deep down inside what it truly was: leverage. Though he always claimed that what he'd done was for the good of us both, he made damn sure I had no choice but to agree.

"So, I stayed silent. God help me, I stayed silent, through the horror of Saville's discovery and the indignity of the subsequent investigation. Though I knew what William had done was wrong, I somehow convinced myself that this would be the end of it:

Now that his thirst for vengeance had been quenched, we would carry on as we always had and take our secret to the grave.

"And for a short time, it appeared I was right. Though our family's reputation was sullied, William and I escaped relatively unscathed. I was sent abroad to finish my education at a convent in France, and William concluded his own in England. But when it was time for me to select a vocation, he adamantly insisted that I come live with him in London. The thought of being pulled back into his clutches was so abhorrent that I was willing to do anything to avoid it. Instead, I took a position at one place I knew he could never reach me: St. Mary's Home for Female Penitents, a reformatory home for unwed mothers and prostitutes. I became a nurse for the newborn babies there, and for the first time since uncovering William's true nature, I began to make an uneasy peace with the God I feared had forsaken me completely.

"For two years, I practised my penance with a sense of duty and devotion. St. Mary's was not a cheerful place, by any means—great emphasis was placed upon obedience, compliance, and discipline, and I could see that for many of the women interned there, it did not heal their tortured souls—but for me, it is what I felt I needed, or perhaps deserved. I would have happily lived out my days there in solemn solitude, but as it turned out, William had other plans.

"One day he showed up at the doorstep of the Home, demanding an audience with the Reverend in charge. Reverend Wagner was a God-fearing and pious man, and he indulged him without question. It was then that William produced my bloodied nightdress and informed the Reverend, who was well aware of my family's disgrace, that he had located it hidden in my childhood bedroom at the estate, and that I was Saville's true killer.

"I was devastated. For three days I pleaded my innocence, but the Reverend's opinion could not be swayed, and William remained firm in his accusations. I begged him to tell me why. Why now? Why here? Why me? But it was only on the evening of the third day of interrogations that he finally agreed to speak with me alone and make his reasoning known.

"William was about to turn twenty-one and come into his full inheritance. But he had discovered that our father was considering changing his will. As it turned out, he still harboured suspicions that William was responsible for Saville's death. William, irate at our father's distrust and shaken at the thought of losing his place as the sole heir to the estate, concluded that the only way to guarantee his future was to obtain a conviction for Saville's murder. And of course, it was only too easy to frame me, as it was my bloodstained nightdress that he'd kept as collateral.

"He was dispassionate as he explained his reasoning to me. I wouldn't be sentenced to death if I would simply confess, he advised me. And if I behaved, I would likely live long enough to be released from prison someday, at which point I could benefit from the inheritance which he would *magnanimously* share with me as a token of his gratitude.

"What choice did I have? The evidence he held against me was enough to convince any court, and if I wanted to escape with my life, a guilty plea was the safest bet. But the most difficult pill to swallow was the fact that it suddenly became very clear that his murder of Saville had been about so much more than a petty bout of jealousy turned madness: As another living male heir, not to mention my father's preferred child, Saville was a direct threat to Wills' inheritance. At the end of the day, it was simply about the money. It always had been." She spat the word *money* as though it tasted sour, her face contorting with revulsion, and she paused to collect herself in the aftermath as the three of us waited in apprehensive silence.

Finally, she continued. "And that brings us here. I shall spare you the details of my stay in prison, suffice to say it was unpleasant in the utmost. Upon my release I came here, to Whitechapel Hall, intent upon continuing my mission of reforming young women with a message of mercy, grace, and compassion, believing that if I could improve the life of at least one pupil, perhaps I could be redeemed: not just for God but for myself. I could repay my debt at last."

To my surprise, a flicker of true emotion appeared upon her face. "But it was not to be. Six months after I arrived here, I received a letter from William, demanding an audience. I ignored him. But his insistence only grew darker, wilder, and more desperate with each letter he sent, yet I foolishly allowed myself to believe that Whitechapel Hall would remain an impenetrable sanctuary within which I could hide. And for a time, that was true . . . until the day of the first murder. I received a note from him that very morning claiming that if I would not speak with him, he would make me pay for my stubbornness with the blood of my 'companions.' That night, Mary Anne Nichols was killed.

"I wanted to believe it was a coincidence. But the pattern repeated itself the morning of Annie Chapman's death: another letter, another murder. And yesterday's events confirm it: I received a dispatch from William in the morning, and last night, he was out on the streets enacting his bloody revenge, as only I could predict. But the trouble is, try as I might, I have no idea how to stop him."

I took a moment to mull this over as my mind fixated on a particular detail of her story. "What does he mean by 'companions,' as he referred to his victims in his letter to you? Did you know them?"

Miss Kaye shook her head adamantly. "I'd never met any of them in my life. As I'm sure Mr. Levy observed, I attempted to do some detective work of my own at the Ten Bells, which is the only known commonality between them. I could make no connection between Miss Nichols and Miss Chapman, but during my investigation, I did make the acquaintance of Miss

Stride—the unfortunate woman who met her end last night on Hanbury Street. She did not admit to knowing either of the previous victims, but I noted that she seemed to fit the profile of my brother's previous targets, and as such, I devoted myself to learning her weekly routine, so that I might catch my brother preying upon her the next time he sent a letter. I learned that on Saturdays, she often drank at a tavern on High Street and would then ply her trade with the men adjourning from their weekly meeting at the Working Men's Club. When I received the letter yesterday morning, I resolved to follow her and thwart my brother's attack. Sadly, I was too late."

"But what of the other victim of last night's atrocities?" Noah interjected. "Did you meet her at the Ten Bells, too?"

Miss Kaye shook her head woefully. "Sadly, no. The press has yet to release her name, but Miss Stride was the only mark I'd made there. Yet now the poor soul has been subjected to the same ghastly fate as the others, and I cannot for the life of me figure out why."

"So why not just go to the police yourself and tell them what you know?" Noah's tone revealed that Miss Kaye had not yet gained his trust despite her tale, and I had to admit that this question gave me pause. Was Miss Kaye boldly preying upon our sympathies?

Miss Kaye was undeterred by his scepticism. "I only wish that I could, but what do you imagine the outcome would be? That they would believe *me*, despite my prior confession and conviction for the murder of a child, over the word of William, who maintains his reputation as a gentleman and citizen in good standing? They would simply think I had relapsed and reverted to my old ways. And the sentence for a second offence would not be so kind. The gallows would be the best outcome I could hope for, but I fear instead they would send me to the asylum in Bedlam, a fate worse than death." She shook her head vigorously as if attempting to clear the mere thought of it. "I had the misfortune of meeting a few inmates that had returned from a stint at Bedlam, and scarcely a scrap of their humanity remained. The prospect of those horrors haunts me; I cannot bring myself to cross the law again."

Noah appeared appeased by this, and his next query was in earnest. "So, what will you do now?"

Miss Kaye sighed heavily. "I'm beginning to fear I have no choice but to capitulate to William's demands and meet him at last."

"You should," I replied simply.

"Dell!" Pippa exclaimed, giving me a mortified glare. "He's a murderer! She can't just go meet with him, he'll kill and maim her, too!"

"Which is why," I continued haughtily, slightly offended that Pippa would suspect me of being so dense, "you must arrange to meet him in a public place, in broad daylight, near a police patrol point."

"And what good would that do?" Noah queried. "It's not as if he'll simply confess his methods and give himself up."

"That's hardly the point," I continued, turning my attention to Miss Kaye. "Your objectives will be twofold: first, to hear whatever it is that he's so keen to tell you. Though he surely won't admit to the murders under such circumstances, it would undoubtedly be beneficial to know precisely what it is he feels is so important to tell you that he's willing to kill to lure you back to his side."

Miss Kaye raised her eyebrow. "And the second objective?"

"To keep him away from his house long enough for the three of us to break in and search the place."

Pippa let out an indignant squawk. "We're going to *what*?"

I waved her off, focusing on Miss Kaye, willing her to trust me. "Any good detective must conduct a proper search of the suspect's house, and this will give us the perfect opportunity to do so!"

Miss Kaye appeared unmoved. "Absolutely not. I cannot in

good conscience put any of you in danger; you've done enough already."

"But we won't be in any danger!" I protested. "You'll see to that yourself. Besides, this is our only lead, isn't it? So far, all we know is that at least three of the victims frequented the Ten Bells, but it's clear from your own surveillance that William doesn't pick them up there. There must be some other connection, but what? If we're to find out, we need to conduct a thorough search of his quarters. And this is our chance!"

Miss Kaye looked torn, but her tone was firm when she replied. "I can't. If anything were to happen to you—"

"It won't," Noah piped up from beside me, much to my delight. "We'll take proper precautions: have a lookout on standby, and a diversion at the ready. There's no risk to any of us so long as we follow the plan."

Miss Kaye did not respond, but she appeared to be wavering, and I seized my chance. "Look, Miss Kaye: We may be young, but we have the knowledge and experience of fiction's greatest detectives on our side. After all, we've been working the case whilst locked in reformatory school for the past four weeks, and we came closer to solving it than anyone else by a long shot!"

"Did you not just confess to suspecting *me* of committing the atrocities?" Miss Kaye fired back.

I refused to relent. "Well, yes, but technically we were only one degree of separation from the true culprit, which is more than the police or Vigilance Committee can say," I concluded smugly. "Besides, what other choice do we have? The headmaster is gone, the Reverend has abandoned his duties, and the police will never believe the likes of any of us. If we don't act ourselves, William will continue to kill innocent women and incite terror upon the streets of Whitechapel forever! Perhaps . . . perhaps it was God's plan to bring all of us together, so that we may thwart William once and for all."

"Do leave God out of this, Miss Morton; pandering is unbecoming."

"Right," I replied, aware that I had perhaps laid it on a bit too thickly, but I was encouraged by the levity of her tone.

A long silence followed. Miss Kaye picked up her spectacles from the desk and polished them with her kerchief, then perched them primly back upon her nose with an air of decisiveness.

"Alright, then."

I could scarcely believe my ears. "Alright? You mean . . . we can do it?"

"Yes, Miss Morton. Against all my better judgement, you're correct: I have no better idea, and for what it's worth, the three of you have proven yourselves to be rather formidable, albeit careless, detectives. We shall make a plan to infiltrate William's residence and search it for clues. I will distract him and trust the three of you to do what apparently you do best: behave badly."

I turned to my co-conspirators for their consent. Noah gave me a resolute nod, his expression determined. But Pippa's face was unreadable, and my heart sank in my chest. Was she perhaps not as committed to the cause as I had let myself believe? Just when I was about to succumb to my doubt, she broke into a conspiratorial grin which required no further explanation.

A thrill of excitement washed over me. "Excellent. Miss Kaye? With your permission, I have some important texts in the annex I'd like to consult before we present you with the official plan."

With a roll of her eyes and the hint of a smile, Miss Kaye dismissed us with a wave of her hand.

Chapter XVI
Adventures of a Notorious Burglar

The Windus House in Stamford Hill was everything that the gothic lair of a villain should be. A dreary, imposing facade of dark grey stone towered over the gated entrance, and wild creepers climbed the exterior walls in a menacing encroachment. The three grand balconies that overlooked the street were cloistered by a series of ornate balustrades, and the doors leading out to them were secured with decorative ironwork. The house was, for all intents and purposes, an impenetrable fortress. Mere days ago, I would have been nothing short of enchanted by the prospect of infiltrating its defences, but I could not shake the lingering fear at the designs of the monster who lived within it. My caprice had nearly cost Pippa her life that night on Berner Street, and I vowed to take our newest caper more seriously.

Pippa and Noah looked more than a little intimidated as we assessed our target from across the street. They had no reason for concern, as our disguises were flawless: Pippa made a convincing (and frankly quite breathtaking) lady of high station. She had donned a silk dress of periwinkle blue and a bonnet crowned with pastel flowers and a delicate lace trim, apparently the ensemble she'd worn on the day of her intake at

Whitechapel Hall, which she'd been forced to turn over to be locked away with the remainder of her personal belongings in some secret location (which Miss Kaye had refused to divulge but had no problem infiltrating to produce the garments in question). I'd known beforehand that Pippa's fair looks would provide an excellent distraction during our caper, but I'd still been struck by her jaw-dropping beauty when she'd emerged from behind her dressing screen in her finery. In her drab Whitechapel Hall uniform, she was beautiful. In full stately dress? She was so resplendent, my eyes barely registered the odd angle at which she cradled her injured arm.

My disguise as her attending lady's maid was considerably less transformative, as I'd merely added one of Mrs. Dolmer's aprons and frilled hats to my standard wool frock. Noah was the epitome of a gutter cleaner, the flat cap and woollen sweater he'd borrowed from Henry giving him a distinctly more gentile appearance than his usual high-collared shirt and apron, and the barrow, broom, and ladder we'd snatched from the gardening shed behind the Hall completed the look.

"Are you sure this is going to work?" Pippa asked shifting uneasily from foot to foot as she took in the Windus home's defences.

"There's no reason it won't," I replied with conviction. "Mrs. Paschal, the Lady Detective, infiltrated a home just like this one in a similar ruse. And Charles Pearce, the Notorious Burglar himself, often took on the persona of a general handyman, just like Noah."

"Besides, we've the perfect plan," Noah chimed in. "Simply relax and play your part."

"Relax. Right," Pippa huffed, and for a moment, I felt distinctly sorry for her. There was no denying that the crux of our operation depended upon her ability to sell our story convincingly, but there was no avoiding it: her blinding beauty made her the perfect distraction from our deception, an opinion that had only been validated by the number of heads she'd effortlessly turned on our omnibus ride from Whitechapel. No member of a reputable household would deny her entry.

"Let's review the plan one more time," I insisted, more for Pippa's assurance than my own. We'd turned it over time and time again prior to the point of engagement, searching for weak spots in our preparations, but outside the safe confines of Whitechapel Hall, the stakes felt distinctly higher.

"Pippa and I will infiltrate the household under the guise of Duchess Rustenburgh and her attendant, Miss Paschal."

"Still think that's a bit cheeky," Noah contested, but I dismissed him. The odds of anyone in the household having read *Revelations of a Lady Detective* seemed infinitesimally small, and conjuring these characters from my beloved fictions fortified my confidence.

"We will demand to be escorted to Mr. Kent's study to await his return. Once left unsupervised, Pippa and I shall conduct a thorough search of the premises for clues. Meanwhile . . ." I gave Noah a meaningful look, which for a moment he failed to interpret until I jabbed my elbow into his rib cage, rousing him from his apparent stupor.

"Meanwhile, I shall be cleaning the gutters of the neighbouring house, which Miss Kaye has confirmed is currently vacant. From my vantage point, I shall keep a keen eye out for the untimely return of Mr. Kent, should he slip through Miss Kaye's clutches. If I observe him approaching, I shall place this red kerchief in my back pocket, which you can clearly observe from the study on the second floor."

"Perfect!" I clapped my hands in enthusiasm and turned to Pippa. "You see? It will be easy, Pippa, I promise. There's nothing to fear!"

"Except the rampaging murderer whose home we are about to infiltrate," she replied drily. Before I could retort, Pippa turned up her nose, tightened her bonnet, and strolled across the street towards the Windus House with an air of haughty indifference. Caught wrong-footed by her sudden surge of confidence, I scampered after her, with nary a wave in Noah's direction lest we draw further attention to ourselves on the bustling street.

Pippa pushed her way through the lavish gate without hesitation, leaving me to secure the ornate latch behind us, ensconcing us completely in William's estate. For a brief moment, terror welled up inside me at the thought of being trapped in such a lair, but I had not the time to contemplate our peril, as Pippa simply strode up to the imposing arched front door and knocked boldly upon it before I could so much as assume my position at her heels.

The door swung open, revealing a small, prim-looking butler, who blinked down at us from over his crooked nose with an air of puzzled indifference. "May I help you?"

Pippa dropped into a perfect curtsy, and I hurried to follow her lead. "I do hope so, sir. I'm in pressing need of an audience with William Kent." Her tone was imbibed with such innocence and urgency that I nearly believed her myself.

The butler's demeanour waivered, clearly affected by the presence of such an illustrious figure upon his doorstep. "Sincerest apologies, madame, but Mr. Kent has just stepped out."

"Would it . . ." Pippa trailed off, her voice a perfect imitation of demure insistence. "Would it be possible for me to await his return? I've come on important business connected with a loan, and it is imperative that I see him today."

The butler considered this. He gave her another thorough examination, no doubt taking in the finery of her silk dress and the fastidiousness of her grooming. "And who might I tell him is calling when he returns?"

At this inquiry, Pippa performed a perfect imitation of a woman disgraced. She issued a frantic glance over her shoulder, lowered her voice, and leaned towards the butler as if divulging a precious secret. "You may tell him it's Duchess Rustenburgh."

At the utterance of the phrase *Duchess*, the butler's eyes flew wide, and he flung the door open in turn. "Why of course, Your Grace! With pleasure. Please, do follow me to the study; Master Kent will return to formally receive you."

And with that, we were whisked across the threshold of Windus Hall with a degree of fanfare apparently reserved for royalty. Up the grand staircase we went, Pippa exuding pompous entitlement with every prim step of her lavish leather boots and swish of her satin gown. I could nearly believe her charade myself, and I was her closest confidante! I focused on keeping my eyes lowered and demeanour proper, for I was not meant to be her ardent admirer but her faithful servant. We reached the landing of the second floor, and the butler led us down a long, narrow hallway to a heavy oak door at its terminus.

"Please, take a seat, Your Grace," he insisted with an elaborate bow as we entered the room. It was a predictably stodgy, formal sort of study, laden with dark wood and dusty tomes and a massive, ornate desk positioned at its centre. "Might I offer you some refreshment? Tea? A bottle of soda, perhaps?"

"No, thank you," Pippa replied with a perfectly put-upon air. "I am altogether too apprehensive to indulge in my current state. Do you suppose your master will be long?"

"Certainly not, Your Grace, if he was expecting you."

"Very well, then. I should like to be left in peace until Mr. Kent returns, if you please."

"Of course, Your Grace. As you wish."

With that, the butler turned and exited the study, firmly shutting the door behind him. We were in!

The moment the door clicked shut behind him, Pippa sprang to her feet, her face flushed with excitement. "Excellent! So where do we start?" I took the opportunity to assess the room, drawing upon all the fictions I'd ever read to determine the most likely hiding places for anything incriminating.

"You start with the bookshelves," I commanded. It was no

small task: they covered the entirety of the western wall, but at least it would not strain her injured arm. "You needn't search each volume in turn; just give it a quick tug to be sure the weight matches its size, and that it is not a false front."

"Right."

"Oh, and do be on the lookout for any hidden doors that may lead to a secret chamber." Pippa's eyes lit up at the prospect, and she gleefully commenced her duty.

Meanwhile, I turned my attention to the filing cabinet wedged against the far wall. Upon finding it unlocked, I abandoned the prospect at once: There was no chance a man of William's cunning would leave incriminating evidence in a location so obvious yet insecure.

Moving on, I appraised the walls. The wainscoting embellishing them was crafted of dark raised mahogany panels. I approached each in turn and knocked lightly, listening for the telltale echo that would signal a disguised cubby behind it, yet once again I came up short.

The desk was next. It was inevitably locked, but a quick twist of my hairpin alleviated the problem. I rifled through the papers inside, but it contained nothing more than the predictable bank statements, ledgers, and deeds, along with a pile of tedious correspondences signed with unfamiliar names. Nothing of help. With a huff of frustration, I checked the backs of the drawers for hidden compartments but once again came up empty-handed.

"Any luck?" Pippa kept her voice low, and I responded in kind.

"Not yet." I rose to my feet to check her progress; she was only a third of the way through her search, so I did not abandon hope at her prospects. Instead, I took the opportunity to approach the window and look across the balcony to the house next door. To my relief, Noah was sweeping away at the gutter, his cap tipped back to allow him maximum visibility as he swivelled his head back and forth, checking the street below for signs of our opponent. Reassured by our lookout, I gathered my resolve and cast my eyes around the room for other points of interest.

They fell upon the large ornate painting behind the desk, featuring an unremarkable pastoral scene of a foxhunt mounted in an audaciously ornate gold frame. Narrowing my gaze, I took in the sheen of the gold, my scepticism mounting. It had an odd, garish lustre to it, at odds with the mellow sheen I recalled seeing upon the similar frames in my uncle's house. I approached the piece and reached up to grasp it, the frame oddly warm beneath my fingers instead of the cool chill I'd expect of metal. The frame was painted wood! With ease, I lifted it away from the wall, revealing . . . *a safe*.

"Pippa!" I hissed, and she was at my side at once, helping me deposit the painting upon the floor so we could better evaluate the small door behind it. It was small, no larger than a breadbox, but sturdily constructed with a thick panel of steel, solid iron bolts, reinforced hinges, and a hardy copper lock, the complex keyhole making a mockery of my paltry hairpins.

"Drat," I muttered as I leaned in to inspect it. "We'll need the key to get in, there's no way I can crack this."

Pippa visibly deflated from the high of our discovery. "I'll keep looking." With that, she returned to the bookshelf with an air of fresh resolution.

For my part, I turned and took in the room with fresh eyes. *Where would one hide a key in a chamber such as this?* I'd already searched the desk, which would have been the most convenient spot. There were no knickknacks upon the shelves beneath which to hide a clandestine object, so that was out of the question. For a moment, my heart leapt as I flipped the painting around to check the back of it, but no key was secured there. There was no other art adorning the walls, either. There was of course the possibility that William carried the key upon his person, but I could not allow such a devastating scenario to derail me.

Think, I scolded myself. *Think.*

I cast my sights upon the statuary, the only other decoration adorning the study. Situated about the room were six small statues displayed upon elegant pedestals. Five were positioned between the towering windows overlooking the balcony on the northern wall, each portraying a different, imposing-looking predator cast in bronze: a lion, a hawk, a panther, a wolf, a bear. Recalling the hidden nature of the man whose study they adorned, a shiver ran up my spine.

But my gaze was quickly drawn to the sixth statue: a plaster rendering of Justice, blindfolded and hoisting her scale aloft, incongruously situated beside the doorway opposite all the others. My intuition drew me to it, and before I could doubt myself, I grasped the statue and pulled it from its base.

"Dell, what are you— "

Pippa's interjection was interrupted by the unmistakable *clang* of an iron key hitting the floor. With a cry of victory, I deposited the statue back upon its pedestal, scooped up the key, and rushed back to the safe. As the lock unfastened and the door swung open, Pippa and I exchanged excited grins, and I reached inside to extract the contents and deposit them upon the desk.

There was a stack of bonds certified by the Bank of London, a small amount of cash, and the life insurance policy for one *Samuel Saville Kent*, whom I assumed to be the family patriarch. Casting these aside, I set my attention upon a stack of letters bound together with a thin string which had been stashed in the furthest corner of the vault. Taking half, I shoved the rest towards Pippa.

"Read these, as quickly as you can. There must be something important in here, for all his other correspondence was stored in his desk. These must be special."

We rifled through the letters as briskly as we could, and the pattern immediately revealed itself: they were letters from his father regarding the state of William's inheritance. From the terse tone they took, it was clear that Samuel was reluctant to bestow his wealth upon his only son, and it was clearer still that William was egregiously persistent on the matter. Yet this was nothing we hadn't known before! And while embarrassing, the contents were hardly incriminating, for there was no evidence of wrongdoing on William's part because of them.

I was about to give up hope when my fingers fell upon an envelope that was quite unlike the others. It was thinner, flimsier, different from the lavish stationery upon which Samuel Kent's letters were penned. Pulling it open, an unfamiliar script met my eye, and the contents made my blood run cold.

> *I now what you have done Mr. Kent your sister Constance revealed all to me. I have proof you murdered little Savil and made your sister taik the blame. You are a wicked man and you must pay. Deliver a sum of 500 pounds to the Ten Bells on Commercial Street, Whitechapel, to the barkeep mister Stokes. By 8 September, or you will be sorry. If you do not I will tell the polis of your cryme.*

"Pippa!" I exclaimed, thrusting the letter at her. I watched her eyes widen as she reviewed its contents.

"Blackmail," she murmured, and I nodded eagerly in affirmation.

"That explains it! Somehow, someone at the Ten Bells found out Miss Kaye's secret, and they tried to use it against William."

Pippa's brow furrowed. "But how could they have known? Miss Kaye insisted she told no one, and she had no association with any of the dead women!"

I bit my lip, turning this over in my mind. "I don't know."

Pippa paused to consider this, but a moment later, her eyes darted to look out over my shoulder, suddenly panicked. "Dell, look!"

I followed her gaze to find Noah hopping up and down upon the roof of the neighbouring home, waving his red kerchief above his head like a lunatic.

"Bloody buggering hell," I muttered, cramming the letter into my pocket and frantically gathering the remaining items from the desk to stuff back into the safe. As I was about to close the door, my eye caught something glittering in the furthest back corner. Despite our predicament, I could not resist the urge to investigate, and I pulled out the mysterious item.

My heart seized in my chest. It was three gold rings tied with a string, the exact description of those stolen from the hand of Annie Chapman.

"Dell, hurry!" Swearing, I thrust the damning evidence back into the safe and slammed the door, turning around just in time to see Pippa place the key back beneath the statue. I hoisted the painting into place before scanning the rest of the study but could see no further signs of our intrusion.

"Quickly," I muttered. "Perhaps we can still take our leave through the front entrance before William arrives." We hurried to the study door and pulled it open, just in time to hear voices echoing up from the entrance hall.

"Indeed, sir, the Duchess. She insisted you were expecting her."

"Shit!" Pippa hissed as we backed into the study. "What do we do now?"

I gritted my teeth, irritated that there was no way to escape without arousing suspicion. We'd have to settle for escaping with our lives, instead. "This way." I grabbed Pippa's hand and pulled her across the room to the great glass door that opened to the balcony. Pushing it open, we fled onto the terrace and straight into the eyeline of a panicked-looking Noah.

"What the hell were you two doing? I've been signalling you for ages!" He shouted across the gap between us, apparently completely disinterested in maintaining our discretion.

"Sorry!" I gasped. "But Noah, we found it! We found—"

"Never bloody mind what you found, William is back in the house! Come on!" With a swift motion, he hoisted the ladder up from the street and swung it over to traverse the space between his rooftop and our balcony. "Pippa, let's go!"

"You have *got* to be kidding me." Pippa was distinctly pale as she peered down over the balustrade at the distance to the alley below.

"Have you got a better idea?" Noah countered. "*Now!*"

"Oh, for God's sake." With that, Pippa swung her leg over the railing, catching the rung of the ladder beneath the heel of her boot in a flourish of satin and lace.

"Dell, hold on to your end, too!" Noah barked, and I rushed forward to steady the ladder.

Pippa pulled her other leg over and secured her foot on the rung, then leaned forward to crawl towards Noah on her hands and knees, no small feat with only one functional arm. Were we not in imminent peril, the sight would have been distinctly humorous, and I noted we had already garnered plenty of attention from the pedestrians passing on the street below.

"Hurry!" Noah shouted. "He'll be up at any moment!"

"Oh, why don't *you* try crawling about one-handed in a goddamned petticoat and see how fast you can move!" she spat back irritably from beneath the brim of her bonnet.

Noah was abruptly chastened. "Right, right, just . . . Come on, a little further! You've got it, almost there . . ." His encouraging tone did appear to influence Pippa, whose movements grew steadier and more determined as she neared the roofline. "That's it, just a bit more . . ." Noah released his grip on one side of the ladder to reach for her hand, which she eagerly clasped. With a triumphant shout, Noah pulled her into his arms and whirled her to safety.

I was about to join in the celebration myself when I watched, horrified, as Pippa's boot heel clipped the furthest rung of the ladder, catching it and jerking it towards her. I tried to tighten my hold, but it was too late: the ladder slipped from my grasp and off the balcony railing, the weight of it pulling the opposite end from the rooftop and sending the whole contraption clattering to the alley below.

"No!" Both Noah and Pippa stared back at me, wild-eyed, the chasm between us now unbreachable.

I would have to find another way. I ran back towards the study, gambling that perhaps I could make it down the hallway and hide in a bedroom until such a time that it was safe to escape. But just as I stepped inside, the study door flew open, revealing the one and only William Kent.

He looked just as he had that night on Berner Street, his dark eyes bottomless in their intensity, and his face a wild mask of fury. Our eyes locked, and for a moment, I was certain I was about to meet my end.

I did the only thing I could think of to do: I turned and sprinted back onto the balcony, launched myself at the railing, and jumped as high and far as my legs could carry me. I did not dare hesitate. And I did not look down.

The next thing I knew, I was being pulled into the arms of my dearest companions, my back foot slipping perilously off the edge of the roof, but my front foot catching me, steady and true. I heaved my weight forward, and Noah and Pippa moved in tandem and yanked me to safety, away from the ledge.

There was no time to celebrate, for the villain was right behind me. "We have to go!" I shouted, and the three of us raced up the pitch of the roof and over to the opposite side. Once out of sight of the balcony, we scrambled across a series of sloping rooftops before locating a downspout that dropped into a small, quiet yard. We shimmied down it one by one, dashed across the yard, and emerged into the blissful anonymity of Portland Avenue.

Noah wiped the sweat from his brow with the red handkerchief. Pippa smoothed the front of her frock and straightened her bonnet. I adjusted my cap and gave them both a curt nod. And with that, we set off for home.

We arrived back at Miss Kaye's office to find her already there, pacing anxiously, a look of palpable relief crossing her face at the sight of us. "Thank goodness! I've been worried sick! I couldn't contain William. He cut our conversation short and stormed off, I feared the worst—"

"We're alright," I consoled her, "but it was a near miss."

Miss Kaye shook her head, looking less than reassured. "This plan was folly; foolish and dangerous. You could have been killed—"

"But we weren't," Pippa piped up unexpectedly, looking rather pleased with herself. "The butler believed our story, we got access to William's study, and Noah bravely alerted us to the danger as soon as William returned, and here we are, perfectly unharmed." None of us sought to mention how nearly it had all gone terribly wrong, lest we undermine her confidence in us completely.

"That said, I'm afraid we didn't exactly make a clean getaway," I confessed. "William knows there were strangers in his study, and there's a chance he'll notice something's missing."

Miss Kaye finally stopped her pacing. "Missing? What would be missing?"

"This." From the folds of my apron, I produced the letter, which I handed to her for review. She stared down at it, eyes flicking across the incriminating words, the crease between her brows deepening as she took it all in. Finally, she lifted her gaze to meet ours once more.

"I don't understand it. This letter—William accused me of this very thing when I met him this afternoon. He insisted that I had confessed our secret to someone, and that he was going to make me pay. But that's just it: I never told a living soul the truth about Saville's death! I pleaded my innocence to William, he called me a liar and left without further discussion."

"And you haven't any idea who else might have found out?" Noah queried.

"There's no one, I swear it upon my life," Miss Kaye affirmed.

"Then there's only one person who knows what's truly going on," I interjected, and all three of their faces turned towards me in tandem. "One Mr. Stokes, of the Ten Bells pub."

The next day found the three of us back upon the streets of Whitechapel, this time with a rather different mission than our last. Miss Kaye had been predictably reluctant to let us continue our detective work after the close call with William, but between the low stakes of interviewing a barman in broad daylight and her obligation to continue running the school single-handedly, she'd had little choice but to capitulate.

I was more confident in our strategy than ever before. Though Miss Kaye had interviewed Mr. Stokes multiple times during her surveillance at the Bells to no avail, the blackmail letter provided us with excellent leverage. Though blackmail was hardly murder, it was still a crime, and I was certain that if pressed, Mr. Stokes would speak to us in the interest of self-preservation—if not to save a life.

The Ten Bells pub was the first tavern in which I had ever set foot, and it lived up to every one of the expectations conjured in my tales of highwaymen and rogues. The ceiling was low, the tables were grimy, and the patrons a haphazard jumble of the city's least desirables. Noah, Pippa, and I turned a few heads as we entered, and I strongly suspected it had more to do with our respectable manner of dress than our age. We sidled up to the bar as casually as we could, ignoring the murmurs behind us.

Positioned behind the bar was a large, portly man with a handlebar moustache, dressed in a pair of festively patterned suspenders and a matching cravat. Upon seeing us approach, he reluctantly recused himself from an animated conversation with a pair of grizzled-looking railwaymen to make his way over to us, a curious expression on his face.

"Good afternoon, sir, ladies. What can I do ye for?"

"A ginger beer for me, please, and lemonade for the ladies," Noah replied with a put-upon air of stoic confidence (the thought of Noah drinking a beer would ordinarily have made me giggle, were we not working a beat).

A look of mild amusement crossed the tender's face, but he procured our beverages without question before turning away, clearly eager to return to his previous conversation.

"Excuse me, sir?" I piped up, and he swivelled his head round, now looking distinctly inconvenienced and reluctant to engage.

"Yes, miss?"

"Are you Mr. Stokes?"

His eyes narrowed. "Depends on who's asking."

I shot Pippa a purposeful look. This was the moment that we most required her charm.

"A friend of a friend," she interjected with a simpering smile.

Mr. Stokes eyed her fair face suspiciously, but he reluctantly returned to stand before us, arms crossed. "And who might that be?"

"The author of this letter," I supplied, and laid my ace upon the bar top.

Mr. Stokes' eyes widened as he took in the contents of the note. "Where did ye get this?" He reached out as if to grab it, but I retracted it before his fingertips could touch it.

"From the aforementioned friend."

"Did *he* send ye here? I told 'im myself, his quarrel's not with me." His tone had gone sharp.

This was an unexpected turn. We had all assumed that Mr. Stokes had simply conspired with one of William's victims and was now living in fear following her death, but it appeared William had already made threats of his own.

I cleared my throat and pressed him. “We’re merely seeking information.”

“Look, I already told ’im everything I know. I gave ’im the list, and it appears ’e listened, based on what the papers are sayin’.”

“Then by all means,” Pippa replied coyly, leaning into her role with a flutter of her eyelashes. “Reiterate that list for us, one more time, so we can be sure we haven’t missed anyone.”

Stokes scowled, then counted off on his fingers. “Nichols. Chapman. Stride. Eddowes. Kelly. The five of ’em met here, and they drafted that bit.” He gestured towards the paper I held firmly in my grip. “Told me they’d give me ten quid if I’d take the deposit. I agreed, I didn’t even know what was in that bloody letter! Better not to ask, when it comes to these things. End of story, I figured, until yer boss came through here and threatened to cut my entrails out if I didn’t tell him everything I knew.”

The three of us exchanged a pointed look. So, William had threatened Stokes with death if he didn’t reveal the conspirators—that would explain how he’d been able to pick his targets so precisely!

I focused on the one piece of information that could still be of use. “The fifth woman, Kelly. What can you tell us about her?”

Stokes shook his head. “Word about town is that she’s left for the continent, what with everything that’s happened to the others. She’ll not be back ’round these parts, that’s all I can tell ye.”

Pippa adjusted her expression into something that could almost seem *dangerous*, taking on the role of aggressor with an aplomb I would not have previously thought her capable of. “But if we urgently needed to, say, *relay her a message* . . . How might we best go about doing that?”

“Hell if I know. But your best bet’s right over there.” He pointed across the room at a young woman dressed in servant’s clothing, her dark hair piled upon her head in a messy bun, her cheeks rosy from the libations. "That's an old friend of 'ers, Miss Harvey. If anyone knows where Mary Jane is at, it's her." Pippa smiled, a slow, calculated thing that seemed more predatory than personal. "Thank you, Mr. Stokes. You've been *such* a help today. Our *boss* extends his gratitude." With a nod of her head, Noah and I followed at her heels as we turned our sights on our next target.

Miss Harvey barely looked up from her pint as we approached her table. Her attention was focused upon the two gentlemen seated with her, both dressed in what at one point must have been rather fine suits but had clearly seen better days. Up close, her fair features were marred with signs of hard living: her skin was ruddy and chapped, her hair an unkempt tangle, her dress worn through and patched. Despite all this, however, her disposition was cheerful, and she appeared unperturbed by our presence.

"Excuse me, Miss Harvey?" I ventured, and she paused in her revelry to at last look up.

Taking in the three of us, her expression turned to one of confusion. "Alright?"

"Pardon the interruption, but we're looking for a friend of yours, Miss Mary Jane Kelly?"

At this, she slumped back into her chair, looking annoyed.

"It's like I told Stokes, told her landlord, told her gentlemen friends, she's gone."

"Where to?"

"Abroad." She took a swig of her drink, a defiant expression upon her face.

"Where abroad?" I pressed, not willing to give up on our only current lead.

"Hell if I know, I'm not her minder."

"Why did she leave?" Pippa chimed in from beside me.

At this, Miss Harvey threw us a smirk. "What's it to you? Doubt she was a friend of yours."

I paused, taking it all in. If Mary Jane Kelly truly were the fifth and final conspirator, perhaps her escape abroad was indeed enough to spare her the current danger. The odds of William finding her were surely slim, if she'd left behind so few clues to her whereabouts.

At that moment, Noah stepped in. "Listen, I'm her brother. I heard she was in a spot of trouble, but I've been unable to locate her. If you happen to hear anything about her whereabouts, could you let us know?"

"Christ almighty, child, how daft do you think I am? Why should I trust you?"

I made a split-second decision. "Because we're trying to protect her from becoming the next victim of the Whitechapel killer."

In that moment, Miss Harvey's pint paused halfway to her chapped lips, hovering in midair as if frozen by a sorcerer's spell. Her eyes finally rose to meet mine, and they were full of terror.

I lowered my voice conspiratorially. "Look, we know she's being hunted, and we're trying to help. If she makes contact, please, I'm begging you: let us help her. Tell her to come to Whitechapel Hall, on Buck's Row. She'll be safe there." Miss Harvey said nothing, but the fear on her face spoke volumes.

"And we'll pay you five quid for any information you pass on," Noah added.

That appeared to do the trick. "Aye, now that's the spirit, dearie," Miss Harvey drawled and tossed back the remainder of her drink, the tender truce between us broken. "You have yourself a deal. If Miss Mary Jane Kelly ever darkens my doorway again, you lot will be the first to know."

Chapter XVII
Tracked to Death

The most infuriating element of our investigation was Miss Kaye's highly inconvenient obligation to run the entire school herself, which meant that from the morning bell through our final meal, she was preoccupied with teaching, supervising chores, or overseeing her newest method of keeping her wards in line: lengthy periods of silent reading in the chapel. Her refusal to allow us to resume our outreach and instead keep us firmly locked inside the Hall inevitably made her a great villain among our peers. Pippa and I alone understood that our isolation was not so much for our protection as it was her own, but we could hardly present that as a defence during Beatrice's nightly diatribe about the injustice of it all.

Instead, we were forced to carry out our days with an aura of casual indifference, mouths sealed firmly shut as the other girls whinged and moaned, until our dismissal from dinner, at which point Pippa and I would nightly be summoned to Miss Kaye's office to continue our detective work under the guise of detention for an unspecified crime (Beatrice had started a rather convenient rumour that the two of us had come to blows, which did wonders to excuse the state of my face and Pippa's arm).

There, we would reconvene with Noah, who would fill us in on all the happenings of the outside world.

For better or worse, Mary Jane Kelly's departure from London seemed to have brought William's reign of terror to an abrupt halt. Though the papers were loath to abandon the tawdry headlines and salacious illustrations, they soon turned their attention away from the crimes to focus on the bumbling incompetence of the police force. There was a blissful flurry of activity when news broke that the fiend had been writing taunting letters to the press, but it took us mere minutes to deduce they were bombastic fakes. After that, there were no further breaks in the case.

The weather turned cold and blustery, the sunlight streaming through the windows paler and more fleeting with each passing day. Pippa's arm healed, and Miss Kaye removed her stitches (under the influence of some much-deserved brandy). Pippa and I still escaped to our perch each night for a smoke, but it was clear that our days of accessing the roof without the peril of ice were numbered. The Hall seemed to grow smaller and smaller as our seclusion dragged on without end in sight, for Miss Kaye did not dare open the doors to the outside world knowing the predator that stalked her would not relent until his mission was complete. Time dragged on in a painful dirge, until not even Noah's visits could cheer us, for the case was trapped in a perpetual impasse.

And then, as all things inevitably do, everything changed at once. It was Bonfire Night, the streets below filled with rowdy and raucous energy, a distinct turn from the grim-faced vigilance of the previous month. Pippa and I had just returned to the annex from our nightly smoke, shivering in the draughty loft as we prepared for bed, when a sudden intrusion caught us both off guard.

"Oi, Batty! Miss Kaye wants to see you. And bring your little pet, too!" Beatrice's voice echoed up from the stairwell, followed by a predictable chorus of *oohs* from the other girls downstairs.

Pippa and I exchanged a pointed look. Our meeting with Noah and Miss Kaye earlier that evening had yielded no new progress, so it was clear that something had unexpectedly changed. As hastily as we could, we pulled on our frocks and boots and clambered down the stairs, ignoring the catty whispers that followed us through the dormitory and out the door. We arrived at Miss Kaye's office breathless with anticipation but disappointingly found her seated calmly behind her desk, thumbing through her Bible with a dispassionate expression on her face.

"Miss Kaye? You wanted to see us?"

She looked up, the light gleaming off her too-flat spectacles, giving her a moon-eyed appearance. "Yes, please, ladies, come in. And do close the door behind you." We complied wordlessly, anticipation heavy in the air as we took our seats across from her.

"I have news on two fronts," she began blandly. Pippa and I leaned in, our excitement generating a current in the air. "First: The headmaster will be returning to Whitechapel Hall tomorrow. He has secured a significant endowment from an anonymous source right here in London, and he believes this will carry the school through its current predicament until the matter of the former instructor fades into the recesses of memory."

My enthusiasm faltered as my mind spiralled around the prospect. "But if he returns, how will we continue our investigation? We can't very well do all our sleuthing in the time allocated for outreach, and he'll no doubt disapprove of our after-hours meetings, and— "

A stern glare from Miss Kaye cowed me into silence. "Secondly, I received an unexpected visitor just now: one Miss Maria Harvey, demanding a sum of five pounds in exchange for an address."

"What?!" Pippa and I cried in unison. "She was here?"

"What did she say?"

"Is Miss Kelly back?"

"Mary Jane Kelly is indeed back in London, having been unable to sustain her stay on the continent due to a purported lack of connections and funds. She has returned to Whitechapel, most likely out of desperation, or perhaps mistakenly believing that the danger has passed. But I know William, and he will not rest until his revenge is complete."

"Will she come here to the Hall?" I inquired breathlessly.

"For now, according to her friend, she has refused. I can't say I blame the girl: she knows nothing about us, only that you were searching for her at the Bells, and for all she knows, you could just as well be on William's payroll."

"We must go to her, then, and earn her trust." Pippa chimed in, and Miss Kaye nodded in agreement.

"Precisely."

I leapt to my feet, inspired by our first break in the case in weeks. "Excellent! We'll grab our cloaks and be on our way."

"We're going *now*?" Pippa squeaked, looking daunted at the prospect.

"Of course we are. Right, Miss Kaye? After all, if we know she's back in town, it's only a matter of time before William finds out. As Noah always says, word travels fast on Whitechapel streets."

Miss Kaye looked torn. "We ought to wait until daylight, and perhaps bring Mr. Levy with us to fortify our strength in numbers—"

"But time is of the essence!" I protested. "Tomorrow the headmaster will be back, and then who knows when we'll be able to sneak out again! We can't keep excusing our absence as detention; someone is bound to notice eventually. Come on, we'll fetch Noah on the way. Please, Miss Kaye, it's now or never."

A resolute expression crossed her face, and she removed her spectacles as she rose to her feet, depositing them on her desk with a resounding *clack*. "Very well. You girls go get your cloaks. I shall lock the dormitory for the night and meet you in the entrance hall."

Pippa and I scurried from her office with fire at our heels. I noticed that Miss Kaye lagged considerably behind us, and I had an inkling her delay had something to do with the knife we had seen her stow beneath her mattress after our last fateful encounter with William.

The streets of Whitechapel were still buzzing with energy despite the late hour, a marked difference from the last time we'd escaped the Hall a seeming lifetime ago. Constables still patrolled the sidewalks in pairs, batons in hand, but the un-uniformed men of the Vigilance Committee had exchanged pitchforks and crowbars for torches to join in the night's festivities. The sailors and rogues gathered outside the gin palaces were more boisterous than usual, and their drunken cavorting enveloped us in a dull roar. Miss Kaye, Pippa, and I passed through all this blissfully unnoticed, the revelry affording us the anonymity we needed. We made our way up High Street at a brisk clip, arms linked, eyes straightforward, allowing no divergence from our mission.

Standing in front of Noah's shop, I recognised a minor oversight in our plan: While pebbles against the window frame had worked to summon Noah's attention in the past, at this late hour I could in no way guarantee that they would rouse our intended target and not his beleaguered mother or short-tempered father. Alas, we quickly concluded that pleading forgiveness was our only recourse: there was simply no way of relaying the direness of our mission without taking the risk. The moment was ours to seize, and it was with a renewed sense of purpose that I flung the first stone.

Four attempts later, the window flew open, and to my relief,

Noah's head emerged, his expression transitioning from bewilderment to utter shock as recognition washed over him.

"Dell! Pippa! Miss Kaye? What in the—What the *hell*?" I could tell from the annoyance and panic intermingling upon his features that our situation was precarious indeed.

"Noah, please," Pippa pleaded from beside me in a frantic whisper. "We need to talk to you."

"Now? It's nearly midnight! And what are the three of you doing outside the school? Have you forgotten there's a damned murderer on the loose?"

"That's just it, we've made a break in the case! Mary Jane Kelly is back in London and—"

Noah's demeanour shifted instantly. "I'll be down in a moment," he hissed, throwing a paranoid look back over his shoulder at the darkened room behind him. "Now go wait on the other side of the street, I'll be brought before the beth din myself if you're spotted hovering around. *Go.*"

"Bring a knife!" I implored before the slam of the window brought our conversation to an abrupt end.

Admonished, Miss Kaye, Pippa and I scurried across the street to wait beneath the streetlamp, where moments later we were joined by a harried-looking Noah, whose disposition could not be any more different than it was during our evening debriefings.

"Noah, thank you so much for coming down, you've got to hear us out—" I started.

Head bowed and collar pulled high, he took us by the elbows and steered us briskly down the street. "Not here, I can't risk being seen consorting with a trio of gentiles at this time of night, come on. Where are we going?"

"Miller's Court," Miss Kaye replied simply, "Off Dorset Street. Miss Harvey was kind enough to make it plain."

"So, she came to you?" Noah asked, his cheeks flushed with what I suspected was excitement despite his initial misgivings about our unannounced visit.

"She did, though she was unable to convince Miss Kelly to join her. Speaking of which, the three of you owe me a sum of five pounds, as I don't recall giving you permission to offer a reward on your fact-finding journey to the Bells."

"Um . . ." I exchanged a frantic look with Pippa and Noah, who were clearly in no position to offer such a sum either.

"Relax, that was a joke," Miss Kaye continued with a look of mild amusement turning up her lips, and the three of us shared a nervous laugh, half relief, half anticipation. "Now, we have no reason to believe that William is aware of Miss Kelly's return to Whitechapel, but even so, we must proceed with extreme caution. When we arrive at her lodgings, the three of you will stand guard until I've determined it's safe for you to enter. Understood?"

"Please, Miss Kaye, as the only gentleman present, I really ought to—"

"Nonsense, Noah. You have risked enough already, all of you, and you have my eternal gratitude. But my own flesh and blood wrought this chaos, and it is my secret that put Miss Kelly in danger. I must be the one to end it."

There could be no counterargument that, and the three of us followed her lockstep in a quiet procession through the crowded streets, our own solemn task so at odds with the jubilant celebrations surrounding us that it all seemed distinctly surreal.

We floated invisibly down Commercial Street, weaving between the late-night revellers spilling from the pubs, dodging the firecrackers and dipping beneath the burning effigies as we wove our way towards our destination. The air was thick and acrid with smoke, which turned every figure into a hazy apparition. To my own frenzied mind, any one of them could be William, knife in hand, prepared to ambush us in a bloody coup. From the safe confines of Whitechapel Hall, saving Miss Kelly had seemed an obvious, practical endeavour, but outside its doors, fear took hold and rattled my heart within my chest.

A sickening sequence of scenes swam before my watering

eyes: the flash of William's knife poised to strike at Pippa's chest, the cold fury upon his face as he discovered me in his study, Miss Stride's palpable terror as her life bled out onto my shaking hands . . . The mirage swirled and danced before me in the flames of the passing bonfires, and I struggled not to swoon.

Turning off the main thoroughfare onto Dorset Street was like emerging from a dream. The narrow road was dark and vacant, a jarring juxtaposition to the bacchanale of Commercial Street. There were no streetlamps, and the only light was that which spilled from lonely windows dotting the dilapidated lodging houses which lined it. I shook my head to clear it.

"Just here," Miss Kaye murmured in a hushed tone, pushing open a rickety gate to our right. We continued through a dim covered passage and emerged into a small, enclosed courtyard, where a single lamp burning in the corner illuminated a decrepit water pump and dented dustbin. The rest of the yard was empty.

"Which number?" I whispered. Though there was no reason to believe we were in imminent danger, the stark stillness of the place had me feeling distinctly on edge.

"Thirteen," Miss Kaye replied. Wordlessly, the four of us separated and spread out across the courtyard, squinting to deduce the door numbers in the low light.

Moments later, Pippa's voice echoed in the darkness. "This one!"

We convened in front of a ramshackle door with the number 13 scrawled upon it in faded paint. Two windows faced outward towards the courtyard beside it, but both were dark. The place appeared empty.

"Perhaps she's asleep?" Pippa offered hopefully.

"Perhaps." Miss Kaye sounded unconvinced, but even so, she raised her hand and knocked.

To the surprise of no one, no answer came. Miss Kaye rapped again, louder this time, but there was no response save an echoing silence.

With a defeated expression, she dug into her pocket, producing a folded square of paper. "I prepared a note. We shall leave this here and implore her to come to the Hall."

"A note?" I protested. "But what good will that do? She'll have no more reason to trust us than she did before, she'll just be terrified that we've somehow found out where she lives. Besides, aren't you curious?"

Miss Kaye paused. "Curious? About what?"

"About how she knew your secret!"

"Of course, but I shall simply ask her in person when—"

"*Or*," I interrupted, "we could have a look about the place for clues."

Miss Kaye raised an eyebrow sceptically. "Clues?"

"Yes, clues! You don't honestly believe that she would blackmail a man of your brother's status without some sort of proof, do you? She must have a piece of evidence at hand; rumour and hearsay wouldn't suffice to indict a gentleman on the word of five fallen women."

Our bickering was interrupted by the sound of the door shaking within its frame, and we turned to see Noah pulling futilely at the handle. "It's locked." He sounded distinctly forlorn.

"Use your hairpin trick, Dell!" Pippa suggested, but a quick glance at the lock revealed it to be double-bitted.

"It's the wrong type," I moaned. "Though maybe . . . Miss Kaye, have you got your knife? We could just jimmy it—"

"Wait, you're carrying a knife?" Noah sounded somewhere between scandalised and impressed.

"Not that it's anyone's business, but yes, I am, Mr. Levy. And to answer your question, Miss Morton, no, you may not use it to break into Miss Kelly's private residence."

"But if we could just have a quick poke about—"

"Oops." Our quarrel was brought to an abrupt halt by the sound of smashing glass. Miss Kaye, Noah, and I whirled around to see Pippa, cloak wrapped around her fist, shaking shards of broken glass into the rough packed dirt of the courtyard. The windowpane directly next to the doorknob was shattered.

"Miss Fitzroy! Did you seriously just vandalise a window to gain entry to her abode?"

Pippa blinked her wide blue eyes with all the innocence of an angel. "My hand slipped."

"Oh, for the love of God—*Miss Fitzroy!*" Miss Kaye looked completely beside herself as Pippa reached her hand through the empty pane and flipped the lock open from the inside.

"Sorry," Pippa replied with a sweet shrug. "It slipped again."

Miss Kaye let out an audible sigh but nevertheless set her shoulders, straightened her back, and reached for the doorknob. "You three wait out here." With that, she pushed the door open and disappeared into the darkness. A moment later, a lamp inside flickered to life, and Pippa, Noah, and I crowded the doorframe to peer inside. Miss Kaye was hovering at the far end of the room, having lit the lantern perched upon the mantle of the fireplace. The space was small and cramped, and we could tell in an instant that it was vacant. With a nod, I led my two companions inside.

Miss Kelly's lodgings were woefully sparse. There was a shabby bed with a ramshackle headboard, a bedside table, and a small table presumably used for dining positioned in front of the fire, populated by a lone chair. There was little in the way of possessions, just a ragged shawl hung upon a peg by the door, a comb, a shard of mirror, a Bible, and a tin cup and plate stashed on the mantle beside the lamp.

The grim surroundings were depressing enough, but a quick glance around the place revealed that there were very few locations in which a precious clue might be stashed. Refusing to be deterred, I took a quick survey and issued my commands.

"Pippa, check inside the fireplace. It doesn't look like it's often lit, so a shrewd woman may use it to stash a valuable possession.

Noah, inspect the undersides of the tables and chair for anything suspicious: a scrap of paper, a mysterious key. And Miss Kaye, would you be so kind as to help me flip the mattress?"

The space was so small that within seconds, we concluded that there was nothing incriminating hidden within Miss Kelly's abode. Unlike William's office, there was not an endless array of clever hidey-holes in which to squirrel away evidence, and there was nary a locked trunk or sealed safe to pique our curiosity. The room was simply as it seemed: plain, drab, and frustratingly, infuriatingly empty.

Miss Kaye broke the disappointed silence. "Alas. It seems we shall have to resort to leaving the note; there is nothing here to explain Miss Kelly's involvement with William." She withdrew the paper from her pocket once more and turned it over in her fingers. "After all, we'd best be getting back to the Hall. The hour grows late." She turned and walked towards the mantle, lifting the note to leave upon it.

An odd creak reverberated through the room as she trod upon the floorboard nearest the hearth. Though none of my companions reacted, in an instant, my mind conjured the tale of Mrs. Paschal's encounter with the Countess of Vervaine, and her secret passage beneath the floorboards.

"Wait!" I cried, and Miss Kaye froze. "Just there!" I pointed to the board positioned beneath the heel of her boot, and with a perplexed expression upon her face, she shifted her weight back and forth. The floorboard let out another hollow squeal.

"Of course," I exclaimed, racing to kneel over the source of the sound. "The floorboards! How silly of me—" With that, Miss Kaye lifted her heel, and I reached down to unseat the floorboard, pulling it from its position and tossing it to the side.

And there, lying in a clumsy hole hollowed from the packed subfloor, was an all-too familiar intricately carved wooden box, inlaid with ivory. It was the mirror image of the one stashed in Miss Kaye's wardrobe, though perhaps half the size, and it was obvious that the two were meant to be companions, matched pieces of a set. With a trembling hand, I reached down and withdrew it, passing it to a stunned-looking Miss Kaye.

"My God." To my shock, her face had gone pale, and her eyes were filled with tears. "My God. Ingrid. *Ingrid.*"

Pippa, Noah, and I exchanged a confused look. Rising to my feet, I asked the next obvious question. "Miss Kaye, who is Ingrid?"

The tears welled over and streaked down Miss Kaye's face, and she did not bother trying to hide them. Instead, she lowered herself onto the bed, staring at the box clutched in her hands as if in a trance. "Ingrid was my beloved." She did not explain further but instead traced the ivory floral pattern reverently with her fingers, as if conjuring a memory from its recesses.

For a long while, we remained in silence, none of us daring to interrupt Miss Kaye, her gaze a thousand miles away despite our proximity within the cramped quarters. At long last, she took a deep breath and spoke.

"Ingrid was my friend, my dearest companion, the only true source of love I have known in my life. I met her my first week working at St. Mary's Home in Brighton. She was my age, but newly with child, and had been sent to stay there for the duration of her condition. Despite our disparate upbringings—I was from a fine household, and she was from destitute Irish stock—we found in one another a sisterhood, a true soul connection, that no earthly boundaries could break. In her company I experienced true joy and purpose for the first time in my young life, and in me she found the same. We vowed that as soon as we could, we would leave the school together and start our life anew. It was that promise that saw me through some of my darkest days.

"But then William showed up and ruined it all. He framed me for Saville's killing and never once flinched as I was arrested, tried, and sentenced for his crime. In doing so, he stole not just my future but Ingrid's as well.

"William took all I had from me, but that was a burden I could bear, for I felt complicit in his evil, despite my prior ignorance of it. I cared not what the public thought, for what consequence would it have? But I could not live if Ingrid thought ill of me. So, the night before Reverend Wagner was to take me to London and deliver me to the police, I penned a letter to Ingrid. And for the first and only time since Saville's death . . . I told the truth."

With that, she pried open the lid of the little box, reached inside, and produced a tightly folded scrap of paper. She held it out to me and met my eye unwaveringly. With trembling fingers, I unfolded it and began to read aloud.

My Dearest,

By the time you read this, I shall be gone, subject to a fate so deplorable that I dare not dwell on it, lest I lose my faith in God and all his Mercies.

But the soul can endure anything, in devotion to the Lord. And I must assure you, darling, my soul is pure, and I am innocent of the crime for which I shall inevitably be convicted. I am the victim of the wicked designs of my own brother, William, who, years ago, murdered our half-brother Saville in a fit of jealous madness. Being the fool that I was, I believed William when he proclaimed the act was one of misguided benevolence. I prayed for his salvation. I believed the Lord had heard me.

But William has returned and framed me for the crime. I could fight the charges and point my finger at him, but who would believe me? I am dour, plain, and unpleasant, and have not the capacity to charm a jury.

Truth be told, love, Saville's death has weighed heavily upon me these past few years. Though I tried to convince myself that my ignorance was innocence, I see now that the Lord has other designs.

So, I shall repent, and serve my time. My penance will be long, but my greatest regret is that it will keep me from you, and the life we envisaged for ourselves so clearly that day out upon the moor. When I close my eyes, I can still see it: the cottage, the garden, a little poppet with your smile tottering about the primrose path. Please know, my love, that in my heart, I am here with you, always and forever.

I know not how long our separation will be. All I can ask is that wherever life may take you, that in your dreams you meet me in our cottage by the sea. I will wait for you there. Always.

Love,

Constance

When I at last looked up, the faces of my friends spoke the multitudes that words could not. Pippa was blinking back tears. Noah looked crestfallen. And Miss Kaye, from her seat upon the bed, looked a thousand miles away—perhaps in her cottage by the sea. In that moment, we were all transported away from the squalor of Whitechapel to another time and place, a moment that should have been but never was, a future stolen by selfishness and greed, a past fractured by regret and pain. The weight of it all was suffocating, the tiny tenement room suddenly even smaller that it initially seemed.

"What became of Ingrid?" I asked. The question felt somehow heretical.

"She died in childbirth. I received word of her passing a month after I was sentenced. I believed her child had died with her, but it would seem I was mistaken. Her child is very much alive. And the Lord has brought her here, to Whitechapel. Here, to me."

I could barely breathe.

Just then, the front door swung open, startling us so

completely that we nearly jumped out of our skins. Pippa let out an ear-splitting shriek, and both Noah and Miss Kaye were suddenly brandishing knives, the reversal of their dispositions so complete that I could scarcely comprehend what was happening. Whirling about, I found myself face to face with a young woman perhaps a few years older than myself. Her skin was fair and freckled, a shock of auburn hair pulled into a messy plait framing the elegant angles of her features, her eyes a piercing blue so stunning that I felt at once entirely exposed by her gaze. It was not until the next moment that I registered her expression as one of abject fury.

"The hell is the meaning of this? Get out! *Out!*" Though she brandished no weapon to counter those wielded by Noah and Miss Kaye, the pure power in her tone was enough to bring my hands into the air.

"Please, Miss Kelly, apologies, we were just— " I attempted.

"*Ingrid.*" Miss Kaye's voice cut through the chaos like the peal of a bell, and at once, Miss Kelly's expression was wholly altered.

"Who goes there?" She cocked her head to peer around me.

"Please. Miss Kelly—Mary—Mary Jane . . . It's me. Constance." Miss Kaye's tone was pleading, a desperate placation to the woman unexpectedly in our presence.

For a moment, Miss Kelly's eyes narrowed. The next, they flew open wide as she registered the presence of the box, haphazardly flung to the side upon the bed. "Constance?" She was breathless, clearly caught off guard.

Miss Kaye's knife fell to the floor as she reached out towards Miss Kelly. "Mary Jane. It's me, Constance. Your mother's companion."

Mary Jane hesitated, her expression still guarded, her tone wary. "What brings ye here, *Constance*?"

Miss Kaye did not falter in her resolve. "William. I have come to save you from William, Mary Jane. He is hellbent on eliminating you, and I shall follow soon after. But you needn't worry, my dear—for I have come to save you. You needn't live in fear of him any longer."

At this, Mary Jane audibly scoffed. "Och, is that so? And what, precisely, do ye plan to do to stop 'im?"

"I plan to bring you to Australia."

"What?" At this sudden revelation, I could no longer hold my tongue.

Miss Kaye didn't even spare me a look, never breaking her connection with Miss Kelly. "Please, Mary Jane. I have the funds and have long dreamt of leaving this place myself. But now I know I was brought here to Whitechapel for a purpose: to find you and bring you with me."

Then the next thing I knew, Mary Jane was pushing past me, rushing into the arms of Miss Kaye, who embraced her with the fortitude of a mother reuniting with a long-lost child.

For a long while, we all simply remained. Noah, Pippa, and I dared not break the holy peace that enveloped us as we witnessed the reunion of two souls torn apart by circumstance but reunited by fate and fortitude. And for the first time in my life, I was privy to the spoils of detective work well done. It was a reward greater than gold.

At long last, the two separated, both wiping tears from their cheeks.

Mary Jane was the first to speak. "Yes. Yes, Constance, I will go with you. It is what my mother would have wanted, of that I am certain."

Miss Kaye embraced her once more, but when they parted, her expression was one of severe consternation. "My dear, I do not blame you in the slightest, but I must know—*why?* Why would you tempt William with the threat of blackmail, knowing his disposition?"

Miss Kelly's eyes filled with unfathomable sadness. "It was desperation, pure and simple. These times . . . these times are hard, and I've struggled so. Ever since I came to London, my life has been nothing but disappointment and misfortune. This box and letter were my sole possessions, and I'd long wondered why I was cursed with such a worthless inheritance. But one night a fallen lady at the pub told a few of us about a blackmail scheme that had landed her a windfall, and it occurred to me I could use your letter to do the same. I employed several of my companions to track down William, and we conspired to squeeze him for his worth. I never thought . . . I didn't think . . . I thought he'd simply pay and be rid of us."

Miss Kaye's expression darkened. "I understand. You greatly underestimated him, but there is no shame in it; no one expects a gentleman to be a monster."

Miss Kelly shook her head woefully. "It was never my intention to cause all this suffering, you must believe me. I can see now that the true fate of the letter was never meant to be for profit. It was to bring us back together once more."

Miss Kaye's face was a portrait of maternal compassion. "Yes, my girl. Ingrid would have willed it." With a sad, slow smile, she regained her composure. "There are arrangements to be made. I shall purchase our tickets tomorrow. There is a passage to Sydney on the Orient Line that departs from London each Friday. Can you ready your affairs by then?"

Mary Jane's face was already lightening with newfound enthusiasm. "Yes, by the saints' graces, yes. I will be ready, Constance."

Miss Kaye beamed. "I must insist you come with us to stay at Whitechapel Hall in the interim. Though we have no reason to believe William is aware of your whereabouts, he is a shrewd, conniving man. You will be safest in our company until the date of our departure."

At this, Mary Jane baulked. "I would, honestly, but I'm afraid I cannot. I have my own affairs to settle."

Miss Kaye looked distinctly put out by this. "Surely

whatever the situation of your affairs, it will be remedied by your convenient disappearance from the city."

"No." Mary Jane did not waver in her insistence. "While I appreciate your offer, there are obligations I must tend to before I go, or it will weigh heavy upon my conscience. Surely you understand?"

Miss Kaye looked reluctant, but to my surprise, she capitulated. "I will be here at dawn on Friday by carriage to collect you. Until then, be safe: tell no one where you are going, do not associate with strangers, and by all means, avoid the streets after dark."

"I understand." There was still fear in her eyes, but it was now accompanied by a brave resolve that inspired me to have faith in the inevitable outcome.

"Until Friday, then, my dear."

"Until Friday."

After such an interminable period of stagnation, the whirlwind that followed our encounter with Miss Kelly was a much-needed change of pace. By all accounts, it should have appeared a return to normalcy: Headmaster Graves returned, and apparently his presence was enough to cajole Mrs. Dolmer into resuming her duties as well. Outreach was reinstated immediately, and Pippa and I found ourselves treading the familiar route to Noah's shop for our daily supplies each morning. The Reverend remained notably absent, but Miss Kaye continued to fill his position as our spiritual leader with aplomb. We fulfilled our post-dinner 'detention' in Miss Kaye's office each evening, ironing out the details of Miss Kaye and Miss Kelly's impending escape. But by night, as Pippa and I sat side-by-side on our perch overlooking the streets below, we could not help but comment upon how different our lives were about to become.

"What do you suppose they shall do about Miss Kaye's resignation?" I pondered the night before her departure, shivering in the bleak November cold and silently wondering whether Pippa or I would be the first to break and declare the weather too inclement to continue our nightly ritual.

Pippa's mouth formed a thin line, and I could tell her thoughts were burdened by her past. "I don't know. Find someone new, I suppose. Hopefully a woman."

She didn't have to clarify.

We arrived at Miss Kaye's office well before dawn the following morning, prepared to execute the final step in our grand plan. I raised my fist to knock, but the door swung open before I had a chance to lower it. Miss Kaye appeared entirely changed: she'd forsaken her spectacles once and for all, and her severe chignon had been replaced by an elegant, loosely woven braid which revealed the warm chestnut of her true hair colour. To my surprise, she looked strangely beautiful.

"Good morning, ladies."

"Morning, Miss Kaye," we chorused.

She stepped to the side, revealing her travelling trunk packed and prepared for departure. Pippa and I each took a handle, and with a curt nod, we smuggled the trunk down the hall towards the kitchen.

Our plan, while not simple, had been well rehearsed. The day prior, Miss Kaye had procured the headmaster's blessing to bring Pippa and me to the Reverend's church to collect three boxes of donated hymnals for the school. The lie was innocent enough and would allow us to accompany Miss Kaye at least as far as Miller's Court, and give us the chance to bid her and Miss Kelly a proper farewell. The two of them would carry on to port in the hackney cab, and Pippa and I would return to the school, claiming we had simply lost Miss Kaye along the way. By the time the headmaster found the note she'd left upon her desk, Miss Kaye would be well out of the city.

The clever scheme to sneak her luggage out via dumbwaiter had been my idea, and I confess it was with an air of deep satisfaction that I assisted Pippa in loading the trunk inside and lowering it to the alley below. *How beautifully poignant*, I thought, *that I once believed this dumbwaiter to be the source of my freedom, and now it will be the conduit to Miss Kaye's.*

Luggage addressed, we scampered from the kitchen out to the entrance hall, where Miss Kaye was already waiting by the door, hood of her cloak pulled up to disguise her hair until we were free of the school. Even so, the lightening of her disposition was so noticeable that it felt entirely incongruous with the woman I'd known before. Wordlessly, Pippa and I procured our cloaks and bonnets from the pegs by the door and gave Miss Kaye affirming smiles. She turned to unlock the door.

"Miss Kaye!" The three of us whirled around in disbelief to find Headmaster Graves descending the staircase, a flustered expression upon his face.

"Yes, Headmaster?" Miss Kaye's voice had once again taken on the cold, businesslike tone I associated with her prior to our alliance.

"Oh, thank goodness I've caught you. I received an urgent correspondence that our new benefactor wishes to tour the school today. He shall be here at eight o'clock sharp, and I must insist you show him the workings of the place, for heaven knows I haven't the time after such a prolonged absence. Can I entrust that you and the girls will return by then?"

Miss Kaye lowered her head as if in subservience, but I could assess that in truth she was angling her hood to hide her changed appearance. "Of course, Headmaster. Our errand will be brief; the girls will be back in time for morning prayer, and I shall be delighted to introduce our new benefactor to the workings of the Hall."

"Excellent, excellent. Very well, then, off with you! You mustn't be tardy!"

The three of us dropped into simultaneous curtsies, and Miss Kaye turned, unlocked the door, and released us into the misty morning air. We didn't speak as we procured Miss Kaye's trunk from the dumbwaiter and spirited it wordlessly out to Buck's Row, where Miss Kaye quickly hailed a cab. It wasn't until we were well down High Street that we breathed a collective sigh of relief.

"The arrival of the benefactor complicates things," Miss Kaye murmured.

"Don't worry," I replied. "We'll stall him as long as we can."

Miss Kaye offered us nothing but a tight smile in return, and we lapsed into silence as we turned onto Commercial Street. The cab slowed as we approached our destination, but we were still nearly two blocks away when it came to a halt, the horse idling skittishly as I peered around its haunch to find us stalled at the edge of a gathering crowd.

"What the bloody blazes?" The cabman rose to his feet, craning his neck to determine the source of the excitement.

Miss Kaye, Pippa, and I exchanged a worried look, before leaning to peer out the sides of the carriage and see for ourselves.

"Oi! You!" The cabman shouted at a paperboy who was weaving his way out of the throng. "What's the meaning of all this?"

"It's the Ripper, sir! Jack the Ripper, he's struck again!"

"No." Miss Kaye's voice was barely audible, but the next thing we knew, she'd flung open the door of the cab and was pushing her way into the gathering masses. At a loss of what else to do, Pippa and I scrambled after her.

Miss Kaye moved like a woman possessed. She threw elbows, kicked shins, and at one point forcibly shoved a man nearly twice her size out of the way as she manoeuvred deeper into the crowd. Pippa and I could do nothing but chase her heels and pray we would not lose sight of her. At last, she came to a stop, where several stern-looking constables were positioned, blocking off the entrance to Dorset Street.

"Officer!" Her tone was so sharp and commanding that the officer nearest her startled and made eye contact as if by instinct. "Officer, what has happened here?"

"None of your concern, ma'am, now please, everyone, move along—"

"But it *is* my concern. I'm looking for my daughter! Please. Of Number 13, Miller's Court. I need to find my daughter."

At the mention of the address, the officer's face blanched a pure white. "Number . . . Number 13, you said?"

"Yes, and I just want to know she's alright. *Please*."

The officer shifted his gaze. "Perhaps you ought to come with me, ma'am. Please, step right this way—"

"No. Just tell me now, is she alright? Is she dead?"

"Ma'am, this isn't the place—"

"Like *hell* this isn't the place! Where is she? Where is she?" Her hysterics were gathering the attention of several other spectators, and the officer was clearly keen to prevent further mayhem.

He straightened his posture, linked his hands behind his back, and leaned his head low. "Ma'am, I regret to inform you that your daughter was found murdered this morning. Now, if you'd please be so kind as to follow me to the station, we have further questions for you—"

But Miss Kaye simply whirled around, grabbed Pippa and me by the elbows, and dragged us back through the crowd, trundling us back into the waiting cab before we could even process what was happening. My breath was coming in hot, uneven gasps. *Mary Jane Kelly is dead.* We had failed to save her. How could it all have gone so terribly wrong?

"Back to Whitechapel Hall. Quickly, please." Miss Kaye's barked orders shook me from my stupor.

"Miss Kaye? What are we going to do now?"

"We're getting back to safety. William could be here. He could be anywhere." She pulled her hood further over her face, and Pippa and I followed suit. "The Hall is the safest place for us now. We can remain there, under lock and key, until I figure out the best recourse."

"Right," I breathed.

Pippa clasped my hand as the cab jerked back into motion, and I bit back the tears that were threatening to well over. "Miss Kaye?"

"Yes, Miss Fitzroy?"

"I'm sorry." Pippa's voice trembled with emotion.

"So am I." Miss Kaye sighed, sounding unbelievably weary as she leaned back in her seat. Her uncharacteristic display of raw emotion dissipated just as quickly as it had appeared, and within moments it was replaced by her signature dispassionate pragmatism. The gloomy facades of Whitechapel began to glow in the dim morning light as we passed them by. "So am I."

We wasted no time. As soon as the cab pulled to a halt, we returned Miss Kaye's trunk to the dumbwaiter and hastened back to the front door as if pursued by the Devil himself. We cared not if anyone found our behaviour strange; all that mattered was sequestering ourselves within the safety of the Hall until William's next ploy could be assessed. Though we could not predict what would happen next, there was a strange solace in the heavy click of the lock as it sealed into place behind us; the place that had once been our prison was now our only refuge.

We were back earlier than expected, and Miss Kaye led us straight to her office. Her first act upon entering was to pick up the envelope containing her letter of resignation, which she'd left strategically propped upon her desk, and fling it into the fire. Pippa and I watched, blinking back tears, as the flames ate away at the only remaining evidence of Miss Kaye's decimated dream. Miss Kaye, for her part, displayed no such sentimental inclination towards tears. Instead, she busied herself reverting to her prior appearance, and by the time she emerged from her bedroom, there was no evidence of her previous transformation. She appeared just as stern as ever as she lowered herself into her chair, clearly deep in thought. At a loss of what else to do, Pippa and I took our places seated across from her.

"I must meet with him again. This madness must stop."

"Miss Kaye, no!" I exclaimed. "You can still leave, right? Your passage is paid for, after all. I know what happened this morning was a shock, but the plan is still a good one. Just leave for Australia next week! Pippa and I can cover— "

"No." Miss Kaye's tone left no room for interpretation. "I will not live the rest of my life in fear that that monster is one step behind me. I can never be free, knowing that he is free. This must end. Here, in Whitechapel. The only question is how."

At that very moment, three sharp raps on her office door startled us all to attention.

Miss Kaye's eyes flicked to the clock. It was precisely eight. "Please, Headmaster, do come in." With that, she rose to her feet and gestured for Pippa and me to do the same.

We turned as Headmaster Graves strode into the room, a wide, performative smile upon his face. "And here is Miss Kaye, venerable schoolmistress and house mother, as well as two of our most illustrious pupils. It's my distinct honour to introduce you to Whitechapel Hall's newest benefactor." He gestured jovially as a man stepped through the doorway, removing his hat. My blood ran cold.

"Kent. Mr. William Kent."

Chapter XVIII
Tales of a Ghoul

"Wonderful, wonderful!" Headmaster Graves, at least, appeared impervious to the fact that a palpable chill had descended upon the room, the three of us frozen stock-still as statues as William eyed us all appraisingly in turn. "Now I do apologise, but I must leave you to it. So much to tend to, at our humble little school! But fear not, Mr. Kent, you are in excellent hands with Miss Kaye. She represents the best of us." And with that, he left, closing the door behind him.

I knew not what to do. It was possible that Miss Kaye had her knife on her, but there was no guarantee; I hazarded a glance around the room in search of an improvised weapon but found none that would defeat William's blade. The best I could hope for was to employ the brass hat rack as a defensive measure, perhaps holding him off long enough for at least Pippa to escape.

Miss Kaye broke the silence, her voice low and dangerous. "So, you have cornered me at last. What will be your play? Will you end me here and now, one final vile, bloody deed? Or are you content to wait, dear brother, for the privacy you so prize? For it has never been enough to *kill*, has it? You must mutilate, dominate, prove your superiority through desecration and deviance. And we hardly have the time for that, now, do we? The pupils are out and about, I fear an interruption is most inevitable."

At this, William simply laughed. To my shock, it was not the cackle of a maniacal villain that haunted me from the night of our attack but instead a wry sort of chuckle reserved for the politest of company. "Please, Constance, let us not be petty about the past. I shall not harm you—are you truly so foolish as to believe I would? Be serious. Come now, sit." And with that, he took his position in the chair normally reserved for Noah and gave the rest of us a look of rapt anticipation. At a loss of what else to do, I sat. Pippa and Miss Kaye followed suit.

"There now, isn't that better? We can all be civilised about this, no need for quarrelling." He turned his attention to Pippa, "Or brawling." His eyes moved to me. "Or thievery." I knew in that instant that he recognised Pippa and me as accomplices just as readily as he'd recognised his own sister. My stomach churned at the thought.

He sat back in his chair, appearing utterly relaxed despite the tension in the room. He was dressed smartly, wearing a coat with an Astrakhan collar and matching cuffs, boots with elegant gaiters festooned with white buttons, and a black tie with a whimsical horseshoe embellished upon it. Were I to pass him on the street, he would appear to me as any fine gentleman one might see in Stamford Hill.

"Now, ladies, it appears we have come to an impasse. As you all know, I was recently confronted with a threat to my reputation, which I have taken the liberty of eliminating."

"You murdered five women, Wills." Miss Kaye was clearly not keen to shy from the confrontation, and I held my breath to gauge his response.

"I eliminated a threat to my reputation. I simply finished what they had the audacity to start."

"And Saville? Was he a 'threat to your reputation,' too?"

"He was a threat to both of us, and you know it." William snarled, for the first time allowing his true nature to seep through a crack in his facade. "Father would have written us out of the will and discarded us entirely as soon as the brat came of age. Don't be obtuse, Constance. It's unflattering."

Miss Kaye appeared unmoved. "I am not being obtuse; I am being honest. I'm sure you've noticed by now that your particular breed of 'justice' doesn't sit well with others."

"Ah, but you aren't 'others,' are you? After the death of our *half*-brother, you were perfectly content to frolic about France and ignore the whole messy ordeal while I remained behind in England. You were hardly put out by it."

"I wasn't *frolicking about France*, I was shipped off to avoid the shame you brought upon our whole family, and the subsequent suspicion Father endured! I was miserable, grieving and alone, and you, whom I'd once believed to be my one true companion in this world, betrayed me, blackmailed me, and then sent me to prison the moment it benefitted you. Don't be obtuse, William. It's unflattering."

At this, William issued a put-upon sigh, spinning his walking stick absently in his fingers as he closed his eyes, as if summoning the patience to endure the very encounter he had initiated. After a pause, he recommenced.

"It is clear now that we find ourselves at an impasse. Though I have successfully thwarted the attempt upon my reputation for now, the problem of you and your persistent little posse of petty criminals has left me feeling most uneasy."

"Your quarrel is with me, Wills. Leave them out of it."

"But they know the truth, don't they, dear Constance? You see, the whole premise of my perfect crime was that you and I were to be the only ones who knew. And yet time and time again, you have gravely disappointed me, flapping your gib with those harlots at the pub, and then recruiting your own students to clean up your mess! Shame, shame, sister mine. Imagine what the headmaster would say if he knew." He paused, perhaps for effect, or perhaps to give Constance a chance to defend herself, but she did not correct his interpretation of events.

"Here's how I see it. There is but one solution, and I find it is both neat and convenient. Constance, you must remain sequestered in Whitechapel Hall for good. It seems a pleasant place, and well suited for you, so it surely will not be too much of a hardship. In my new role as primary benefactor, I shall be a permanent presence at your illustrious institution.

"Yet if you endeavour to leave your designated sanctuary, I shall have to kill you on sight. It appears you are not to be trusted, and that is perhaps the greatest regret of my life. For I do love you, more than anything in this mortal world, which is why I go to such lengths—time and time again—to spare you, though any sane man would undoubtedly have done away with you long ago. And do not bother with your pedestrian trickery; I have seen you out in your mourning veil, as if a scrap of lace could disguise my most intimate companion from me! So, I implore you: If you value your own life, do not stray from the Hall." Miss Kaye's jaw clenched, but she did not protest.

"Now, as for the two of you." At this, his empty gaze shifted from Miss Kaye to Pippa and me, and we both stiffened in our seats. "You shall serve the remainder of your sentence here at Whitechapel Hall and conduct yourselves as if nothing is amiss. Do not deviate from your assigned routine, including your morning market duty—oh, don't look so shocked, you aren't the only ones capable of a bit of surveillance—and conduct yourselves with utmost discretion. As soon as you are released from your incarceration, you will leave London and never return.

"Now, I'm sure I needn't explain to you that to report me to the authorities would be an exercise in futility due to your unfortunate station and my significant clout, a fact which I imagine has been the impetus to hold your tongues until now.

But should you find yourself tempted to venture such a folly, do remember: if I catch so much as a whiff of suspicion from the authorities, or if I witness you put one toe out of line, I will come straight here to this office and kill my sister."

Pippa and I blinked back at him, horror-struck.

"I won't kill *you*, for that would be difficult and messy and I loathe the thought of killing innocents—"

"And what do you call the women you slaughtered upon the streets?" Constance shot back.

"*Conspirators against me*, Constance dear. Those women chose their course of action, whereas these two lost lambs were clearly victims of your predatory scheming." Constance let out an indignant huff, but William simply carried on. "As I was saying, you needn't be afraid of me, so long as you follow the rules. During my visits to Whitechapel Hall, I shall check in with you regularly to personally ensure your compliance. Understood?" Pippa and I nodded, for what choice did we have?

"Excellent!" William rapped his walking stick briskly against the ground, as if giving himself a round of applause for his role in the negotiations. "I'm so glad we've reached an understanding. Now—"

He was interrupted by a knock at the door. "Miss Kaye? Miss Kaye, it's Beatrice."

Miss Kaye shot William a warning glare. "Yes?" I noted that she pointedly did not invite Beatrice to enter.

"Cook has sent for Miss Morton and Miss Fitzroy. They're late for outreach."

"Of course, they'll just be one moment." Lowering her voice, she faced the two of us, an earnest expression upon her face. "Do not be afraid. Carry yourselves with purpose. And tell no one." She need not mention Noah by name.

"Yes, Miss Kaye." With that, we rose from our seats, and to my surprise, William did so as well, issuing a regal bow.

"Ladies, it was a true pleasure to meet you. I eagerly look forward to our next meeting."

"Yes, Mr. Kent," we replied, and hastened towards the door.

"Oh, and one more thing—Miss . . . Morton, is it? If I ever catch you in my study again, I shall eviscerate you and eat your kidneys for breakfast."

I had no reason to doubt him. "Yes, Mr. Kent." And with that, we once more narrowly escaped the clutches of the Whitechapel monster.

Noah stared at us, utter disbelief etched upon his face. "He came *there*? To *Whitechapel Hall*?"

Pippa nodded miserably. "And what's more, he's apparently the new 'anonymous benefactor' that the headmaster has entrusted with saving the school from financial ruin!"

"He has total control over all of us now, especially Miss Kaye," I continued.

Noah shook his head. "How is she? I imagine the loss of Miss Kelly has devastated her."

I shrugged helplessly. "She hasn't had time to dwell on it. We'd barely made it back to the Hall from our ill-fated trip to Miller's Court when William arrived. The savagery of that man, to kill Miss Kelly last night and then show up at Miss Kaye's doorstep this very morning!"

"He's a beast," Pippa chimed in with a shudder.

"Well, I think it's clear what we must do," I announced.

Pippa and Noah stared at me blankly.

"We have to capture him ourselves, of course!" I did not make this declaration lightly, having witnessed William's evil firsthand. The look upon Elizabeth Stride's face as the light left her eyes still haunted me nightly as I waited for sleep to overtake me; it was not something that could be so easily shaken as my penny bloods had led me to believe. But the torture her final moments had inflicted upon my soul had only strengthened my resolve to bring William to justice, and now was hardly the time to back down from our cause.

Pippa leaned against the counter and buried her face in her hands. "Dell, for the last time, are you out of your goddamned mind? This is hardly the time for one of your detective schemes! William's nearly killed us twice already; if we try to capture him and fail, he now has full access to the Hall! There will be nowhere safe for us to go. Not to mention Miss Kaye—"

"And what's your solution, then?" I argued. "Say we comply and let him go free. How long will it be before he grows so paranoid that he kills Miss Kaye? Or one of us? He isn't a normal man, Pippa, he's insane, you saw it in his eyes—"

"Of course I did, but what else can we do? It's not like we're going to kill him before he kills us!"

I rolled my eyes. "Of course we'll not resort to murder, Pippa. We'll do what all good detectives do: rely on what we know."

"And what is that?" Noah interjected.

"We know that William has vowed to kill Miss Kaye on sight if he witnesses her leaving the Hall."

Noah cocked an eyebrow. "And?"

"And we've observed the path of every policeman and Vigilance Committee patrol in all of Whitechapel."

"But we've been through this before, they'll never believe us—"

"We won't have to convince them of anything if they catch him in the act."

"You want to use Miss Kaye as bait?" Noah's scepticism was palpable.

Pippa scowled. "She'll never comply, she's far too prudent."

"Who said anything about involving Miss Kaye?" I retorted. "We have access to the dumbwaiter, which means not only do we have a means of escape, but we have access to the contents of her travelling trunk to boot. I'll don her garments and sneak out of the Hall and lead him to a designated location. Noah, that's where you come in. You've been attending the Vigilance Committee meetings, haven't you?"

"Of course, me and every other able-bodied young man in Whitechapel."

"Then you're familiar with the band that patrols High Street each night?"

He nodded. "They pass my father's shop once every thirty minutes, like clockwork."

"And you're familiar with the constable that walks the beat on Prescot Street? I've observed him from our perch making his rounds."

Noah shrugged. "I know him, not by name, but his face is familiar enough."

"That's all we need. For based on the timing of his beat and the patrol of the Vigilance Committee on High Street, the two converge on either side of Minories Street each night at precisely half past midnight."

Noah's eyes widened. "Right beside my shop."

I grinned. "Exactly. William won't attack me—or, Miss Kaye, rather—in the middle of High Street. He may be insane, but he's no fool; he'll wait for an opportunity when he can commit the deed without detection, just like he did for the others. I'll deviate from the main thoroughfare here, just outside your shop, and hide in the shadows of the cross street; William will surely be in pursuit. But before he can catch me, I shall scream murder, and by the sheer perfection of our impeccable timing, there shall be a policeman at one side of the street, a mob at the other, and you among them to alert them to my presence. He will be well and truly caught!"

"And I'm supposed to sit back and let you both put your lives in danger while I, what, twiddle my thumbs?" Pippa protested petulantly.

I paused. Admittedly, I would prefer to keep my dearest

companion away from the danger, having nearly lost her once before, but I knew her as well as I knew myself, and she would never stand for it.

"You can be my guard—from a distance, of course. Noah will arm you with a knife, and you will follow William, who will be following me. In case anything goes awry, you will be my protector."

Pippa shook her head. "It's mad, Dell. William is no ordinary foe: he deceived his own family, he tracked down five anonymous women in the chaos of Whitechapel like a bloodhound, and he's cornered Miss Kaye in the very place she sought refuge. What chance do we stand in outwitting him?"

"Don't you see, Pippa? We have no other choice! We have no voice, no power, no other recourse than to stop the monster in the very place he lurks. You heard Miss Kaye: If we don't stop him now, we will spend the rest of our lives looking over our shoulders, always wondering if he's one step behind. This is our chance! We must seize it, or the opportunity will be lost forever."

Pippa closed her eyes and took a deep breath. "I can't believe I'm saying this, but you're right. Though it may all be for naught, we'll regret it if we don't at least try."

"That's the spirit! Noah?"

To my surprise, Noah looked considerably more enthusiastic about the prospect than I'd anticipated. "I'm in. Let's take him down once and for all."

"Excellent!" I clapped my hands. "Now, Noah: what kind of knives have you got lying around this place?"

Chapter XIX
True to Each Other

My hands trembled more than usual as I fumbled with the dormitory lock. Despite having Pippa beside me to hold the lantern steady, my composure was noticeably rattled. Neither of us spoke a word, but I could feel her silent urgency: *Come on, hurry up, we can't be late.*

I know! I snapped back at my own inner monologue. *I'm trying!*

"Are you leaving?"

A quiet voice from directly behind us made us both jump. Whirling around, Pippa shone the narrow beam of light from our covered lantern in the direction of the sound. *Don't let it be Beatrice, please don't let it be Beatrice!* I internally begged. To my dismay, it illuminated none other than our sworn nemesis, who was blinking owlishly back at us from her bed.

"Don't be daft," Pippa whispered harshly. "We're checking that the lock is secure."

"So, you're planning to stay here and let Mr. Kent murder you?"

My jaw dropped. "You *heard* that?"

"Obviously. I'm not deaf, and I arrived at Miss Kaye's door

this morning just in time to hear him announce his plot. He was hardly coy about it." Beatrice shrugged. "So, I assume you're escaping from school. And I just wanted to let you know that as far as I'm concerned, I saw you both go upstairs to the annex directly after supper and haven't seen you since."

It was difficult to hide my shock. "You'd cover for us?"

Pippa sounded even more incredulous than me. "Why?"

Beatrice rolled her eyes. "Please, Batty. I might give you a bit of lip now and then, but I hardly want to see you both gutted. Besides, then I'd have to feel guilty, which sounds utterly tedious and no fun at all." And with that, she rolled over and pulled her blanket up over her shoulders. Wordlessly, we returned our attention to the lock and continued to the kitchen without further incident.

At the drop of a veil, I was battle-ready. Miss Kaye's garments fit me well enough to be passable, but it was the reappearance of the familiar mourning veil, washed and purified of Pippa's blood since the night of William's attack upon us, which fortified my resolve. Beside me, Pippa was solemn and stoic as she secured Noah's boning knife beneath the folds of her cloak. Our plan had been timed to the second; there was no room for deviation. Just as the bell of Whitechapel Hall tolled midnight, I pulled open the door of the dumbwaiter.

"Dell?"

Pippa's voice, though soft, felt startling in the lingering silence of the pantry. Pausing, I turned to her. Even now, in our most precarious moment, the sight of her face was enough to warm my heart. "Yes?"

"I . . . I just wanted to say . . . to say . . ." She faltered, her eyes suddenly refusing to meet mine. It was not fear that I saw in them but something else entirely, and I drew her hands into my own and pulled them to my bosom.

"Say nothing," I said. "There will be time enough for talking when all of this is through."

She gave me a tight-lipped smile, then lifted my veil and leaned in to place a soft peck upon my cheek. I squeezed her hand once more, memorising the feeling of her palm against mine, recalling the now-familiar weight of her grasp at the crook of my elbow as we sauntered down High Street, the warmth of her arm around me as we peered down from our perch at the whirring world below us, the press of her head upon my shoulder as we dozed off to sleep at night, and suddenly, I realised just how much I had to lose.

But this—*this* was worth fighting for.

"Be safe." I lowered my veil and turned from her before I could lose my nerve. Moments later, I was back in the familiar enveloping darkness of the dumbwaiter, descending into the very danger we'd once so foolishly believed we could defeat.

The alley did not frighten me anymore. The vagrants that lined it were no threat at all compared with the true beast that stalked me, and as I made my way out into the streetlight of Buck's Row, I reflected upon the irony. That the police were so caught up in blaming someone, *anyone* besides a high-stepped gentleman—*No Englishman could have done it!*—that they refused to see the fiend that lurked in their very midst. Though my vision was obscured by the veil, I could see Whitechapel more clearly than ever before as I made my way to High Street.

My pace was swift and purposeful. I skirted the pools of light cast by the lamps, occasionally tossing a glance back over my shoulder, feigning paranoia but revealing enough of myself for William to be certain of his target. Once or twice, I thought I spied Pippa in the distance, mingled amongst the late-night pedestrians, but I refused to let myself dwell upon her. She was well out of harm's way, I reminded myself. William's target was me, and me alone.

I slowed as I approached Minories Street, casting a glance up at the clock tower in the distance. In precisely two minutes, the Vigilance Committee members would emerge onto High

Street from their turning point at the square, and the constable would pass by the south end on his way towards the terminus of his route at the station. Taking a deep breath, I turned into the narrow passage and assessed my surroundings.

The small shops on either side were all shuttered, but I instantly spotted one with a recessed doorway, which offered the perfect hiding place. Ducking inside the arch, I disappeared expertly into the shadows and dropped into a crouch to wait. It was imperative that William follow me, but not so quickly that I'd be found out before help arrived.

I counted the seconds. Ten, fifteen, twenty. Forty. A minute. Then another. My legs grew stiff, and my back scraped uncomfortably against the rough brick of the alcove. I yearned for any sign of life—William, the Vigilance Committee, something, anything besides the damp darkness and ominous silence—but none appeared. I breathed and counted some more. I began to shiver, whether from the chill or the compounding dread, I could not tell.

A leaden feeling was forming in the pit of my stomach as I realised just how fragile my brilliant plan had been. Though William was nowhere to be seen, neither was the Vigilance Committee, their assumed presence such a linchpin in my scheme that their uncharacteristic absence seemed a dire omen. They had patrolled the streets nightly since the very first murder in September—what could possibly have detained them on this night of all nights? I consoled myself with the fact that Noah was among their ranks tonight and would doubtlessly steer them back onto the right path, but when, *when*? I prayed it would not be too late.

No sooner had the thought crossed my mind than I spotted a flash of movement at the end of the street. *William.* The figure moved effortlessly through the shadows, the sum of his image no more than the flutter of a cloak and the scrape of a boot against the cobblestones. And yet no sign of the Committee!

I cowered where I hid, and willed William to pass, leaving me unnoticed. Despite my better reason, I squeezed my eyes shut, for I could not bear to witness what would happen next.

"*Dell? Dell!*"

The familiar hiss of Pippa's voice shook me from my self-imposed blindness, and I scrambled to my feet, bewildered by her unexpected presence.

"Pippa?" I stepped from the doorway, and she squealed and whirled to face me, brandishing her knife in front of her.

"Jesus Christ, you scared me!"

I was in such a state of shocked confusion, I could scarcely form a sentence. "What the hell are you doing here? Where's William? Where's the Committee?"

"That's just it!" Pippa's voice was high and frantic. "The Committee is nowhere to be seen! I heard word on the street that they were planning some sort of protest against the new police commissioner! I don't know where they are at this hour, but Dell, they're not here."

"Shit. We have to return to the school right away, maybe we can try again tomorrow—"

"No, Dell, we can't." Pippa's face was a mask of terror, her eyes wide and wild. "William. He's tracked you."

"What? Where?" I cast my eyes frantically towards each end of the street, but it remained disconcertingly dark and vacant.

"I don't know! He followed you this far, watched you turn the corner, then he just sort of . . . stood, and waited, and then he kept walking!"

"Why didn't you follow him?" I insisted.

"Because I came here to save *you*, you stupid arse!"

I wanted to berate her; after all, a good detective never abandons her mark, and we were at a severe disadvantage now that we'd lost sight of our target, but I had to admit it was hard to quarrel with her logic in the heat of the moment.

"Fine, never mind all that." I glanced around, willing myself to remain calm and think of the next cleverest thing. "Come on, this way. We have to get to safety before William corners us." Taking her hand in mine, I pulled her out onto High Street, straight to the door of Noah's shop. Plucking a hairpin from beneath my hat, I set about picking the lock. "Keep watch. And keep your knife out."

Pippa didn't need to be told twice. Her back pressed against mine, I could feel her breath coming in short, aborted gasps as I worked the lock. It felt like an eternity to get my fingers to cooperate, but it was no more than a few short seconds before it gave way. I yanked the door open, and we both stumbled inside.

The store was dark and eerily still, the dim lamplight shining through the window making the familiar space feel foreign and strangely sinister. "This way." I slipped into one of the aisles and stooped into a crouch. Pippa immediately followed, sinking into place beside me with an unsteady sigh. I pulled up my veil and pushed my bonnet back on my head, taking in the scene properly for the first time.

At last, Pippa spoke. "What now?"

"We'll wait here for Noah to return from wherever he is. And pray that his father doesn't wake and find us hiding." Pippa bit her lip. "Right."

The rattle of the front doorknob jarred us both to attention. In a singular, sickening moment, it dawned on me: I had not relocked the door behind me.

It's just Noah, I told myself. *Just Noah, returning home from his failed patrol, with a wild tale of how it all went wrong. He'll embrace us both and be so glad we're safe, and we'll simply stay here until morning, until the danger has passed—*

The squeak of the hinges was deafening juxtaposed against the stillness surrounding us. A footfall. Then another.

And then the unmistakable *click* of a walking stick against the floor.

Pippa's hand flew to mine, the squeeze of her fingers leaving no room for doubt that she knew as well as I that this was not Noah coming to save us. The door slammed shut, and the two of us flinched, but we remained mute.

And then, silence. It lingered so long that I began to wonder if perhaps I'd gone mad, and there was no one in the shop at all, and this was all some sort of terrible hallucination, and any moment I would blink open my eyes and it would all be gone.

"Come out, come out, wherever you are." William's voice was low, nearly a whisper, but it echoed through the space like a roll of thunder.

More footfalls. He was moving slowly, pacing the space in front of the display windows, cutting off any hope of egress. Wordlessly, I released Pippa's hand and, with a jerk of my head, gestured towards the counter. Rolling onto my hands and knees, I began to crawl silently towards it, Pippa following close behind.

"Come now, my dears. Now is no time for games. I think we're rather past that childishness, don't you?"

My breath caught in my throat as his footsteps turned to tread the aisle beside ours. Glancing between the shelves, I could make out his smart boots and gaiters, white buttons glinting menacingly as he strode past. I held up my hand, and Pippa froze, listening for his next move. To my relief, he took a right at the end of his aisle and continued to canvass in the opposite direction. Pippa and I resumed our silent scramble towards the counter.

"It's a pity, really." William's voice rumbled in the stillness. "We could have put an end to this with our little chat today and left it all in the past. But you simply couldn't let it go, could you?" His walking stick clacked menacingly with each stride, and I mentally tracked his progress past the tinned fish as Pippa and I at last reached the counter.

"What is it that drives you to such flights of fancy, hmm? Do you truly believe yourselves cleverer than the police, wittier than the press, braver than the Vigilance Committee? What makes you think that *you* could be my undoing, when none before have suspected me of more than a disagreeable disposition, hmm?" I caught Pippa's eye and pointed towards the curtain leading to the back of the shop. She nodded in affirmation.

"But you do know what this means: You are no longer innocents, my dears. You have endeavoured to betray me. And I regret to inform you that such a transgression results in only one sentence: death."

At the utterance of that simple phrase, I reached onto the shelf beside me, procured a jar of potted meat, and rolled it with all my strength towards the display case beside the front door.

My diversion worked. The jar knocked against the wooden framing with an incriminating clunk, William's footsteps falling double-time as he rushed towards the source of the commotion. Taking advantage of his distraction, we scrambled frantically under the counter and through the curtain, seeking sanctuary in the butchering room.

The moment we entered, respite was replaced with revulsion. I had never comprehended that Noah intentionally kept the dirtier elements of his work from us, but standing amidst the carnage for the first time, it all became apparent. Huge slabs of raw, glistening meat hung from enormous hooks affixed to cables spanning the length of the room, and the floor was caked in blood-soaked sawdust. A dizzying array of knives and cleavers lined the near wall, and in the centre of the room, a bone saw rested against a large cradle and a crate of spare hooks. The smell of the place was beyond comprehension; while the front of the shop had never smelled particularly pleasant, it was nothing compared to the pungent, sour stench of death that permeated the butchering room.

I paused to collect myself. My visceral disgust for slaughter was of no use in this moment; I must be calm, rational, practical.

Think, Dell. What would Mrs. Paschal do?

Assess. I took in the size of the room. It was considerably larger than I had previously imagined, extending perhaps a hundred feet beyond the point where we stood, with a high ceiling and exposed beams from which the hanging cables were affixed. At the far end was a wooden staircase leading to a narrow balcony with a rickety railing that ran the length of the room. The balcony beckoned temptingly, but I knew better than to run *up* when being pursued—my penny bloods had been perfectly clear on that point.

"Look!" Pippa gestured eagerly towards a sliding door built into the wall to our left, clearly the access point for the unlucky livestock being driven there. My heart leapt, but an instant later, it was broken once again.

"It's padlocked. I can't pick it fast enough."

"Then what do we do? Hide?"

I ran a quick calculation. We were rapidly running out of time; it would take William only moments to discover the jar was a distraction and to clear the rest of the shop. From there, it wouldn't take a genius to deduce where we'd gone.

I shook my head. "We fight." From the rack on the wall, I took the first item that drew my eye: a long, slender knife measuring nearly a foot and a half in length, with a rectangular, smooth blade. Though the lack of a pronounced point was less than ideal, the sheer length was appealing in maintaining the distance between myself and my aspiring murderer. Pippa clutched her borrowed boning knife valiantly in front of her, but I could see the tremble in her grasp.

"This way." I darted towards the curtained door frame and positioned myself behind the nearest hanging rack of meat, with Pippa right behind me.

"What are we going to do?" she whispered as we waited, both shaking with tension.

My plan fell into place as the words tumbled off my tongue.

"We're going to ambush him with the meat. Catch him off guard, compromise his balance. If he falls, we make for the door and run. If he doesn't, we . . . attack."

Pippa's eyes widened. "With a *knife*?"

"Well, what precisely do you think he's about to do with *you*?" I hissed back.

"I've never stabbed anyone before!"

"And you think I have?"

"Well, no, but you've read so much about it— "

"I hardly think it's an academic endeavour, Pippa!"

"But— "

Our quarrel was abruptly aborted by the sound of footsteps approaching the curtain, and we lapsed into tense silence. The curtain withdrew, and a sliver of light spilled into the cavernous room as William at last made his entrance. He stood, his shadow a ghostly silhouette upon the bloodstained floor, taking in the scene before him. And then he laughed.

I knew better than to hesitate. To give a villain opportunity to wax poetic upon his designs was a folly straight from the pages of my novels that I had no desire to emulate. Instead, I opted for action. With all my might, I threw the weight of my entire being at the dangling side of beef in front of me, propelling it directly at William. Much to my surprise, it glided effortlessly along the cable and caught him on his blind side, knocking him akimbo. With a roar of fury, he staggered to right himself, and from the handle of his walking stick he produced a bespoke knife, the sight of which I recalled all too clearly from our prior encounter on Berner Street. So that was how he obscured his weapon following each crime to guarantee an anonymous retreat! It was a clever ruse, and I experienced a moment of disorienting respect for my adversary before recalling my imminent peril.

In the next instant he was nearly upon me, knife aloft and fury in his eyes as he swung wildly in my direction. Afforded the advantage of preparation, I ducked away and thrust another dangling slab in his direction. His knife pierced the flesh with a sickening squish, and he swore violently as he struggled to withdraw the blade and continue his pursuit. Seizing the opportunity, I turned and gripped Pippa by the elbow, pulling her deeper into the slaughter room, dodging the dangling racks of meat as we wove our way past them, frantically searching for an opening to gain the upper hand. Suddenly, the stairs at the far end of the room seemed as decent a chance as any, and we made a break towards them with all the speed we could muster.

Mere feet from the base of the staircase, a yank at the hem of my petticoat tripped me in my tracks, and I was torn from Pippa's grasp. I flailed frantically, barely maintaining enough balance to shield myself with my knife as William descended upon me, his own weapon held aloft. By some miracle, his first blow glanced off my blade and sent him stumbling, giving me just enough time to pull free of his grasp and grab the first defensive weapon I could lay my hand upon: a rack of ribs hanging from the nearest hook. Wielding it like a shield, I whirled around just in time for William's knife to plunge through them, the tip of his blade coming to a stop mere inches from my breast. I wrenched the ribs sideways to disarm him, but his knife was far too sharp and simply sliced through the gristle with a grotesque crunch. In desperation, I threw the severed meat at him and made to run, but his reflexes were too quick, and he once again caught my skirt in his clutches. With a scream, I pulled away as ferociously as I could, but it was no use. He let out a maniacal cackle and raised his blade once more.

Just as I prepared to meet my maker, William was suddenly bowled over by a full side of beef descending upon him from above like a bloody, moist plague sent by a vengeful god. Bewildered by this turn of events, I looked up to see Pippa balanced daintily upon the beam above me, knife in hand, having severed the slab from where it was tied and grinning from ear to ear.

"Cheers!"

"Thank me later! Hurry up!" Her eyes widened as she pointed beside me. Sure enough, William was already struggling to his feet, and I hadn't a moment to spare. I sprinted up the staircase, then quickly volleyed myself over the railing to follow Pippa's lead onto the beams traversing the room.

It wasn't until I was halfway across the beam she was waiting upon that I looked down. Suddenly, the world swayed in and out of focus, the floor dropping away as if melting into a bottomless pit. My knees quivered, and I nearly released the knife still clutched fervently in my fist, willing myself not to faint. I stood frozen in place as somewhere in the distance, I vaguely registered William's footfalls on the stairs.

"Dell!" Pippa's voice shook me from my spiral, and I looked up. "Come on, let's go!" She smiled and beckoned to me as casually as she had that first day in the annex when I'd blindly followed her to our perch for the very first time. "Just like at home, yeah? One foot in front of the other."

I obeyed as if under a spell. First one foot, then the other, I recommenced traversing the beam with grim determination. I refused to look down, but more importantly, I refused to look behind me: William was inevitably in pursuit, and I would have to trust my balance if I had any hope of escaping with my life.

"That's it! This way." Just as I almost reached the point where Pippa stood, she leapt gracefully over to the next beam. Though it was only a few feet away, it seemed to me an impossible act of acrobatic skill. There was no way I could follow her!

"No, no, I can't do that. I have to turn around."

"*No!*" The sheer terror in Pippa's voice confirmed what I already knew: William was quickly gaining on me. Jumping was the only way. "Look at me. Jump to me, only me. Come on."

I could not refuse her. I launched myself from the beam, and in the next instant, I was at her side. She caught me with one hand, bracing her other against the low ceiling to stabilise us. I was shaking from head to toe, but I was alive, and we shared an elated smile. Our relief was rudely interrupted by the familiar timbre of William's drawling baritone behind us.

"You think a few fancy circus tricks will be enough to save you? Foolish, pitiful, *tsk, tsk.*" I turned to see him making his way determinedly down the beam I'd just jumped from. His progress was far slower than mine had been, the low height of the ceiling forcing him to hunch, and he was struggling to clutch his knife in one hand while bracing for balance with the other. I was delighted to have finally caught him wrong-footed, but despite this, he showed no signs of hesitation as he progressed in our direction.

"We have to keep going," Pippa implored. With that, she released me from the comfort of her embrace and took three delicate steps before hopping to the next beam. I followed her lead, refusing to look down, and before I knew it, we'd put four more beams between ourselves and William. Despite this success, my panic continued to grow: what was our endgame? We could not simply engage William in a merry chase forever.

No sooner had the thought crossed my mind than my eyes settled upon what I knew in an instant was Pippa's grand design: a ladder wedged against the wall directly beside the curtained door. If we could get that far, we could descend the ladder and escape the shop before William had a chance to catch us! Hope washed over me in a rush of warm relief, and I was fortified in my pursuit of Pippa's progress as she expertly charted our course towards our destination. I did not bother to look back at William: wherever he was, unless he had gained a gymnast's skills in a matter of moments, he was hardly a threat.

Before I knew it, there were only three beams between us and the ladder. Triumph was so close at hand I could taste it, and I allowed myself a giddy shriek of excitement as I took yet another leap. Pippa turned to smile at me, and I watched uncomprehendingly as a flash of silver streaked past me, coming to lodge itself in her side. And then, she was gone.

I blinked. I could not comprehend the scene I had just witnessed. All I knew is that when I looked down, her body was crumpled on the blood-soaked floor twenty feet below. Pivoting where I stood, I came face to face with William, who still stood six beams behind me, but his hands were now empty. He had thrown his knife and found his mark.

"No. No." The words were more a plea than a protest. My eyes flicked back down to Pippa's unmoving form, then up to meet William's once more. His expression revealed no glee in his triumph.

"Now, my dear, why don't we simply end this once and for all? I shall give you two choices, neither of which are superior to my blade, but sadly, your little friend received that honour. You can either fling yourself from the beam on which you stand, which seems a perfectly dignified end, and not particularly painful. Or you can carry on with this imprudence, and when I catch you—for make no mistake, I *will* catch you—I shall throttle you with my bare hands. So. Decision time! Which will it be?"

For a split second, I was tempted to simply launch myself from my beam and join Pippa on the unforgiving floor, for what was the purpose of saving my own life if she was no longer in it? But no sooner had the thought crossed my mind than a wave of rage so potent that the sheer power of it overwhelmed me. *How dare he take her from me?* I would not give him the satisfaction of surrendering without a fight.

Before William could detect my newfound resolve, I turned and bolted down my beam towards the balcony as fast as I could, abandoning my reliance on the ceiling for balance. Footfalls to my left indicated that William was in parallel pursuit, but I could not be bothered to care. I reached the railing and swung myself over it onto the safety of the balcony, racing to the base of William's beam just as he approached the end of it. Raising my knife before me, I held it aloft at the height of his throat, the implication clear. For once, he was the one trapped.

He pulled to a reluctant halt, balanced on his beam ten feet from the edge of the balcony, and shook his head. Once again, he began to laugh.

"What's so funny?" Rage had untied my tongue, and I was biting to enact my revenge. "I suppose it is a bit ironic, isn't it? The very choice you gave me is now yours. Either you jump, or I take your life the moment you step foot on solid ground." Distantly, I noted that my knife was no longer shaking as I held it aloft.

William cocked his head, his bottomless eyes locked with mine. "Don't be silly, child. You don't have what it takes to do what's necessary."

"Necessary?" I spat incredulously. "None of this is necessary. You got everything you ever wanted: your family name, your money, your precious reputation! All your sister ever wanted was freedom, and your greed wouldn't even allow her that!"

"You know nothing of my sister." His voice was low and dangerous.

"I know her better than you do," I countered. "She is kind and good, and she believes in redemption! You cost her everything, even her one true love!"

At this, he cackled. "Love? Constance doesn't know how to love."

"She does," I replied simply. "She just doesn't love *you*."

He charged at me with reckless abandon, and his lack of weapon did not hinder him. He flung himself over the railing and was upon me before I could take a single swing of my blade. I staggered backwards, stunned at the suddenness and speed of his assault, but not quickly enough: his hand gripped my forearm and twisted it, a searing pain spiralling up past my shoulder, and my fingers unclenched on instinct, sending the knife clattering to the ground. William's eyes flashed with maniacal glee as he bent to retrieve it.

I saw my fleeting advantage and took it. In one swift motion, I kicked the knife out of reach and watched as it skittered down the length of the balcony, coming to rest at the top of the stairs. William's head snapped to the side to watch its trajectory, and I exploited his distraction by raising my knee to connect squarely with the side of his jaw with an unholy *crack*. Reeling and howling, he arched upright and released my arm to grip the side of his face in apparent agony, but I did not pause to gloat. Ducking past him, I pelted in a full-blown sprint towards the staircase, now the source of my last, best hope.

I did not make it far. No more than three paces in, something wrapped around my throat, and I was pulled to a gasping halt, my feet nearly going out from under me. The constriction tightened, and the next thing I knew, I was fighting for breath.

The veil. William had caught the end of it where it hung loose behind my bonnet and was using it to strangle me outright. My hands flew to my neck and my fingers clawed to find purchase between my flesh and the damned black lace, but William's hold was too strong, and I could find no separation in the two. The world spun and dimmed; an odd black vignette dotted with stars clouded the edges of my vision. I flailed against his grasp, but the harder I struggled, the tighter my noose contracted, and the more desperately my lungs screamed for relief.

There was only one solution. I dug my heels into the ground and threw myself backwards as hard as I could at my assailant, catching him by surprise. I felt him stagger backwards and slam into the railing, and the sound of splintering wood was the only warning I had before the pressure around my neck resumed tenfold and I found myself yanked backwards towards the edge of the balcony. I reached out for anything that could save me, and by some miracle, my fingers came to wrap around the dangling end of a suspended cable, halting my descent.

William apparently had the same idea, but unfortunately for

me, the only lifeline within his grasp was the veil around my neck. I was trapped in an impossible choice: either release my grip on the cable and allow William to drag me over the edge of the balcony to our mutual deaths, or hold tight and simply be strangled until I met my inevitable end. Through the hazy edges of my sight, I looked around frantically for a means of escape, but there were none. There was no recourse left. This would, quite simply, be the end of me. I closed my eyes and wondered if I would still be conscious when my fingers lost their hold.

"*Dell!*"

I was startled back to lucidity by the most unexpected and welcome sight I'd ever seen: Noah, my knife in hand, charging towards me with the fervour of a hero on crusade. I tried to cry out to him, but my lungs simply clenched in silence, and my hands began to quake as the cable slowly slipped through them.

"*No!*" Noah's hand caught mine at the last second, just soon enough to save me from plunging backwards over the edge of the balcony. But William's grip still held firm upon the veil around my throat, and Noah's eyes widened as he took in my predicament.

"Hold still." Noah's voice was soft and firm as he lifted his knife. "Trust me." With that, he lowered the blade to my throat and in one smooth, elegant motion, sliced the veil away from my flesh.

I did not see William fall, but the frantic scream cut short by an abrupt silence was sufficient to communicate his fate.

Noah pulled me up and into his arms, and for just a moment, I allowed myself the indulgence of consolation, but I could not maintain it. The reality of what had just transpired was too awful to bear alone.

"Oh, Noah, Pippa's *gone*," I wailed through the tears that had erupted the moment I knew I had truly been saved.

Noah did not pull away but simply held me tighter, stroking my hair as I shook from shock and anguish. "What do you mean?"

"She's dead," I sobbed. "William stabbed her, and she fell, and she's *gone*." The words were garbled by my grief, but to my shock, Noah laughed.

"What are you on about? She's not dead, though her ankle's a bit worse for wear. She was hobbling her way to try and save you when I got here."

I stepped back from him, smearing the tears from my cheeks with the back of my hand as I rushed to the edge of the balcony, scarcely daring to believe him. Sure enough, waving up at me was none other than Pippa, very much alive but leaning heavily against the bannister, her hunched posture revealing her obvious pain.

"Pippa!" My heart felt fit to burst as I dashed down the stairs as quickly as my legs would carry me. Coming face to face with my cherished companion after believing her gone was a privilege so profound, I could not verbalise my gratitude. Luckily, I didn't need to; Pippa simply pushed herself upright and staggered the last few steps into my arms, and we embraced as if for the first and last time all at once.

"Oh, God, Pippa, I thought I lost you. I thought you were gone," I murmured into her golden hair.

"Don't be foolish, Dell. I'd never leave you. Never." She held me tighter, and for a long while we simply stood, lost in the profound joy of one another.

At long last we separated, and I took in the entirety of her appearance for the first time. "Are you truly quite well? Did his blade not pierce you?"

"It was a near miss. It pierced my cloak, but in the effort to dodge it, I lost my balance."

"And your ankle?"

She winced. "Broken, it seems, and perhaps a rib or two as well." I noted that she was holding her chest in an odd, defensive embrace, her breathing shallow.

"We have to get her to the hospital," I said as Noah descended the stairs to join us.

"Of course we do, but first, there's the matter of . . . this." With a jerk of his head, he gestured towards the centre of the room. I had known in my heart what had become of William, but it was with reluctance that I turned around to take in the harsh reality of it.

It was worse than I could have written even in my grisliest penny blood. For William had not simply fallen to the ground and ended in a heap of broken bones and a shattered skull. Instead, he had landed in the bin of hooks, which impaled his body a dozen times through, mutilating his flesh into a ghastly mass of blood and gore. As if in a trance, I approached his corpse and stared down at it with numb disbelief, watching as the blood seeped from his wounds, a sensation dangerously close to satisfaction settling in my chest at the sight.

Behind me, Pippa audibly retched, and I turned around to find Noah rushing to support her. "What are we going to do with him?" she managed meekly.

"I could . . . Maybe I could . . . cut him up a bit, and we could toss him in the river?" Noah sounded reluctant at the prospect.

"Oh, God." Pippa swayed unsteadily on her feet, and Noah bent to drape her arm around his shoulders for better balance.

I bit my lip. "It's risky. We'd certainly be spotted."

"Never mind all that, Dell. You take Pippa to the hospital and leave it to me."

"No. Leave it to me." We all whirled in unison towards the curtained doorway to find none other than Butcher Levy taking in the scene before him.

"*Tate!*" Noah breathed, his eyes wide in shock and fear.

Butcher Levy took a few steps towards us, his eyes locked on William's corpse. At last, he spoke again, his thick accent rendering his words guttural and strange. "This is the man who has been causing the problems. Yes?" The three of us nodded, still too surprised to speak.

"And you have stopped him. This is good." We nodded again.

"Good. I am glad to see it end. Now, go. Noah, *nemt ayere Mame*; get your mother. Take her to the rabbi. Get your friend to the doctor. Go, now."

Noah blinked back at his father, a look of incomprehension on his face. "What are you going to do?"

Mr. Levy stooped and picked up a can of paraffin from a low shelf beside him. "What I should have done long ago." With that, he removed the cap and turned the can on its side, watching with a dazed expression as its contents splattered across the sawdust-coated floor.

I wanted to protest, to demand an explanation, but I hadn't the time to open my mouth before Noah was sweeping Pippa into his arms and making a break towards the door. "Come on," he ordered. I scurried after him, turning back one final time before disappearing through the curtain to see Mr. Levy dousing William with the remnants of the can.

Moments later, we burst out to the street with Noah's mother in tow, the frigid night air a shocking awakening. We were no more than a block away when the plume of smoke enveloped the Whitechapel sky.

Chapter XX
Fought for and Won

The hospital was mercifully uncrowded, and Pippa was tended to immediately. Because we presented ourselves under the guise of servants involved in a carriage accident, our youth and unaccompanied status roused no suspicion. I was even permitted to remain at Pippa's bedside when she emerged, ankle splinted and ribs wrapped, an hour later.

We were too exhausted to talk. The events of the night had already taken on a dreamlike quality, the relief coursing through me a soporific so potent that I nodded off in my chair without bidding Pippa good night.

I was stirred to wakefulness as if from a nightmare. Muted sunlight shimmered through the windows, illuminating the ward in a golden glow. Sitting up stiffly, my heart fluttered in my chest at the sight of Pippa, angelic as ever in her slumber. Despite her injuries, her cheeks were flushed with health, and I smiled at our good fortune. We were here, alive and well, our villain vanquished, a victory hard-fought and won.

My pleasant reverie was interrupted by the sound of footsteps in the corridor. Much to my surprise, I looked up to see none other than Miss Kaye stride into the ward, her face as stern as ever, stalking straight in our direction. My heart sank. In the flurry of activity, I had not yet considered the inevitable consequences of our recklessness, and I found myself suddenly confronted with the prospect of expulsion. After all, what could we possibly tell the headmaster that would account for our actions?

Miss Kaye came to a halt at the foot of Pippa's bed, taking in her splint and bandages before turning her glare to me. "Miss Morton, dare I even ask?"

"I'm sorry," I started. "We didn't mean for it to happen, we just wanted to protect you, and then William came after us and—"

Miss Kaye held up her hand. "Say no more. Noah delivered a note to the Hall this morning reporting your whereabouts and that William is unfortunately deceased. That is all I need to know."

"It was an accident, truly, but—"

Miss Kaye would hear none of it. "Take it from someone with prior experience, Miss Morton: The less you say on the matter from this moment on, the better off you shall be."

I nodded wordlessly. Then, to my surprise, she smiled. Lowering herself to sit at the edge of Pippa's bed, she gave her a fond examination. "How is Miss Fitzroy?"

"She'll be alright," I confirmed. "A broken ankle and a few cracked ribs, but they believe she'll be discharged in a week."

"Honestly, the girl has the most dreadful luck. You must keep a closer eye on her from now on."

I nodded earnestly. "I certainly intend to." Inwardly, I wondered if this meant that we weren't about to be banished from the school forever.

"Nonsense, you're the one always talking me into your hair-brained schemes." Pippa's eyes fluttered open, and she winced as she pulled herself into a sitting position. Miss Kaye leaned over to prop the pillow behind her with a fond smile.

"Miss Fitzroy! How are you feeling?"

"As well as can be, considering."

"I'm glad to hear it. You must rest up and take your recovery seriously. I shall speak with the headmaster about preparing a temporary room for you on the ground floor of the Hall, as I fear your annex will be quite inaccessible to you for the foreseeable future."

Pippa and I exchanged a nervous glance. I gathered my courage and asked the obvious question. "Does that mean we're not expelled?"

"Not if I have any say in the matter."

Pippa furrowed her brow. "But the headmaster—"

"I have reason to believe that my opinion will have considerable sway with the headmaster from here out."

I was about to inquire further, but our conversation was cut short as Pippa sat bolt upright, eyes fixed upon a point behind me, a glowing grin on her face. "Noah!"

I was on my feet embracing him in an instant, and he squeezed me tight before relinquishing his hold to take a seat on the other side of Pippa's bed and pull her hand into his, a look of immeasurable fondness upon his face. He had dark circles under his eyes and a tight set about his lips, but his demeanour still seemed lighter than I could ever recall it before.

"How are you?"

"I'm fine, Noah, you needn't worry. Just a bit banged up. But how are *you*? How is your family? The shop?"

Noah sighed. "The shop is gone. We were able to salvage a few of our belongings from our rooms, but the rest is a total loss."

His words pierced my joyful heart with sorrow. "Oh, Noah, I'm so sorry."

He quirked a half-hearted smile at me. "Don't be. I'm not. Whatever happens now, it will be different. For so long I have endured my existence because change appeared impossible. But now?" He paused, a hopeful glimmer in his eyes. "Now we will have no choice but to change."

I hesitated. "How is your father?"

"The police found him at the scene of the fire, still holding the paraffin in his hands. He was returned to the asylum in Essex this morning. I do not believe he will be discharged again."

"Oh, no," Pippa breathed. "How is your mother?"

"In all honesty? Relieved, I think. She's already making plans to leave for Paris. I'm happy for her: She'll be better off there than she's ever been here."

"Paris? Are you going with her?" Though I knew that his heart had never been in Whitechapel, the thought of losing him was bittersweet.

He shook his head. "No. Not to Paris."

"Somewhere else, then?"

He shrugged. "I'll have to stay here for a while, find employment, save some money. Henry believes he'll have the funds for his own passage to Australia by the end of the year. God willing, I want to join him there in the new year, if I can come up with the price of a ticket."

"Australia?" Miss Kaye chimed in for the first time since Noah's arrival.

He turned to her, a bashful smile on his face. "It's been a dream of mine for years. But my father was ill, and the shop fell to me, and I believed myself too entangled to go. But now? My future is wide open."

An odd look came across Miss Kaye's face. She reached into the folds of her cloak, and from her pocket produced two ornately embellished envelopes. She held them out to Noah.

With a curious expression, he opened one. Reading the contents, his eyes flew open wide. "These are . . . these are tickets to Sydney. You must be joking."

Miss Kaye shook her head. "I am not. Your assistance has

been invaluable to my cause, Mr. Levy, and I do believe I have you to thank for saving the lives of these two young women, and bestowing upon me a freedom which I have never before possessed. I have no desire to leave London now that William is gone, and it seems to me that perhaps fate brought us together for a particular purpose, indeed."

"I can't . . . I can't . . . I can't believe this! You're actually serious?" Miss Kaye nodded. Noah leapt to his feet with an exhilarated hoot, tickets aloft above his head. "Thank you, thank you, a million times thank you!" A sudden change came over him as he looked down at Pippa and me, who were staring at him with expressions of intermingled fondness and sorrow. When he spoke again, his tone was distinctly melancholy, a mist of tears welling up in his eyes. "I shall miss you both more than anything. You have changed my life, and I will never forget you."

"Nor us, you," I professed. "We never could have done any of this without you."

He reached down and took my hand, then Pippa's. He gave them a tight squeeze, then joined our two hands together. "Take good care of one another."

"We will," we vowed.

"And you," he turned to Miss Kaye. "Take good care of them."

Miss Kaye smiled. "I'll certainly try, though they do test my wiles. Best of luck to you, Mr. Levy."

"Write as often as you can!" I implored.

"Don't get eaten by cannibals!" Pippa added.

"Or kidnapped by a highwayman!" I concluded.

"Kidnapped by a highwayman?" Noah scoffed. "Surely you know by now, I intend to *become* one." And with a wink and a grin, he was gone.

Our return to Whitechapel Hall was heralded with a swirl of petty gossip, savage rumours, and a healthy dose of impolite scepticism. We were on strict orders to keep our heads down as Miss Kaye pleaded our case to the headmaster. Nearly a month passed with Pippa and me in a perpetual state of anxious anticipation, worsened by the fact that her temporary lodgings on the ground floor kept us separated each night. Even so, we remained hopeful that Miss Kaye was as good as her word, and her sway over the headmaster would spare us expulsion.

It just so happened that the day Pippa's splint was removed was the very day we were at last summoned to Miss Kaye's office to hear the headmaster's verdict. My stomach was a churning pit of trepidation as we made our way up the stairs, Pippa's gait uneven as she adjusted to her renewed mobility.

"It's surely not expulsion, or else our guardians would be here," Pippa posited, clearly hoping to sound more confident than she felt.

"Do you think they even told them we escaped at all?" I wondered aloud.

"Probably not. Reputation of the school and all." She had a point. The very fact that no one had heard a word about our caper was indication enough that the staff had every intention of hushing up the whole incident.

We reached Miss Kaye's door and paused. Pippa linked her hand in mine, then raised her fist and knocked.

"Come in!"

We entered to find Miss Kaye sitting primly behind her desk, a pot of tea and three saucers already set. The scene was reassuringly familiar, and the tightness in my chest began to loosen.

"Please, ladies, do sit down." She gestured, and we sat.

"I appreciate your patience during this transformative time here at Whitechapel Hall. There have been many changes these past few weeks, and I'm pleased that today I'm finally able to inform you of their nature."

Pippa and I exchanged a confused look but said nothing. "As you know, Whitechapel Hall recently lost its newfound financial benefactor, which put the status of the school's operation back in peril." My heart sank at the thought of this. Until that moment, I had failed to realise the grander implications of William's death: the school could no longer rely on his funds to operate. Was the reason we weren't being expelled? Because there was soon to be no school from which to expel us?

"Luckily, it turns out that I was listed as the executor of my brother's estate. Due to his prolonged and unexpected absence, his power of attorney has been turned over to me, until such a time that Mr. Kent reappears." She paused diplomatically. "Until then, I have taken the liberty of arranging myself as Whitechapel Hall's official financial backer, in exchange for the title of executive director. The daily operations of the school will now be under my complete discretion."

My eyes flew open wide. "What?!"

"Miss Kaye, that's fantastic!" Pippa was grinning from ear to ear, and a small smile tugged at the corners of Miss Kaye's lips in turn.

"But does the headmaster know your true identity?" I queried.

She shook her head. "He does not, and I intend to keep it that way. I simply told him I had unexpectedly come into a large inheritance, and that I was eager to secure the financial standing of the school. As you can imagine, he was all too keen to comply and save himself the mess of recruiting another backer."

"Do you have to keep wearing your disguise?" I asked, disappointed. The memory of the pretty, wavy-haired woman I'd seen the morning of Miss Kaye's attempted departure stuck with me. She had looked so happy and free.

Miss Kaye shrugged. "I'm afraid so. But to be honest, I do not mind it. I believe Constance Kaye's personality suits me and is a better match for this institution than Constance Kent would be. Besides, after enduring the horrors of the press for decades, it is a distinct relief to live in anonymity."

Her response appeared sincere enough. "So . . . we aren't expelled, then?"

At this, she laughed, and Pippa and I finally joined in. "No. After careful consideration, the headmaster and I have decided that detention will do. The two of you will be assisting me with some very important work: designing an academic curriculum for the pupils of Whitechapel Hall."

I could scarcely believe my ears. Pippa was the first to gather her wits and respond. "An *academic curriculum*? Here? You're serious?"

"Very serious indeed. I've informed the headmaster that it is my belief that young ladies would greatly benefit from academic learning to engage their impressionable young minds. While it is true that domestic servitude is a practical pathway to a noble livelihood, a well-rounded grasp of scholarly matters may inspire them to more high-minded pursuits."

"Miss Kaye, this is amazing!" I could hardly contain my excitement.

"I was hoping that the two of you might have some recommendations of books to include in our curriculum."

I grinned. "I'd start with *Eternal Hope*."

Miss Kaye was clearly startled. "You actually read it?"

"Indeed. I found it a most fascinating companion piece to a favourite penny blood of mine, *Ada the Betrayed* . . ."

Epilogue

Spring

I entered Miss Kaye's office with the envelope in my hand, surprised at the tremor in my fingers as I clutched it. My dismissal interview was hardly a cause for concern, for I had fulfilled the requirements with aplomb: The judge had signed my discharge papers the week prior, I'd received the headmaster's official recommendation the day before, and now at last, I possessed the final element to secure my freedom.

"Ah, Miss Morton! Good afternoon. Have a seat." Miss Kaye's voice was warm and familiar. Throughout the course of our time creating the curriculum, she had gradually dropped her stern demeanour in the presence of Pippa and me, allowing her livelier, lighter side to shine through. It was a glimpse of intimacy that I valued dearly.

"Good afternoon, Miss Kaye." I settled in my chair and smoothed my skirt, still nervous for reasons I could not completely define.

"First and foremost, a package arrived for you today." She produced a rectangular parcel wrapped in brown paper and passed it to me.

"For me?" I ripped open the paper, and my jaw dropped open. Inside was a weathered copy of *The Lady Detective*, the familiar font and saucy flash of her petticoat conjuring the fondest memories of my childhood. Breathless with emotion, I opened the cover to see a note scrawled there.

> *Found this in a shop and thought of you. I'm sure the postage will be ten times the price of the book, but finding it halfway around the world feels like destiny. Good luck detecting!*
>
> *Your highwayman, Noah*

I was mortified to find my eyes suddenly brimming over with tears. Hastily wiping them away, I regained my composure. "Thank you, Miss Kaye."

She smiled. "Of course. Now, on to the most important business of today: your official discharge from Whitechapel Hall." She plucked my file from her drawer and placed it in front of her, rifling through its contents. "I see here we have the court papers, as well as your approval letter from Headmaster Graves."

"Yes."

She paused. "But it does seem we are missing the letter from your guardians confirming their continued stewardship."

I took a deep breath. "I don't have it."

She glanced up. "But Miss Morton, the only alternative is an offer of employment from a reputable source. We cannot simply turn you loose on the streets."

"I have this." With as steady a hand as I could muster, I passed her the envelope.

"It's a contract of employment from *Belgravia* magazine." Miss Kaye's eyebrows rose as she took my offering and quickly perused its contents. "They've purchased the first six instalments of a serial I've written for them and given me an advance for twelve more. The money's enough for a room of my own and to sustain a reputable lifestyle. That will fulfil the requirement of employment, will it not?"

Miss Kaye blinked up at me, gobsmacked. "Why, yes indeed, Miss Morton. This is quite extraordinary, my dear. You should be extremely proud of yourself."

I blushed. While Miss Kaye was now considerably friendlier than she had been when we'd met, she was never one to lavish praise upon me. "Thank you, Miss Kaye."

"What is your serial about?"

I summoned all my courage. "It's called *Wicked Wills.* It's the story of a fiendish deviant who gleans pleasure from torturing and controlling his sister. It's about how she gains her freedom from his sinister clutches. She's . . . she's the heroine, you see."

Miss Kaye's eyes were suddenly as wet as my own. "That . . . that sounds quite fascinating. I shall be eager to read it."

"I brought you something," I continued earnestly, before I could lose my nerve. "An unpublished instalment, as it were." From my pocket, I withdrew six folded pages and passed them to her.

She peered down at them, reading the title aloud. "*The Incident at Road Hill House.*" Her expression darkened as she glanced through the pages.

"I wrote this for you," I hurried to explain. "It's the true story of what happened the night that Saville died. Just as you told it to us."

Miss Kaye looked up, her eyes filled with fear. "You cannot publish this, Dell. I've no desire to have my family thrust back into the national headlines. I've spent the last twenty-five years distancing myself from the events of that fateful night. I cannot endure any more public scrutiny than I've already been subjected to."

I shook my head. "I won't ever publish it. This is just for

you. Your truth. Your story. It's yours now, to tell or not tell, to hold or to publish or to burn in your fireplace the moment I walk from this room. It's all up to you."

A look of unspeakable tenderness crossed her face. "Miss Morton . . . Dell . . . Thank you. I've never— "

A knock on the door interrupted her mid-sentence, and I heard Pippa's voice echo down the hall outside. "Dell! Are you nearly done? Hurry up! The cab will be here any minute!"

"Miss Fitzroy! If you have something to say, please join us and say it at an appropriate volume. Shouting is unbecoming of a lady."

The door swung open, and Pippa appeared, flushed and breathless. "Apologies, Miss Kaye, it's just that we're on a rather tight schedule— "

Miss Kaye raised an eyebrow. "*We?*"

I cleared my throat. "I should probably mention I'm bringing Miss Fitzroy with me. As she's a voluntary boarder, I assume a guarantee of her lodging with me will be sufficient for her discharge?"

Miss Kaye's expression was one of resigned amusement as she cast her gaze upon the two of us, scarcely able to contain our enthusiasm at the news. "Yes, Miss Morton, Miss Fitzroy. That will be sufficient. I shall mark it in Miss Fitzroy's file that she has been released upon discretion of the school."

Pippa and I shared a jubilant grin. "Excellent. So . . ."

"So, I believe that concludes our business today, ladies. I wish you both the best of luck. Do keep in touch." We rose and for a moment hovered in silence. It felt too abrupt an ending for such a lengthy saga, but there was simply nothing more to say. Pippa and I curtsied, and with one final nod to our dear conspirator and confidante, we departed.

Pippa had already donned her travelling cloak, and she was practically bouncing from foot to foot with excitement as we made our way down the stairs. "You were taking forever. I nearly thought Miss Kaye was going to deny our discharge!" She thrust my own cloak at me, and I swung it over my shoulders as we crossed the entrance hall.

"She seems happy for us."

"As she should be! Look, the first two graduates of Whitechapel Hall's *academic curriculum*!"

She took my arm in hers, and together, we stepped out into the world to begin our own story at last.

Acknowledgments

A million thanks to Elizabeth Trout and the Kensington Publishing team for their unwavering dedication and enthusiasm. To my agent, Laura Bradford, for her steadfast support. To Gila Green, Jimmy Chang, Tiffany Wey, and Carolyn Nishon, for their thoughtful feedback. To Speakeasy Bookmarket in Idyllwild, California, for renting me their attic so that I could brood in solitude. To Amy Huntley, for her generous wisdom and encouragement. To Audrey, Jess, Tiff—as with everything in life, I couldn't have done it without you. To my father; my #1 cheerleader, confidant, and trivia partner, for reminding me what matters. To Rolyn, for emotionally manipulating me into hitting my deadlines, no matter how hard I fight back—this manuscript would be lost without you. And to Brendan; words can't express all the wild and wonderful ways you have changed my life. Thank you for coming on this journey with me.

Author's Note

Let me be the first to admit: I hate Jack the Ripper. The murderer himself, obviously, but the case itself never enthralled me the way it does so many others. I've never found the appeal in Ripperology, as to me this case has always simply seemed to be the sum of its parts: it's the story of a deviant sadist, bad-faith victim blaming, a bungled police investigation, and lurid exploitation by the press. Tale as old as time.

But what draws me to a particular crime is rarely the nature of the crime itself but the social, economic, and political conditions that conspired to allow it to happen. While Jack the Ripper's personal motivations do not interest me, the London police force in the 1880s was the perfect storm of xenophobia, homophobia, antisemitism, and misogyny that utterly derailed any chance of a proper investigation. I do not believe that Jack was a brilliant and cunning psychopath; I believe he was a sloppy, crude, opportunistic killer that eluded police only due to their own prejudice. *No Englishman could have done it*, the chief inspector is reported to have said. A century and a half later, knowing what we know now about criminal profiling, we can bet an *Englishman* probably did.

The Five: The Untold Lives of the Women Killed by Jack the Ripper (2019), by Hallie Rubenhold, is one of the best modern accounts seeking to turn the traditional narrative of the case on its head. In humanizing the Ripper's victims and contextualizing their lives within the social and economic conditions of London at the time, Rubenhold drew me back to the case after years of turning up my nose at it.

The more I reinterpreted the case through a modern lens, the more determined I became to redeem the reputation of the much-maligned Whitechapel neighbourhood. Contrary to popular folklore (and what the proprietors of most Jack the Ripper-based tourist attractions would have you believe), Whitechapel in 1888 was not a seething den of squalor and filth perfectly poised to provide a poignant backdrop to the century's most famous crime. Instead, it was a mixed-class neighbourhood where upper-class merchants, middle-class shopkeepers, the working poor, and the city's most undesirables rubbed shoulders daily. While there were indeed entire streets labelled as "Vicious [and] Semi-criminal" by the census takers of the time, they were mere footsteps away from streets labelled "Wealthy," "Fairly comfortable," and "Good ordinary earnings" (*Map of London Poverty, 1889*). Religious evangelists from the Salvation Army were as common a sight as Jews from the established Orthodox community there, and above it all rose Buck's Row Board School, the real-life location upon which Whitechapel Hall is based. Studying the imposing brick structure which stands to this day at 6 Durward Street, it's impossible not to imagine what a vibrant slice of life would have been visible from its roof sixty feet up.

Placing Dell and Pippa squarely at this intersection of poverty and privilege felt like an obvious choice, but including Noah in the narrative was imperative to provide an additional perspective to their investigation. Antisemitism and the resulting violence against the Whitechapel Jewish community played a large role in the Ripper case, and I wanted to bring focus to the people impacted by it. Noah's father, Jacob, is based upon a real-life individual who lived in Whitechapel at the time (and has even been suggested as a suspect in some Ripperologist circles). Researching his life was one of the most fascinating elements of this story for me; a third-generation British citizen of Dutch Jewish heritage, Jacob and his family lived at a time of cultural assimilation and religious reform within the established London-based Jewish community, a stark contrast from the more Orthodox eastern-European Jews who were just beginning to arrive and settle in Whitechapel at the time. For the purposes of this narrative, I have positioned Jacob and his family in the midst of the reverberating tension between anglicized and Orthodox; while the shop follows kosher customs and practices, it services a gentile institution, and the family does not have strong ties to the Orthodox synagogue. Placing Noah at such a transformative point in his family's journey, I wanted to portray him as straddling two worlds, while never feeling quite at home in either. His search for his own identity and sense of belonging, much like Dell's and Pippa's, only commences at the conclusion of this narrative.

And what to say of the Road Hill House Murder tie-in? I must confess, for a writer such as myself, the timeline of Constance Kent's incarceration and release is the fodder upon which my particular brand of "historical fanfiction" thrives. I stumbled across her name in a long list of Jack suspects during a late-night Ripperologist deep-dive and did a double-take. While in my opinion there is no reason to treat her as a valid suspect in the Whitechapel murders, the details of her real-life case have stuck with me throughout my years as a true crime fan. Her criminal profile is so unlike that which we would expect from a perpetrator of familicide, and the fact that she never committed another crime after the one to which she confessed has always struck me as noteworthy. I knew right away that I did not want to portray Constance as a killer, but the potential to tie her into the narrative was irresistible. I am not the only murderino who remains sceptical of her conviction; throughout the years, it has been posited that she was covering for her father or brother. For the case of this fiction, William seemed the best prospect.

Do I truly believe that William Kent was Jack? No. Following Constance's conviction, he went on to lead a thoroughly fascinating life as a marine biologist in Australia, and there is no evidence linking him to any of Jack's crimes. But I focused on him as a convenient stand-in for who I truly believe the Ripper to be: an ordinary gentleman of considerable means, whose gender, race, class, background, and privilege would have provided him the perfect shield from the scrutiny of Victorian police. In other words, *an Englishman*.

Discussion Questions

These suggested questions are to spark conversation and enhance your reading of *The Dreadfuls.*

1. As a true crime enthusiast, Dell Morton's take on the case unfolding in Whitechapel is coloured by her exposure to lurid tales. How does this help her detective work, and how does it hinder it?
2. As Dell insists in her conversation with Miss Kaye, fascination with true crime is hardly a recent phenomenon. How does modern society's obsession with the genre differ from that of the Victorian era? How is it the same?
3. For Dell, Miss Kaye, and Pippa, their status as women makes them both vulnerable and powerful as burgeoning detectives. How do they use their gender to their advantage, and in what ways does it work against them?
4. Noah is portrayed as a close friend to the girls, but at the same time, his connection with his Jewish identity is never openly discussed with them. How might you as a reader find out more about the lives of Jews in Whitechapel at the time and better identify with Noah and his family's experience?

5. Miss Kaye and Dell often debate the morality of Dell's chosen literature. Do you believe the tropes and mores of penny dreadfuls are helpful or harmful in forming a moral compass?
6. As summarized by Dell in the Epilogue, *The Dreadfuls* is not her heroine story; instead, it is her origin story. What do you think happens to Dell and Pippa after the conclusion of the book? What clues are provided in the text that led you to this conclusion?

Read on for a sneak peek at A. Rae Dunlap's

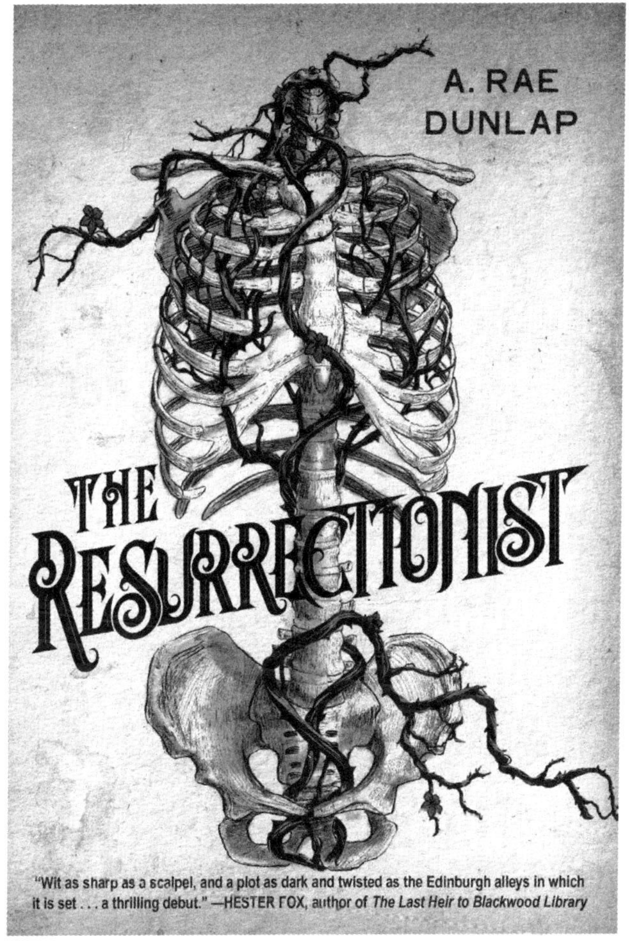

The Resurrectionist

i. An Introduction

To hear my mother tell the story, my decision to abandon my studies at Oxford was enough to disgrace my father into an early grave. Regardless of his habits—his drinking, his gambling, his debts—in her mind, it was my own act of reckless rebellion that finally put him under for good.

To that end, it's perhaps for the best that he wasn't alive six months later, when I was nearly arrested for smuggling a naked corpse in a wheelbarrow down Chambers Street at half past midnight, but I fear that's getting rather ahead of myself. The point is, my father's shame in me apparently drove him to death out of sheer mortification, making the events which transpired in the wake of his passing the fault of no one but myself and myself alone.

In all fairness, my father never had particularly high aspirations for me, so the fact that I was able to underwhelm him so completely was quite the accomplishment indeed. As the third son of a modestly landed family, it was impressed upon me from an early age that I would require a livelihood—and not just any livelihood, but one becoming of a man of my station.

In my early childhood, my father assumed that I would follow my uncle's path into the military, but it quickly became apparent that neither steadfast leadership nor brazen feats of daring were amongst my stronger suits, as I exclusively pursued activities of a much gentler persuasion. I would notoriously steal away from my brothers' reckless exploits and wild marauding about the grounds of the family estate to hide inside the library with a book, more content in the company of words than my siblings. What's more, my diminutive stature made athletic competition too humiliating to endure, so I therefore declared it outside my natural inclination and avoided it whenever possible, much to my father's dismay.

So it was to be a clerical vocation for me—the Church being the next best chance for an unlanded gentleman to excel in society—and preparations were made for my attendance at Oxford, where I could procure a degree while maneuvering my way to a prominent parish position. This edict of intent was dictated to me by my father in his unmistakable blithe monotone across the mahogany expanse of his desk three days before my departure for University in the summer of 1828, along with a comprehensive summary of my weekly allowance and the names and titles of class-appropriate peers with whom I was explicitly instructed to rub shoulders.

However, it quickly became clear to me that life in the Church could never suffice. As ill-suited as I was to be a leader, it was evident that I was a considerably worse follower and uniquely repelled by both mundanity and tradition. Classics bored me, rhetoric confounded me, and the few Theology lectures I attended failed to ignite wonder. I abruptly began to realise that I could no more devote my life to legend and myth than I could take up arms and command a battalion. To me, military maneuvers and ecclesiastical quandaries paled in comparison to the passion that I felt when reading about the biological facts of life. The insuppressible notion began to dawn on me that I was, in my core, a man of Science.

And not just any science: *human* science, the study of the body, of man *himself*, of sinew and bone and humour and blood. The essence of life, the very organs that granted our *being*, that was the *wonder* of it all! To unlock the mysteries of the human form was to behold God's masterpiece firsthand, and *that* is what sparked the fire within me for the very first time. Turning each riveting page of every volume in the University's well-curated collection of anatomy texts, I knew then and there that my calling was to be a physician.

And to a modern man, a call to be a physician was a call to *Edinburgh*, shining beacon of medical discovery, home of Hume and the New Enlightenment, a city unparalleled even on the Continent in its quest for progress on the scientific front. To be a truly contemporary physician of the era, one could aim no higher than a diploma from the University there.

And so as the withering chill of autumn descended, I repacked my trunks, settled my debts, and returned to the family stead brimming with fervor and bursting with pride to announce my new career with all the careless haste of a young man possessed. Much to my chagrin, my intentions were met with staunch opposition from all parties involved, yet I persisted. From teatime through dinner, my resolution was brought under fiercest scrutiny, but I refused to allow my temper to get the better of me, civilly commanding that the relentless interrogation cease. The remainder of the evening was spent in a predictably grim and heavy silence as I held firm in my resolve.

On that very night, my father died in his sleep. So it could perhaps be said that my mother's less-than-equitable placement of blame was not *entirely* far-fetched, though I maintain that perhaps it was a small mercy that he did not survive to see the deepest depths of my eventual moral compromisings—the aforementioned corpse in the wheelbarrow being the least of it. Little did I know that that brush with death would be my first of many, and at the time, it both consumed and compelled me in a way that only one's first encounter with mortality can.

Yet I must insist that, in the end, this is not a story about Death. It is perhaps a Life story—or even, yes, a Love story. It is the story of how I clawed my way from the decay of a crumbling legacy into the modern era of Reason and Science. It is the story of how I escaped the prison of archaic superstition to the freedom of enlightenment. It is the story of how a rose can blossom from even the bloodiest soil, of how light can grow from shadow, how love can grow from despair.

This, dear reader, is the story of my Resurrection.

I. An Invitation

My arrival in Edinburgh was heralded, quite fittingly, by a deluge of rain the volume and frigidity of which took me embarrassingly by surprise. I'd ventured that far North only twice before in my life, both times in the basking embrace of summer. Unfortunately, this experience had filled my head with romantic notions of Scotland based upon hazy recollections of carefree days spent upon sun-kissed moors with the temperate winds of the rugged highlands ruffling my hair, heather and thistle beneath my feet.

The reality of Edinburgh, however, was a harsh contrast to my fond memories not just of the untamed countryside, but to my sparse experience of city life thus far. Juxtaposed against Oxford's dreaming spires, the jumbles of soot-singed bricks slicing jagged black angles into the sky appeared primitive to my discerning eyes, to say nothing of the coal-black sludge lining the cobblestone streets. I'd arrived the first week in November, just in time for the start of Winter Session, and was quickly forced to admit that the sly expressions of amusement exchanged amongst my acquaintances at home upon hearing of my intention to disembark for the North in such a season may not have been without merit. It was staggeringly obvious that my tweed overcoat was sorely lacking before I'd even set foot outside my carriage.

I'd resolved to take a room based upon an advertisement posted in the hall of the Royal Medical Society, which was the first stop upon my arrival. This would have undoubtedly horrified my mother, who was already offended enough that, unlike Oxford, the University here provided neither porters nor bedders, so I would be responsible for maintaining my own accommodations. But it would seem luck was on my side, as there were plenty of vacancies listed that boasted proximity to the lecture halls and a set-rate fare for breakfast and tea, and I'd simply pointed my coachman towards the first lodging house on the list.

In any other circumstance, my initial impression of the Hope & Anchor Inn would have been one of profound revulsion: The windows were caked in several layers of grime; the door handle was disconcertingly slippery to the touch, the interior dim and smokey. But following the interminable journey from Bath, coupled with the disorientation of a stranger in a foreign city and the demoralisingly inclement weather, it seemed to my weary eyes to be the coziest, quaintest lodging house imaginable. The barman was endearingly gruff (just as I'd imagined every native Scotsman to be), and I was charmed by the prospect of living amongst the local populace. I secured a room, then promptly returned to my coach to await a porter.

It soon became obvious, however, that porters were not part of the standard service at the Hope & Anchor Inn. What's more, my coachman declined to provide any further assistance besides depositing my trunk and valise unceremoniously upon the rain-soaked street and stealing off into the descending night with barely a tip of his hat in my direction. Thus it was with the strength of my own two hands and the gritty determination of a man in the throes of newfound independence that I made my first official entrance as a resident of the Hope & Anchor Inn.

It was not, truth be told, a particularly graceful entrance. I was unable to completely lift the trunk due to its cumbersome shape, so I was relegated to dragging it behind me as the brass tacks securing the underframe screeched in protest against the wooden floor. The handle of my valise had grown slick with rain, and I fumbled it no fewer than three times as I wove my way between the densely packed tables filled with wary-eyed patrons hunched over pints of dark ale. A disconcerting silence seemed to follow me, but I resolutely ignored it and made my way to the interior staircase and proceeded to ascend.

Well, I *attempted* to ascend. As it turned out, scaling steep stairs beneath the weight of my luggage was considerably more challenging than the porters of my past had led me to believe, and I had barely struggled past the halfway point when I lost my grip on the trunk entirely and whirled in horror to watch as it thundered down the stairs in a deafening cacophony—and to my compounded horror, directly into the outstretched arms of a young, curly-haired stranger who'd had the misfortune of rounding the corner into the stairwell at the least opportune moment possible.

With a startled shout, he braced himself just in time to bring the trunk to an abrupt halt, still perched at a precarious angle and threatening to continue its descent as he strained against its unwieldy bulk. To his credit, the stranger recomposed himself in the blink of an eye, his expression turning from surprise to amusement as he cast a glance up the stairs in my direction.

"Drop something?" His lip was quirked in the hint of a smile, but his blasé attitude towards nearly meeting an untimely end beneath a piece of rampaging luggage did little to fade the blush of humiliation I could feel scalding my cheeks.

"Sorry, so sorry, a thousand apologies—" I somehow dropped my valise *again* in my haste to retreat down the stairs to free the young man from his current quagmire, and to my relief (and perhaps mild indignation), he *laughed.*

"Keep your head on, I've got it. Why not pop your bag up on the landing, then come back here and we'll hoist this *beast* up together, yeah?"

"Oh! Um, yes, of course, quite right you are . . ." I hastily followed his directive, and we were soon working in tandem to shepherd the offending *beast* up the stairs, which proved to be considerably easier than maneuvering it solo. The stranger showed no hesitation in providing me instructions as I struggled awkwardly backwards up the stairs, and I in return duly hid my chagrin at his continued sniggering at my clumsiness. An unspoken gentlemen's agreement reached, we summited the staircase with a collective shout of triumph and gave The Beast a final heave in the general direction of the bedchambers before collapsing on either side of it in mutually undignified surrender.

The stranger was still grinning, his amusement apparently unimpeded by exertion. I found the sentiment to be contagious and grinned back.

He recovered his breath first. "So. I take it you're new in town, and not just carting this about for the entertainment of local bystanders?" He gave the trunk a good-natured pat.

I took a gulp of air and mopped the sweat from my brow with the back of my hand, only to discover it had mixed with the rainwater to form a rather unsavoury salty sheen. "Just arrived from Bath. I'm starting at the Medical School this week."

His smile grew even brighter. "You, too? Brilliant! There's a whole group of lads here from the new class; we were just enjoying some pints downstairs. You ought to join us."

Transferring the sweat from my hand onto the twill of my breeches, I shook my head forlornly. "Look at me. I'm clearly in no state for socialising. I haven't even dressed for dinner, let alone—"

To my surprise, the stranger let out a bark of laughter. "Listen, mate. Not sure what pubs were like in *Bath*, but around here, we tend to be a bit more casual."

I eyed him appraisingly, attempting to suss out his backstory in the few details illuminated by the sparse lamplight of the hall. His accent sounded civilised enough—London, or thereabouts at least—his boots well-cobbled, and his shirt finely tailored. But he wore no jacket or waistcoat, his cravat was loose at his throat, and his sleeves were rolled above his wrists. After months of the rigorous cap-and-gown standards at Oxford, to me he appeared nearly charlatan in his approach to propriety, and a part of me wanted to doubt his seemingly earnest intent.

But that said, there was no malice in his eyes, no judgement in his tone, and no hesitation in his speech. What reason would he have, I concluded, to cause me more indignity than what I'd already suffered as a result of my own poor coordination and physical ineptitude at something as simple as wrangling my own valise? After all, I was a stranger in this town—no family name to honour, no tradition to uphold. I was, at last, *free* from the rigid mores of my past! It suddenly seemed that the very *least* I could do was indulge in a well-earned pint with my new peers.

With a curt nod of assent, I extended my hand. "In that case, it would be a pleasure to join you. My name's James, by the way." This didn't seem to be the proper place for titles.

He took my hand and, much to my surprise, rose to his feet and pulled me up bodily with him. "I'm Charlie. Now, let's get *The Beast* to your room and head back downstairs before we miss all the fun."

We made quick work of depositing my trunk into the darkened chamber whose number coincided with that of my newly acquired key. I admittedly made no effort to assess my new abode, as Charlie seemed keen to rejoin the revelries at the pub and I had no wish to detain him further. Mere moments later, he was leading me back into the smokey din, a flush of excitement on his cheeks—a condition I found mirrored in my own. For this, *right here*, was to be my new life! A life of independence, of personal discovery, of raucous barrooms and newfound *mates*, of loosened cravats and rolled-up sleeves, of dark ale and smudged glasses and sticky floors, high-minded ideas and low-minded gossip and everything in between. For while it was the sanctified surgical theatre that had called me North, it struck me then and there that it was only the base of the bargain. For the first time ever, my life was *mine*, and I was determined to live it to the fullest.